My
Guardian Angel

To : Patrick
He's watching over you!

Eric Lee Allen

My
Guardian Angel

Eric Lee Allen

Northwest Publishing, Inc.
Salt Lake City, Utah

My Guardian Angel

This is a work of fiction.
All characters and events portrayed in this book are fictional,
and any resemblance to real people or incidents is purely coincidental.

For information address: Northwest Publishing, Inc.
6906 South 300 West, Salt Lake City, Utah 84047
JC 11.8.94

PRINTING HISTORY
First Printing 1995

ISBN: 1-56901-220-2

NPI books are published by Northwest Publishing, Incorporated,
6906 South 300 West, Salt Lake City, Utah 84047.
The name "NPI" and the "NPI" logo are trademarks belonging to
Northwest Publishing, Incorporated.

PRINTED IN THE UNITED STATES OF AMERICA.
10 9 8 7 6 5 4 3 2 1

To Grampa

Thanks, Chad.
You are a great angel, and a neat kid, too.

Wayne Finley, *My Guardian Angel*

Preface

Kids can be so amazing; it is very often fun to just sit and remember what it was like to be one. For all you adults out there who may long for the unclouded, neat-feeling, anything's possible kind of curiousity we all had at one time in our lives, well...enjoy this story. It is for you. If there's a screened-in porch nearby and a thunderstorm's on its way, it's the perfect reading spot. Or maybe you'd prefer that big recliner in the family room. Or maybe nowhere in particular. But wherever you read, get ready to let a kid take over for awhile—and see the miracles that happen. You may even find yourself glancing next to you, every now and then, just to see who's there.

E.L.A.
North Syracuse, New York
February, 1993

1

Any second now.

Mortal danger would be here any second.

Number seventy-seven recalled his orders as he stood ready, muscles tensed.

Your job is to guard and protect. Always and at all times...

Then it came.

Ripping through the air at its target with ferocious speed and deadly accuracy.

No, he thought. *I won't let it!*

He lunged sideways, throwing his full weight against it as it struck him with equal fury, knocking him backwards seemingly with the force of a thousand cannons...

For a moment, he lay totally disoriented. Had he stopped it? Yes, yes he felt *something* in his hands. He clutched it tight to his stomach, determined it would not elude his grasp.

It didn't.

Another goal saved! Every Angel on the field, and most of the bleachers, erupted in cheers. Barely able to breathe, the goalie lifted himself from the ground and was quickly engulfed by euphoric teammates.

"Whooooiii!"

Whistles blew, and it was halftime. The goalie brushed his thick, dirty-blond hair back over his ears and managed a weak smile himself. Walking—almost *staggering*—he made his way to the touchline amid a pandemonious exchange of high fives and tossed the grass-stained soccer ball to assistant coach Stevens, who congratulated him.

"Hey, that was quick *work* there, Shortstop!"

"Shortstop" grinned, rubbing his newly tender stomach. He'd *learned* to be quick—someone with *his* job *had* to be.

He was suddenly shielded from the hot summer sun as another, much *taller* figure moved in front of him.

He looked up. There was the Big Guy himself.

"You *bet* it was fast!" He was grinning, too. "Good work, Chad! Good work." His strong, gentle hand came to rest on his shoulder. "You okay, there?"

Chad's grin broadened into a full smile. "Sure am, Coach. Thanks a lot."

"Well go get yourself some juice. We're gonna need ya again here, pretty soon!"

"You bet!" Chad raced over to join the rest of the Angels, most of whom had already gathered around the snack stand. He waved up to his father and brother as he passed the bleachers; Mr. Thomas smiled and waved back.

MUNCIE, INDIANA
1973

It had been a pretty mild summer day thus far—about eighty degrees, or so the old rusty thermometer on the phone pole said. Still, it was plenty warm and Chad always looked forward to halftime. It usually ran about fifteen minutes, out of an entire *hour* of playing time, so he wanted to get off his feet as soon as possible. He sat down on the grass and gulped down some cool, cherry ade.

He was already anticipating the second half. It would be the Panthers' turn to kick off, and now the Angels would take aim at the very goal he'd just defended. That was one of the ironic things about soccer. Fight to keep a goal safe, then switch sides to attack it. But it was *his* kind of play—quick, fast-moving, *relentless*. And he loved it. Any kind of action in the world, he *loved* it!

And he loved the game itself. Not for the scoring, or the competition, or even knowing that a win this afternoon would send his team to the Delaware County Junior Soccer Finals on Tuesday.

It was for the *fun* of it. For the activity. For the companionship. For just being with other kids his age and having fun in the summer.

He even loved the smell of the field—*mmmm, yes.* That fresh, summery smell of mowed grass. He brushed some loose blades from his dirty white socks.

Back in the bleachers, his father again read his stats on the back of his team card, even though he knew them by heart:

NAME: Chad Warren Thomas   ANGELS # 77
AGE: 10   HOME TOWN: Muncie
HEIGHT: 4' 8"   WEIGHT: 75 lbs.
HAIR: Blond   EYES: Blue

And below it, scrawled with pen in Chad's handwriting:

FAV. FOOD—P. Butter   FAV. COOKIE—Snickerdoodle
FAV. DRINK—Root Beer   FAV. GUM—Spearmint

Mr. Thomas smiled. What a kid.

Chad was startled by teammates running by. He looked at

his watch—over *ten minutes* had already passed! Quickly he got up and joined the rapidly swelling huddle around the Big Guy.

It was strategy-plotting time.

Coach wasted no words. "We're down seven to nine," he said. "You all know how it gets at this point. They're really gonna be trying hard now to stay ahead and run down the clock." Quickly he called each player by name, what position they'd fill, what course of action they should take if needed. Craig would be the center forward. Chad was to be an inside forward.

Coach looked over at him. "You'll switch with Craig when the time comes," he said. "Then we're gonna need your shoot-in."

Chad grinned in eager anticipation.

The shoot-in. His favorite moment of the whole game. Maneuvering, positioning, maneuvering right up to the enemy's goal with the ball firmly in his possession, then spinning around and launching one into the net with a powerful, lightning-fast kick. But he had to be, as he put it, very "precisionly" about it—he got few second tries, and everything had to go almost perfectly up to that moment for it to even happen at all.

And he was *always* practicing the shoot-in. At the playground, at home, on walks, anywhere he could stand up. Most of all he liked to practice in his bedroom, while listening to his parents' Carpenters record, his favorite music in all the world. He'd spin around, holding his hand like he was clutching a microphone...

"Okay, guys! Let's do it!"

The team smacked hands, fanned out onto the field, and took their positions.

The game was fast and furious. The Panthers scored again, the Angels did the same.

Still down by two.

Kick after kick, save after save, time after time the teams went at it, neither able to gain ground. But the Angels had to. They *had* to.

Here came the ball.

Chad ran for it, reaching with his legs, stretching, *almost touching it—*

Smack! He collided with a Panther, knocking them both to the ground. *Mmmf.* He just missed it. Well, he'd try again.

Then the tide turned, at least a little bit. The Hawkeye got the ball; he managed to blaze a trail deep into Panther territory and kick it into the net off the goal post. A few high fives were given—now they were down by only one.

But Chad was growing concerned. Time was rapidly running out. They now had less than three minutes to make two goals—and that was assuming the Panthers wouldn't score any more. Considering how much tougher the second half had been so far, it wouldn't be easy.

The intensity picked up. Back and forth, back and forth…

Craig took it!

Chad's heart leaped. Could he do it?

On the inside, on the inside…

Yes! He launched it in. Again the field and bleachers erupted in cheers.

The game was tied.

The Panthers' coach blew his whistle. He wanted a time-out. The Big Guy motioned for the Angels to come over; quickly they gathered around him.

"Good work, you guys!" He looked at Hawkeye and Craig. "You got us this far, and now we're gonna take it all the way!" He gave Chad a wink. "Ready to go there, partner?"

Chad didn't hesitate. "You bet!"

"Okay, then. *Center forward!*"

Chad grinned. This was it. The moment he'd been waiting for. *Hot diggity,* he thought. *I love this job!*

He followed the team back onto the field.

How much time's left, anyway? In his initial rush to the huddle, he hadn't even bothered to look at the stop clock. His eyes traveled over to the scoreboard above the bleachers, to the digital numerals ablaze under the teams' names.

Fifty-nine seconds.

Fifty-nine *seconds* to score.

This would take immense concentration. It would take a *miracle.*

Chad cleared his mind of everything except the ball and the net it *had* to hit. *One more to go,* he thought. *Just one more.* His lips pressed together in utter determination and his legs tightened, ready for action. Everyone—the whole field, the coaches, the bleachers, *everyone*—was pumped, the tension thick.

The whistle sounded.

And the push was on.

Again the ball went back and forth, changing possession over and over...

Hawkeye made a wild pass from the left and Chad felt something bump his ankle.

It was the ball!

Now it was *his* turn. His adrenaline surged and he ran with it.

Forty-three seconds.

There was no stopping now. This was it. Do or die. He could *not* lose the ball. He wished he could see into the future, to just *know* what was coming next and what he'd have to do, where he'd have to go, what was going to happen. But he couldn't, so he'd have to rely on experience and his senses— feel, sight, sound, thought. Maybe he couldn't see the future, but he *could* think ahead.

And he *was* thinking ahead—looking around carefully, studying the situation, mapping out strategy in his mind—all as he raced forward, cut back, pushing the ball along with his feet. Nothing escaped his eyes. Every bit of activity, every relevant movement on the field, he noticed. He kept driving toward the goal, continuously, methodically...

Thirty-one seconds.

Behind the touchline, the Big Guy was watching Chad.

He couldn't *help* but watch him. Not only because the game now depended on him; no, it was more than that.

It was the way he handled himself.

He was amazed at how Chad remained so tremendously calm and collected under pressure. Such concentration, with precious few seconds ticking away, was—as he'd coined the phrase himself—a "semi-impossible" job. But not for Chad. He never panicked, or lost his judgment, or forgot exactly what he was doing. It was *remarkable.* Such single-minded determination was rare in any *adult,* let alone a *ten-*year-old, and no doubt it was something he would always be known for.

Nineteen seconds.

Chad moved in on the Panthers' goal. So did most of the Panthers.

Things were growing difficult in a hurry. A goal now would indeed be nothing short of miraculous. Once again, the Big Guy's advice came back to him.

Wait until the last possible second to act, then wait a couple more.

Twelve seconds.

Chad thought fast. He glanced around—yes, there was Craig—and passed the ball to him.

It worked. Several Panthers moved away to counter him, giving Chad his opening.

Eight seconds.

"Now, Craig!"

Craig whipped it back to Chad.

Shoot-in time.

BOOM! The ball cut through the air past the goalie like a rocket and slammed into the net with such force it wobbled the goal posts.

It was over! Every Angel on the field went nuts.

For a moment, Chad only stood there in amazement; he didn't even realize he'd done it.

Then it hit him.

"Holy *wow!"*

Before he knew it he was riding the shoulders of high-fiving, yelling, *cheering* teammates!

A pair of strong hands lifted him off and held him in the air before setting him down.

It was the Big Guy.

"Good work! I knew you could do it, Chad. And ya *did it!*"

He could barely be heard. The team was euphoric, almost beyond help, yelling and whooping and carrying on in an outbreak of what Chad called "spastic adrenalitis"—so loudly, in fact, that Coach had to shout at them to speak only with their voices if possible, to keep their excitement below the danger level. But he was plainly happy, too.

And so was Chad. He knew he'd made the goal, but only now was he really beginning to realize they'd *won*. Only now, after he could stop and catch his breath and think about it, was it all sinking in. He smiled again, a great *big* smile.

Yes, it felt *good!*

All the Panthers came over to congratulate the Angels. Chad shared a handshake and a high five with Travis, one of their goalies—he was also their most powerful kicker and the one who'd launched the ball into Chad a little earlier. It was neat to be such good friends with the other side. Chad was almost sorry they'd lost. Almost. Many of them were his schoolmates. And they'd all done a great job and they'd tried hard. Chad always admired that.

Dad and brother Carson joined him as the bleachers emptied onto the field—and for a few moments, it was completely interwoven in Angel white and Panther purple, coaches, spectators and players alike. They all stood and listened as the Big Guy spoke.

"Wow! What a great game it was! Everyone worked hard, on both sides—"

"You bet, Coach!" Every team member on the field faced a player from the other and applauded them.

"Well, all right then!" Coach chuckled and wiped his forehead on his sleeve. "There's not much more to say, I guess—just all you Angels be here on Tuesday, and let's score another one!"

Another loud cheer went up from the Angels.

"See you all then!" The Big Guy tossed the ball to Coach Stevens, and everyone slowly started back toward the parking lot. Chad started to leave too, but not before the Big Guy signaled for him to come over.

Dad grinned and kept walking with Carson. "We'll see ya back at the car—by the hill."

Coach went down on one knee to Chad's eye level. "So how was *that* for the hi's and wows of it all, Chad?" He chuckled and Chad did, too.

"It was *great,* Coach!"

"Lookin' forward to this Tuesday?"

"Sure am."

"Good. I just wanted to say thanks to ya, for bein' here and doin' such a good job."

"Sure, Coach. Thank *you,* too."

They shook hands.

Coach stood and gave Chad a wink. "Just take care of that property like you did today," he said, motioning toward the goal net. "And don't forget to have fun doing it."

He chuckled again. "Got it?"

"Yes, sir. Got it!"

"Okay, see ya then!" He gave Chad a pat on the shoulder, then stopped once more. "By the way, you gonna be at singing practice on Monday night?"

"You bet! I'd never miss it."

"Great. I'll be there, too."

Chad wondered what was up. The Big Guy rarely ever made to the *practice,* with all his work...he obviously knew something Chad didn't. Oh well, it'd have to wait.

"I'll see you Monday, Chad."

"Okay, Coach. Bye!" Chad turned and raced for the parking lot.

He caught a glimpse of the stop clock, still frozen at five seconds.

2

Chad was *exuberant.*

The win really *did* feel much better than even *he* thought it would. He sat on the passenger seat with the door open and changed into his battered white high tops (almost a habit by now—he *loved* those shoes!), pausing just long enough to dislodge chunks of dark, coffee-ground soil from his soccer cleats with his fingers.

And then it was homeward bound.

Chad looked down at himself. His hands were dirty, he was covered with grass stains, and his grubby white uniform was damp, but he felt *good.* He was hot, tired, sweaty, and dirty as the underside of a mop, but he felt *good.* Everything about him was either hamper or shower fodder, but he felt *good.* He clenched his fists in triumph, drumming them on his knees, drumming his heels on the floor—oh, *yes,* it felt *sooo good!*

Mr. Thomas looked over and smiled. The famous rapid drum was Chad's way of showing his excitement. "Well, all-star," he said. "Congratulations—ya done great! Third in a series and I'd say it's been going pretty good so far."

Indeed, Chad's two big brothers had played before him, and now it was his turn. Chad glanced over the seat at Carson, who paused long enough from his counting ritual to smile and give him a thumbs-up. Chad smiled back. Other brother Aaron, whose afternoon paper route had kept him away, would be happy, too.

Dad scratched vigorously at his arms, shifting his hold of the wheel from one hand to the other. *"Crazy* mosquitoes!"

"Mm! Gotcha too, huh?" Chad noticed the itchy red welts on his own arms.

"Yeah, a few of 'em sunk wells. But this is their season, all right. Humid."

Chad giggled. "Want me to drive for ya?"

"Naw, not yet. Ya still have a *few* more years to go." Dad chuckled, too. "Anyway, your Mom sure would have loved to see the game. But she had groceries to get and, well…your little brother would've kept her hands too full to notice much of it. Besides, he wouldn't have lasted the afternoon."

Chad grinned. Likely the same could be said for the only girl out of the five Thomas kids. "Is that why we left Katie with her?" he asked, jokingly.

"Sure is. She's a good little helper."

Chad had to suppress his euphoria. He couldn't *wait* to tell Mom. And Katie. And Ethan, too!

He untucked his shirt, whisked his dirty white baseball cap from his back pocket, and set it on his head.

Backwards, of course.

The cool smell of fresh salad greeted him as he walked into the kitchen. Mom was scraping carrots at the sink; she turned around as he came in.

"Mom! We won the game—and I made the winning goal!"

"You did? That's wonderful!" She put down her work and wiped her hands on her apron. "What was the score?"

"Twelve-eleven, with *five seconds left!*"

Mom looked amazed. "Mmm! Pretty close!"

"Sure was! *Nothing* could get closer than that. I barely almost didn't!"

"I'm really happy for you, dear. I see you got some sun, too."

Chad looked down at himself again. He *had* tanned, slightly. "Where's Katie?" he asked.

"Taking a nap. She and Ethan played hard all day—I think he wore her out."

The radio on the refrigerator was on. Chad picked up a carrot, holding it like a microphone as he sang along with the familiar words of "Yesterday Once More."

He whirled around, giving the shoot-in another practice.

"I wish I could have gone this afternoon," Mom continued. "But I'll sure be at the next one! When is it, again?"

"On Tuesday."

"At the same field?"

"Uh-huh."

"Great! We'll be watching the fireworks there on Wednesday night, too. This should be an exciting week."

"Hot diggity!" Chad couldn't wait for that. He *loved* fireworks.

"Well, go get yourself cleaned up. Supper will be on in a little while—out back on the picnic table."

"Okay!"

Eating outside. Another of Chad's favorite summertime events. He took a bite of the carrot and walked into the living room.

There was Ethan, sitting on the rug in front of the fan, talking into it and laughing at the distorted sound of his voice. Chad laughed, too—he'd done the same thing when he was younger. "Hi, Eeth," he said, taking another bite. "What's up?"

His brother looked back at him. "Ith my fan cub," he answered, repeating a phrase his siblings often used. He talked good for a three-year-old.

"We won the game," said Chad. "We did it!"

Ethan yelled into the fan again. "Yaaaaay!"

Chad grinned and headed upstairs. Now for a nice, cool shower.

The smell of grilled hamburgers filled his nose as he stepped into the backyard.

Dad was busy cooking on the patio. Mom was setting the picnic table, Katie was painting water pictures on the concrete, and Aaron and Carson were involved in a game of badminton on the grass. A light breeze was blowing, but it was still sunny, warm, and humid.

Chad breathed deeply—he enjoyed this *so much*. He sat down on the reclining lawn chair as he waited, stretching out, closing his eyes and daydreaming.

It was summertime.

The time of year for *everything*.

Like a cool sprinkler to run through, then some ice cream to cool off on the inside; things like endless hours of sunlight, muggy days filled with the sounds of lawnmowers or locusts or june bugs or mourning doves, warm nights filled only with the sounds of crickets and the quiet hum of a fan propped in a window—everything from sweltering humidity to cool breezes.

Ah, summertime.

A time for open fields ablaze with lightning bugs or swarming with mosquitoes or thick with cottonwood seeds; entire months rich with the smells of grilled steak, corn-on-the-cob, homemade donuts, clean laundry on the clothesline, fresh-mowed grass, wild onions growing in yards, the aroma of charcoal, the smell of garden hoses, the tinge of chlorine at the swimming pool.

Summertime.

A time for playing soccer or tug-of-war or swelter-skelter (hide-and-seek on a hot afternoon). Or playing baseball in the big lot beside the house—hearing the dull thud of a bat hitting the ground as a player dropped it and ran for first amid the muffled thump of footsteps on dirt and grass.

Or riding Aaron's skateboard and helping him with his route or helping Dad wash the car.

Or just having some homemade peach pie and fresh farm cream.

Summertime. One huge vast array of sight and sound and smell and activity and fun.

Like sitting up in the screened-in porch and watching a thunderstorm—his favorite thing of all—or of going to sleep listening to one.

Or going on evening bike rides in the country, listening to the crunch of gravel under the tires, and then back home for the ultimate root beer dessert—"black cows." He'd literally *melt* as he'd watch Dad put two big scoops of vanilla ice cream in each person's glass and then pour cool root beer over it, making a rich, creamy froth.

Mmmmmmm.

It was *summertime.*

A time for running and playing and being outside and having fun and an endless million other things. Summertime through the eyes of a ten-year-old.

He *loved* it.

Things like…

"Chad! Supper's on."

Startled, he opened his eyes and looked over. Everyone had gathered at the table and was starting to sit down.

He joined them and said the blessing.

So this is how it was on this hazy Saturday evening, with July, the best month of all, just a few short hours away.

3

July!

And how *quickly* the morning went. First days of the month were always like that, especially Sundays. Before anyone knew it, the afternoon had rolled around and they'd all fallen victim to an onset of the post-lunch "stares," for which there was no cure except to sit and sleep it away (the extra thick humidity which had set in overnight made it even easier). Chad picked his favorite spot for this ritual—the big green recliner in the family room. It was the perfect place to relax, unwind...and just get *bored,* the best thing of summertime.

And it was also Abraham's favorite spot. He jumped into Chad's lap as he sat down, settling in and purring quietly.

Chad leaned the chair back all the way and shut his eyes.

17

Not a sound.

It was amazing how *quiet* the house could be with four other sibs, considering two of them were even younger than him. He smiled. What a bunch. One big brother who'd be *driving* in less than three years, another who liked to see how many times he could count to fifteen before the car passed the next sign post, a sister who'd once used white correction fluid as nail polish, and a little brother with a chuffy-sounding laugh who liked to yell into fans. No doubt, a unique bunch.

And then there was him. The only blond-haired, left-handed one, smack in the middle of the pack, no adulthood within eight years of him. He felt, well…different, too.

And they were a *fun* bunch, especially the younger ones. Chad practically felt like a dad already. At ten, he was already plenty experienced at babysitting and diaper-changing, having literally "grown up" with the smells of strained food, diapers, ammonia, and the sound of little palms slapping the floor in a crawl. He remembered holding Katie on his lap when she was a baby (even though he could *barely* remember—he was only four!). Chubby, round, and with what he'd called "fat, scrawny little legs," she'd been equipped with a vast arsenal of nicknames—words like Buttertubs, Katiecakes, Sugarbricks and Ring-Chin-Chin abounded. Chad laughed out loud as he remembered them. She'd been a character, that Katie.

Then came Ethan, and the cycle started all over again (Wuggers, Wifflebeans, and Beebers were a few of *his* aliases). Chad recalled when he'd first learned to walk—it was several days of slip, crash, bang and bump. Then he'd gotten the hang of it and everything was up for grabs; it had to be put up high or he'd grab it. Even now, Chad would follow him almost *everywhere* to make sure he stayed all right. So much, in fact, that Mom had dubbed him Ethan's guardian angel. Chad thought that was *neat*. And indeed, he'd often been right there to rescue his brother from many a minor calamity. Often he wondered what it'd be like watching an *older* person!

What a fun job that would be, he thought, smiling again.

And of course, there was Dad. Kind, laughy, and with his own brand of dry humor, he was the funniest Dad that *Chad* had ever known. It was the way he always *said* things, Chad figured. He'd say how he could hold something and carry it at the same time, or how he could do two things at once—as long as he did one before the other, or how he could buy anything in the world—as long as he didn't have to pay for it, or how he liked to jog because he was too lazy to walk, or how skinned knees should be avoided because they hurt, and so on and so on. He said stuff like that all the time and it had rubbed off on Chad; he'd grown to love it, plain and simple.

And Dad could build almost *anything* with wood. He'd even made a somewhat elaborate jungle gym in the backyard which Chad *loved* to play on, even now that he'd grown a little.

Most of all, though, Chad liked how Dad always made the evenings fun. Chad wasn't a night person and never had been. But Dad always found a way to make that last little while before bedtime the best part of the whole day. The dusk hours would be filled with a backyard game of badminton (until the mosquitoes decided it was enough), or swing era music or ragtime on the record player (was that *Make-Believe* or *Maple Leaf* Rag?), or an involved board game, or the sound of a card deck getting shuffled (which Chad *still* couldn't really do) before play. Chad *loved* playing cards. Crazy eights was his favorite game and he could beat almost anyone at it. Solitaire, on the other hand, was a whole different story. Many a time he'd watch Mom or Dad play it, but he could never figure it out—even after it had been explained to him.

But by far his *favorite* evening activity was when Dad read a story from the Bible. No other book in the world was so fun or neat or *fascinating*. Everyone would sit enchanted as they'd hear about Baalam's talking donkey, or the Tower of Babel, or Noah and the Flood, or the Apostles in Jerusalem, or most importantly, of course, the Lord Himself and the Good News He brought. And what a *funny* Book—many a character, many a line had been spawned during the readings. Chad laughed out loud yet again as he recalled some:

"The Lord wants us to walk *up*rightly. That's why he didn't put our legs on our heads."

"And He doesn't want us to go first. That's why He commands us to 'go forth.'"

"What was Jay's last name?"

"Jay *who?*"

"That's it! Jehu!"

"'Titus' was really a *middle* name, ya know. His first name was 'Derma.'"

"The Philistines had the world's toughest court system. It was either make Baal or die."

"Is that pronounced Phil-*IS*-tine or *PHIL*-is-tine?"

"Who's Phil Istine?"

Of course, this sparked others, Phillip-Pie, Phil Lipians, Phil Ofitall, Phil Osofical, Phil Erup, Phil Ingstation, Phil Bert, etc. Then there was the Axe of the Apostles, Knee-High Miah, Bildad (Bill Dad?) the Shoe-Height, King Hair-Ud, and Gauze-Uh. And who could forget all the tribes—the Caananites (Cain and Abels!), Amorites, Jebusites, Hittites, Stalactites, Goflyakytes, Fraidofhytes, Skeeterbytes, Toobigabytes, or the Outtasytes?

Chad roared. *What a book!*

He was instantly reminded of some of his *own* characters, which he was constantly making up—there was Sir Vey (who loved to ask questions), Sir Real the Painter, Miss Take (who could never do anything right), Miss Ulaneous (who did any *number* of odd things), Miss Fortune the Accident-Prone, Aunt Arctica (a very cold person), Size McWaves (the Quaker from California), Evan Gelist the Preacher, Saul Right (whose name was always said twice—first like a question, then an answer), Patty Cakes, Polly Esther and her dog Cotton. And, of course, there was Dun Roony (an ancient tennis ball Chad had drawn a face on and made a slit for a mouth).

Chad couldn't *help* making so many things up—words were so *incredibly* fun! And he'd literally developed his own entire language, having coined a word or phrase for almost everything. When a tooth fell out it was *gap*itated; when the new one came in it was *de*gapitated. When there was more than one grouch it was *grice;* being lost in thought was *ponderizing.* Potatoes were *tato-spuds,* and when something tasted yucky—like licorice or watermelon—it was *churky.* A lady mailman was a *femailman,* and a space-consumer was a *bulk-taker.* Paper clips to bend out of shape were *doodleclips,* and "correctly on the button" meant simply, "right!"

Sometimes, though, words—*real* words—got tough to pronounce or understand, and would occasionally confuse him. "Ecstatic," for instance, was the condition reached after scuffing on a rug in winter. An "exhaustive concordance" meant a book was exhausting to carry, and a "thesaurus" was some kind of dinosaur. "Misled" was pronounced "mizzled," "hypocrisy" was "hippo-crissy," "pothole" was "poth-hole," "infrared" was "infraired," "mishap" was "mish-hap," "humid" was "hummid," Milk Duds (the candy) were "Milk Dudes." Then there was stuff like lead and *lead,* tear and *tear,* minute and *minute,* record and *record,* bass and *bass.* Chad was usually content (was that content or *content?*) with what he *did* know of the language, but he was always trying to better himself. And he *loved* learning new words. He'd asked Aaron one time what "opposite" meant.

"Well," he'd replied, "it's like the other thing of whatever you're doin' or sayin'—you know, like the 'opposite' of the same thing."

"Oh yeah, *I* know."

"Good! So then what's the opposite of *specific?*"

"Atlantic."

"Right!"

Chad felt great that day—yet another new word learned.

But words weren't the only things he had fun with. He was extremely inventive—*always* thinking of something new— and had already tried many different things (with varying degrees of success). Like reading two copies of the same newspaper at once to get his own homemade stereo sound, or planting Cheerios in the backyard (thinking they were donut seeds), or mixing paint with glue to make it stick on the wall better, or shutting a door open, or giving the supper bell only half a ring, or mixing two cans of the same pop to get twice the fizz, or mixing two glasses of water to get twice the thickness, or even trying to pour water backwards!

One time Dad accidentally locked the keys in the house and Chad had asked why they couldn't just go in and get them. Dad stifled a laugh when he mentioned it but nevertheless helped Chad—then the smallest one—squeeze through the kitchen window where he retrieved the keys (before coming back out the same way).

Chad wasn't sure why he was such a pragmatist. Impossible or not, maybe, he felt everything was worth trying. And everything that *did* happen was for a reason, whether it was even pleasant or not. Even every "mistake" had a reason.

Abraham stirred in his lap. Chad petted him on the head. *What a fun life,* he thought. *And it's all the little things that make it fun. All the little things that make this place home.*

He thought how he'd playfully try to hold his bedroom door shut against Dad (even though Dad usually won!). Or how he'd turn the doorknob the *opposite* way the person on the other side was turning, preventing an entry. Or trying to walk up or down the stairs without making a single creak (he'd yet to succeed). Or trying to shut the stapler lid without ejecting one. Or seeing how far he could throw an empty styrofoam cup. Or singing along with a record playing at high speed. Or touching metal things fingernail first to muffle the effects of static electricity. Or watching the fuzzy screen on TV and make-believing he could see all sorts of things in it.

He chuckled again.

Pretty tidily stuff, maybe, but *he* thought it was neat. All tricks of the trade in the life of a ten-year-old. All fun and games. There were a *thousand* of them.

And, of course, there was soccer.

Chad thought of all his teammates, everyone who made it so enjoyable. Craig, his closest friend who lived right down the street. And the Hawkeye (his real name was Shawn— originally from Iowa, he was called "the Hawkeye" because he could hawk louder than anyone else). And Kevin, Keith, and Kit, triplets on the same team who had to wear color-coded armbands because they had the same differences. And Brian and Mitchell and Zack and Ian and half a dozen others, each with their own way of adding to it all. And assistant coach Stevens (also Craig's dad), who always called Chad "Short-stop"—probably on account of his baseball cap, he figured. He added an extra spark to the whole game, too.

And then there was the Big Guy.

Coach Anderson. Aside from his own parents, Chad felt Coach was one of the biggest influences on his life. He was almost, through sheer force of his presence, the game itself. With his tall height, brown beard and mustache and kind, almost *fatherly* attitude the whole team had affectionately called him the Big Guy, and while most coaches could probably be thought of as ruthless and hard-nosed, the Big Guy was nothing but ruthlessly *kind.*

To Chad, he was practically a second dad—on *or* off the field. He knew how to communicate; he spoke Chad's language. And he was good at it. He'd say how nothing could be done on a routine basis without it, too, becoming routine (a good thing to remember during practice!); or how a talent should never be overregulated; or how certain moves during a game could prove to be insignificant yet important; or (that if a player chooses a strategy, it's best to stick with it,) or, ultimately, to dot all the t's and cross all the i's and just enjoy the game for what it was—a game. Chad had received the lasting extent of his advice. And it was that kind of advice that had made the team and got it where it was now. Chad loved every minute of it, and he couldn't wait to see the Big Guy again.

And soccer was only *one* of his many, many interests. Geography was another. Chad was a geography *buff*. Sure, it was unusual for a kid his age, but he didn't mind. Everyone had their interests (Aaron was a history buff, and Dad said he used to be a floor buff). There weren't many places he couldn't find on a globe or map. He was an *avid* studier of them, and was delighted an entire country halfway around the world shared his name. The interest had sharpened his "navigational" skills, too—he could memorize every single detail of new surroundings with only a couple of glances.

But by far his favorite interest was *computers*—or robots, or *anything* electronic. Stuff like that was *fascinating.* Any pictures of robots or anything related to them, he saved. He'd even asked to see the new "Western World" movie, but Dad said he wasn't quite old enough for it (he did, however, build a wooden "robot" for Chad in the basement, using old radio parts for the "inside"). Dad knew all about computers at his job (he was an electronics specialist) and even had a new *calculator* to help him do taxes with. It was an *incredible* little thing—and it fit right in his shirt pocket!

"They're already trying to make whole computers—small ones—that'll fit on top of a desk," Dad had told him one day. "With no big wires or anything else."

"Really?" Chad was astounded.

"Sure," said Dad, himself a little wide-eyed. "And people will get to buy them and use them at *home.*"

"Can *I* use one?"

"You bet, eventually."

Chad couldn't *wait* for that day to come. Operating a *computer.* Pushing those big, lighted buttons, pulling the levers, watching the tape come out.

But, for now, it would all have to wait.

"You know, Abe, someday I want to live in a place with all that neat stuff." Chad stroked the shiny black fur. "A nice, quiet house, out in the country. With a family like I have now. And a couple horses. And a cat like you. And a screened-in porch, of course."

Abraham stirred again, making him giggle. He was very *ticklish!*

So much to do in his life—so, so much. Chad liked it so far. And he still had so much ahead of him.

It was such *fun* being a kid. Chad almost didn't want to grow up. He recalled that he'd once been concerned his younger sister and brother would somehow get older than him. Now, he almost wished that was the case. Almost.

That's what I want to be when I grow up, he thought. *A kid!*

The supper bell was ringing. Chad awoke with a start.

He smiled.

Holy wow, the afternoon sure goes fast.

4

Practice, practice, practice.

A *lot* of practicing.

He stood in front of the mirror on the door in his bedroom and *practiced* every soccer move he knew, over and over, again and again.

The shoot-in was looking better and better. Wearing his soccer clothes seemed to help. He felt more comfortable, more in place with them.

And his anticipation was growing.

Tuesday was almost here.

"Still workin' on it, huh?" Dad noticed his uniform as he walked into the dining room. Everyone was just sitting down for breakfast.

"Oh, yeah," Chad answered, grinning. "Morning's the best time."

"Gettin' tired of it?"

"Sort of. It's kinda gettin' worn out to a frazzle, but I still like it." He took his seat.

"I'll be home from work early today," said Dad. "Maybe we can practice together."

"Sure!"

"I wish I didn't have to go anywhere at all—but that's how it worked out with the holiday in midweek. I have the *next* two days off, though."

"Mm." Chad was looking at Ethan, perched in his high chair against the table. He found it amazing how he could crumb when he didn't even have his food yet. They bowed their heads and Mr. Thomas said the prayer.

"Could you pass the juice, please?" Chad called to Aaron as he opened his little box of cereal.

His brother reached for the juice. As he leaned forward on his other arm, his elbow bumped the end of his spoon, catapulting the cereal it held into the air. Thrusting out a hand to catch it, he knocked over the carton of milk, spilling the whole thing all over the table and into Chad's lap.

For a moment Chad sat there, a look of absolute surprise on his face. Then he laughed.

So did everyone else. "I hardly ever see you get spilled on sometimes," said Katie.

"Aw, it *always* happens, every now and then," said Chad, as he stood and mopped up his front with some napkins. He went back upstairs to change and Mom got his uniform in the laundry right away.

Phew, it was hot. And *humid,* too! What Chad would call "unfathomably unbelievable" humidity, what Dad called just plain *thick.* It had indeed been humid Saturday—even more so yesterday—but nothing like this. Chad was only glad it had waited until after the game; they might even have called it under such conditions, for all he knew. He could only hope it would break before the next day.

Nevertheless, it was good summer weather. Chad looked up from his dirt mural back across the lot toward the house—Mom was hanging his freshly-washed uniform on the clothesline with the rest of the laundry. He grinned and looked back down.

This was his favorite spot in this lot. Situated at the far edge with an old, red wooden bench (which worked as a shield from the hot sun for anyone squatted in front of it, like now), it served a variety of purposes: dugout and fort, base from would-be taggers and spy station (whenever "suspicious" cars were going by). Today, however, the little dry, grassless area was a canvas. Equipped with a small branch, Chad was working on a scene from a city street, with buses, cars, skyscrapers, shops, the works. He'd never *seen* a really *big* city before, except in pictures.

Someday, he thought.

Craig, sitting right beside him, was drawing his own: an ocean with a beach and a pier.

Chad was exultant. "Boy! I can't *wait* for tomorrow!"

"Me neither," said Craig, carefully adding lines to a seashell. "Dad and me will be here to get ya, as usual. We'll get here a little earlier."

Chad heard someone over on the sidewalk and looked up again. There was Ethan, busy skipping along, stopping every so often to pick dandelions.

He wasn't very far from the street.

Have to watch him, thought Chad. He finished putting the windows in a skyscraper, taking care to avoid the tiny ants frolicking around their mound nearby. He stared at the grains of dirt that made their little house, imagining they were grains of sand, like on a beach in Craig's picture. Normally they resembled cereal or malt mix or something, but today, sand.

The cruel blare of a car horn jolted his mind back.

He looked up.

Suddenly he saw Ethan darting into the street after a dandelion the wind had caught—a big car coming straight at him—

No!

Chad grabbed his brother by the arm, half-pulling, half-tossing him back onto the grass just as the vehicle roared by, so close its wind almost knocked him backwards. He staggered to regain his balance…

Ethan started to cry. It was the most *wonderful* sound Chad had ever heard—and only then did he really notice where he was. He couldn't even remember running to the street. He sat down on the curb, still shaking a little, breathing hard.

Craig ran over from the bench. Mom rushed over from the patio. Se looked a little shaken herself—she picked up Ethan and hugged him.

"You *are* his angel, Chad!" She looked at her other son and smiled. "Good eyes! Thank you!"

Chad's adrenaline was still racing too hard for him to answer. Mom carried Ethan back to the house and took him inside. He was probably going to be spanked.

Chad was slowly catching his breath.

Craig was wide-eyed. "Wow, Chad! That car almost *killed* him! And *you,* too!"

Chad's heart jumped at the realization—he could hardly believe it. "Yeah, I know," was all he could say right then.

He got up. They both walked, silently, back to the old wooden bench and sat down.

Craig had a funny look on his face. "Hey Chad," he said, finally. "Have ya ever thought what it'd be like to *die?* Even when you're still a *kid?* When you're not even grown *up* yet?"

Chad picked up the branch again and stared down at his drawing, now smudged with the hurriedly-made imprints of his high tops. No, he *hadn't* thought. Never in his life. Such a thing just seemed too…*unbelievable.* At least until *now* it had.

"No I haven't," he answered, not looking up.

Then, suddenly, he *smiled.*

He smiled with the confidence of one who had suddenly remembered something—something so neat as to render all worry and uncertainty and insecurity utterly needless.

He looked over at Craig.

"But I know where I'm goin' when I do," he said, "so I'm as ready as I can be."

Craig smiled, too. *He* knew what Chad meant.

He looked at his watch. "Wow! I gotta be gettin' home!" He started off toward the house for his bike.

"Gonna be at singing practice tonight?" Chad called after him.

"Naw, afraid I can't make it."

"Okay, then. See ya tomorrow morning!"

"Eight-thirty!" Craig shouted as he disappeared from view. "We'll be here with bells on!"

"All right! See ya then!" Chad yelled back. Then he thought, *Naw, he won't really. It's too hot for long pants.*

The bright afternoon sky had suddenly grown darker—a wall of clouds had covered the sun.

Chad stepped outside again. Though it was still quite humid, a light breeze had picked up and a familiar smell hung in the air. He breathed deeply.

Rain.

It was going to rain. A nice, cool, midwestern thunderstorm was rolling in.

His eyes lit up. "Hot diggity!"

He went back inside, back to his favorite place and waited.

Mr. Thomas got home from work just as the first drops started to fall. Mrs. Thomas had just finished hurriedly bringing the laundry in. "At least they got dry first," she said. "Now I can iron."

She told her husband what happened—what had *almost* happened—earlier.

He looked around. Chad was nowhere to be seen.

"Where is he?"

"Heef upstaws wathing the thunder." Ethan had just come into the kitchen.

His father looked down at him and smiled—Ethan, alive and well. "Thanks there, young sir."

He gave him a pat on the head and started toward the stairs.

He should've *known* where Chad was.

Slowly he made his way up.

The familiar "Rainy Days and Mondays" drifted out from the porch as he reached the top, accented by a small clap of thunder and the patter of rain on the roof. He walked in. There was the little portable record player, neatly sitting on the old footstool.

And there was Chad. In one of the lawn chairs from the patio, facing the row of big, screened windows that spanned the porch. His hands were folded behind his head, under the bill of his backwards baseball cap, his crossed legs were propped on the window sill in front of him.

Mr. Thomas smiled. It was classic Chad. His favorite way of sitting, favorite music, favorite event in all the world. Chad looked up. Their eyes met just as the melody peaked in beautiful, harmonious splendor—then reached its calm, gentle climax. They *both* smiled.

Chad reached over and turned the machine off, setting the needle back in its perch. He looked back up at Dad.

For a moment, neither of them said anything. Dad carefully lifted the player off the footstool and sat down.

He's always here when I need him, Chad thought, looking back out the window. *He always knows.*

They both watched the rain for a little while.

"You really like watching thunderstorms, don't you?" said Dad, finally.

"Yeah." Chad's gaze was fixed outside, almost *captivated.* "A lot."

Did he *ever* like it. Nothing was more fun than sitting up in a screened-in porch, listening to the thunder, watching the rain pelt the sidewalk, the street, the grass, and smelling the fresh, crisp air it always brought. It almost seemed...*magical.*

He watched the dark clouds move across the surrounding timber, the farmland, over his neighborhood.

"Yeah, they are fun." Dad sounded lost in thought, too. "I liked to do this same thing when *I* was a kid. I think thunderstorms run in the family."

They both chuckled.

Chad looked down at his lap and swallowed. He knew what Dad was going to say.

"Your Mom told me what happened today." He gave Chad a pat on the knee, then brought his hand to rest on his shoulder. "Thanks, little guardian. Your quick reflexes come in handy, in more than one way."

Chad grinned. Then he thought—he'd ask *Dad* the question.

"Have ya ever thought what it'd be like to *die,* Dad?"

Mr. Thomas smiled. "Well, can't say I've ever spent a *lot* of time thinking about it. I've never really died before."

They both chuckled again.

"Actually," Dad continued, "I did think about it once. But like you, I now have the assurance I need so I don't have to anymore."

"Oh yeah," said Chad. "That was the best day of my life, when I got that. But it's still nice to be alive anyway. So I can do all the neat stuff I'm doin'."

"Like just havin' a good attitude and laughin' a lot?"

"Yeah, *that* kind of stuff." Chad's smile slowly turned into an inquisitive look as the question aroused yet another long-standing curiosity in his mind.

"Why *does* everyone always make me laugh?" he asked.

"Because ya have such a neat-*sounding* laugh," said Dad. "It's really contagious. It's fun to listen to and it makes other people feel good. And you—"

A brilliant flash, followed by a sharp crack of thunder, momentarily interrupted him. He continued.

"—and you have such a good outlook, besides. Everything's fine for ya. You're just inconsolably happy."

"I hope I make everyone else feel the same way," said Chad, staring back outside. "Besides, if I ever…*left* like that, then Katie and Ethan would get older than me."

They both laughed.

"You wouldn't really *mind,* would ya?" said Dad.

"Well, naw, not really. Because then I'd be a kid forever."

The smell of ironed clothes crept into the porch.

Their eyes met again.

"Thanks, Dad. Thanks for bein' here."

His father smiled and laid an arm on the back of his chair. They both watched the thunderstorm.

It was so *cool* outside.

For that first initial period after the storm had passed, the air was so fresh, so rain-washed, so *crisp* that Chad could even see his breath as he walked to the car.

He breathed deeply. *Mmmm,* yes. Cool, clean air.

> *I've got a home in Gloryland*
> *That outshines the sun*
> *I've got a home in Gloryland*
> *That outshines the sun*
> *I've got a home in Gloryland*
> *That outshines the sun*
> *Way beyond the blue*
> *Hey! (Clap)*

Everyone on and off stage broke into applause and cheered loudly—it was almost like winning a game all over again!

Chad *loved* singing practice. And they sounded way better tonight than ever before. With a piano, two guitars, a big bass (or *bass?*) fiddle and an eager "choir" of twelve clapping kids, it was indeed fun to see and hear—hardly a person could pass up just sitting and listening to it. And the pews *were* nearly full—and this was only practice!

The Big Guy was there too, all right. Chad could see him from the corner of his eye, sitting by Dad near the far end of a row about halfway down. He *was* up to something. Chad could *feel* him grinning. It took everything he had to keep from swinging his head around to see him better, but he had to keep his place on stage.

"Okay, everyone! That's it!"

Another loud cheer filled the auditorium, and the pews began to empty out. Coach walked down and met Chad at the front; he stood silently with his arms crossed, smiling, waiting for everyone else to leave. Chad sat down on the edge of the stage, his curiosity rising fast.

"Well!" Coach gazed down at him as the last of the crowd wandered out the doors. *"I'm* here, and *you're* here, so…"

Chad noticed he had something under his arm. *What was it?* It looked like a—

"Yep! It's a *package.*" Coach had a gleam in his eye. "And it's for *you,* Chad. Here."

He lowered the plain brown, neatly-tied mass into Chad's outstretched hands. "Go ahead, you can open it now."

Chad could hardly contain his excitement—he hadn't been expecting anything like this. Getting his own *package* was almost enough in itself. It was even better than getting a present, because *they* were usually known about in advance, in anticipation of birthdays or Christmas. But not this.

What in the world was it?

He laid the soft bulk in his lap. That one, big, *wonderful* moment of anticipation.

His hands trembled as he slowly removed the string. His eyes widened and his mouth fell open as he pulled away the paper, revealing a brand-new, clean, *perfect* soccer uniform.

Chad couldn't believe it. Again he could feel the Big Guy grinning from ear to ear as he held up the pristine white shirt, matching shorts and new socks. Emblazoned on the back of the shirt in brilliant yellow letters was the name THOMAS. *His* name. Directly below it in jet black was the number 77. *His* number.

His very own *personalized* soccer uniform.

He absolutely didn't know what to say. He looked up at his coach.

"Thought you might enjoy it," he said. "You'll wear it for me tomorrow, of course, won't you?"

Chad flashed him a smile—the second biggest smile he'd ever made. "Yes, sir, I sure will! I'll be there, and it'll be there, too!" He stood, holding his sparkling new uniform close to him.

Then both he and Coach laughed. Chad gave him a big

bear hug, as big as could be expected of a ten-year-old.

He barely even noticed the bright flash as Dad, who'd been tipped off in advance, caught the moment on camera.

Chad walked out into the now *warm* summer evening, his new treasure neatly tucked under his arm. There was not a sound, except for the crunch of gravel underfoot in the parking lot and the steady, quiet hum of locusts. He couldn't *wait* for the next day. The second best day of his life.

5

Oooh, yes!

The wonderful smell of crisp, freshly-printed fabric filled his nose as he slid the brand-new shirt down over his head. *Ahhh.* It had even been prewashed so it didn't feel stiff. It was *so* comfortable—and perfectly *clean!* He almost didn't want to wear it.

He finished dressing and stood in front of the mirror on his door. He could hardly believe what he saw. The little guy before him stood completely *immaculate* in white from head to foot, save for battered high tops and baseball cap. He was *awestruck.* It was amazing how much difference a new uniform could make. He took a step back—the whole room lit up as it reflected the morning sunlight streaming through the window.

Holy wow!

He turned and stared wide-eyed at his bedroom, newly ablaze in brilliant splendor. He'd never really noticed just how pretty it was. And he *loved* it—*his* room, *his* home. He was already looking forward to coming back, in a way.

He again faced the mirror, and gave the shoot-in one more practice before going downstairs.

The big day had finally arrived.

"My *goodness!*" Mom and Dad seemed as amazed as him when they saw it. "Look at *you!*"

Chad did—he looked down at himself again.

"That's gotta be the *whitest* set of clothes I've ever seen!" Dad exclaimed. "How do ya like it?"

Chad grinned from ear to ear. "It's *perfect*. Makes me look brand new."

He walked to the table and took his seat, studying his reflection wherever he could—in the windows, the stove front, even the distorting metal lid covering the pan of home-made brown sugar maple muffins.

He said his prayer and ate a couple. *Mmmm*. Nothing quite like 'em.

Craig would be arriving shortly. "Where's everyone else?" asked Chad.

"They haven't come down yet," said Mom. "But then, you're up a little earlier, too—at least for a *summer* morning." She pointed to his soccer shoes, still on the old newspaper by the front door where he'd left them Saturday. "Just remember to grab those on your way out."

"Uh-huh! I sure will!"

"I don't imagine you'll be *in* them until the game starts," said Dad, chuckling.

Chad laughed, too. "No, of *course* not!"

A car horn sounded in the driveway. Chad looked at his watch. Yep—eight-thirty exactly on the dot.

Time to go do it.

Chad rose, kissed his parents, and headed out the door, his cleats in hand.

"Whoa!" Coach Stevens exclaimed as Chad crawled into the back seat beside Craig and dropped his shoes in the footspace. "I see *you're* ready to go there, Mr. Thomas!"

"You bet!" answered his eager little passenger. "Ready as I've ever been!"

Craig was staring at him, too. "Wow! Did *Coach* give you that?"

"Sure did."

"It's fantastic-looking," said Coach Stevens. "Only problem now is, all this *grubby* stuff'll look outta place with ya." He laughed and patted the big, dirty equipment bag on the passenger seat.

The familiar "Candyman" came on the radio. Chad and Craig looked at each other.

"You ready to go?"

"You bet! Let's go do it!"

"Yeah, let's go score another one for the Big Guy!"

They both whooped and gave each other high fives, as high as they could in the car—first on their right hands, then their lefts, then again on their rights, then both at once; then one, then the other, then both again.

The car pulled out of the driveway, and they were off.

Chad looked out his window. He could see Mom and Dad, waving at him in the front yard—along with Aaron, Carson, Katie, and Ethan. And they were all still in their pajamas!

He rolled down his window and waved back as the car moved down the road. "Bye, Mom! Bye, Dad! Bye, guys!"

"See ya there!" Dad shouted back.

Chad couldn't *wait* to see them again. He only hoped he could keep his uniform clean until his brothers and sister saw it.

He watched his family through the back window until he couldn't see them anymore. Then he turned around again and settled into his seat.

It was still noticeably cooler than it had been, compliments of the previous day's thunderstorm—puddles were everywhere, vapor was rising from the rooftops, and there wasn't a cloud in the sky.

Perfect playing weather.

Craig yawned and Chad did, too—he couldn't see anyone do it without doing so himself. And strangely enough, he *was* starting to feel a little…*sleepy.*

The car stopped at a traffic light. Chad watched a workman's chainsaw clearing away some fallen timber. *What a fast three days it's been,* he thought. *And what a life it's going to be.* So many things to do, so much to look forward to in a lifetime. He liked it so far. And he still had so much ahead of him.

He grinned. He couldn't *wait!*

Buzzz. He watched the thing effortlessly carve into a tree trunk. *And I'd love to hold one of those, too,* he thought. *Someday.*

The car moved on.

They finally arrived at the field—the gravel crackled beneath the tires as they parked in the usual area, at the base of the steep, grassy embankment below the highway. The field wasn't very full yet. The Lions' coach was already there, helping the groundskeepers set it up. A few Angels were there, too—the Hawkeye, and Zack, and…yes, that looked like Mitchell practicing by the touchline.

And, of course, the one Chad had been waiting to see most of all. The Big Guy.

He hadn't seen *them* yet. Chad wanted to surprise him. He started to walk up behind him, slowly, and almost made it—until Zack gave him away.

"Wow! That's a *cool* uniform!"

The Big Guy turned around. For a moment, he just…*looked* at Chad, scrutinizing him from top to bottom, squinting against the glare of sunlight off the bright material. Then he smiled…*big.*

"That *is* a good-lookin' one, stranger! Where'd ya get it?"

They both laughed.

"Well, it *does* look good on ya, Chad—*really* good. And it's definitely your color, no question. Thanks for wearin' it for me."

"No problem, Coach. Thanks for *gettin'* it for me."

"You bet! Now we can have the games at night." They both chuckled again and Coach gave him a playful knock on the head "So, ya wanna go kick the ball around for a while, or just wait a bit?"

Chad thought. He was feeling a little sleepier now. "Could I sit down for a little while?"

"Sure! Go find yourself a spot on the bleachers. They're still in the shade."

"All right, Coach."

Chad walked over. He sat down, spreading his arms on the floorboard behind him, savoring the cool shade of the elm trees above. He swung his cap around and lowered the bill slightly. Another yawn came—he seemed especially vulnerable to them this morning. He wasn't even sure why; maybe getting up a little earlier had done it.

He heard others arriving. He raised his head—yep, more of his teammates—and watched as a couple of them practice with a Nerf soccer ball, while the rest stretched or talked among themselves. A few pointed at him and waved; he waved back.

But he was growing *sleepier* by the minute. Even considering his early start, he couldn't understand it.

Boy, I'd love a quick nap. He rarely ever took one, but now he cherished the thought. He looked around groggily and his eyes landed on Coach Stevens' grand Omega, back in the parking lot where they'd just left it.

He sighed dreamily. Those seats sure would be more comfortable than hard wooden bleachers...

"Whoa! Still with us there, Shortstop?"

Chad lifted his bill. Coach Stevens was looking down at him, grinning.

"Well, yeah, *sort* of," he answered, grinning back weakly. "I guess part of me's still in bed."

Coach laughed. "Sandman's still after ya, huh?"

"Yeah. I can't shake him this morning." Chad couldn't help glancing over at that wonderful car again. "Um...could I..."

Coach's grin gave him away—he knew *exactly* what Chad was thinking. He reached into his pocket and pulled out his car keys. "Here," he said, singling out the large one with the square end and handing it to Chad. "Go rest yourself in the back. Ya still have some time."

"Wow! Thanks a lot, Coach!"

"No problem! At least it'll be *quieter* in there for ya. Just don't drive off with it, all right?"

He winked and pulled Chad's bill down again before heading back to the field.

Chad chuckled. Yes, driving was another thing he was immensely looking forward to. He went over, keys in hand.

Ahhh. The back seat was even more comfortable than he'd anticipated. He stretched out on it, pausing only to study his uniform once more in the rearview mirror—it was so *white,* so *neat.*

I'd love to look like that all the time, he thought, yawning yet again. He tipped his cap down over his eyes and folded his arms behind his head. *And what a fun day this is gonna be. This is great!*

He could hardly believe it. In less than thirty short minutes, it would all start *The* big game. Mom and Dad would be arriving anytime, and so would the rest of the bunch. And he couldn't wait—he couldn't *wait* for it all. And he wasn't even nervous, like he thought he'd be. Not one bit. He was totally calm.

For but a moment, he lifted his cap and opened his eyes, deeply lost in thought.

So, so sleepy.

He could vaguely see cars passing on the hill up the embankment, he could hear the occasional slam of a car door and the crunch of gravel underfoot as more players arrived. But none of it really registered. His eyes again came to rest on the vinyl ceiling above him, and then he shut them once more.

Up the road a ways, the truck driver noticed how *slippery* the puddles were making it. He slowed a bit. He had to be very careful with a full load on a full-size tractor-trailer, especially on a gradual, downhill slant—things could get pretty sticky in a hurry.

Little by little, Chad dozed off, the Big Guy's words running through his mind over and over.

Guard and protect. Your job is to guard and protect. Always and at all times...

The semi started to pass the field, and the parking lot below. Suddenly there was a car coming the other way, swerving to avoid a fallen tree branch and veering *directly into its path—*

No! The trucker steered hard to the right and slammed on his brakes. The monster skidded on the wet surface and tore through the metal guardrail, ejecting him onto the grass—it thundered broadside down the embankment and smashed down on the Omega, instantly crushing it like a piece of tinfoil with the horrible, gut-wrenching sound of metal on metal; both vehicles exploded in a blinding fireball that rocked the whole area.

It all happened in an instant.

And Chad was gone.

Just like that.

6

I'm dead.

I'm dead!

I can't believe this has happened to me. When will every-one find out? It's only a matter of time. But they can't find out. They just can't...

Are you there? called a distant voice.

What was that? Did somebody hear me? They can't find out! I won't let them! But what can I do—I'm dead!

Can you hear me? said the voice again.

Somebody hears me! Help me, please! Someone's...

"Are you there, Finley?" The voice was a little louder this time.

Huh? Slowly he opened his eyes and raised his head.

Vinnie was standing by his table.

"I'm ready for your order, Wayne."

"Oh." Suddenly he remembered where he was—his "favorite" booth in the diner. He sighed and looked back down at the gritty, scratched surface in front of him. "Yeah, yeah, no, yeah, no."

"All right—the usual." Vinnie turned and left.

Now where was I? Wayne's mind started searching again. He hated having his train of thought derailed, especially while so exhausted. He knew it had *something* to do with his restraining order—he pulled the tattered police form out of his wallet, unfolded it, and laid it on the table.

Almost done with that crap, he thought, staring down at the ancient creases and faded ink. *Almost. Just two more days.* He ran his hands through his prickly, dark-blond brushcut.

NEW YORK CITY
PRESENT DAY

Yes, just two more days—midnight Friday, in fact—until the order expired and he'd be free to leave the city limits. But to go *where,* though? To start all over again? What a laugh— he'd already tried that once. And twice. And again, and again. And now he had no money, no family, *nothing.* Two days? It might as well have been two years.

He momentarily wondered why he even *had* the stupid thing at all and then he remembered. And he hated himself for it.

Here he was, under threat of sudden and violent death if it ever became known what he'd done. He picked up the paper and stared at it, subdued. Had it really been worth it, going to the cops with what he knew? Yes, it had been. Just being a simple cash runner between the street dealers and the chief guns had given him a first-hand look at what drugs did to people and it sickened him to even think about it. He couldn't *believe* some of the human vermin he'd dealt with. People— *alleged* people—who'd utter despicable threats at him for simply being there doing what he was "supposed" to do when they just didn't want him to be. His own vindictiveness toward them now almost surprised him, but he'd grown to resent the "business" and anyone involved in it. He'd grown tired of the dishonesty, the double-standard hypocrisy, the human suffering the "business" caused—that and all the garbage, the sleaze, the half-baked, pressure-cooked loony bins it was rightfully synonymous with. He'd been taken by liars, and he wanted to at least *try* giving them back what they deserved.

But had it been worth getting involved with in the first place? No, it hadn't. Why couldn't he have just gotten a *regular* job, like anyone else? Why couldn't he have just stayed *clean?* Six years in this town and *still* he couldn't find a decent living. Not even one. He'd tried to hold down a few, but like hot potatoes he'd dropped them almost at once. Dishwasher, paper deliverer, sidewalk-sweeper—they just didn't fit him, they weren't what he was looking for. But at least they were *clean.* So why *had* he gotten involved in such a damn fool thing? He'd asked himself a thousand times over but *he* knew the answer. He'd been a scared, insecure kid who was tired of struggling to get by, who just wanted to make enough money to live on for the first time in his life, that's why. It had sounded so good at first. And he'd gotten money, all right—plus a lot more he hadn't counted on. He just hadn't realized what he was stepping into. And he hated himself for getting suckered in so easily.

And now here it was, two months after he'd started informing and there was nothing he knew the cops didn't already know. His "services" were done, and he'd been living on edge ever since. It wouldn't take Glitch long to whittle down his list once he knew he had an informer on his hands; his suspicions had probably only been raised now that Wayne had abruptly "quit."

Wayne shivered at the thought. Glitch had such a *ferocious* temper, and he was viciously paranoid. He was so violently predictable, capable of doing anything to anyone for the slightest reason—and usually with quite lethal results. Wayne knew he needed protection, but he didn't know how to get it. He had *nothing*. And he couldn't get any more exposed if he wanted to. Carry a gun? No way—they were virtually illegal, and he couldn't afford one anyway. Even if he *could,* he wouldn't. He didn't like them—he'd already seen *enough* of them, and the kind of people who had them. Police protection? Couldn't happen. He'd agreed not to have it as part of the deal to stay with Glitch for a time and inform—it was either that or testify. He *could* have gotten it, if he'd chosen the latter and gone public with what he knew at that point; it would certainly have ended this cruel guessing game. But then he couldn't have done as much damage to the trade. Besides, he'd also been allowed to keep a small amount of his "profits" to live on (the rest he had to fork over to the court system)—and although it hadn't been much for fancy room and board, it was at least better than none at all.

With that in mind, the deal had looked appealing at first. But now the money was gone, too, and what few personal items he had were rapidly disappearing as he'd been on a selling spree, growing more and more desperate to just *make* it from day to day. Now he practically had less than when he'd first come, something he never would have dreamed possible.

And he knew Glitch wouldn't care—it wouldn't matter to him if Wayne had been a snitch, even if *years* passed before he discovered it. Once he knew, he'd come after him until he'd been eliminated. And that was that.

Wayne buried his face in his hands. The nail-biting suspense of it all had really taken its toll on his nerves. What he'd give for just one day of excitement—*real* excitement—free from the day-in, day-out dreariness and uncertainty. It was such a *depressing* combination. His *worthless* life on one side, the possible *threat* to his life on the other. He was so tired of going on like a blind fool, never knowing what was coming next…

"Okay—oops."

Wayne looked up with a start. Vinnie had his plate ready. "Sorry, I thought maybe you were…"

Wayne glared at him. *"You* know I don't pray. Set it down here."

His eyes followed the plate as it was lowered to the table and then he noticed his police form—lying face-up, smack in the middle of it. Instantly his hand shot out and covered it; he tried to look inconspicuous as he whisked it under the newspaper. He trusted no one—he had to be *careful* with that thing.

Vinnie said nothing as he turned and walked away, but not before his eyes momentarily met Wayne's.

You don't have to hide it, his look said. *Everyone knows already.*

Wayne stared down at his plate, a nervous sweat suddenly running down his back. His appetite had vanished. Suddenly, it seemed, everyone *did* know. Another regular had once told him to start out sick when he ate, that way the food couldn't make him any worse. Now that was almost the case with him.

He needed something—anything—to calm himself, to get his mind off it. Uneasily he started to browse the classifieds. Certainly there was something *somewhere* he could do for a living. His deep-set eyes scanned the pages in no particular order, searching through the myriad of categories…

Professional.

No, definitely not *his* category. He moved on…

Arts.

Ha, he thought. *That's funny.* At twenty-two, he could draw no better than he could in third grade. And he drew *then* like he did in kindergarten. He *was* good at drawing a couple of things—namely breath and bad luck—but nothing else. He kept looking…

Poetry.

Wayne stopped, suddenly reminiscing at the word. Yes, poetry. He actually *smiled* as his mind wandered back—back to his first grade classroom in Philadelphia, to the one and only time in his life he'd written his own "poem" for a homework assignment. He could see it all clearly—the rows of desks, the green tile floor; he could even *smell* the place and feel the lump in his throat as he recalled facing the throng of kids and uttering his infamous words:

Roses are red
Violets are blue
My friend owns a lawnmower
Can you swim?

Wayne chuckled. The whole *class* had roared that day, so apparent was his lack of rhyming ability. *He* hadn't thought it funny at the time; quite the opposite. But how things could change. That one brief memory, almost at once, seemed the best thing that had ever happened to him.

And the sudden good feeling it brought him—the first he'd felt in a long, long time—produced a flood of other childhood memories. Like when he tried to chew the moldy pipe tobacco he'd found in the trash and accidentally swallowed some, resulting in a bucket by his bedside all that night.

He laughed. He'd been so afraid he was going to die, then afraid he wasn't.

Or the time he tried some paste at school and quickly discovered—like soap or coffee—that it only *smelled* good. Or when he had to memorize the Preamble—he'd told the teacher he couldn't do it because he couldn't remember which parts he might forget.

Yes, it was little, bothersome stuff when it happened, but now it all sounded so neat. And Wayne was astonished. It all seemed so long ago—practically another lifetime.

Amazing thing, time is, he thought. *Passes slowly, goes quick.*

Other memories came. Like when he tried to play the Scotch tape in the recorder. Or when he'd been dubbed "Wayne the Profane" for the embarrassing cussing problem he'd developed and never really kicked. Or even avoiding Todd, the neighborhood bully. All these seemed so distant, so innocent now…

His mind was jolted back as the guy at the next booth unleashed a coughing spasm.

He groaned.

Back to *reality*. Just when he was starting to forget it. He couldn't even escape it for a few moments—it was *every-where*. And he *hated* it because it made him think about the one fact he'd been struggling to hide from himself for as long as he could remember; the one thing that lately, he'd had to face.

He had failed at everything, and failed miserably.

And now he felt like a fool for even wasting his time thinking about a life that never really was, of hanging onto little pieces of a distant past he hardly even knew. But it was all he had.

He remembered his brief days of home, so, *so* long ago— of the little boy seeing his daddy drive off in his pickup one day and never seeing him again; of his mom being unable to afford raising him. He fought back tears as he recalled kissing her goodbye at the foster home, of crying for her at night, of long summers spent virtually alone in his room or on the play-ground, no siblings or friends to play with, of being too shy and quiet and sad to even utter a word. Even after Mom started visiting on a regular basis, it hadn't helped—all those endless months and years had already taken their toll. A little kid's mind, like soft clay, had been permanently imprinted. He'd gone in a shy and scared youngster; he'd come out a restless and bitter adolescent, too independent for his own good. At sixteen, he figured he'd had enough of it all and he wanted out. He hadn't even waited to see Mom that morning as he boarded the bus; he hadn't even waited for the surprise she said she'd have. Then he'd fallen asleep and woke up in the Big Apple, a whole new start, a whole new *life* ahead of him. He'd been *so* excited. For the first time in his life, he was on his own, *he* was in control. No more shattering disappointments, or guilt, or separations, or unbearable, heartbreaking loneliness. He'd left everything that could cause them far, far behind—or so he'd thought.

How wrong he'd been. That one first mistake—leaving— had merely been a prelude to many others; now he felt his whole life had been wasted in a moment of ignorant ambition. *Everything* was tougher than he'd anticipated—even getting his driver's license, for which he had to wait until he was eighteen to avoid the parental notification he couldn't get. And from the sobering reality of getting his first speeding ticket (which ate every penny he'd managed to save for weeks), to being consistently sporadic at holding jobs, to being twice evicted from his rooms because he just couldn't make enough fast enough, he'd learned and learned hard that life was far more involved than he'd expected. And he'd come to realize no matter what kind of a life he *tried* to make for himself, there were always a hundred better ones he couldn't. So *both* ends of the stick had turned out short for him.

Six years ago it all happened. And it's taken me six to accomplish nothing. He could only figure the *next* six—if he even *lived* that long—would be no different. It was a damper on any further expectations, but he really hadn't any left. He already felt older by the day, more like a seventy-year-old than a young person. He was completely used up and devoid of any more motivation, having spent his whole life thus far just trying to get started, dealing with mistakes only after he'd made them, hoping against hope he'd do something right for a change. Yet somehow, he felt time had already run out for him. It was *insulting* how fast it went. He wished he could replace it with something slower, or find someone with considerable influence to make it stop. But it *hadn't* stopped, and he had failed. The time that had passed was gone forever; he'd never get it back.

Again he buried his face in his hands, not even daring to moan, unable to hear his own voice without getting further depressed. *Jeepers,* he thought. *My life should be just beginning. It feels like it's just ending. I just have no satisfaction...no, no...huh?*

He blinked as he realized the jukebox was on and once again he was back at the diner. He sighed. Keeping his mind with it sure was hard sometimes. But he didn't want *that,* either—being aware of things as they really were wasn't much nicer.

He stared down at his soup, now almost as cold as the

frigid March weather—it looked like liquid dust, with a skin thicker than elephant hide. He took a spoonful anyway; maybe it tasted better like that.

His blurry reflection came into view as he broke the surface; he automatically drew away from the bowl. He *hated* mirrors. To him they were but another reminder of how differently things might have been, *could* have been—and how they were now. Occasionally, though, he'd override his instincts and stare into one. And he never knew whether to laugh, cry, or just stare in silent pity at what he saw, and think it fitting his name was a four-letter word, not counting the silent e.

He swallowed the lumpy soup and cast his eyes toward the front windows. It had grown dark out and the air was full of glittering snow, almost sparkling with it—quite a pretty sight for sore eyes, actually. Had his whole body not been aching from exhaustion, he'd have found it even more enjoyable. He'd *grown* to be a night owl in recent years, his days now reduced to little more *than* mourning and evenings.

But maybe a walk "home" would do him some good. Wayne's head already felt like it'd been in a beehive—he was tired of the talking, the smoke, the incessant banging of pots and pans, and of being overwhelmed by his past. Besides, his legs had fallen asleep and he needed to stretch.

He stood and refolded his old police form; he stuck it back in his wallet and put it in his back pocket. Normally it went in his *shirt* pocket (a trick of the trade he'd learned in avoiding would-be thieves), but he didn't even have the motivation to reach that high. Besides, it'd be one *less* thing on his chest.

He made his way to the register and laid his last five dollars in the world on the counter. Then he zipped his coat and made his way out the door into the frigid night—suddenly just another dreary night, like he knew all the others would be.

"Good night," Vinnie's voice called out behind him.

"No it isn't," he muttered.

Stay out of trouble, now. The classic phrase, often repeated to him by Mom and almost everyone else he'd ever known, hit hard. He *hadn't* stayed out of it. He was up to his neck in it, trying desperately not to go under.

And he still had a very real and dangerous *possibility* to contend with.

7

Wayne picked up his pace a little; he didn't want to be outside any longer than necessary. It *was* cold—bone-chilling, biting cold, unusual even for the late winter it'd been so far—and snow was already getting into his lightweight coat. Yet somehow he was in no hurry to get back "home;" an eerie feeling had cropped up in his mind and he didn't know what it was.

He shivered and kept his eyes to the pavement as he tried to ignore his surroundings. He *loathed* this place. Not just *this* place, but the whole scene in general. He'd grown to know this street, this familiar route all too well—he knew everyone on it, the who's and who-not's, who to watch for, who to watch out for. And tonight seemed *especially* dark and gloomy. As usual, the foot traffic was…well, heavier than normal—the same bunch of typical-Wednesday-night, dead-from-the-feet-up Neanderthals, people who looked like they'd stepped on their heads all day, drunks busy hamhocking along, jabbering, jawing, mumbling to themselves, doing nothing. And a Civil War photo had more smiles. Wayne had learned all the telltale looks—a scowl, a glare, a revealing glance of some kind—everyone always had a way of letting everyone know what everyone thought of everyone else. And it sure wasn't much. Anger, fear and mistrust were all staple foods around here, and like Wayne himself, the whole atmosphere seemed to be constantly depressed; the *hopelessness* was so ingrained.

Brrr, it's cold. He suddenly realized he hadn't removed his coat indoors and now it wasn't doing him any good. The street noises became part of the background as he briskly made his way along.

This whole place was so *mercilessly* spread out—by now snow was everywhere in his coat and he was shivering almost uncontrollably. He hated being so thin. He rattled around in his clothes like a pencil in a barrel and the weather always took full advantage of the excess. Such non-weight could never do him any good, he figured, but being under stress all the time probably wasn't helping.

Almost there. He stared down at his battered tennis shoes as he walked, watching them literally glide across the slippery concrete with their smoothened soles. And he found himself thinking once again that if *only* he hadn't done certain things, none of this would have ever happened, he wouldn't be here like this, everything would be different. His life had been a process of trial and error—he'd try something and make an error. And he was *sick* of it.

Yet to his astonishment, he actually found himself struggling to think that for every exception, there must be a rule somewhere. Certainly, he figured, *something* would go well for him *sometime.* If that would only happen once. Just once.

He arrived at the plain, drab brick building and sighed—back at the old homestead, so to speak. He stuck his hands in his pockets and then he felt them. His face sank as his fingers closed around his car keys.

He'd *driven* to the diner.

Why couldn't he do *anything* right? He turned and made his way back down the dark, cold street.

It was almost half an hour later before the rusty blue Toyota pulled into the gravel lot next to the building. Wayne left it and quickly made his way inside, pausing only to collect several days worth of "mail" from his box before proceeding up the echoey, rank stairwell.

God, I need sleep. He only wanted to see his bed; maybe that—*if* he could even relax enough for it—would help ease his mind.

He reached the sixth floor and made the all-too-familiar nine steps down the dimly-lit hallway to the first door on the left. He glanced about as he fumbled for his key. There was no one else around. The Slammer wasn't home yet, either—a rolled-up newspaper still lay in front of the door opposite Wayne's.

He entered and flicked on the light, looking around the tiny, yellow, carpetless, nearly bare room as his eyes adjusted. Good. No break-ins. Everything was exactly as he'd left it— his night stand (an old crate) with the little portable radio, his cot with the old blue and purple-checkered bedspread he'd grown up with, his combination dining-telephone table, on which sat the cheap cigarette lighter (the only "stove" he had), the partly-nibbled "snack pack" (he'd quickly discovered potpourri didn't taste good, but it *had* made the room smell better), the half-a-six-pack of root beer (all he could afford), and the shapes of his recently-pawned mini-refrigerator and flashlight in the dust beside them.

And, of course, the answering machine. Wayne *hated* that thing. He wasn't even sure why he'd gotten it—even used, it was his biggest investment ever, next to his car. He figured it was the intense paranoia he'd developed recently; he just didn't like talking with anyone over the phone anymore.

The slow, methodical blink of the message light caught his eye as he crossed the room.

No, he thought. *Not now.* He'd listen to it *later,* if at all.

He flicked on the radio and tapped it lightly to get it going. He needed to hear something, *anything* to break the eerie silence; he still felt uneasy, like something awful was about to happen.

So now what? He sat down on the cot with the stack of mail and breezed through it, tossing pieces over toward the trash as he went. Nothing important. Three or four old Penny Savers, another last-chance sweepstakes entry, a couple doorhanger flyers, and an expired coupon booklet addressed to "COW JENKINS." Wayne glared at it—his mail was getting weirder all the time. He also found a scrawled note from the building's cleaning person, who he'd never yet seen:

Sorrycouldntgettrashtoday

But

willgetitsoon.

Yeah, right. Wayne looked at the wastebasket—it was overflowing and everything he'd tossed had landed on the floor around it. He stood and scooped up the mess, tossing it back onto the cot. Maybe it'd give him something to read later on, anyway.

He sat down with an old Penny Saver and then he noticed the radio had cut out again. Reflexively and without looking up, he reached for the first button his finger could find in his haste to fill the silence and unwittingly activated the playback on the machine. It gave a whir as it rewound, then a loud click which jolted his eyes up from his lap.

Oops.

"No one can answer right now, so please leave your name, number, and a brief message…"

The sound of his own voice sent Wayne's heart pounding, his muscles tense. For some reason, though, he couldn't bring himself to shut it off.

The beep sounded.

"*Your* name and number's well-known, you little stoolie,"

said a strange, monotone voice. "And here's the 'brief' message from the G: *You're dead trash.*"

Click.

The newspaper fell from Wayne's hands. For a moment—an *eternity,* it seemed—he sat there, stunned, not certain if he was dreaming. But the deafening silence told him otherwise...

BANG!

He jumped to his feet—his neighbor was home. And then he *knew* he wasn't dreaming. He'd heard it, all right; it was real.

They know. Glitch knows!

No longer just an unsettling possibility, his worst fear in all the world had happened. Suddenly he felt terrified, sick to his stomach, *nauseous.* Suddenly he felt helpless, totally alone, out in the open and exposed to a menacing evil he could do nothing about; he felt they were watching him, from every dark corner, from *everywhere,* all at once. Like the cat, hiding nearby, was ready to pounce on its prey at any moment, without warning.

And there was nowhere to hide.

My God, I'm going to die. And I'm not ready yet.

Panicked, he bolted to the door. What should he do? They were coming after him—and *soon,* because they'd even let him know in advance. He had to get out and get out *now.* He *had* to. But where?

He didn't *know* where. All he knew was that he was *running*—running out the door, back down the hall, down the rank stairs; running from that building, that room, that table, that machine, that awful, *awful* message. Back out to the parking lot, slipping and sliding. Back to his car, already half-covered with snow.

He fumbled for his keys, blinded by panic, oblivious to the cold sweat suddenly drenching his clothes, the steam rising from his sleeves.

And then he was driving. He didn't know where, he didn't care where.

You're dead trash. You're dead trash.

The chilling words, the monotone voice rang through his mind over and over. It wasn't merely a spoken *threat* against him; it *described* him perfectly. He was worthless, he was a failure. And now he was going to die, besides.

He rolled his window down, hoping the cold air would shake him from his shocked daze; freezing gusts of wind slammed him in the head.

You're dead trash.

He'd tried to hide the only good thing he'd done in his life and he'd failed miserably. Now the whole world knew; it might as well have been everyone else. And the undercurrent of anger and hatred in that voice told it like it was. He was not only nothing, he was *despicably* nothing.

Dead trash.

A rush of sewage smell riding the wind added force to the words. He blinked back tears, his eyes growing red. They didn't *have* to say it like that. But it was so accurate.

The panic slowly gave way to subdued silence. He barely even noticed the car horns, or driving on the wrong side of the road. He tried to think clearly. He tried to think. He *couldn't* think.

Beeep!

Wayne was oblivious to it all now. The fear, the terror, the depression had consumed him, numbing his senses. Was the light red or green? The red looked brighter. He came to a stop.

Helpless, unprotected.

Both at once.

Fear, terror.

Completely consuming him.

Out of chances, out of hope, out of time.

Doomed.

And God Himself couldn't do a thing about it.

Then Wayne's eyes moved ahead and he saw it. Appearing out of nowhere as if in answer to his thoughts, an ominous, gray concrete wall loomed across the intersection ahead.

For a moment, he only stared at it blankly. Then a crazy thought crossed his mind, a *crazy* grin spread over his face.

Yes, of course. Yes!

He almost giggled. Shoot, he'd beat them at their own game and end this nightmare now. Why drag it out any longer? He had nothing to lose, anyway—his fate was already foregone. Maybe *God* couldn't do anything, but *he* certainly could.

Right now, he thought. *Right now. Quick and painless. The only painless thing in my life.*

He started to rev the engine. *I'll do sixty straight into it. Clean and easy...clean and easy...*

He was already savoring the moment of impact as he waited for the light. *Just a few more seconds...a few more...*

The green lit up.

Wayne hit the gas with all his might. The engine roared, the smoke rose, the tires screeched and then he was going—

Nowhere.

Stuck in the slush.

"No, please!" he shouted desperately, fighting a sudden flood of hot tears. He floored the pedal again, spinning, sliding, determined to finish what he'd started. "Go, goddamn it! *Go!*"

The car didn't go.

Seething with fury, he pounded the wheel with his fists, setting off the horn again and again as he struggled to get a running start at oblivion. The car only fishtailed, spinning around and jumping the curb into the snow, hopelessly stuck.

He wasn't going anywhere.

He burst out crying, hanging his arm through the open window, literally reduced to a state of infantile hopelessness. *Jeepers,* he thought. *I can't even end it all. I can't even do that much.*

His nose was running, his nerves were shattered, he was shivering uncontrollably in his cold, damp clothes—every possible emotion *except* happiness was raging through his mind. If ever there was a lowest of depths, he'd sunk *below* it. And this is how it would end, with no friends, no one there to help him or care about him.

He shut off the car and buried his face in his hands.

Oh God, I need help!

Can I help you somehow? a voice answered.

Yes! I wish someone could help me. I'm such a mess!

Is there something you need?

Yes! I need to go back and start over!

Is there any way I can help you?

Yes! Get me a new life!

"Are you all right there, buddy?"

Wayne felt a hand on his shoulder. It took him a moment to realize somebody *was* there; he looked up with a start. A black guy was standing by the car, peering down at him through the window and tugging at a coat he'd obviously donned in a hurry. Wayne could see his face by the sickly pale glow of the street lights; it was full of concern. He almost turned away again as he couldn't imagine what his *own* leaking face must have looked like.

"Would you like to come inside?"

Wayne was taken aback. No one had ever asked him that before, let alone so *quickly.* And a complete stranger, too.

"I heard a horn and a bump," the guy continued. "I didn't know if maybe, well…"

One look at me and I'll bet he can only guess, Wayne thought, suddenly embarrassed.

The guy lifted his hand from Wayne's shoulder and lowered it in front of him. "I'm Doug Waters. I'm kinda the 'pastor' here at out congregation."

Wayne recoiled at the word. As if to put him at ease, the guy smiled. "Please, just call me Doug."

Wayne *did* feel a little more comfortable. Slowly, he reached up and grasped his hand. "I'm Wayne—Wayne Finley."

He was astonished to find *himself* smiling.

"Good to know ya, Wayne. You okay, there?"

"Uh…uh…y-yeah," Wayne managed to stammer out. "I…I guess so." He felt rather awkward—it was so *weird* saying that, considering what he'd just tried.

Doug's smile remained. "Well, seein' as you're on our front lawn…"

"Oh." Wayne grew even more embarrassed as he realized where he was.

"…I thought ya might want to come in and join the family."

"Family?" Wayne didn't know what he meant. "You mean you *live* here?"

"Well, not *exactly.*" Doug motioned behind him at the plain, one-story brick building. "We have a Bible study here every Wednesday night. Want to come in?"

Wayne was hesitant. *Of all times in the world,* he thought. He'd always hated religion, or anything to do with it. And he certainly didn't like pastors. But in just talking he'd noticed *this* guy was different. He wasn't at all the kind of person Wayne would ever associate with a *church.* He had a sense of…*peace* about him that Wayne had never seen before. And he'd already shown more kindness to him than anyone had ever done.

It was enough to convince him. He wanted to see more of it, and anything was better than sitting out here alone.

Doug stepped back as he opened his door and got out.

"Yes," said Wayne, "I'd like to go in."

8

They walked together up the old cement steps and entered.
Wayne was astounded. This place didn't even look anything like a church—just a simple, windowless room surrounded by a dull blue curtain, with a tile floor and some metal
fold-up chairs loosely arranged in rows and facing a podium.
About thirty or so black people sat in the ones nearest the front,
heads bowed, listening to a...a *prayer* from somewhere among
them. And it didn't *feel* like a church, either. The mood was
warm, calm. Wayne had never felt anything like it.

A few people looked up as he followed Doug past the
chairs toward the far wall; Doug signaled to them that everything was okay before directing Wayne to a door, near the
corner where the curtain had been pulled aside. He followed

Wayne in and turned on the light.

It was a small, carpeted room, with a ceiling lamp, two armchairs and a little table in between, on which sat a Bible.

"Go ahead," said Doug, nodding toward them. "You can sit down."

"Uh, am I keeping you…?"

"No, not at all." He shut the door behind him and removed his coat. "They know why we're in here. Most of them have been here, too."

Wayne wondered what it all meant. He took one of the chairs; Doug took the other. Only then did Wayne notice he'd stopped shivering. His nose was still running a little, his clothes were still damp. It was the first time he'd looked, really *looked* at himself in a long, long while. And he wasn't very impressed.

Doug handed him a handkerchief from his pocket. "Do you need anything?" he asked. "Coffee, water, anything?"

Wayne shook his head and blew hard. He slid his coat off and laid it on the floor beside him.

"Anything you want to talk about?"

Wayne's heart sank. He'd been so attracted, so inspired by this new and different atmosphere that he'd momentarily— and *completely*—forgotten about the events of just a few minutes before. But now it all came back in an instant.

Before he knew it, he was crying again. He hated doing it in front of anyone—especially someone he didn't know—but he couldn't help it.

Doug's hand came to rest on his shoulder once more. "It's all right, Wayne. You can tell me. You can tell it all."

Wayne reached up and laid his hand on Doug's. Never, it seemed, had his need for another human touch been greater than at that moment.

He *did* tell him everything. Every single thing there was to know about him. His past, his present situation, the terrible phone threat—even why and how he'd ended up sitting backwards in the yard outside. *Everything* came out. Every circumstance, every frustration, every fear; not one pathetic little detail went without mention.

Doug listened intently, never once interrupting, never removing his hand from Wayne's grasp. Even going on like he was, Wayne could not understand why he cared to hear him. No one ever had before.

At last he finished. He let go of Doug's hand and blew his nose again, sniffling profusely. He felt better, *much* better, now that he'd *finally* let it all out, but deep down he knew that no one could help him, no one could possibly understand all he'd gone through or the kind of life he'd had.

To his astonishment, Doug was... *grinning.* "Oh yeah," he said, a reminiscent look on his face. "All *that* sounds familiar."

Familiar? That was almost too much. "But how could anyone *else* be that miserable?" Wayne tried not to sound rude as he wiped his eyes on his hand. "It's *impossible!*"

Doug unfastened the buttons on his sleeves and rolled them up. He held both his arms out at full length, revealing long, thin scars across his wrists.

"It's not quite *impossible,* Wayne," he said, pointing at them. "*I* was that bad off, for sure. That's where I tried to end it all twelve years ago."

Wayne was shocked. *This* guy? At the point of *suicide?*

"I was a living, walking mental case," Doug continued. "*Shot* some guys for that same kind of 'business' *you* were involved with. Spent some years in the big house for it, then a couple more tryin' to wean myself from the stuff. Finally thought a piece of glass would solve it all for me." He rolled his sleeves back up. "Mercifully, though, I failed."

Wayne couldn't believe it. Someone who'd been through all that, who'd had it as awful—no, *worse*—than even *he* had...and who could sit in front of him so calmly.

He pondered how to ask it. He didn't *know* how, but he had to, he *had* to know.

"Um...then, uh..." He wet his lips as he tried to think of the right words. "Then what—what *happened* to you, Doug?" How'd you *change* so much? What made you so *different?*"

Doug's smile broadened. He looked right at Wayne with a look he'd never known—the compassionate eyes of a father.

"It's simple, Wayne. I found that I was cared about, that I *could* be happy and secure—forever and ever—and that I was *worth* something, I wasn't just another piece of trash on the earth."

Wayne didn't understand. *"Religion* did all that for you?"

"'Religion' had nothing to do with it, Wayne."

Wayne drew back—now he was really confused. "It *didn't?"*

Doug shook his head. "Nope. Not at all. My life, this place, those people out there, the reason we're all here—has nothing to do with 'religion.' If it was that, I wouldn't have wanted it in the first place, and I'd be *dead* now."

Wayne's curiosity had never been higher; he *had to know!* "Then what *was* it?"

"It was Someone I met Who showed me that all the garbage in my past, all my mistakes, all the hate and bitterness and depression that was eating me up didn't matter. All I did was trust Him, and it didn't matter anymore. He took it away and gave me my *life* back—plus a whole lot more, too. And I've never been the same since."

Wayne's mouth was watering; he was on the edge of his seat. Everything he'd just heard was exactly what he'd been waiting to hear all his life. A chance to start over, to begin fresh all over again. A way—the *only* Way, he suddenly realized— to just forget all the lousy, *endless* screw-ups he'd made, forget the past, leave the crap where it belonged and start new. And now, what had seemed impossible, *unthinkable* only a short while before suddenly seemed *within reach.* The only difference was that Doug had it and he didn't.

He wanted to have it, too.

He looked right at his new friend.

"Is it anything that could ever happen for me?" he asked, unable to hide the eagerness in his voice.

"Anytime *you're* ready," said Doug, glancing upward, "He's ready."

Wayne knew Who he meant. "I'm ready," he said. "I want to have what *you* have, Doug. I want to change like that. I don't want to be like this anymore."

He paused, then swallowed. "What do I do?"

"Just do like I did, Wayne. Just pray and ask Him into your life."

"That's *it?* It's that *easy?*"

"It's that easy."

Wayne, who had never prayed before, didn't hesitate. "Let's do it, then!"

They both lowered their heads as Doug's hand again came to rest on his shoulder.

They prayed.

Wayne felt it immediately.

Freedom.

9

Freedom!

Wayne was *awestruck*. At that moment, every rotten thing that had ever happened to him, anything he'd ever done— every disappointment, regret, sorrow and hurt; all bitterness, uncertainty and fear—vanished. A huge burden had instantly been lifted from him, a hardened shell had fallen off—he felt like a *person* again, *happy* for the first time in his life, brand new, clean, *rejuvenated.* Suddenly he had hope—*real* hope. Suddenly he knew he didn't have to *worry* incessantly anymore. All the terror and insecurity he'd been so powerless against, all the frustration and anger that was slowly consuming him like a cancer—*was gone!*

He raised his head and looked at Doug, who was smiling

even bigger and warmer than before.

"Welcome to the family, Wayne. You have a new life now."

New life. They were absolutely the only words that could describe it. Wayne *knew* he'd changed forever, completely, totally, permanently. The *assurance* he felt was overwhelming; the peace, the sheer *calm* it brought was so extraordinary it almost unnerved him—he was so *unused* to it!

He smiled, too—and then he laughed. Tears of *happiness* streamed down his face.

"It's *real,* isn't it, Doug?"

"It sure is, Wayne. You're not for rent anymore—the *Owner* just moved in, and *you're* His permanent residence." His new friend stood and motioned toward the door. "Come on, let's go meet the rest of 'em."

Wayne got up and followed him back out.

> *Amazing grace, how sweet the sound*
> *That saved a wretch like me*
> *I once was lost, but now am found*
> *Was blind but now I see.*

Wayne had never heard a more appropriate melody; in fact, he'd never heard it before. But it was so *beautiful*—the goose bumps rose on his arms as he followed Doug to the podium. They stood and waited until the congregation was done with the old hymn, then Doug spoke.

"I thought before we all left this evening, I'd introduce you to the newest member of out family." He laid an arm around Wayne's shoulder. "This is Wayne, everyone."

A collective exclamation of delight went up from the throng; every face in the room smiled.

"Wayne, this is our—this is *your* family, now."

The whole place broke into cheers and applause. Wayne smiled and waved back. He felt wonderful—a whole *roomful* of people who had what he now had, and who even liked and appreciated his presence. He'd never seen so many smiles at once.

Doug drew close to him. "Should we let 'em in on it? Your situation, I mean?"

Wayne thought for a moment, then nodded. Yes, that would make him feel even better.

Doug motioned for everyone to come up; they all left their seats and gathered around.

"Wayne's in trouble," he said. "A little *serious* trouble." He outlined Wayne's plight amid quiet expressions of concern and support. "He needs help."

Wayne looked at him, surprised. *"Help?* But you've *already* done more for me than I could possibly—"

Doug wasn't listening. He was already talking with several people who had approached him; he spoke barely above a whisper, motioning toward Wayne and nodding.

What was going on? Wayne swallowed, half-flattered, half-embarrassed at being the source of all this attention. He lowered his eyes to the floor, trying to look inconspicuous...

His head shot back up as Doug faced him.

"You know, Wayne, we'd be glad to have you stay with us for a while, until things cool down for ya."

Wayne's mouth dropped open—he couldn't believe this. First shown the Way to a new life, and now offered asylum. *Asylum.* Shelter with other people who understood his situation and cared about him and wanted to be with him—all such brand new things. He didn't know *what* to say.

But then another thought entered his mind, one that sent a burst of cold chills down his back. He thought about the drug men, their sheer viciousness and determination. And suddenly he could see it all too clearly. They'd track him down, find out where he was, everyone here...

The room had fallen silent; everyone was waiting for his response. He swallowed again. He knew what he had to do—and although he desperately didn't want to, although it ran against every inclination and instinct and desire he had, somehow, he still felt comfortable letting them know.

He faced the small throng.

"You folks mean a lot to me," he said. "More than you'll probably ever know. I'd *love* to stay here, and I want to badly. But...well...I couldn't involve you like that. It'd be too dangerous. These guys are capable of stuff no *animal* could do. It'll be better if I just keep on the move until I know where to go after my order's lifted. But thanks for offering..."

He fought back yet another rush of hot tears, almost choking over the words. "Thanks so much. I'll never forget it."

Doug looked at him for a moment, then he smiled. "All right, Wayne. We trust your judgment. Thanks for thinking of *us,* too."

He laid both hands on Wayne's shoulders. "We'll all pray for you and for your safety."

"Uh-huh." "We sure will." "You bet!" A chorus of voices went up at once from the gathering—and then Wayne and Doug embraced. A long, warm embrace.

"I love you, Doug."

"We all love you too, Wayne."

The two stepped apart and gazed into each others' faces. "Take care," said Doug. "Hope you find what you're looking for."

"I already have," said Wayne, smiling. "I already have." He felt a dozen different hands on his back as everyone clamored to offer support.

A big guy holding a gas can walked up. "You were kinda low, so I put some more in for ya." He handed Wayne the keys and grinned. "She's out back."

Wayne blinked—only then did he realize he'd left them in the ignition. *And it hadn't even been ripped off!* He figured someone must have been watching it.

Another guy came up with his coat, which he'd left in the little room. Doug took it first, inserting a small, brown Bible into the pocket before handing it to him.

"It's yours," he said. "Consider it a gift from all of us."

"I will. I'll keep it forever," said Wayne.

"And always remember," said Doug, gazing at him again, "The Lord sends His special agents to watch over us, wherever we are."

Wayne looked at him curiously; Doug's eyes sparkled with the same warm confidence he'd grown to love.

"*Angels,* of course."

Wayne flashed him yet another huge grin. "I *will* remember, Doug. Thanks again, and thank all of *you,* too."

He walked back out into the cool night air—the nice, *cool* night air—and made his way down the sidewalk to the building's rear. He felt so good, so…so *neat,* inside and out. He laughed. Several people were walking past and gave him a strange look; they probably thought he was either stoned or plastered. But he didn't care. He even bumped into a guy—or was it the other way around?—but he felt too good to notice. The peace hadn't dissipated one bit. It was no temporary euphoria. It was *real.*

For the second time that night, he couldn't remember getting into the car—only this time out of sheer happiness—but next thing he knew he was driving again.

10

I'm free. I'm changed.

Wayne couldn't help chuckling again; only now was he really beginning to fully realize just what he had. And it was then he knew what he'd been missing all his life—for someone to say, "I love you a lot, you know, and I'll never let anything happen to you." No one ever had before. He'd grown up skeptical and untrusting of anyone or anything, and all his attempts to remedy things had only made it worse. But now Someone *had* told him that. And that Someone was right inside of him.

Thanks, Lord.

He looked down at himself and shook his head in disbelief; he was astonished to see the same clothes, the same body.

Yet…he *was* a different person now. He looked at his eyes in the rearview mirror—no longer tired and afraid, they were calm and warm. The absence of misery, which he was so unused to going without, was clearly visible—and it was one bunch of baggage he was glad to leave at the airport. Quite simply, he'd needed a miracle, and a miracle he'd got. And it erased from his mind forever the myth that they couldn't happen.

The car skidded a little, jolting his mind back to the road.

Where was he going, anyway? He hadn't even thought about it until now. He pondered, suddenly aware of the importance of his decision. A hotel? He had no money for it. Back to his *room?* Well, that's where all his stuff was, but…

Good as he felt, he didn't kid himself. He was still under a death threat, and he still wasn't very interested in seeing it carried out. And who knew how long ago that *message* had been left?

He knew he had to decide soon; he couldn't keep driving all night.

And then, suddenly, another sense of peace came over him—flooding his mind as if to alleviate any new fears about this latest little problem.

It's okay, said a small voice. *You'll be safe in your room for tonight.*

He didn't know how, but he could *hear* it, like he was being told directly. All right, then—it was settled. He was going back to his room.

The car skidded again. Wayne cut his speed down. He always dreaded slick roads like this—the darn thing would lose its traction if someone so much as *spit* on the road, and in *this* weather, every direction could be up for grabs.

He started to think about the next day, where he should go, what he should do. Regardless of what he ultimately decided, he knew he couldn't stay in one place for long. He'd have to keep moving constantly, always being careful, and of course he'd need *money* for it…

The car skidded again, this time badly. Wayne tried to steer, but to no avail—it was out of control. Panicked, he hit the brakes. Nothing. The wheels locked up on the slush-covered surface, sending him skidding, sliding, spinning sideways into the intersection ahead and right into the path of a huge semi truck. Its deafening horn screamed as it skidded, bearing down on him, unable to stop—

No! "Dear God, *help!*"

Guard and protect him. Always and at all times...

Special Agent Number Seventy-seven recalled his orders, directly from The Big Guy Himself, as he put his hands out. The truck slammed into him, pushing him backwards along the snow-covered surface in front of it as he stood solidly, slowing its mad drive, altering its course—

The monster's powerful backwind shook the car as it roared past; Wayne sat frozen in terror as the heavy vibrations consumed his being. Then, slowly, he opened his eyes—and was astonished to find himself *still there!*

He looked in his rearview—the truck had come to a stop behind him. He got out, suddenly gasping, shaking, sweating profusely; the other driver was already standing there, obviously *plenty* shaken himself.

"You—you okay?" he asked.

Wayne could barely nod. "Uh-huh, I...I sure am—I *think.*" Dazed, he looked at his car—and himself—once again. Nope, no pieces missing.

He followed the semi's tracks with his eyes. The thing had suddenly veered to the side, missing his car by just *inches, millimeters.* But how?

Wayne knew how. His desperate cry had been heard and answered.

He had a *protector.*

He glanced upward, then got back in the car.

The other driver said nothing. He was staring wide-eyed at the *second* set of skid marks alongside his own. Beginning right where he'd started to swerve, they were much smaller and narrower than the truck's. And the funniest thing—the prints left at the ends looked almost like they'd been made by...well...*tennis shoes.*

Wayne felt a presence as he drove. He couldn't explain it; he hadn't stopped shaking yet. But from what had just happened, he *knew* what it was—he knew he had a protector, right there with him.

He most certainly did. He was sitting right beside Wayne, in the passenger seat, immaculate in white from shoulders to high tops. Wayne couldn't see him, but he was there. He didn't see him smiling, but he was there. He didn't see him clenching his fists in triumph, or hear him rapidly drumming his heels, but he was there.

Chad was *so* there!

He looked over at Wayne, The Big Guy's brand-new property he'd just taken care of, so alive and well. He laughed as he brushed dirt from the truck off his hands. *Hot diggity, that was fun! Way* more fun than stopping a soccer ball. And the second time tonight he'd looked after this car. He *loved* his job already. Being an angel was great. Being a *ten*-year-old angel was even better. Wayne had been in trouble, big time, and now he had a little defender, big time. Oh, *yes,* it felt *sooo good!*

He looked down at his outfit—his untucked, loose-fitting shirt with half-length sleeves, baggy white pants and beautiful, immaculate, *perfect* high tops. They were so *neat!* Such a uniform was not to be found anywhere.

Thanks, Lord. Makes me look brand new.

He slipped off the shoes one at a time and examined them. They weren't dirty at all. He laughed again and settled into his seat for the rest of the way, never forgetting his instructions.

Guard and protect him, always and at all times...

He'd be plenty busy doing so. He knew who was nearby, and what had already happened.

Wayne swung into the familiar gravel lot. Yes, "home" again. As differently as he saw things now, he still found himself fighting a sudden small wave of drudgery—and a feeling there were much safer and better places to be. Quickly he made his way in and back up the stairs; he didn't want to be out in the open by himself any longer than necessary.

He wasn't.

Chad was right beside him. He was taking three steps for Wayne's every one—he was so much *taller,* his stride so much *bigger*—but he stayed with him.

And he was scanning everything. His eyes were darting back and forth, searching for *anything* of danger to Wayne. *Nothing* was hidden from him. Every step, every corner, every detail was clear to him—anything Wayne didn't see, he saw.

They reached the sixth floor. Chad entered the little room just ahead of Wayne; it was all clear, he would let him come in.

A safe block away, Glitch sat and waited. He ran a palm across his short, black hair, then gave his cold legs another rub. Not much longer. Wayne would certainly be there by now, he figured; he'd driven right past him a short while before. His fingers impatiently drummed the steering wheel, his small, hardened eyes glanced at his watch.

Twelve minutes.

Just twelve more minutes and he'd be rid of his problem. This was actually going easier than he'd thought. The idiot had even left his *door* open, sparing him a break-in.

He uttered a slow, sinister laugh.

Wayne couldn't believe how differently the room felt— this same place he'd fled in terror only a little earlier now seemed so calm, almost friendly. He walked over to the once-dreaded answering machine, its light still blinking. He picked it up and shut it off, chuckling, astonished at himself for having ever feared it.

But this was no time to stand around. He set it down and quickly got ready for bed, again pondering what to do. He couldn't stay *here* after tonight—he'd be insane to. He was probably crazy for being here *now;* he was actually surprised they hadn't tried to nail him already. But he had to make a decision soon. He knew Glitch's "accidents" never happened gradually. He'd *already* had a close call that evening—and it wasn't even them!

He shut the light off and laid down, not even bothering to

pull the covers up over him. He desperately needed rest, but he couldn't—not with so much on his mind.

What should I do...what should I do...

He tried to reassure himself. Maybe, he figured, maybe after tonight there wouldn't be anything more. Maybe somehow he'd decide what to do and avoid any more excitement. Maybe a *threat* was all the farther it'd get...

Chad knew otherwise. He stood by Wayne, laying a hand on his arm.

Just go to sleep, he said. *Go to sleep. I'm here.*

Suddenly Wayne felt calm again. Although it was pitch dark, the room seemed aglow with a warm *presence,* the same one he'd felt in the car. He laughed at himself for fretting again so quickly.

He fell asleep.

Directly underneath him, affixed to the underside of his mattress, the time bomb was ticking. The tiny red numbers grew smaller and smaller as the last few precious seconds slipped away.

Three...two...one...

Chad turned it off. They'd have to do a lot better than *that* to get by him. He laughed—what a *fun* job! Deadly serious, yet so, so fun. These were the kinds of things he waited for, anticipated, loved.

Wayne would be safe for the night. Chad quietly scooted the chair over from the table and swung it around with the back toward Wayne. Then he sat down with his arms across the top, his feet hooked around the front legs, pointing down. He'd stay right here until morning.

He watched the sleeping person in front of him, Wayne Lawrence Finley, acutely aware of his every move, his every breath. And he was *fascinated* by him. There was something just inexplicably *neat* about the living *person,* the living *soul* that could walk, talk, feel and think, and that was *his alone* to look after, no one else's. And he would never let anything happen to him, no conditions, no strings attached. He wouldn't ever let anyone bother him or hurt him or anything. Not while he was here. And that was for all of Wayne's life.

He smiled. Holy *wow,* it was fun being a guardian angel. There was nothing else he'd rather do in the whole world—he *loved* it.

Wayne stirred. Chad reached over and pulled the covers up over his shoulders.

Good night, Wayne.

Then he folded his arms once again and laid his head on them.

It's sure gonna be fun to look after him.

11

Chad laid an icy hand on Wayne's arm. Wayne awoke with a start.

It was morning already.

He rubbed his eyes and yawned, suddenly remembering what had happened the night before. He smiled, recalling the transforming chain of events one by one—and then he remembered the *threat*.

The thought came back to him so strongly it jolted him out of bed. He sighed. He'd have preferred not to remember *that* part at all, but of course he couldn't *un*-know it; it was something he had to deal with, and fast.

Quickly he got dressed, his mind already far ahead of him, planning in detail the first thing he needed to do above all others: get out of the city. He could already see himself on the road, leaving it all far, far behind...

Wait a minute.

He checked his watch...eight A.M., Thursday morning.

He *couldn't* leave yet—his restraining order wouldn't officially expire for another forty or so hours. Well, he *could* leave, but at the risk of being caught and hauled to the slammer, something that didn't exactly top his list of priorities. No, it wouldn't be worth it, not this close. And besides, it just wouldn't be right anyway.

He decided. He would stay within the city limits until then, and trust the Lord to give him continued protection.

Chad grinned. He couldn't wait to honor that trust.

Wayne sat on the cot and pondered his options; he knew there weren't many. Moving around was really all he could do at this point. He couldn't help wondering if there might be an easier way to do it—mobile as he was, he hated living like a hunted animal trapped in a giant cage. Maybe, just maybe, he could talk some sense to Glitch, maybe he could somehow call a truce...

He almost laughed at himself. Of *course* he couldn't do that. With the threat alone, Glitch had already called the first shot; he had no intention of stopping. The wheels had been set in motion, and now Wayne had a very real and scary situation to live with. Or so he *hoped* he'd live.

But he also knew lamenting it to himself was useless and wouldn't make it any less real. There were much better ways of wasting his time; right now he had to spend it wisely. And right then and there he told himself that he would not fret over it anymore.

Nevertheless, he couldn't *ignore* it; avoiding sudden death until he could leave was a priority. He'd have to be very, very careful.

Time for some fast and calculated planning.

Quickly he thought of every little third-rate hotel, every boarding house he could remember, ones he'd stayed in, ones he'd seen, places where he could, well, *hide* for the next couple of days. He thought of the ones that were farthest from each other; maybe he *could* use the city's huge size to his advantage.

Yes! He picked out several different locations in his mind, taking care not to utter them aloud. He couldn't ever let anyone know where he would be next. He chuckled. He'd never been one who could stay for long in one place anyway; hopefully the tendency would serve him well.

Now to pack.

He pulled the old green backpack from under the cot—brushing the strange *wiring* out of the way—and quickly filled it with everything he could get his hands on: the machine, the radio, his bedspread, another change of clothes (his *only* change of clothes), everything on the table, all his mail. He peered in at the pathetic, jumbled heap. It looked as if it'd been ripped together, a landslide that had collapsed all over itself. But it was only for a short while, and then...

And then *what?* In all his haste, he hadn't once thought of what to do *after* he left the city. For that matter, he didn't even have any money. And he couldn't eat, let alone *stay* anyplace, without it.

But that was something to deal with later; right now the priority was getting out of *here.* He'd just have to pawn what he could of his stuff, when he could.

He slipped the pack on and turned for the door, habitually laying a hand across the shirt pocket where he kept his wallet.

He didn't feel anything.

It was gone.

Then he recalled placing it in his back pocket instead and he felt there.

Nothing.

Suddenly uneasy, he checked all his other pockets. He looked on the cot, around the room. He slid the backpack off again and checked all through it.

No wallet.

Chad only stood by, grinning, watching this whole scene intently. He waited...

Now Wayne was really getting nervous. He *had* to find that wallet. Everything he needed—his license, his restraint form which he was supposed to have with him at all times—was in it. He tried to stay calm; perhaps he'd merely misplaced the thing. He thought back, trying to recall any instance, any time the night before where he might have done so. Suddenly he remembered leaving the church, walking to his car, the guy "brushing" into him. He hadn't even considered…

No, he thought. *Please, no.*

He started looking all around the room again, searching every square inch, under the cot, under everything. *It's gotta be here somewhere,* he thought. *It's got to.* He groaned. He didn't *need* this—not *now,* just as he was leaving. Not with so much *already* on his mind.

Chad couldn't help chuckling. *Guess it's time to relieve him.*

He walked over to the table and calmly laid his hand on it.

By now Wayne was desperate. Slowly he got up from his hands and knees, a sullen look on his face. He couldn't for the life of him figure where…

His eyes landed on the tabletop.

There was his wallet, neatly sitting in the middle.

"Jeepers." He breathed a huge sigh of relief as he whisked it up and tucked it safely into his shirt pocket. *Have to hire someone to watch it for me,* he thought. *When I can afford it.*

He laughed.

So did Chad—he was faster than any pick-pocket in the world.

He slipped Wayne another message.

Wayne suddenly felt that he should look in his coat pocket. He wasn't even sure why—he'd already found what he needed, and besides, he'd looked there before. Oh well, an urge was an urge…

He felt inside it and his hand closed around something. He pulled it out; it was a folded piece of paper with a note scrawled on the back:

You'll always be in our prayers, Wayne. Don't worry—it's not a dream! Hope this will help you.
                                                    Doug

Wayne opened it; attached was a check for one hundred dollars.

Made out to *him.*

He was shocked—how had he *missed* the thing?

Keep looking, said Chad, eagerly. *There's more.*

Wayne saw something else in his palm. He studied it closely—it was…it was an old *photograph,* the one of Mom and him sitting together on the old swing in their backyard, when he was but three or four. He was astonished. It must have somehow fallen from his wallet, where he'd kept it all these years, completely forgotten. But how did it end up in his *coat?*

Chad knew how.

Wayne's eyes grew red as he stared at it. *Mom.* He couldn't imagine what his sudden disappearance must have done to her, how much she was probably worrying about him. He'd left so abruptly; he hadn't said goodbye or told her where he was going or anything. He realized just how long it had been since he ran away and then, suddenly, he knew where he wanted to go.

I've gotta find her. I've gotta find Mom and go home.

Go back *home.* So obvious, really, yet he wouldn't have thought of it in a million years if he hadn't seen that picture.

Chad only stood there, watching him silently. It wasn't time to let Wayne know yet, but at least now he felt ready to leave.

He pulled on Wayne's arm *Come on, let's be going.*

His mind now settled on two big counts, Wayne picked up his pack and walked out the door—with Chad right beside him.

He thought he should leave the back way, just to be safe; the exit there was partially hidden by a dumpster and he felt the less noticeable he was, the better. He had everything set: leave the building, get in the car and go straight to the first hotel he'd chosen. Simple, clean and easy.

But Chad knew better. The whole thing had already begun—and danger was fast approaching. He got ready, quickly hustling outside ahead of Wayne...

Wayne stepped into the alley. It was empty and quiet...except for a creaking, bending, snapping sound that had abruptly arisen somewhere in the distance. He hardly noticed—there *was* a lot of construction in the area.

He started walking. Suddenly his ears were assaulted by a terrible, *loud* scraping noise, like fingernails on a chalkboard, screeching metal, wood splintering.

What the—?

A hailstorm of broken glass fell all around him. He looked up, horrified, as a huge metal *thing* crashed down toward him from the sky, scraping the building, shattering windows—*no time to run—*

BOOM!

Then blackness. For a moment, Wayne thought it was the last sound he'd ever hear—and then he realized he *wasn't dead!* His adrenaline was racing; he slowly opened his eyes and stood up.

"Ouch!" His head hit something.

Barely four feet off the ground and as big as a car, a huge air-conditioning unit had crashed down from the roof; one end had landed on the steel dumpster, crushing it to half its size. The other end—

There was nothing under it! Only an area of shattered pavement on the ground beneath, as if something had been violently driven into it. He looked at the small, shoe-shaped cracks. Perhaps the thing had smacked the ground and ricocheted back up. No, it couldn't have; he'd have been crushed in the process. And that still didn't explain—

The unit made a rumbling noise. Quickly he darted out from under it and started walking again. *Maybe it's just leverage,* he thought, glancing back. *I don't even remember ducking...*

Chad laughed—Wayne was so *funny* when he said things like that. He waited until he was a safe distance away before letting his end of the unit drop. Wayne jumped and walked even faster.

Chad rejoined him at his side. He had to get him to the car at once, before he…

Wayne heard footsteps behind him and started to look back. Chad tugged on his arm.

No, Wayne! Don't!

Wayne did—he heard a low *whir* and kept walking. He glanced back again; the footsteps had stopped and no one was there now.

He had an ugly feeling he shouldn't have ignored that little urge not to.

He reached his car and got in; Chad settled into the passenger seat and they were off.

Glitch was irritated.

He couldn't understand why the time bomb hadn't detonated, or how the air conditioner had missed. Two failures in a row were *unheard* of, for him. But no matter. His guys would have the problem fixed soon enough.

Even so, he was taking no chances—he wanted some back-up, just in case. Hots had been very receptive, so had Wall Street. And now, well…

He turned back to Grubman, still busy polishing the rifle in his lap, slowly, methodically.

"So anyway, I might be needin' ya tomorrow, Howie. I'll let ya know exactly when and where."

Grubman didn't look up.

Glitch shifted his weight from one leg to the other, restlessly glancing about the dark, windowless tool shop. He wanted an answer.

"So…do we got somethin' here? Think you can handle it?"

Grubman's quiet, emotionless voice drifted upward. "It's a long shot, but that's why I always use a *scope.*"

He raised the rifle and pointed it right at Glitch, peering through the eyepiece. "And I never hit anything except what I'm aimin' at."

Glitch swallowed nervously; he tried to smile. "Never miss, huh?"

Grubman's finger slowly closed around the trigger and started to squeeze. "Only thing I ever *miss* is a welshed reimbursement."

The gun clicked.

Glitch suddenly felt faint. "Don't worry. Hold up as good as ya *say* ya are and you won't miss anything."

Grubman laughed.

Glitch did, too—weakly. "You'll be needin' some visual ID, then."

He started to pull out the freshly-developed snapshot his street photographer had given him. "See? He even grinned for us!"

Grubman held up a hand. "Don't need it. I play by *this.*" He pointed at his ear.

"Oh." Glitch nodded. "*I* know. I'll have what you need by this evening."

12

Leave the car here and walk the remaining distance.

Wayne was glad he'd followed the urge this time and done so; the more spread out everything was, the harder he'd be to hit. He nodded silently to himself as he left the small parking area far behind him. He *had* to listen to those urges more often, anyway. It was a hard habit to form—new as he was at it—but he had to remember that a Higher Power was now in charge of him and always knew what was best. It would just take time, that's all.

He'd already spent a *lot* of it merely getting here…it was almost ten A.M.! He sighed. Remembering a *place* was one thing; remembering the *way* there, years later in a town *this* size, was entirely different.

Chad said nothing as he walked alongside him. "Forgetting" had been for Wayne's good, too—with *their* Boss, everything was always for his good, it always had a reason.

Wayne reached the hotel.

The room was small and warm, situated on the second floor. Wayne surveyed it as he walked in. Good. It even had a desk with a big window behind it for natural light.

A good place to write a letter to Mom.

He reached for the backpack and then suddenly realized he'd left it in the car. Oh well, he'd get it later. The desk already had a pen and pad and he wanted to get started right away.

He sat down, trying to think of what to say to her. He only wanted to let her know that he was all right, and mention in advance he was coming home. But how could he *put* it to her…how could he possibly do *this,* after running away? What nerve! And besides, he had no idea when, or even *if* he could locate her—he didn't know her address yet, let alone if she was still in the same *state* or not. He gave a perplexed shrug and shook his head. Hopefully, he could find all that out later. And writing now was at least better than *nothing*. He paused, groping for words…

Chad sat on the bed and watched him. He knew how much Wayne was ponderizing, and he badly wanted to let him know what he *needed* to know, to just…well, to just *tell* him, at least. But he couldn't—it wasn't time yet.

A calling came.

Immediately Chad knelt. *Yes, Lord.*

There was imminent danger. He knew what had to be done. Quickly he stood and reached for Wayne's hand, the one holding the pen…

Wayne couldn't believe what a limp-wrist he was. The pen twisted from his grasp—smudging a word—and fell to the floor.

"Aw, *shoot!"*

He leaned over to pick it up.

The window behind him shattered as two bullets tore through, grazing the sleeve on his coat.

Terrified, he flung himself to the floor as Chad drew a hand from between him and the chair's back, a slug flattened against his palm. He'd stopped it *just* in time.

Wayne was panic-stricken. They'd *followed* him, they knew where he was. He had to get out *again*. But where—?

Never mind, said Chad, pulling at him. *Just get out of here! Come on!*

Wayne crawled to the door, trying to stay as low as his thickness—then he stood and ran.

He ran to the stairs in the hallway and the floor had been mopped. Slippery as waxed ice. He felt his legs going and tried to stop himself but was too late—his hands missed the railing and he was falling...

Instantly Chad leaped forward, seizing Wayne around the middle in a solid grip and cushioning him with himself as he tumbled end over end, head over heels down the entire length of the stairs.

Wayne hit the bottom with a grunt; he scrambled to his feet and bolted out the door toward the road. Chad raced after him—*man,* he was fast—and jerked him aside as he reached the curb.

The truck roared by.

Again Wayne staggered to his feet. He slumped against a hydrant, gasping, the wind knocked out of him from his fall. He looked up. A strange brown car had appeared around the corner and was coming toward him, two guy inside.

Wayne knew at once.

It was *them.*

He panicked—he had to get out of the open!

Go back in, said Chad, urgently *Go!*

Wayne did. He ran back into the hotel and up the stairs again as the car raced past; he heard the sound of the engine fade away as it kept going. But *where?*

Determined to elude them, he headed for the stairs at the other end of the hall, the ones leading to the alley entrance.

Chad ran alongside him, pulling on his arm. *No, Wayne! Don't! Go back down the front way!*

Wayne stayed his course—he was sure they'd be waiting for him anywhere else. *I've got to be calm,* he told himself. *I've got to keep my head in the game.*

He started down the steps. Chad moved in front of him, arms outstretched, ready.

Wayne reached the door and ran out—the brown car roared around the corner and plowed smack into him. Chad leaped in between, cushioning the impact again with himself as Wayne staggered backwards, half-sitting, half-falling to the ground.

He scrambled back up again, but not before he saw a *towering,* menacing figure—a huge guy in dark clothes with fiery-red hair and sunglasses—step from the car with something black and shiny in his hand. Wayne turned and bolted for the alley as a burst of rapid, loud cracks from a semiautomatic went off behind him—

"Ouch! Ow!"

Several sharp jabs struck his back, almost knocking him over; he thought he'd been hit but somehow he was still running. He hadn't been—he'd only felt Chad's fist recoiling into him from the force of the slugs he'd snatched.

Wayne kept going. He could hear footsteps echoing off the damp brick walls behind him, sporadic shooting, yelling. He tried to recall where he'd seen the tall guy before—that red, pony-tail hair seemed awfully familiar.

He stormed around the corner into a big, open lot and the ground was a vast sea of thick, slushy mud. Again he saw it coming but was too late—he lost his footing and fell headlong into it.

Quickly Chad pulled him up, propping him on his feet, tugging at him. *Come on, Wayne! Keep going!*

Wayne felt himself regain his balance. He ran, wiping mud from his eyes.

Chad dropped back. He waited until the two pursuers came around the corner, guns aimed, ready to fire. He stuck a leg out. Both tumbled face-first into the mud, dropping their weapons, cursing.

Chad snapped the triggers off.

Wayne kept running and running and running, his panicked mind racing ahead of him, desperately trying to figure out where to go next. And now, suddenly, he knew where he'd seen the tall guy before.

It was Moose.

Glitch's right-hand man and sometimes-bodyguard. At least seven feet tall and completely ruthless, he specialized in delivering "messages"—usually quite *permanently*. And Wayne had already signed for one.

Where to go? His eyes landed on the construction site, near the railroad tracks up ahead. A crane was busy demolishing one of two old buildings; maybe he could lose them there.

He raced toward it.

Chad rejoined him.

Far behind, the two would-be killers looked up and saw where he was going. Their weapons now useless, they resumed the pursuit on foot.

Moose ran far ahead of the other, carefully keeping Wayne in sight. He waited until he'd narrowed the gap, then reached into his coat and started to pull it out...

Chad knew what was coming. He seized Wayne by the wrist, steering him off his intended course around the buildings and directly toward one of them.

Wayne was startled—his legs had suddenly changed directions! He looked over his shoulder and there was Moose—he had come to a stop only a short distance away, a raging snarl on his face. He drew his arm back, getting ready to throw something; Wayne only needed to see the flash of a lighted fuse against the dark clothes and he knew it was a stick of dynamite.

Oh my God.

Desperate for shelter, he turned and lunged for the building—but not before he heard the dull *thud* of the stick as it hit the ground right behind him.

It exploded.

BOOM! The tremendous shock wave ripped the air from

his lungs and sent him flying through space, clean through a boarded window and onto the floor inside with a crash.

For a moment, he lay dizzy and completely disoriented as the blast echoed all throughout the cavernous wasteland. Then, dazed and moaning, he sat up and looked at himself— his throbbing eyes could barely focus—and was amazed that no part of him was missing! There must have been something, some kind of *shield* behind him when it blew…

He slumped against the wall, holding his ringing, pounding head in his hands, trying not to be sick. He tried to regain his bearings. Through his still-blurry eyes he could make out the gaping hole his body had just made in the wall clear across the hollow room; bright sunlight was streaming through the thick dust. He was on the third floor, at least.

Good grief, he thought, coughing. *What else do I have to go through?*

Chad got ready.

Slowly, unsteadily, Wayne pulled himself to his feet; he was suddenly aware of an ominous whir of machinery outside. It grew louder—

Chad lunged at Wayne, knocking him sideways just as the huge, iron wrecking ball smashed through, sending bricks and plaster flying everywhere.

Wayne staggered back up, horrified, only to be thrown down by Chad again as the thing swept back through the other way.

Chad threw an arm across him. *Stay down,* he said. *Don't try to stand up!*

Wayne was almost in shock. He crawled, *pulled* himself toward the hole, gasping, hoping to get some idea, *any* idea, where it would strike next. He couldn't see out…too much dust…he had to rise—

No! Chad grabbed at him. *Don't!*

Wayne did.

Chad leaped in front of him, cushioning the impact again as the ball tore through and smashed into Wayne, carrying him across the room—Chad swung himself around so he was first

through the other wall, head down, fists clenched in front of
him like a battering ram, punching through before Wayne ever
touched it. He did the same as it continued through a second
wall, then a third before pulling Wayne off and moving under
him as he plummeted…

"Ooof!" Wayne landed flat on his back on a soft pile of
dirt; he was on the ground outside.

Back on the other side of the building, Moose grimaced.
He thought he'd nailed the little rat—but he saw no blood, no
arms or legs lying anywhere to confirm it.

He wanted to be sure.

He whistled to his companion as he reached the lot,
panting and breathless. "Hey, McKernan! Get your tail around
to the other side—see if you can find any bits of him there!"

McKernan glared at him as he brushed mud from his
stubby, round frame; old weeds and chunks of filthy snow
clung to his yellow hat. "Don't *whistle* at me, idiot! I'm not a
dog!"

Moose grabbed him by the trench coat. "Shut up and get
moving, or *you'll* be the tire block this time!"

He shoved him away. McKernan sighed through his teeth,
then trudged off around the building, muttering.

Wayne rose from the dirt pile, only to fling himself flat
again as the ball came through yet *another* time high above—
Chad stood over him, garment outstretched, shielding him
from the torrent of debris as it rained down. He knocked the
bricks from his back and took hold of Wayne's arm.

Come on, Wayne, let's go. We have to now!

Wayne hesitated. He wasn't even sure if he was *alive* yet;
he was shaking uncontrollably, his head was still ringing, the
hair on the back of his neck was still on end from the blast's
intense heat. He wanted to *check* himself first, just to see if he
was all right.

He got up and stumbled away from the building to a large
cement block, then sat and unzipped his torn, muddy coat. He
was covered with dust.

A yell of profanity caught his throbbing ears. He looked up

to see a short, heavy-looking guy with a hat jump out of the way as yet another storm of debris from the wrecking ball crashed down; he shook his fist at the thing, straightened his coat and slowly scanned the area, stopping cold as his eyes landed on Wayne.

He started running toward him.

Wayne stared at him for a moment, then he saw the mud on the guy's clothes and he knew.

Chad pulled on him urgently. *Run, Wayne! Hurry!*

Wayne ran again. He ran to the other side of the second building and came face-to-face with a solid *wall,* stacked high with wooden crates on one side, rolls of chain-link fence on the other. He looked around frantically—the darn place was shaped like a U and there was no way out; it was a dead end.

He had to hide!

This way, said Chad.

McKernan plodded around the corner, out of breath, coughing. He looked around suspiciously—he didn't see Wayne anywhere, but he *had* come in here.

He cursed and started looking.

Crouched on his knees inside the crate, Wayne could hear him. He peeked through the boards and saw the guy clearly now as he searched, toppling roll after roll of fence and sending poles clattering all over the ground. It was the first time he'd really *seen* him and he almost laughed. He'd never seen such a *flat*-looking face—the guy must have been hit with a sidewalk or something. And with that round build and dirty yellow hat and trench coat, he looked almost the perfect combination of Elmer Fudd and Dick Tracy. Perhaps the two had conspired and created this poor disaster.

Wayne tried not to laugh; he slapped a hand over his mouth as a chuckle escaped through his nose.

The guy paused and stared at the hopeless mess he'd made; he shook his head, threw his arms up and sighed deeply before turning to leave. Wayne couldn't understand it—he hadn't even searched the crates. He laughed silently as he watched the stunted ball of a man stumble over the rough ground.

Then his stomach growled. *Loudly.*

McKernan stopped dead in his tracks. Slowly, he turned back around and faced the crates.

He'd heard it.

He started walking toward them, drawing a huge *dagger* from under his coat.

Wayne's heart sank. Suddenly the guy wasn't funny anymore. His face was expressionless, his eyes were stone-cold. He was *quite* serious, he was a killer.

Don't move, said Chad. *Stay put.*

He squeezed between Wayne and the boards in front of him.

McKernan approached the first crate in the bottom row and plunged the shiny blade right through the wood, directly in the center. He pulled it back out with a grunt and examined the point before moving on and doing the same to the next crate.

And the next one.

He was working his way down the row, getting closer and closer.

Wayne sat huddled, terrified, not knowing what to do. He could probably bolt and outrun the guy, but a knife hurling through the air would be slightly harder to beat. Maybe he could distract him somehow—

Too late. He was already at the crate.

Wayne tensed as he saw the stubby arm draw back; he shut his eyes, waiting for the screaming pain of a knife plunging into his heart—

McKernan drove the dagger into the wood, clear to the handle.

It snapped against Chad's chest.

McKernan pulled it out and looked at what was left of it, his face growing bright red. He threw it to the ground and stalked over to the scattered mess of fence poles.

Huh? Wayne hadn't felt anything. Slowly he opened his eyes—just in time to see the guy pick up a crowbar and run at the crate with it like a javelin.

He tried to scream, "No!"

Chad snapped off the point as it tore through and whacked the rest of the thing into pieces, section by section like a wooden toy.

Wayne couldn't believe it—again he opened his eyes, suddenly falling over as McKernan punched and kicked at the crate, cursing, fuming.

He started to pull on the latched front and then stopped abruptly.

"You stupid bowling ball!" yelled a voice behind him. "I've been lookin' all *over* for ya! Quit fonchin' around and get back there! We *missed* and we gotta find him!"

Wayne's view was obscured by the guy; he couldn't see who was talking. All he could see was a stubby finger pointing his direction.

"I already did," came the answer. *"In there."*

A terrible moment of silence followed.

"Go get the car," said the first voice, suddenly calm. "Bring it here and wait for me."

Wayne shut his eyes again—he didn't *want* to know what was coming. He heard two sets of footsteps walk away, and then it was silent once more.

Had they left? Wayne opened his eyes and looked; there was no one. He started to climb out, but not before the sound of footsteps coming back sent him scurrying in again.

He heard someone climb up on the stack of crates beside his; it shook slightly as the one above him was lifted off and hurled to the ground, sending thin beams of bright sunlight streaming through the planks into his eyes.

Wayne swallowed nervously, instinctively crouching down low. *What in the world was going on?*

Again Chad got ready, climbing on top of Wayne and facing the top of the crate.

The roaring jackhammer exploded through the flimsy wood, ripping it into splinters and exposing the towering figure of *Moose* as he plunged the vibrating point toward Wayne's head.

Immediately Chad grabbed it, muffling the end with himself, never once letting it reach Wayne. He laughed profusely as it pounded his stomach—he was *sooo* ticklish!

He was laughing so hard he couldn't reach for the thing's cord. He rapped Wayne's knee with his fingers; the reflex shot him up to where he could grasp it firmly.

He snapped it.

The jackhammer stopped dead in Moose's hands. He cursed and hurled it against the wall before jumping down and ripping a large, nail-studded board from one of the crates.

Wayne saw it coming. He tried to climb out and run but didn't make it—Moose had already lunged at him with it.

Again Chad acted, seizing a fence pole and throwing it across the top of Wayne's crate just as the board crashed down on his head. It struck the pole, splintering on impact and sending Moose in the other direction, yelling, moaning, clutching his arms in agony.

Bweebweebweebwee...

A sudden noise arose from around the building. Wayne tried to ignore it as he took his opening and ran.

He didn't get far. A huge earthmover suddenly appeared from around the corner and backed across the entrance just as he reached it, sealing him in at the one critical moment.

No!

He looked back—Moose was coming.

Hurry, said Chad. *This way.*

Wayne followed his urge—he couldn't *believe* he was doing it—and ran back *toward* the wall as Moose stormed past him the other direction.

Where was he going?

Wayne reached the wall again; he looked back as Moose climbed aboard the earthmover, jerking the startled workman off the seat and tossing him over the other side like a rag doll. He sat and started to mess with the gears. His sunglasses had come off and Wayne could see his eyes—they were wild with determination.

He wasn't going to miss this time.

The thing backed up, swung around, and started toward him.

Wayne was trapped. A brick wall behind him, a solid wall of steel closing in from the front. He couldn't believe it—he'd finally listened to an urge and *this* is what he'd got. He was panicked. There was nothing he could do.

The thing picked up speed, pushing fence rolls and crates ahead of it. Moose laughed as the gap grew smaller... smaller...yards apart...feet apart—

Chad knew what had to be done.

He did it.

The blade met the wall with a thundering, ear-splitting bang that jolted Moose right off the seat into the safety mesh in front of him. He cursed but then grinned, satisfied that he'd finally succeeded. He climbed back into the seat and set the gears into reverse.

He wanted to *see*.

Slowly the machine lumbered backwards, revealing the entire face of the wall. Flattened crates and pipes clung to the brick surface like pancakes.

Wayne wasn't there.

Impossible.

He wasn't there!

Seething, Moose looked all around the wall. A small, narrow hole near the base, one that *hadn't* been there moments before, caught his eye.

He jumped down and ran to it, doubling his huge frame over as he peered though sideways on his hands and knees. He could see Wayne, running away...

The brown car swung around the corner. Moose stood and bolted toward it—clearing the machine's blade in one leap— flailing his arms and pointing behind him. "McKernan! Take it around back! He's blowin' us off! Move it!"

He jumped in and grabbed for the door, nearly falling out as the car backed up with a screech; it spun around and took off like a rocket.

Wayne glanced back as he ran. He couldn't remember

seeing a *hole* in that wall, let alone *ducking* through it. He must have fallen—it felt almost like he'd been *pushed*—through...
Never mind that, said Chad. *Just keep going.*

Wayne hardly needed the reminder. Already he could hear the sound of a car engine growing louder. He spied a narrow tire path winding between an embankment and some trees and bolted toward it.

He couldn't understand how he was still going. After all he'd been through, he was still going. He was panicked, he was *terrified;* his energy was gone and he was completely spent, but he was *still going.*

Of course he was. Chad was helping him along.

He had a hand firmly grasped around Wayne's arm, leading him; his eyes were constantly scanning, his mind constantly planning. So many things could happen.

Wayne looked back again. The brown car was now hot on his trail, rapidly catching up like a tank homing in on its prey.

He couldn't outrun it. He had to get out of view before he was flattened...

Chad knew what he was thinking. *No, Wayne! Go the other way!*

Wayne didn't. He veered off the path and stormed up the embankment.

He went over the crest and the other side was much steeper than he'd thought. He couldn't stop himself; his legs went out of control and he tumbled forward down the cliff-like hill—

"Ooof!" He felt dirt and grass, dirt and grass, then jagged gravel and cold, hard metal. The ground started to rumble.

Where was he?

Shaking the dizziness from his head, he looked up to see Moose start down the hill toward him on foot—then quickly stop and back away.

Why?

Then Wayne heard it. The terrible, nerve-shattering scream of a *train's horn.* Horrified, he realized he was on a double set of tracks with *it* bearing down on him.

He didn't even know what happened in the next instant.

All he knew was that he was *racing* into a tunnel just ahead of the thing, faster than he'd ever run before. He tried to jump out of its path, but not before a *second* train roared by the *other* direction—it was too close, he couldn't leap clear without hitting it.

Run run run! Wayne heeded the voice as he focused all his energy, his mind, his entire *being* on outracing the screaming monster at his heels, oblivious to his own screams above its blaring horn, made even louder by the tunnel walls. His only other path still blocked, he raced for the tunnel's end a ways ahead...it went on forever...all happening in slow motion...

Right behind him, Chad was slowing it down.

His hands were out against the train, his high tops braced against the rails, sending sheets of brilliant yellow sparks flying outward as he was pushed backwards down the tracks ahead of the thing. Slowly it dropped back from Wayne, a little more, a little more...

There. That was just enough.

Wayne reached the tunnel's end as the second train's caboose passed—he lunged sideways off the tracks just ahead of the monster, tumbling, somersaulting, falling down a slope into debris-strewn brush with a powerful thud that knocked the air out of him.

The train's horn continued to blare as it roared by; its vibrations shook him as he laid on the ground with his head in his hands, gasping, crying, hyperventilating all at once. His heart was thundering, his legs were burning almost unbearably, his adrenaline was racing.

But he was *alive.*

I outraced a train. I outraced it. He kept repeating it over and over in his mind, as if to prove to himself that he *was* still there. He *had* beaten it, or it had slowed just enough, to allow him the split-second he'd needed. But *how?*

Slowly, painfully, he sat up and looked back at the tracks, easily twenty-five feet away. And how had he *jumped* that far?

Chad grinned. He knew how on *both* counts.

He sat up beside Wayne, brushing dirt from the train off

his hands, knocking trash from his hair and clothes; he did the same for Wayne, who was shaking his head in amazement.

But there was no time for in-depth speculation. Here came Moose again, running out of the tunnel, scanning the tracks ahead of him foot by foot.

Wayne couldn't believe it—didn't that guy *ever quit?* He flung himself down among the brush as the killer raised his eyes and scanned the area.

I will never, ever complain about a dreary life again, he told himself. *Never.*

Chad laughed. Something good came from everything, no doubt.

The ground started to shake again. Wayne raised his eyes and saw a slow-moving cargo train lumber out of the tunnel toward Moose, closing in on him as he stood looking the other direction. Wayne wanted to yell at him but he didn't dare. Horrified, he saw Moose whirl around just as it reached him— and then he disappeared.

Wayne felt sick. He started to look away but then saw Moose reappear as he scurried up the embankment above the train.

Wayne froze. If Moose turned and looked around from up there, he'd see him for sure. He had to get out and get out fast.

Chad scrutinized the situation, his eyes landing on the street intersecting the tracks about a half-mile farther down. He had the whole thing laid out in seconds; he whispered to Wayne.

An idea suddenly popped into Wayne's mind. Quickly he got to his feet and darted *toward* the cargo train, running alongside it, carefully staying within the long, distorted shadows of the boxcars. It was so ironic, really. First chased by one of these things, now pursuing one. But it was a good idea—he didn't know where it'd come from.

The train picked up speed a little; Wayne ran faster. He couldn't let it get ahead of him!

Moose reached the crest of the hill and turned around, huffing. He watched the train passing below. As his eyes followed it, he caught a glimpse of *someone* passing through the thin line of sunlight in between the shadows of the cars.

He started to follow it.

McKernan followed *him,* on the other side of the hill.

Wayne was starting to run out of train. It kept moving faster, he kept dropping back another boxcar. He could hear the clanking sound of the caboose rapidly approaching. *Please,* he thought. *Not yet.* If he could just stay with it long enough to reach that street up ahead.

Moose kept following. He saw the image flash through the light again, then again a few seconds later. Now he knew for sure, he knew it was Wayne.

He kept his eyes on the last two boxcars as the thing entered a trainyard, moving between other stopped cars. Wayne would appear behind it any second.

Wayne looked over as the caboose started to pass him. He wasn't quite at the intersection yet. *Please,* he thought desperately. *Just a little more train!*

Chad grinned with an unmistakable calm.

More train he'd get.

He made his way to some idle cars along a side track and grabbed hold of them, pulling, *dragging* them to where they merged with the main tracks...

Wayne heard a clank and looked over, startled to see *two more* cars behind the caboose. Suddenly re-energized, he picked up his pace as they lumbered by, slowly, slowly...

He reached the intersection and veered left just as the second car passed; he ducked under the guardrail and took off down the road.

Moose saw him. He stormed down the hill to the car and got in, tossing McKernan into the passenger seat.

"Hey! What the—?!"

"Stay outta the way and let *me* drive this time, bunghole!"

He slammed on the gas.

The car went nowhere.

"What in blazes—?"

He tried again.

Still nothing.

Moose's face turned red, as red as his fiery hair. He floored the pedal with every bit of strength in his leg.

Nothing but a thick, acrid smell of burning rubber.

Coughing, he flung the door open with such force it ricocheted back and hit him in the side as he got out. He cursed vehemently and looked at the tires.

Someone had poured water all around them and over them; they were completely iced.

Chad laughed. *Oops. Wonder who could've done that?*

He rejoined Wayne, now long gone.

Oooh, maaan! Wayne heaved an enormous sigh as he sat down stiffly in the driver's seat and gingerly leaned his head back. For what must have been several minutes he just *sat* there with his eyes shut, catching his breath. He was so numb, so drained, so…so utterly *exhausted. Never* did he think he'd live to see another quiet moment, let alone his car, again. But he had.

Chad watched him from the passenger seat; he laid a hand on his shoulder.

It's okay now, Wayne. You can relax for a while.

Wayne felt the warm presence again, the same soothing calm he'd already grown to love. And after what he'd just been through, it was the most welcome feeling in the world.

He smiled. "Thanks," he said, not really sure who he was talking to. "Thanks a lot."

Chad smiled, too. *No problem, Wayne.*

Wayne opened the door and set his legs down on the ancient, oil-stained pavement. *Oooh, so sore.* Slowly, carefully, he unzipped his battered, muddy coat and slid it off his arms. He shook it. Shards of broken glass, wood splinters, gravel, bits of brick and dried mud fell out all at once. Part of the back had been seared away, blackened.

He untucked his dirty flannel shirt, examining his arms, feeling his front and back, searching for any injury at all.

Again, he was astounded.

Nothing.

Not even a cut or scrape.

Save for tired muscles and absolutely *no* energy, he had slipped through everything completely unscathed. And he couldn't believe it.

So, so tired... He shut the door, crawled around to the back seat and collapsed. It *never* felt so good.

The comforting presence filled the car as he lay there. *What an angel I must have,* he thought as he drifted off. *Hasn't even seen his first full day with me and I can't believe what a job he's done.*

He shook his head in awe. *My angel must be huge.*

Chad laughed as he looked down at his pristine white outfit and high tops. Wayne was so *funny* when he said things like that.

I'm sure glad I have one. Wayne breathed another huge sigh of relief.

"Thanks again, buddy," he said out loud.

Chad reached around and patted his arm. *Anytime, Wayne. Thank you.*

Wayne fell asleep.

Chad kept watch.

13

It was almost three in the afternoon when Wayne awoke—he'd been asleep for *hours!* Well at least—yes, at least it was still Thursday. He gave his watch a pat. Good *grief,* what a packed day it'd been already. *Brrr!* And still cool, too. Why, he'd have probably half-froze if he hadn't pulled his coat over him...*huh?* He couldn't recall doing that. Oh, well, he must have in his sleep. He sat up and hurriedly threw it on; he had to get to his next room.

But which one was next? Considering how easily they'd found him earlier...

He climbed up front, started the car, and retrieved the broken plastic spoon from the floor beneath the seat. This was still a very precarious situation, he realized as he scraped away the layer of frozen breath from the inside of the windows. He—was that a picture of a *race car,* scratched in the ice on the passenger window? No, he was seeing things; drawing was something he did *not* do, awake *or* asleep. He chuckled.

So anyway, about his next location. He couldn't be careful *enough,* where he went now. He thought carefully as he drove off, running over and over through the list of places he'd made in his mind. He pondered briefly before settling on the farthest place he could think of—clear on the other end of the city. Yes, it deviated from the loose "order" he'd set, but he desperately wanted to avoid a repeat of recent events. Hopefully they'd find it a little harder—if not *impossible*—this time.

Still beside him in the passenger seat, Chad said nothing. He knew better. Wayne was already being followed.

It was a much *bigger* hotel now; they'd expanded since he'd last been here. Wayne took only his bedspread with him as he checked his backpack at the counter. He didn't need the extra bulk, but he did want *something* familiar with him.

He crossed the lobby with his key.

Take the elevator, said Chad. *Take the elevator.*

Wayne veered right and took the stairs. He didn't *like* elevators.

The room was small, along a quiet, narrow hallway and across from a laundry chute. There was a locked door to the adjoining room with a wool throw rug in front of it.

Another eerie *feeling* cropped up in Wayne's mind as he shut the door behind him and locked it. There was absolutely no one else around; it was *too* quiet.

He began to wonder if he *should* have used the elevator.

Uneasily he tossed the cover across the bed and sat down. He *hated* feelings like this, and he hated being distracted by them.

His eyes landed on the notepad by the phone. Shoot, he hadn't even written to Mom yet. Of *course* he hadn't—he'd spent so much time just keeping *alive* that he hadn't yet had a single moment to think about it. And his time for doing so was growing short in a hurry.

Chad stood and watched him. Poor Wayne—he was really getting himself worked up. But he would let him go on for a minute; it was for his own good.

Wayne stood and paced, wondering how to proceed with his search. Forget *writing* to Mom; he wanted to *find* her and *get* there. But how? He had no idea where to even *start* looking. But he *had* to start—just a little over a day now before he could leave and he certainly couldn't stay *here* any longer than that; he'd have to go *somewhere.* In fact, he had nowhere *else* to go but home. Besides, his money would soon run out again…

"Ouch!"

He'd scuffed across the wool rug and brushed the metal door handle. Furious, he shoved it under the adjoining door with his foot so only a corner was sticking out.

"There!" He resumed his pacing.

Chad paced along with him; he could calm him now.

"Why can't I have just one *minute* of spare time?" said Wayne, irritated.

Chad grinned. *Uh, Wayne…*

"This is so ridiculous! At this rate I'll never—"

…Wayne…

"—I'll *never* find her! And I don't even know where to look…"

Wayne, you're fretting again.

Wayne stopped and looked at the floor, suddenly feeling rather silly.

He *was* fretting again.

He'd told himself earlier that he wouldn't, and he'd meant it. But here he was doing it anyway. Years of habit were just plain hard to break, he figured. He smiled—*boy,* did he feel silly. After all he'd been through, after all the times he'd already been looked after, how could he *possibly* complain now?

He laughed and so did Chad.

Jeepers, what a twit I can be sometimes. Wayne reached down to pull the rug back under the door.

Chad clamped a foot over the corner. *Naw,* he said, *you want to leave it there.*

The rug wouldn't move. Wayne couldn't understand it—but he suddenly felt he should leave it alone.

Oh, well. He stood and made his way to the bed once more, pulling the phone onto his lap, mapping out a strategy to locate Mom. Let's see…first, there was information in Philadelphia …certainly *they'd* know something…

Chad said nothing. He positioned himself by the adjoining door and waited.

A long sigh escaped through Glitch's nose as he packed the recorder away in the dark stairwell. He glanced up only passively as Moose approached him.

"Got it?" asked the giant, staring down at the thing.

"Yeah, got him climbing 'em." Glitch rose to his feet. "Let's *hope* we won't be needing it, though."

They started up the stairs.

"Got here as soon as ya called," said Glitch, visibly annoyed. *"This* time we'll *both* be right there—I'll have to blow it a couple *more* times before I move on to the other, more expensive guys."

He glanced over at Moose. "But I don't intend on *having* to, right?"

Moose only looked ahead glumly.

"Now let's get up there and get it *done* this time," said Glitch. "Got the room number?"

"Yeah—what if he slips out again?"

Glitch laughed. "He *can't.* I already got a guy on every floor watchin' the stairs and elevator. There's no way out."

"How about the lobby?"

"Naw, we don't need the extra publicity. But it doesn't matter—he'll have to get by one of us first."

They both laughed; it echoed eerily off the cold, brick walls.

Wayne hung up the receiver, his shoulders slumped.
He was discouraged.

This was already tougher than he'd thought. It seemed *no* one in Philadelphia had ever heard of a Ruth Guilford, or had any information they could give. He'd tried everyone he could think of—directory assistance, the phone company itself, the post office, city hall, city auditor, even the police.

But there was no trace of Mom.

She hadn't been listed as missing, so he could only figure she must have moved—probably far away, years before. And he had no idea where.

And even if he *could* find her, he again realized just how hard it would be to face her. What would he *say?*

If he could just *do* it and get it over with. If only their last names matched, his search would be so much easier. But she'd only been married once, briefly, before he was born and...well, she'd always kept the same name.

Wayne suddenly found his eyes growing hot. He blinked rapidly as he recalled asking Mom about it once, why he wasn't like all the other kids who had the *same* last name as their mommies. He remembered listening as she tried to explain why, as best a mother could to a five-year-old. But it hadn't helped; he'd only grown more confused, more inquisitive. Was that her last name when she was little like *him,* he'd asked. No, she'd said, her last name began with a J when she was little. He'd almost cried. As simple as she'd tried to make her answers, it was all so mixed-up to him. He'd hated seeing Mom like that, so obviously embarrassed and uncomfortable with the subject, and he'd hated himself even more for asking. But he'd been *teased* about it so much...

Wayne stopped his mind cold. That was all in the past now; it needed to be left there. Again, he felt silly—it was so *easy* to get distracted. He smiled and resumed the search, his mind back on track.

Chad smiled, too. He really admired Wayne, his desire to keep going, his rapidly improving character. He wanted to walk over and lay an arm around his friend's shoulder, to just...*encourage* him, and give him all the emotional support he could handle.

But he couldn't leave the door. Danger was fast approaching…

Wayne heard a noise and looked up. Footsteps were crossing the next room.

He heard them muffle and saw the corner of the wool rug move slightly as they stopped on the other side of the adjoining door. He didn't think much of it until he heard the loud static snap and then a yell of profanity.

And then he knew right away.

It was *Glitch.*

Get out of here, Wayne! Chad set his hands against the door. *Go now! Hurry!*

Terrified, Wayne sprang to his feet and bolted from the room.

"Come *on,*" Glitch snarled at Moose. "Get *in* there!"

Moose pressed on the door, trying to cave it in. It was a *lot* sturdier than it looked; he strained and heaved, cursing vehemently.

Chad didn't budge.

Out in the hallway, Wayne could hear the racket. *All* of it. He couldn't believe this was happening again—it seemed mistakes from his past kept finding him wherever he went. He looked around frantically; he didn't know where to go. If he went for the stairs, they'd hear him—and he certainly didn't want to stand around waiting for the elevator.

What, then?

A sheet falling past in the laundry chute caught his eye.

Try as he might, Moose could not budge the door—it felt like a *truck* had been backed against it.

"*Break* it," Glitch hissed. "Rip the damn knob off!"

Moose turned the knob with all his strength.

Chad turned it the other way.

And vice-versa.

And vice-versa.

The door didn't move.

Down the chute Wayne clamored, hands and feet braced

against the sides for traction. The crazy thing couldn't have been much more than twenty inches wide—for the first time, he was *glad* he was so thin!

Phew, it smells graphically. He looked beneath him as best he could. He didn't know where he was going; the passage was pitch black except for a small patch of light every so often where a floor was.

"Aaiiyyy! Aw!" Moose cursed the static shock as he continued wrestling with the door knob.

Chad was having *immense* fun. He laughed, listening to the giant struggle against his iron grip, hearing the *pop* every time he touched the thing. Now he was *really* ecstatic.

Moose groaned, throwing his entire weight down on it.

Chad didn't move.

Moose ground his teeth, throwing every fiber of his strength into it.

Nothing.

Wayne passed another flap as he carefully made his way down, inch by inch; a hand tossed a crushed beer can through it, which tumbled past and caught on his shoestring, clattering against the side every time he moved. He tried to shake it off, almost losing his grip.

Perfect, he thought. *Now the whole building will know I'm here.*

A sheet fell down over him and muffled it. He breathed a sigh of relief—but then it caught between his hands and the sides.

"No!" He lost his grip and plummeted.

Stationed on the third floor, one of Glitch's men heard a noise in the chute behind him and whirled around.

Nothing but a sheet fell past.

He turned around again, shaking his head.

Glitch was furious. "Break it!" he screamed at Moose. "Smash through it!"

Moose drew an arm back and drove his fist into the door—then turned away in agony.

Chad laughed. He moved his hand to a different place as Moose used his other arm.

The same thing happened.

Chad laughed again, placing his hands over and over wherever Moose struck on the other side. The poor fool. If he was trying to *impress* anyone, then he certainly wasn't succeeding very well.

Wayne managed to free his legs from the sheet—he jammed them against the sides, slowing down more...more...stopping just as he reached a flap.

Good a place as any, he thought. He climbed out with the sheet still over him, grunting, struggling, trying not to catch himself on the edge.

He was on the main floor, in the lobby.

"Whew!" He stood, suddenly realizing he was the focus of several odd stares. He grabbed the can from his shoestring.

"Um, uh, just collecting these," he said, then quickly headed to the front counter for his backpack. He whisked off the sheet which had entangled him.

He looked at it.

It was his old blue-and purple-checkered one.

But who'd thrown it down?

Wayne was now safe. Chad took his hands off the door and stepped aside just as the two men rushed it head-on from the other direction.

A tremendous crash ensued as they broke through and landed flat on their faces, Glitch on top of Moose.

Wayne was gone.

Glitch screamed with fury and pounded his fists on Moose's back.

Chad laughed hysterically and rejoined Wayne.

"My brother tells me the other day how much trouble he's

having gettin' a *loan,* right? I says, 'What's so tough about that? Just go off someplace by yourself!'"

The whole place roared and applauded as the comic finished his routine; so did Wayne. And *mmmm,* what a good meal—he hadn't realized just how famished he was.

He looked around as he scraped his leftovers into an aluminum container. The cafe was *packed* with the evening crowd, from the front windows clear to the little area with the microphone at the back; the mirrored wall behind it made the whole room look twice as big.

He shifted in his seat as he again realized he was getting some funny looks; his still-sensitive ears buzzed from the sound of a hundred different, loud voices going at once. But even so, he was *glad* to be out in the open. He preferred the crowded calm, the company of other people—even if they were complete strangers—to being alone. He'd *already* seen what could happen then.

Chad said nothing. He sat across the table from Wayne, ever alert.

Wayne stared at the mirror, again thinking through his list of places. He caught his own reflection as he pondered and then he could see why he was getting looked at—he hadn't even *changed* yet! His battered shirt and pants were still covered with a dusty film of dried mud; he hadn't had one spare moment to clean up since certain events put him in such a state. He smiled, embarrassed. He must have looked like he'd just crawled from under the floor.

He settled in on another location.

Then it hit him—another strange, eerie *feeling,* like he was being watched. Not just looked at, but *watched,* like his every move was being scrutinized. He sighed uneasily. He was growing *weary* of such feelings; without fail, they were always preludes to near disasters. But maybe it was just edginess, maybe his sensitivity was over-inflated from the day's events. He tried to preoccupy his mind with something more pleasant, like how to locate Mom...

Another calling came to Chad.

Immediately he knelt. *Yes, Lord.*

An upcoming scenario was presented to him, and then his orders came.

Alter it.

He opened his eyes and grinned, then stood and momentarily left Wayne's table.

Alter it he would.

A few tables away, the man in the gray business suit studied Wayne closely. His eyes moved to the snapshot he'd been given, neatly paper clipped in a corner of the newspaper his gloved hands held; his graying head moved ever so slightly as he peered back over the top edge of the thing, again focusing on Wayne through the gold-rimmed glasses.

Yep, same guy.

He set the newspaper down and got his .45 ready, pulling the long, cold silencer from inside his coat and fastening it in place under the tablecloth. He laughed quietly. Now to simply aim and squeeze.

The strange *feeling* was growing impossible to ignore. Wayne could feel it clearly now, a cold stare burning right through him...he couldn't *stand* it. He bolted to his feet, prompting several startled patrons to glare at him.

Good. That was exactly what Chad had told him to do.

Wall Street lowered his gun, a frustrated sigh escaping under his breath. A standing target was too obvious; he'd have to follow him outside, or wait until he sat again—whichever came first.

Chad pushed his chair out and swung himself part-way around, laying an arm on the table. He tugged at Wayne's shirt.

Leave now, he said. *Leave right now and don't look at the back wall.*

Uncomfortable enough with the feeling and all the attention he was getting, Wayne picked up his food and walked out, carefully avoiding the mirror.

Wall Street rose and started to follow.

His shoelaces were tied together.

He fell forward, crashing into a table and landing flat on his face.

Chad roared. He'd been *waiting* to try that on *someone*.

Infuriated, Wall Street staggered to his feet and tried to walk again.

Chad hooked a foot under both of his legs, lifting them right off the floor and sending him crashing headlong into another table.

The whole *place* roared.

And Wayne was gone again.

The air had cooled back down, significantly.

Wayne stamped the fresh, thin dusting of snow from his shoes as he entered the hotel and made his way to the counter. His arms were already getting tired—the dinner bag and other set of clothes were slipping from his grasp after that brisk walk from the car. He noticed the desk clerk glancing at him as he approached; he only half-consciously returned the glance to the small-framed man with dark hair, a mustache, and heavily-tinted glasses. It was possible they'd seen each other before—Wayne had, after all, stayed there once, several years back.

He set his load down and rubbed his arms. "Brrr! Guess winter ain't over yet."

The clerk smiled. "Nippy out, huh?"

"Yeah." Wayne smiled back. "No such thing as too much heat in *this* weather." He blew on his suddenly burning hands.

The clerk handed him the key. "Don't worry. Your room will be *well*-heated, I assure you."

He motioned toward the stairs. "Number twenty-nine, safe—er—way at the back of the building."

"Whew, thanks!" Wayne filled his arms again and started across the lobby.

Chad drew close beside him.

Hots watched his "guest" a moment longer, then checked the little photo behind the counter once more. A *perfect* match. He laughed gleefully—this would be *so* simple. In fact, it'd be a classic, showcase model for all the other guys who preferred the fancier methods. Nothing like the old-*fashioned* way to use plastics, he figured; hell, any *other* way was just flat demeaning, both to the stuff itself *and* his line of work.

He grabbed his coat and raced out the door. He'd come back and see the damage the next day, at his leisure—over coffee as usual.

Wayne cringed as he climbed the steps—he'd forgotten just how old and *dingy* this place was. And it certainly hadn't improved with age. Every ledge, railing, even the *floor* was covered with a gunky, oily residue to which clung a thick layer of dust. It scattered as his movements stirred the air; both he and Chad sneezed at once.

What a skunk hole. He reached the hallway and started walking. He'd never *heard* such a creaky floor—every step sounded like a herd of elephants getting strangled.

Chad quickly moved ahead; he knew what had to be done.

Wayne reached door twenty-nine. *Ah, finally,* he thought. *Now to clean up and get some sleep.* He piled his stuff in one hand and started to insert the key.

Directly behind the door, still within the folded, brown paper bag, the half-pound of C-4 sat waiting for the slightest movement of the knob to close the connection on the mercury switch…

Wayne was startled as a small rush of *wind* suddenly came from nowhere and zipped between him and the door. He felt the key slip from his grasp but didn't hear it fall anywhere.

Great, he thought sarcastically. *This really saves me a lot of trouble.*

He set his load down on the floor and started looking.

The key was nowhere to be found.

Inside the room, Chad was disconnecting the bomb. He was following his instructions with care and speed, pulling the switch away from the other wire and lifting them both off the knob…*ah, there we are.*

He grinned and glanced up. *Thanks, Lord.*

He picked up the whole thing and stashed it safely behind the little table in the corner. Then he pulled the chair out, planting it squarely between the table and bed, where he would stay all night. The bomb would not go off while *he* was there; he would keep Wayne or anything else from getting near it until he worked on it further. Oh, one more thing: he climbed to the little window high above the bed and pushed it open, ever so slightly.

All set. Now to give Wayne his key back.

Down on his hands and knees in the hall, Wayne couldn't understand it. That stupid key had simply vanished off the face of the earth.

I give up, he thought, sighing. *I'll have to go back and get another one.*

He rose and picked up his bag.

There was the key, under it.

He stared at it wide-eyed for a moment, then stifled a chuckle. *Figures,* he thought. *Only I could leave it someplace so obvious.*

Chad roared.

Wayne yawned as he slipped into his second set of clothes. *Boy,* was he tired. He draped his damp shirt, pants, and coat over the end of the bed. Hopefully they'd be dry by morning— the sink washing hadn't completely rid them of all the grime, but they looked acceptable.

Then he sat and started to do what was quickly becoming routine: pondering. There was only one thing on his mind now, one big, nagging, all-important thing.

Finding Mom.

He *still* didn't know where she was. And in the meantime, his desire to get out was growing more insatiable by the day— were his sheer existence not at stake, he'd have probably found it a lot easier. He needed patience.

But that still wouldn't solve his *second* problem: even *if* he found Mom, even *if,* miraculously, he *could* locate her and get there safely, he still didn't know what he'd say to her. What would he *say,* after leaving her like that?

"Aw, *jeepers,"* he said, abruptly. He stood and pulled the

covers back, chuckling. He was fretting again.

Chad stood beside Wayne and looked up at him. He smiled. Wayne *was* trying, he *was* making an effort not to fret. But Chad also knew his job was not to counsel Wayne on personal matters, at least where his safety wasn't concerned. He could lend *emotional* support, but he couldn't counsel. Much as he wanted to, he couldn't. Wayne needed to seek a Higher Help for advice on that.

And it still wasn't time to let him know yet.

Wayne stared blankly for a moment. So *now* what?

Sleep, that's what. He was *exhausted.* He'd never been accused of being overly physically active, and now he was feeling every single thing that had happened in the roughly twenty-four hours since his life was changed. And what a day it'd been.

Yet tired as he was, he couldn't unwind. Repeated—and potentially *lethal*—interruptions from calm scenes like this had produced a near paranoia, a *fear* of relaxing. And Wayne didn't kid himself. He knew Glitch would be even *more* desperate now, *more* vicious. He'd pull out all stops, spare no expense to eliminate his living, walking scourge and maintain his lovely reputation.

Wayne shivered. Already his mind was racing ahead, his adrenaline rising…

Shhh. Chad whispered to him. *It's all right, Wayne. You're safe for now. I'm here.*

Wayne suddenly felt the *presence,* the same one he'd felt so many other times. He breathed easy. *What a twit I am,* he thought as he climbed into bed. *I did it again. It's so easy to worry and fret!*

He stared down at the shape of his body under the covers, again amazed it was all still in one piece. Indeed *glad* it was, but nevertheless amazed. He couldn't figure how they'd missed him so *much.* These guys were *professionals.* He recalled the old adage, that when a bullet has a person's name on it, they can't do anything to stop it. Well, he could only figure his name must have been *crossed* with someone else's because the disasters marked for *him* had been missing entirely.

Chad laughed—he was *glad* to "cross" them!

Wayne fell victim to another big yawn, recalling all the times that day he'd slipped, tripped and dropped things; all the times he'd told his hands to do one thing and they'd done another. They'd all seemed so insignificant, almost *maddening*, when they happened. But now he could see that if even *one* of them had gone differently in any way, he probably wouldn't be alive now. He was really quite shocked—he'd never made so many mistake-free goof-ups before. Even the times when he hadn't listened to his urges (which was *most* of them), he'd always come out unscathed.

He shook his head. What he would have called infinite *luck* only a day earlier, he now considered nothing short of *miraculous*.

And then, suddenly, he remembered the reason he'd gotten through it all—he shook his head again, in disbelief at how easily he'd forgotten.

He had a *protector,* that's how he'd survived. And *boy,* was he glad!

Chad grinned, but it was a tempered one; there was still one more little thing Wayne would have to endure. He sat down on his chair and waited. He didn't want to see it happen—but like so many other things, it was for Wayne's own good.

Ahhh. Wayne settled into the pillow, his tired body savoring every minute of it; nothing, it seemed, ever felt so comfortable. He started to fall asleep...

A loud roar sent it scurrying back again.

A plane was going over.

Perfect timing. Annoyed, Wayne pulled the pillow over his head.

Another plane came.

Then another one.

Wayne started to mutter, then stopped himself. Maybe it would subside.

It didn't. They kept coming.

Wayne was rapidly growing irritated; only now was he realizing just how much quieter it'd been when there was no noise. He knew he had a tremendous grasp of the obvious—but he needed absolute quiet to sleep, or at least *something* in the general vicinity of it. And *this* certainly was not. He tossed and turned, throwing his arms over his head a dozen different ways as he tried to ignore the incessant, loud rumble.

Another plane…another plane…another plane…

It was plain to see he wouldn't be sleeping for a while. And he was *disgusted.* Now his whole system would be thrown off; he'd be late getting up, he'd be awake well into the next evening. He pressed the pillow down hard against his ears, hoping to muffle it.

An even louder one went over.

Wayne couldn't believe it—no matter what he did, they adjusted the volume to counter it. Every time he thought it was letting up and he started falling asleep again, *another* one came along and filled his head with that stinking, gunky roar. He was *really* starting to get aggravated.

The planes kept coming and coming and coming…

"Aw, *Jesus!*" he yelled, finally. *"Shut up!"*

Chad winced. A pained look covered his face, tears welled up in his eyes.

Please, Wayne. Don't say that. It hurts me deeply and it hurts Him even more.

Wayne already felt rotten. He sat up in bed and glanced upward, then lowered his head and apologized. Some old habits were hard to break.

Chad smiled again. *Thanks, Wayne.*

The window suddenly fell shut with a bang; the noise stopped at once. Wayne jumped—he hadn't even known it was open. He checked his watch by the moonlight: almost one A.M. He had endured conveyor belt noise for nearly two hours straight.

He laid back down, feeling silly for complaining and for his outburst.

Don't let it bother you, said Chad. *You don't have to now.*

Wayne smiled. Indeed, he *had* taken care of it, and that was that. And besides, he had nothing to complain about and everything to be thankful for. He was alive, and he still had God on his side. And what else could possibly matter, then? All the seemingly pesky things that had happened thus far were ultimately for his benefit—maybe *this* was, too.

He drifted off to sleep.

Chad crossed his arms on the back of the chair and rested his chin on them. Again he watched Wayne, The Big Guy's property he was guarding, so alive and well for another night. He smiled, too. He knew Wayne was fallible, that he wasn't perfect and never would be. But his duty was to guard and protect him, regardless of what he said or did or whether he always listened or not. Period. And he loved every moment of it.

And Wayne was fast becoming his closest friend, besides.

He pulled the covers back over his shoulders. *Good night, Wayne.*

Wayne shifted positions; for a moment, his eyes opened wide. By the dim reflection of the moonlight, he could make out not one, but *two* shadows on the wall beside him—his own, and what looked like another one *sitting* there...

He was too drowsy, too eased by the comforting presence to care.

He went back to sleep.

Chad laughed quietly, then resumed his all night vigil.

Much more lay ahead.

Glitch was growing more furious by the minute.

He couldn't wait any longer—not on Hots or his bombs, or Grubman, who hadn't even tried yet. No more messing around or waiting for any more flubs. It was the last straw. He'd had *enough* of the *normal* guys.

Time for the sickos.

He took a deep breath as he entered the dimly-lit night club. Even *he* didn't like this place—it felt so inexplicably *evil.* He glanced around the stuffy room. It was practically empty, except for a few low-lifes—mainly hookers and drunks—scattered among the tables in the middle, totally oblivious, either laughing or stoned or asleep.

He looked beyond them toward the windowless back area, completely dark except for the steady, red glow of a single overhead bulb. He swallowed as he scanned the far wall, and then he saw who he needed—sitting alone in a corner booth, chewing on a celery stalk.

Slowly and carefully, he approached the man dressed in black with the partly-drooped left eye. He *had* to be careful. He didn't want to set him off—a dangerous thing to do, if he was surprised.

The guy's head turned and he spied him; he laughed almost inaudibly as Glitch approached. That *laugh,* tinged with insanity, sent shivers down Glitch's spine.

"Well, who left the lid off the trash can?" he almost shouted, his strange eye twitching slightly. "Look what just blew in! Long-time-no-see, Goof-Up! Got somethin' *new* for me?"

"Hold it down!" Glitch hissed.

"Who, *me?*" The guy drew back in mock surprise. *"I'm* not getting excited! *I'm* not getting loud! Nope, not me! I'm not I'm not I'M NOT!"

"Shut up!" Glitch fumed. "And don't *call* me that!"

"What's the matter, Botch? Don't like synonyms?"

"I like my name *right,* psycho!"

"Then stop stickin' an *O* on *mine,* geek!"

Glitch was already sorry he'd come. He spoke quietly, hoping to get the same in return. "Yeah, I got work—"

"For *moi?*" Sykes interrupted. "Oh, you *shouldn't* have!" He bit off a chunk of celery.

"Just swallow your cud and quit yappin'," said Glitch, impatiently. "I got somethin' for ya, one I think you'll really enjoy. Now listen up."

Sykes leaned forward on his hands. "I'm wired for sound, Sam! Go for it!"

Glitch thought out his words carefully. Sykes had to be enticed or he'd quickly lose interest, like a baby with a rattle.

I got this problem that keeps goin' away," he said. "Your, uh, *professionalism* is needed to *fix* it."

"*Ooo,* must be a *tough* one for ya, schoolboy!"

"Let's just say it *eludes* things well," said Glitch, irritated. "But that's right up your alley. And there's a lot in it for ya this time—you could retire on your payment alone."

"Mm. Somethin' *extra* then, Botch?"

"A substantial royalty's involved."

Sykes looked almost insulted. "Just a 'royalty?' I've *killed* for more than that!"

"'Royalty' bein' a place on my board of collectors—*you* know, makin' sure the dues get paid and all."

Sykes hesitated. He wanted more.

Glitch thought fast—he didn't want to lose him, not this close.

"*Any* means necessary to get it done are fine by me."

The magic words.

Sykes slammed his hands down on the table. "Sold!"

Glitch blew through his mouth, relieved. He handed Sykes the snapshot.

"Here he is."

"Ooo, a *pretty* boy! Can I frame it and keep it?"

"Just try not to be quite so *messy* this time," said Glitch.

Sykes only laughed eerily again.

14

Oh, yes.

The lighter did the trick. It was all ready now, everything was just right.

And now for the fun part. Get it out of his hands and where it belonged before it exploded—

There!

Wayne set the heated aluminum container down on the table and blew on his fingers; he pushed the chair out of the way and dragged the whole thing over beside the bed, where it'd be more comfortable to sit.

Reheated leftovers for breakfast, at...yes, twelve noon Friday, already. *Man,* he'd overslept!

He took his seat and opened the lid, filling the room with

the aroma of steak, potatoes, and peas. *Mmm,* it smelled good. But he'd sure have loved a homemade cinnamon roll.

He started to eat. Chad reached across from the chair and tapped him on the shoulder.

Wayne was forgetting something.

"Oh, of *course.*" He smacked his forehead. "Guess I should pray."

It was a habit he was still unused to, considering he'd only started Wednesday—but nevertheless, one he wanted to learn. He put his hands together and lowered his head.

Chad did, too.

"Thanks, Lord, for this food and for everything You've given me. And thanks for guarding and watching over me everywhere I've gone and will ever be…"

A big smile spread across Chad's lowered face.

"…Thanks, Lord. Amen."

Amen, said Chad.

Wayne sighed and looked up. He was *amazed.* As if his own prayer had just brought the fact home to him, he'd actually survived the night without a single incident. Shoot, no one had even *tried* anything since yesterday afternoon!

Chad laughed.

Wayne started eating—he indeed felt happy for his safety, yet not *entirely* easy. Even after such a remarkable night, it still seemed things were going just a little *too* smoothly. He knew the lull wouldn't last forever and he'd need to leave again soon.

But eating was one thing—*the* one thing—he refused to be hurried or pressured in. He'd told himself he wouldn't fret, and besides, it'd give him at least a *little* time to think about finding Mom. And that was *certainly* something that should avoid a hurry-rush job, if it was to be done right. No, he *wouldn't* let anything distract him.

Chad felt happy for *Wayne;* he *was* improving dramatically.

Let's see…who to call…what to look for… Wayne pondered, his mind probing, digging, hunting for any clue, anywhere, anything he might have missed before that would aid in the search. There wasn't much left. He'd already exhausted every option *he* could think of; he'd called every place there was to call. But no one had known. Yet there *had* to have been *someone...*

"Oops—*yuck!*

He'd taken a forkful of globby, warm jelly. He swallowed it and grimaced, then scooped up the rest and aimed at the wastebasket. "Does anybody *else* want this before it goes?" he asked out loud, glancing around the room at imaginary people.

Naw. Chad frowned and stuck his tongue out. *Never did like it. Tastes churky.*

"Fruit punch with rigor mortis, far as I'm concerned." Wayne tossed it and stared back down at his "plate," once more lost in thought. Habitually, he hooked his feet around the front legs of the chair and pulled it toward the table; it pressed against Chad's stomach and tickled him.

He giggled and pushed himself back out.

Wayne looked up. *"Huh?"*

He pulled the chair toward him again and looked back down.

The same thing happened.

I'm losing it, thought Wayne. He couldn't even recall moving it by the table in the first place. Well, what the hey, he needed the leg room—he'd leave it out.

He reached for the little carton of milk. As he leaned forward on his other arm, his elbow bumped the end of his fork, catapulting the mashed potatoes it held into the air. Thrusting out a hand to catch it, he knocked over the carton, spilling the whole thing all over the table and into Chad's lap.

For a moment Chad sat there, a look of absolute surprise on his face. Then he laughed.

"Aw, *jeepers.*" Wayne's face grew red with embarrassment as he reached for the roll of tissue paper. Yet somehow, he could feel...*laughter* as he mopped up the table and chair— a funny, neat, *contagious* laugh! He found *himself* chuckling, too—already relishing his new found ability to find *humor* in little things like this that he would have hated so much before.

And look at the bright side, he told himself. *At least no one was sitting there.*

Chad roared.

He hadn't gotten *wet* this time, either.

So anyway, back to Mom again. Wayne's mind resumed its endless search as he sat down once more and felt into his pocket for the pack of gum. Certainly *someone* in Pennsylvania *somewhere* knew *something* about her. But who and where? That was a pretty big state, with an awful lot of places. He'd already called so *much*…there was simply no one left, no where else he was familiar with.

He popped in a stick.

So what could he do? *Maybe I should just call her and get her number,* he thought, before laughing at how ridiculous that sounded.

Chad laughed, too. *Sounds like something I'd try.*

Wayne thought for a moment longer, and then it struck him.

Her number. Her *phone* number.

That was it! The one single thing he *hadn't* thought of. Shoot, it was so *simple!* He could call someplace in Philadelphia that kept records of old phone books—yes! the public library—and see if he could find Mom's most recent number there, and then…and then maybe an old address! But certainly *something.* Maybe nothing would come of it, but *he* certainly didn't know that yet and he really had no other options, anyway. It was worth it to him.

Chad said nothing. It still wasn't time.

Wayne wanted to get started as soon as possible; first, of course, he'd need a room with a phone. He gathered up the mess on the table and tossed it into the trash, but not before Chad slipped the aluminum container into his shirt. It might come in handy later on, considering all that was coming…

Stay here a bit longer, Wayne. Just a little more.

Wayne ignored the feeling as his hands kept working. The sooner he was out, he figured, the better.

He folded his nightclothes and stuffed them into his shirt. *I'll be so glad when this is all over,* he thought. *So, so glad. I hope it all ends…*

He was still somewhat sleepy. He yawned and the gum went down his throat. He leaned forward, panicked, unable to breathe—

Quickly Chad moved behind him, seizing him around the middle and squeezing hard.

The gum popped out.

Stay here, Wayne, he urged again. *Don't go anywhere yet.*

A level below, crouched on one knee in the dark hallway, Grubman silently pushed the playback and waited for the sound of footsteps in his headphones. It was the first time he'd ever listened, the last time he needed to. He liked these things fresh in his mind, without distraction.

The faint sound came on, filling his ears with a steady, almost rhythmic beat:

Chk-chk-chk-ka-chk-chk-chk…

Mm. That was enough. He shut it off and raised his gun to eye level, aiming at the underside of the stairs above.

Now to wait for the same sound in real life.

Wayne was almost ready to go—he only had to move the table back and the room would be in order, so to speak.

He started to pull it. The darn thing was *heavy,* much heavier than it felt before. He groaned as he picked up an end, straining with it, half-pulling, half-dragging it away from the bed.

Chad remained sprawled across the *other* end; he *had* to slow Wayne's advance.

Lead bricks, this thing's heavy. Just a few more seconds, though, and he'd have it back—then he'd be out the door and down the stairs.

Down the *stairs!* Chad had to act fast. He leaped forward onto the end of the table Wayne was lifting, instantly ripping it from his grasp and slamming it down on his foot.

"OUCH!"

Moaning in agony, Wayne lifted the leg and pulled himself free and fell backwards.

"Aawww…oh, f…Je…*awgh!"* He grasped his head, biting his lip, trying desperately not to curse. He staggered back up and limped toward the door, stumbling, walking sporadically, struggling to hold his throbbing foot up…

Grubman heard a door open and shut.

His finger closed around the trigger, ready, as the horrendous *creaking* in the hall above grew louder, closer.

Someone started down the stairs.

Pum-pum-pumpum-pum-pumpum…

Nope. Wrong ones.

Grubman stayed frozen in position, waiting for the footsteps he knew.

Hots approached the hotel haltingly. He took another sip of coffee and peered down the side of the building…*had* that thing gone off? Everything looked completely *normal*—there were no fire trucks, or sirens, or anything. And the police band he'd been monitoring sure hadn't mentioned any unusual events…

No, he figured, it *must* have gone off. He'd never failed before; perhaps the walls were much sturdier than they looked and the blast had been localized, completely *inside.* Yes, yes *that* was what happened—the place had been gutted. But wouldn't that have at least blown the *windows* out?

He shrugged. Such minor details didn't concern him at the moment.

Right now he wanted to see it for himself.

Wayne tried to conceal his limp as he crossed the lobby. The clerk was just walking in the door and he saw him; the styrofoam cup slipped from his hand, his eyes bugged out and he seemed amazed, almost *afraid,* of something.

"It *was* warm." Wayne grinned as he laid his key on the counter. "The room, I mean. I sure *slept* well…"

He chuckled and turned for the door. "…once the *airport* gave up, that is."

The guy only nodded, staring at him with a dumbfounded look as he passed by.

His day sure didn't start with a bang, Wayne thought. *He should trade places with me.*

He walked outside and started the short distance to the car. His attention was quickly riveted on a red pickup truck, speeding toward him from the street; it suddenly pulled to the curb across from him and a tall guy stepped out, glancing around nervously.

Then he looked Wayne's direction.

He reached into his coat and pulled out something *small* and *black.*

Wayne panicked. He didn't wait to see that it was only a comb; he was already running back into the hotel.

Chad ran alongside him, tugging at him. *Wayne, stop! There's nothing wrong!*

Wayne didn't. He stormed back through the lobby past the clerk—still standing there with a shocked look on his face—and toward the stairs. *I've gotta hide,* he thought.

He ran up.

Still waiting underneath, Grubman heard it.

A perfect match.

"Ooof!" Chad pushed Wayne sideways as the blast tore through the stairs and grazed his pantleg.

Grubman fired again.

Now Wayne's *pantlegs* matched.

He reached the top and bounded down the hallway as yet another blast, then another, tore through the floor behind him, almost inaudibly under the monstrous creaking…

"Uh!" He barreled smack into the *wall* at the other end. He staggered back from it, dazed, grabbing for the first door he saw.

Locked.

The kind that locked whenever it was shut.

He leaned forward on his knees, panting, as he realized all the others were the same.

There was nowhere to go.

He was *stuck.*

His shoulders slumped—he turned around slowly, distraught, almost reserved, fully expecting to see a gun barrel aimed at his head.

There was no one.

But they're probably coming up right now.

He stood and waited. He *waited* for the dark form of a killer to appear above the stairs at the other end and do his deed. It was the most uncomfortable thing he'd ever done in his life. He couldn't *believe* this, he *hated* himself for standing there like a helpless dolt, waiting for his own death. But he couldn't do anything *else.*

Still no one came.

Wayne didn't move. For the longest time he stood there, frozen in terror, not flinching a muscle.

Not a sound from *anywhere.*

He began to wonder. *Was* there anybody? Had he even been *shot* at? His eyes moved down to his legs and he could see the holes, the two black scorch marks on the sides of his pants. Yes, there most certainly *was* someone.

But *where?* Had he *left* or something?

He clamped a hand over his nose as it suddenly grew tickly from the dust he'd stirred up. If only he *knew.* He hated standing here so *uncertain* like this…

Wayne had already given Chad an idea. He scooped up a handful of dust and went downstairs.

Wayne almost jumped as a sudden, loud sneeze echoed from beneath the stairway up ahead.

So *that's* where the guy was.

Waiting for *him,* not the other way around. And probably listening for the slightest noise or creak.

Wayne's heart sank as he realized his new knowledge wasn't helping much. He knew the killer was *there* now, sure; but he was still trapped. Whoever it was obviously meant business, and probably couldn't be outlasted—and if he tried to get silently across *this* floor, which anyone *light-years* away could hear, well…

He almost cried. Again he hated himself for acting in a moment of blind panic, for getting himself into this mess.

Don't worry about it, said Chad. *Just follow me.*

Wayne suddenly felt the urge to start walking. He couldn't understand why; it was *crazy.* Yet he felt...no, he *knew* he should.

Before he even realized it he'd taken a step, placing his foot ever so gingerly, ever so softly on the floor again. He took another one with equal silence, then another one...

Chad was muffling his steps.

He was walking *backwards* in front of Wayne, one hand on his belt, the other on his arm to steady him as he placed *his* feet under Wayne's, padding, cushioning the pressure...

Take it slow and easy, Wayne. Keep your stride short.

Wayne couldn't believe it—he wasn't making a sound! He was stepping on the floor and yet...and yet he *wasn't,* it was like his feet weren't even *touching* it. Still, he had to resist the temptation to bolt and run—

Shh. Don't think about it, Wayne. Keep going just like you are.

Chad continued to guide him, slowly, slowly, head turned, eyes scanning every dangerous inch of the floor ahead of him, acutely aware of every spot where any pressure at all would set off a deadly barrage of sound. He steered Wayne to the left, then right, then left again...

Wayne carefully moved around the two gaping bullet holes in the floor...he was almost there...

His foot landed on the top step.

He proceeded down, sweat already dampening his clothes. The keys in his pocked started to rattle, but he was too busy concentrating on being quiet to notice—

Chad clamped a hand over them as he steered Wayne around the second pair of holes in the floor.

Another step...another step...*another step...*

The whole thing seemed like an eternity, happening in slow motion.

Then he reached the bottom. *Finally.*

Don't look around, said the voice. *Keep walking.*

Haltingly—almost feeling faint—Wayne made his way to the lobby once more.

Only then did Chad draw his feet out from under Wayne's.

Say nothing, just get outside and go straight to the car. Wayne listened this time as he kept his eyes straight ahead; he again breezed past the clerk toward the front door.

Hots was furious—first the wrong key, and then *two walkouts?* No, he *wouldn't* mess up again! He started to reach into his coat for his .357, equipped with a silencer.

He froze, his mouth falling open in terror.

Carefully spiraled around his arms was the terrible, red wiring. The mercury switch, teetering precariously, was ensnared in the connecting end; the folded brown bag, still attached, sat on the floor at his feet.

He gasped.

Chad grinned and stuck his tongue out at him as he followed Wayne outside. It would be a safe while before the guy discovered the bag was now filled only with trash.

Wayne reached the car and got in; Chad paused just long enough to empty the putty-like stuff from his pockets into a grate before joining him.

Wayne took off for the next location.

He breathed a huge sigh of relief—yet *another* close call he'd escaped completely unscathed. He shook his head in amazement.

Thanks, Lord. What a guardian You've given me.

Chad laughed. *No problem, Wayne. You're a fun one to watch.*

Wayne smiled, too—in anticipation. Now to get to a phone and keep looking for Mom.

An ever decreasing distance away, Glitch waited on the rooftop.

His eyes scanned the street below; he could see for miles in every direction. He rose up on one knee, focusing his aim so the rifle's scope was centered directly on the passing lane beneath.

He was *disgusted.*

He already *knew* Grubman hadn't done it, without even hearing first. Given the way things had been going, *that* was a certainty.

But *he* was ready. Yes, he was *so* ready! It was all going to stop right here, right now, with just he by himself. No more of this endless aggravation or anyone else screwing it up.

He raised his head above the scope and looked down the road, careful not to move the weapon from its position. Any moment now...

Yep, sure enough—here came the little blue car. He peered back through the scope. Now to simply wait until it passed the building.

He snickered.

He had no intention of nailing the rat *himself;* no, that would be too easy, too plain. This had to be more *creative* than that. Just a well-aimed shot into the gas tank, and presto: instant barbecued snitch.

Only a few more seconds...

Wayne looked at his watch—it was now one P.M. All the oversleep and activity had already taken a big hunk out of the day; he realized his order would now expire in roughly *eleven hours.* Not much time to find Mom. His speed increased—he *had* to get to that phone!

He approached the last side street for another block.

Turn right here, said the voice. *Don't ask why; just turn.*

Wayne slowed and took a right.

For a moment, Glitch didn't move—then he slowly looked up. His eyes widened, his chin quivered as he realized it...no, it wasn't possible...no...he'd...*he'd missed again...*

He went *ballistic.*

Screaming obscenities, he slammed the gun to the rooftop, discharging a round and sending him leaping repeatedly as it ricocheted several times off the brick rim; he slipped on the slick, metal barrel and fell flat on his nose.

"He wasn't supposed to *turn* there!" he bawled, pounding his fists. "Why did he *turn* there?"

"Why *did* I turn there?" Wayne wondered aloud.
Chad only grinned.

"I'm sorry, sir. Could you repeat the name, please?"
Wayne grimaced. He pressed his hand tight over his open
ear, loudly and carefully speaking into the receiver.
"RUTH ELIZABETH GUILFORD! G-U-I-L-F-O-R-D!"
"Last name is *Guilford,* with 'g' as in 'girl?'"
"YES!"
"Just a moment, please."
Wayne sighed. Yet *another* wait. And he wished the
construction noise outside the wall would quiet down just a
little; it seemed everything in the world was making this as
difficult as possible. But hopefully he was onto something
here—hopefully, they'd know *something.* It was his last
option, really. It was this or nothing. He could only wonder if
he was even having the *right* phone book checked—he had no
way of knowing which, if any of the few they kept, might have
her name. *Last* year's book seemed a good starting place, he
figured; though pretty unlikely, he wanted to be as recent as
things would allow—
"Sir?"
"YES!"
"I'm scanning the listings under 'Guilford' now—there's
quite a few, a big section of 'R' names alone..."
"UM...IS IT THERE?"
"Well, I'm looking...I can't seem to locate that particular
name right off hand. But even if it turns up, I can't say for sure
there'll be an address with it—so many of them don't list one.
Hold on, I'm almost through it..."
Wayne's heart sank. This was already looking futile.
"Wait a minute, here we are. Yes, it's...Guilford, Ruth
Elizab...yes, the abbreviation's Elizabeth...uh, one, no there's
another name like it, but the middle initial's different."
Wayne swallowed nervously. "Does it have an address
with it?"
"Excuse me, sir?"

Wayne couldn't *believe* the racket—seems he'd just been through this the night before!

"IS THERE AN ADDRESS?"

"Yes, indeed there is."

Whew! Wayne hung his head in relief. "COULD I HAVE IT THEN, PLEASE?"

"Just a moment, sir...okay, here it is."

"MM-HMM...YES...THANKS! THANKS A LOT!" Wayne jotted it down and hung up. It was a street in Philadelphia *he'd* never heard of before. But she'd probably moved around quite a bit since he'd left; she'd always had trouble finding affordable rent.

He dialed the number for the main post office there and waited for the connection; his eyes traveled around the room as he remained seated on the bed. It was so *small.* And *isolated,* too—on the third floor, clear at the far end of a Z-shaped hallway and right around the corner from a boarded-up door, one of only two exits. Again, he wasn't entirely comfortable with it; he seemed to have an uncanny knack for getting weird rooms like this. And having a work area right outside the wall—where an old section of the place had been torn off and demolished—didn't help.

He sighed again. The noise had subsided somewhat; he wouldn't have to shout *quite* as much now. But it was still plenty loud.

"Philadelphia post office, main branch."

Wayne's mind jumped back. "Uh, yes, I'm looking for an address, and I have an old one here. Is there any way you could trace it?"

"If the party has moved from that location within the last eighteen months, and has a forwarding address, we can."

So many ifs. *Please,* Wayne thought. *Please know.*

He started to give his information but was put on hold again before he could finish. He moaned. Even a *momentary* pause at this point was excruciating.

Please, God, he prayed silently. *Please let them know. Let me find out and go home.*

Chad sat beside Wayne—he laid an arm on his shoulder and said nothing. He wanted to tell Wayne what he knew, but he could not. He could say or do nothing more on this matter.

The voice came back on.

"All right, sir. You said you wanted to find a forwarding address, using an old one?"

"Yes."

"For a business or resident?"

"A resident."

"Okay, sir, we can't do that type of thing over the phone. You'd have to bring it in here and pay the standard minimal charge in person, or drop us a written request in the mail."

Wayne was stunned. He felt the hot tears coming to his eyes and blinked them back, trying to hide the quivering in his voice. "Uh...uh..."

"Sir?"

"Uh, can...is there any...any other *possible* way of finding out?"

"No, I'm sorry, sir. That can only be done through the mail, or in person at the post office."

"Oh, God..." Wayne was desperate. He didn't know how else to go about it; he explained his situation, where he was calling from, who he was looking for.

There was a pause.

"Well, I'm afraid there's not much I can do, but...hold on, let me check on something I just thought of. It's a pretty long shot, but—"

"Could you, *please?*" Wayne couldn't hide his disappointment any longer.

"Uh, I'll try...could I have the person's name, and the old address?"

"Yes." Wayne repeated his mother's name and the information he had.

"All right—this may take some looking, and I certainly can't guarantee there'll be anything...would you like to hold, again?"

"*Yes,* please." Wayne bit his lip and shut his eyes. No, he would *not* fret. He was *determined* not to. He would wait here for as long as it took, and he would accept any news that was given to him. He'd been disappointed many times before in his life; certainly he could handle it now. But still, *this* time was so different. He was trying to find *Mom.* The one who'd *raised* him almost single-handedly for as long as she could, the one who'd done so much for him even when she couldn't. The one he'd *wronged* by leaving like he had. The only one he had left to go to. And now he didn't even know if he'd ever see her again...

"Sir?"

Wayne jumped—he hadn't been expecting anything so soon. He braced himself for the bad news.

"Yes," he answered weakly.

"I've found the change-of-address orders with that name."

Wayne's heart leaped. "You *did?*"

"Yes, in the files. The original was only a couple days from *expiring,* in fact, now that I'm looking at it."

Wayne almost fainted—the overwhelming *relief,* plus this latest round of on-again, off-again uncertainty, were almost too much to handle.

But they *had* it!

"Please, what's next, then?" He tried not to sound demanding.

"Well now—they're like I was thinking of, sure enough—now I can give you the new address."

"You *can?*" Wayne was taken aback by the sudden breakthrough. "How'd...how'd *that* happen?"

"Well, looking at the second form, it seems the person is maintaining a post office box here under 'business,' which allows us to give a street address over the phone. I can't say for sure, but it's very possible she's hoping someone—"

"Will call up and try to *locate* her!" Wayne interrupted before apologizing. "I'm sorry, I didn't mean to cut ya off...I just blurted that out as it struck me."

"That's all right, it was my guess, too. It would be really unusual, I might say—but actually very clever."

Wayne smiled in shock as the novelty of the idea began to sink in. Yes, that was *exactly* what Mom had done—she'd left him a way to find her again!

Chad only nodded silently; that was true.

"Let's have it!" said Wayne.

"All right, sir…"

Wayne wrote it down with trembling hands; he almost dropped the receiver as he was told the city and state. Had he actually *heard* right?

"Could you repeat *where,* please?"

"That's New York, New York."

"The *city?* You mean the *city itself?*"

"Yes, that should make your search even easier."

Wayne could hear the smile in the voice; he trembled with excitement. "Um, thanks! Thank you very much for your help!"

He hung up and then he laughed.

He couldn't *believe* it—*Mom,* right here in the *city!* He didn't even have to *go* anywhere! And what a simple, clever, *thoughtful* way she'd found to help him!

He lowered his head. *Thank you, Lord. Thank you so much!*

Still Chad said nothing.

Wayne stood. He thought about it for a moment, and then…yes, and then he knew what to do. He went to the mirror on the wall and brushed his prickly hair as best he could with his fingers; he tucked his shirt in and reached for his coat.

I'm gonna go see her, he thought. *I'm going over there right now.*

No, said the voice. *Stay here. Stay put for now.*

But I've found her, Wayne thought in reply. *So why wait a moment longer? I know about the drug men. I'll get police protection now…*

He put his coat on.

Don't do it, the voice said again.

But why not? thought Wayne. *I'm ready. And I'm tired of playing hide and seek like this.*

Don't do it, Chad repeated, his voice growing urgent. *Not right now.*

"I *have* to." Wayne started toward the door. "And it'll sure get me away from this noise."

He walked out and shut the door behind him before strutting off down the hall.

Chad opened it again. He also opened several others.

Don't! Wayne kept hearing the voice over and over. *Don't do it! Go back! Go back!*

He tried to ignore it as he walked around the first corner. Something was going to happen. He didn't know what, but he could *feel* it. Yet he didn't stop. He'd found her, and he would not, he *could* not wait anymore.

He rounded the second corner and not thirty feet away, right in front of the stairs, was *Glitch.*

With *someone* Wayne had never seen before.

Holding a long, orange and black *thing.*

Wayne's mouth fell open in horror. He ducked back but didn't make it.

They'd seen him.

He turned and ran for his life again. His exit blocked, there was now only one place to go—back to his room.

He bounded down the hallway, acutely aware of the heavy footsteps, the demented *laugh* that had suddenly arisen behind him. And it *wasn't* Glitch. He didn't know if the guy was crazy, or insane, or maybe both—and he didn't care.

He rounded the first corner again, nearly storming past his room; before he knew it, he'd caught the doorway with one arm and recalled himself back through it. He landed inside on the floor with a thud, literally yanked backwards like he'd suddenly run out of cord.

Only then did Chad let go of his arm.

Half-staggering, half-crawling, Wayne lunged for the door but was too late—they were already too close, they'd hear it slam and know where he was.

Where to hide?

Chad acted. He pushed Wayne behind the door just as the

two pursuers raced past, sending heavy vibrations up through the walls.

Wayne sat up, startled. He heard the footsteps stop abruptly as they reached the dead end, then retrace amid a barrage of profanity. He heard other rooms being entered, things getting shuffled, thrown, tossed.

"Who left all these damn *doors* open?" Glitch's voice shrieked. "Where are you?" a crazy-sounding voice sang out. "You are here somewhere! We will find you! I have something for you!"

Now Wayne was *really* unnerved. *You fool,* he thought to himself. *Why didn't you stay? Why didn't you listen?*

He stayed crouched behind the door, frozen, trying desperately to control his heavy breathing. His back was against the wall, the door was barely a foot in front of him.

Not until then did he notice the construction noise outside had ceased entirely; the only sounds now were those of his thundering heart and the would-be killers rapidly searching room after room outside, getting closer, closer. It was only a matter—

"We're running out of *rooms* now, *aren't* we?" said the crazy voice, finishing his thought.

Wayne *prayed* they'd miss him. *Just stay put,* said the voice. *Don't move. Don't do anything.*

Wayne's leg was falling asleep. The tickly agony slowly grew worse...*worse*...

He couldn't bear it. He started to shift positions.

No! Chad put his hands out against him. *Don't!*

Wayne did and lost his balance. As he thrust a hand sideways to catch himself, he bumped the springy doorstop.

Boioioioioioiiiiing

Horrified, he jammed his foot against it.

Several moments passed. Several *awful* moment of absolute silence.

Wayne felt sweat running down his back. His heart was pounding, his hands were trembling, he was shivering with fright. He tried not to breathe, move, or think.

Then he heard them.

A set of footsteps racing back toward his room. They entered, stopping *directly* on the other side of the door; they were quickly joined by another.

Laughter.

"Fighting again, boys?" said Glitch's snarly voice.

"Yep! Sure are!" said the crazy voice.

Chad got ready, positioning himself between Wayne and the door.

"So cut it out!" Glitch continued.

"Okay, daddy!"

Then Wayne heard a *sound.* It started as a low whirl, then quickly rose to a deafening scream—the sound of a *chainsaw* starting up.

My God, he thought, adrenaline rising. *Is he really that sick?*

His answer came. The long, whirling chain ripped through the door amid a hailstorm of sawdust, sending him choking, gasping, lunging sideways as it bore down on him.

Instantly Chad was on it, grabbing the thing with his hands, angling it away from Wayne and into the wall behind him, steering it around him, over him, around him…

Blinded by sawdust, disoriented by noise, Wayne was helpless. He tried to scream, getting only a mouthful of plaster and suffocating motor fumes. He coughed violently as he feebly tried to cover himself, acutely aware of the insane laugh over the roar.

Chad held firm to the chain, pulling and steering, pulling and steering—

There. That was all he needed.

He let go of the chain and slammed his body hard into Wayne's, knocking him backwards through the perforated wall like it was a dotted-line cut-out.

"Ooof!" Wayne found himself on the hallway floor. He sprang up, brushing debris from his eyes, leaping for the door in front of him.

It was the *boarded* one.

No! He pulled on it for dear life; he heard the chainsaw stop and the demented voice yelling.

"No oil! No oil on the dipstick! There's no red!"

Wayne heard them coming…he pulled *desperately…*

Chad helped him out.

Wayne suddenly fell backwards as the board snapped in his hands; he scrambled for the knob. *Please, God, help!*

He pulled it open and ran out into—*nothing!*

He was outside, falling three stories onto a spiked metal fence—

"Aaahh!"

Chad steered him between the spikes and cushioned him as one ripped his shirt up the front, another up his back under his coat.

Panicked, Wayne tried to free himself. He started to pull his coat off,—but not before he saw the lunatic appear in the doorway above, whirling chainsaw in hand, preparing to jump down after him.

Chad acted again. He ripped the impeding spike loose and pulled it up through Wayne's coat, hurling it into the building like a javelin just as the guy came down. He bent himself sideways in mid-fall to avoid it and landed flat on his back on the rocky ground, stunned.

"Uh, I think I'm disoriented!" he gasped. "Who! What! Me! How!"

Run, Wayne! Get out of here! Chad already knew. *This guy's different! He won't stop!*

Wayne got off the fence and ran, the noise, the fumes, the demented *laugh* still fresh in his ears.

Sykes stood and picked up the chainsaw. He laughed again. "Whew! That felt *good!*"

He raised his head at Glitch, standing in the doorway above. "So you comin' too, or *what?* Are ya gonna *what* on me? Come on, Botch! Try it! It's nifty!"

"Keep your snide blurbs to yourself, idiot!" Glitch bellowed down. *"I'm* not goin' with ya—I just had *lunch!* I'll wait on ya!"

"But aren't you *coming?*" Sykes sang out. "I *need* you, Botch!"

"Quit it out!" Glitch shouted. "I mean—aw, just shut up and get after him!"

Sykes laughed dementedly. "Your command is my wish!"

He took off after Wayne.

Where to go? Wayne looked about hurriedly as he kept running. This was a bad part of town; even in broad daylight, the streets were deserted, everything along the sidewalk was boarded up. But maybe that was *good...*

He heard distant footsteps pursuing him, the buzz of the chainsaw steadily growing louder.

And a *voice.*

"Don't run from me forever, cuz I'll *find* you forever!"

Wayne thought frantically. Maybe he couldn't run, but he *could* hide. But again, *where?*

This way, said Chad.

Wayne heard a snap. He looked over as the padlock broke in two and slipped off one of the boards in the building he was running past.

There was a *door* behind it.

He couldn't even tell until that moment. Quickly he pushed it open and slammed it shut behind him.

Phew! A foul odor met his nose as his eyes adjusted to the darkness. He could make out a few tall, empty shelves, standing in rows in front of a counter. There were bare display cases lining the walls; a few wheelless shopping carts were scattered about. He was in some kind of old grocery store. It sure *was* dark—the windows all along the front were completely boarded up.

No time for standing around, said Chad. *Come on, Wayne.*

Indeed, Wayne could already hear the footsteps approaching outside. He darted toward the back of the store, Chad's hand firmly clasped around his arm, guiding him through the blackness. He could hear the guy yelling.

"He he! I know you're in one of these places! Time for some exploratory surgery!"

The sound of wood being carved away met Wayne's ears. Then the entire back wall was suddenly ablaze in sunlight; he could hear glass shattering as the chain continued through the window.

He ran through the large cargo doors now visible in front of him.

The stench inside was even greater. Wayne clasped a hand over his mouth, trying not to gag as his eyes raced around the warehouse and the maze of crates, cardboard, and boxes.

He bolted toward them.

Sykes walked through the store. He could see Wayne's footprints clearly in the layer of dust on the tile floor; he followed them back, back...

He came through the cargo doors and inhaled deeply.

"Ooo, *dawg!* Garbage *stink* that reeks! Someone sure died in *here!*"

He held the chainsaw aloft. "Or is *about* to, that is!"

He started toward the boxes.

From his hiding place behind the far back row of crates, Wayne could hear him. He heard the weapon effortlessly carving into box after box as the guy walked along the first row with it, four aisles ahead of Wayne, laughing maniacally. The cutting sound stopped every so often as he checked the chain.

"Nope! No red yet!"

He passed by and Wayne could momentarily see him, clearly, through the space between the stacks. His face was crazy, totally bananas. His expression was wild and the half-drooped eye he'd caught a glimpse of earlier was now wide-open, more so than any *normal* eye.

Wayne shuddered.

The weapon's roar echoed throughout the huge room as the guy continued around the end of the first row and started down the second, still cutting a single, deep line through the crates. He was slowly getting closer. Wayne would have to move again before long—but if he did that, he'd be...

Just stay here, said Chad. *Don't make a sound.*

The guy appeared in the space again, this time an aisle

closer, going the other direction. Wayne could see the clouds of sawdust flying up as the thing continued its deadly course, sending rotting tomatoes and heads of lettuce spattering all over the floor. The *smell* was unbelievable.

"Aw, come on!" the guy yelled, pausing from his walk. "Stop hiding and *gimmee* yourself! You've been so *cooperative* so far!"

He laughed as he revved the engine. "The work crew back there was nice enough to loan this to me. And *you* saved us some trouble, too, boy! Good you showed up when you did! We weren't even sure we had the right *place!*"

Wayne shut his eyes and sighed. He didn't need the reminder of his stupidity; his present situation was enough of one.

The chainsaw started to sputter, then cut out. The guy's grin disappeared as he yanked on the cord again and again.

Nothing happened.

The guy cursed. He threw it to the ground and dropped to his knees over it; he tried to move the chain by hand. He unscrewed the gas lid and stuck his nose down over the hole, inhaling deeply.

He put his tongue in it.

He sat up with a dejected look on his face. "Aw, shucks. Outta gas." He held up the blade. "But at least I got some *red* on it!"

He laughed as he licked off some tomato juice.

Maybe *now* was a good time. Wayne started to rise.

No, said Chad. *Don't move yet. Wait here.*

Wayne heeded this time.

And he was glad he did. The guy had already risen and was staring down at something ahead of him. He walked out of view…

Wayne suddenly heard a light scraping noise, like metal on the floor—then a high-pitched, twangy, boingy sound, almost like a saw being bent. Only it was too quiet for that.

The guy jumped back into view, hands down, arms moving out and in against his sides every time the noise sounded.

It looked almost like he was stretching something, but Wayne couldn't see what.

"Ha ha! Gotta pick up where I left off!"

He started forward again. "You in here somewhere?" he sang out. "We'll soon find out, right?" He laughed hysterically. "We'll soon find *out, right!*"

He continued down the aisle. Wayne kept hearing the boingy sound.

"Let me introduce myself," the guy bellowed. "Just take 'sicko' and make it 'psycho' and drop the 'O' and add an 'S' and you have *me!* Simple, isn't it?"

Wayne swallowed. The boingy noise continued.

"And I leave my niche if you snitch on Botch—oops!" More laughter. *"That* don't rhyme!"

Wayne shook his head—what a jabberwocky! The guy's mouth must have been the other end of a black hole or something, because everything was coming out of it. And yet in hearing him, Wayne finally knew what it was that made him so different.

His *laugh.*

Totally crazy, yet…*giddy,* almost…almost *likable.* Both Wayne, and even *Chad*—each to their own amazement—found themselves *smiling* at it. It was strange, hearing someone so *unnerving* and yet…so downright *funny.* For Wayne, at least, it made knowing he was a fruitywhacko—and deadly *serious*—hard to remember.

But Chad knew it. *Cover your ears, Wayne.*

Wayne started to reach up, then stopped. He couldn't bring himself to do it.

The guy rounded the corner and started down the third aisle, kicking crates, knocking stuff over. "Yeah," he hollered, "I'm behind a block and down another alley, no doubt!"

More boingy sounds.

"Ate a fruitcake once and got locked up for cannibalism!" He laughed insanely again.

Wayne tried not to.

"Aw, come on! Don't make me waste my time lookin' for ya…"

He appeared in the space again.

"...cuz I'll find ya anyway!" More laughter. "And why would you hide from *me?* I'm just a good, fun guy!" He paused. "A good *fungi!* HE HE HE!"

Wayne shut his eyes. It was getting harder to keep quiet.

Chad was growing more concerned. The guy's strategy was working; he was slowly softening Wayne's alertness, lowering his guard.

Don't listen to it, he repeated. *Cover your ears and don't listen to it anymore.*

But Wayne couldn't *help* listening. There was something almost hypnotic, weirdly fascinating about it. He felt almost spellbound...

As if the guy could sense it, he started to crack jokes as he rounded the stack to the last aisle.

"You know, I was told I have a unique strand of DNA in my genes? And *I* thought it was just lint!"

Wayne bit his lip. It was getting harder...

Don't listen. Don't listen, Wayne...

"I told my boss I needed a vacation. He said, 'Okay, take a week off and come back tomorrow!'"

Wayne clamped a hand over his mouth. The guy was almost right across from him.

Cover your ears! said Chad.

Wayne didn't.

"I felt sick and my doctor said my food had been poisoned. But that was impossible cuz all the safety buttons popped just fine!"

Wayne couldn't hold it any longer—a snicker escaped through his nose.

"AH-HAAA!"

The guy suddenly pushed through the stacks and stopped right in front of Wayne—they *both* screamed insanely and Wayne could see all the fillings in the guy's teeth.

Chad acted, seizing a rotten tomato and lobbing Sykes in the face with it; he fell backwards, coughing and sputtering and wiping the stinking mess from his eyes.

Run, Wayne! Chad grabbed him by the arm. *Run now!*

Wayne bolted toward the stack of boxes near the back wall…maybe there was an *exit* behind them…

He stormed around the pile and almost fell down the cement steps to the loading area before Chad pulled him away from the edge; he heaved Wayne up over the flimsy metal railing and behind the flattened sheet of cardboard against it.

"Oooof!" Wayne sat up—he realized he was momentarily hidden and looked for a door. He saw one, not twenty feet away, bright sunlight streaming through the crack underneath.

It was also padlocked.

And out in the open.

Stay put, said Chad. *Wait here for a minute.*

He reached into his shirt and pulled out the aluminum container he'd saved earlier.

He set it where it needed to be.

Sykes stood and picked up the metal shipping strap again. Now he was *mad.* He stretched it tight between his hands, filling the room once more with the light, plucky sound. All right, where *was* he? Where was the *rat?*

Wayne sat motionless, trying to ignore the barrage of instantaneous cramps in his legs. He could hear the sound, he could hear the guy walking about, aimlessly. He tried not to breathe…

His stomach growled again. He glared down at it in horror.

Sykes whirled around, facing the boxes near the far wall. A cool, sinister laugh escaped from his lips as he started toward them.

Wayne heard the footsteps growing closer, closer. They were so *agonizingly* slow; he could hear the guy chuckling, hear him *breathing* the whole time. He shut his eyes and lowered his head into his lap, once again waiting for the inevitable…

The whole room fell silent. Wayne looked up with a start. No guy.

He slowly looked to one side, then the other.

Still no one.

He lowered his hands to the floor and started to push himself up.

No, said Chad. *Wait here!*

Wayne slowly rose...

The aluminum pan popped back into shape; an insane yell rang out.

Wayne dropped down again—the guy was right across the steps on the other side of the boxes!

Sykes picked the thing up and banged it a couple more times with his hand. He laughed. "Clever! I like...I mean I *really* like that!"

He started forward again.

Wayne could hear him coming around the stack. His head shot sideways—had someone just peeked at him? He sat frozen as footsteps made their way down the stairs to his back.

Chad grabbed him. *Okay, Wayne! Run now!*

Wayne was slow to respond. He began to rise, but not before the two arms tore through the cardboard on both sides of him and looped the strap around his neck. His eyes bulged out, his face grew red as it tightened—he clawed at it, writhing, gasping for air that wouldn't come...

Sykes laughed dementedly—now for the *fun* part.

He started to twist.

Chad grabbed the strap in his hands and snapped it in two, sending Wayne flopping forward, Sykes tumbling backwards down the stairs. Then he kicked the door open.

Hurry, Wayne!

Wayne staggered to his feet, coughing, sputtering. He raced out, wiping his burning eyes.

Sykes landed at the bottom with a grunt, moaning and laughing at once. "Ooo, stairs down which to fall!"

He bolted to his feet and ran back up, stomping loudly. *"Gee,* I love cement!"

Wayne bounded down the dirty, gravel walk path behind the place, heart thundering. He could only go straight ahead; there wasn't a single gap between the back of the buildings that lined the sides. *When will this end?* he thought.

Apparently not anytime soon—he could already hear the guy behind him. "He he! I see ya there! Thanks for the drop, pal! Made me aware of *reality* for a minute!"

Wayne couldn't believe it—*nothing* phased this guy. Nothing at all. Like he'd been permanently set off or something. How in the world could he lose him?

Keep going, said Chad. *Just a little farther.*

Wayne kept running.

"Tryin' to *lose* me, huh?" the psycho wailed. "Come on, admit it! *Nooo,* yes you are! But I'm good at this, you know! With near flawless perfection!"

The rear of the small metal hangar—an old auto repair place—came into view. Through a partly-broken window, Wayne could see the large, open garage door clear at the other end and *civilization,* the busy street at the end of the block, nearby. A scene reminiscent of the day before.

Go through the window to the front, said Chad.

Wayne didn't—he'd had enough of dark buildings or anything to do with them. He veered right toward the side of the place; he'd go around *that* way.

Sykes saw him disappear around the corner.

He laughed.

The skunk was finally trapped.

He raced to the hangar and dove through the window.

Wayne stopped cold. He'd made yet *another* deadly error—the stupid place had been built at an *angle,* completely pinching off the space between it and the brick building next door. And right at the *front,* of course. He leaned forward on his knees, panting, bemoaning the situation. He couldn't go back, there was no way out...

Go through the window, said Chad.

But that's clear back there, Wayne thought, staring at the debris around his feet. *I can't go back there.*

No, that window, said Chad, pointing. *Break it and go through.*

Wayne looked up. He hadn't even seen the small, mesh-covered window in the hangar, right at his head level.

Break it, said Chad.

Wayne found a loose brick and hurled it through the glass;

Chad gave him a boost as he hoisted himself…

Jeepers, what a tight squeeze! Wayne lowered himself back down—right onto a pile of old exhaust pipes, which clattered loudly all over the place as he stood and raced for the opening.

The demented laugh caught his ear and he whirled around.

There was the *guy,* in a doorway across the dark room, an *ax* in one hand, the other raised to a button on the wall—

"Adjusted for speed!" he yelled. "Bye bye blackbird!"

He pushed it and Wayne heard a loud buzz—he looked up, horrified, as the steel garage door came crashing down on him.

Instantly Chad wedged a pipe under it, slowing it for the millisecond he needed to push Wayne outside before the door crushed the thing and slammed to the floor.

It started to rise again.

Wayne scrambled to get out of view—he bolted to the side and unwittingly entangled himself in the loop of power cable as it lowered around him. He could hear the psycho coming.

"Did I *miss* you? Shoot, yes! Gonna *get* you, though!"

Wayne panicked. He bolted from his place and ran across the doorway—too late realizing the guy was already there.

He laughed wildly as he swung the ax out.

Chad yanked the cable still around Wayne's leg, toppling him over just as the blade cut through the air above him.

"Hold *still,* you dummy!" Sykes raised it over his head.

Not to be outdone, Chad seized a rock and flung it across the room into the switch—

Again the door came down with a whir, catching the blade just before it struck Wayne and sending Sykes reeling from the piercing sound. He shrieked madly as he pulled it loose and swung under the rapidly-closing door, again missing Wayne as he was hoisted upside down, high into the air by the cable.

The door hit the ground.

Hanging by one leg, Wayne could hear the lunatic yelling as he crossed the room for the button. He clawed frantically at the cable—he had to get down immediately!

Chad snapped it with his hands. He again cushioned Wayne's fall with himself.

Wayne rose and bolted for the street. He knew the door wouldn't open now and the guy would have to go clear back through the building and around all the other places to keep after him. Good. He'd need every minute of it.

This way, said Chad.

Wayne kept looking over his shoulder as he approached the car. Apparently he *had* lost the guy, at least for now. Still, though...

He couldn't help wondering if maybe he should go to the police and get some protection first before going to see Mom. They'd continuously found him so *easily;* every place he'd gone for any length of time had been fair game. He *shuddered.* The idea of being at Mom's and then having an unexpected *guest* suddenly show up at the door...

Good grief, he thought. *I couldn't do that. It'd be totally irresponsible.*

He reached the car and got in. *I'm going straight to the cops first.*

Chad got in beside him. He laid a hand on Wayne's shoulder. *No,* he said calmly, *that isn't necessary, Wayne. You don't have to do that.*

Wayne heard the voice, felt the soothing *presence* once again. It was the same voice that had guided him, despite himself, safely through the last, well...*bizarre* day-and-a-half, the same presence he'd felt ever since that moment he'd prayed with Doug.

He smiled.

Only when he could stop like this and reflect did he really realize they'd been with him all along. And now, suddenly, *he* felt totally calm again, at peace, secure in knowing he had nothing to fear by going there.

He pulled the little piece of paper from his pocket, the one with the address on it.

It was settled; he was going to Mom's.

Even so, he would take no chances. He'd drive around for a little while, then park a safe distance away from her apartment and ride the bus the remaining distance.

Chad smiled. All that would be fine—in fact, that's exactly what he'd just told Wayne to do. Yet he said nothing else. He looked over at Wayne, so happy and content, enjoying the only time he'd had to finally *pursue* what he'd been looking so long and hard for. And he didn't want to see anything shatter it for him.

But Chad knew otherwise.

He was *already* feeling sorry for Wayne, he could *already* feel the pain, the hurt that Wayne would soon feel. And it was *tough* for him, tougher than anything he'd faced so far as his personal guardian.

But it would all be for Wayne's safety, ultimately...

Wayne glanced at himself in the rearview as he pulled away, again amazed he could see anything at all. He'd probably been through more already than anyone else, anywhere. And yet here he was again, alive, breathing, and completely unscathed. He couldn't help wondering how *much* more he could go through—although, he hoped, no more at all— before it would finally happen...

He laughed at himself.

Infinitely more if necessary, that's how much. He had a *protector.* And he felt silly for ever thinking anything that would even *hint* otherwise. After all he'd been through, wasn't it the most obvious thing in the world?

He prayed silently.

Thanks, Lord. Thanks for looking after me, despite all my shortcomings.

He looked over beside him, at the passenger seat.

Thank you, too, angel. You're lookin' after me well for Him. Thanks for all your help, even when I didn't listen.

Chad beamed. *No problem, Wayne. Great to be with ya.*

"That was one *thick* cable you broke," Wayne added.

It was? said Chad. *Which one?*

"Well, *both* of 'em, I guess. You must have some *powerful* teeth."

I do? Chad felt his jaw, then laughed.

15

It had started to snow again.

Wayne's excitement rose as he stepped off the bus in front of the drab, brick apartment complex. This was it, finally. His search was over. No more running or looking or wondering or anything.

He was coming home.

He walked down the sidewalk between the buildings, tugging at his backpack (he'd had an *urge* to bring it with him), and taking in his new surroundings as best he could. Boy, they *were* drab. Every structure in the place was exactly the same—three stories tall, box-shaped and flat-roofed, with no trees or anything. There were hardly any people around; only a couple kids playing by a dirty, half-melted snowbank in the grassy middle area.

Wayne tried to piece together what he was going to say. He wasn't exactly pressed and groomed, and his clothes were battered, ripped, and covered with a new layer of danger-induced grime. But he was *home,* he was safe, and that was all that mattered. *Home,* right here in the city, where the long melodrama he'd endured was about to end. Shoot, he didn't *care* what he'd say; he'd say it when he got there. Quite frankly, he felt too good to care about anything at this point.

He found Building Five, toward the rear of the complex, and entered. Chad walked in with him, saying nothing.

The landing inside was dark and echoey. Let's see...*was* it the right place? Wayne checked the row of rusty, black mailboxes—yes, he saw the one marked *R E Guilford, Apt. 307,* penciled into the little slot on a scrap of paper. Never before in his life was he so glad to see that name; it sent *chills* down his spine just looking at it. He stood there and studied it a moment longer before proceeding—and even *then* it was hard to keep going. He wanted to just stand and stare at it, to confirm over and over what he already knew.

He started the climb up the stairs. He'd climbed a *lot* of stairs recently, but this time was different. He felt stronger, more *renewed* with each step, almost...like they were battery chargers, keeping his spirits at the highest level possible for those last few feet.

And this whole crazy thing's almost done, he thought, smiling from ear to ear. *Mom won't believe it when I tell her.*

Yet even in all his happiness, Wayne was astonished to find a pocket of uncertainty, *uneasiness* still occupying a tiny corner of his mind. He wasn't sure if it was simply a paranoia he'd developed (given recent events, it was altogether likely), or indeed legitimate. But there was something...*strange* about this place; for some reason, it...it just didn't seem like Mom. And he had no idea why, exactly.

But this was no time for any of that. He was already at the top floor. He trembled as he walked down the hall and stopped in front of door number 307, savoring every *wonderful* moment of the suspense.

This was it—home at last!

He knocked. Then he stood and waited, hurriedly straightening his shirt, brushing half-melted snow from his prickly hair, anything to keep his hands busy. His mouth watered as the smell of freshly-baked chocolate-chip cookies suddenly filled his nose.

He knocked again.

He heard footsteps inside, slow, quiet footsteps coming to the door. His heart started to race, he could hardly contain his excitement as he stood straight and tall, ready.

Chad drew close beside him. Wayne would soon need every bit of emotional support he could get and he wanted to be right there with him through the whole thing…

The door opened, ever so slightly.

Wayne caught a glimpse of someone peering up at him from behind the chain stretched across the small gap, studying him suspiciously before closing the door again. He heard the thing slide off, and then it opened all the way.

An elderly black lady stood before him, leaning on a short, metal cane and staring up at him with half-a-smile on her face.

Wayne smiled back—Mom must have had a friend, maybe a neighbor over.

"I knew you were safe the minute I saw ya," she said, chuckling. "I can tell a saved person when I see one—just like that." She snapped her fingers. "Thought maybe you were my son, at first."

Wayne swallowed. He was glad it showed, but he needed to ask…

"Is there something I can help you with, young man?"

She'd taken the words right out of his mouth. "Uh, yes," he began. "Is, um, is Ruth Guilford at home?"

The woman nodded slowly. "Oh yeah, she's here."

Wayne felt immense relief. "Well, um, could I see her, please? I'm—"

He glanced behind her and lowered his voice to a whisper, trying to conceal his presence. "—I'm her son Wayne. She hasn't seen me in over six years and, well…I've finally found her again and I-I've come back."

The woman's mouth dropped open for a moment; she raised a hand over it and she appeared to be hiding a chuckle. Her face bore an expression of humor, and yet... embarrassment, *pity* as she looked up at him.

"Oh my goodness..."

Wayne swallowed, suddenly uncomfortable. "Uh, is...is something wrong? Can...can I see her now?"

"Oh, you poor boy." She shook her head and moved her hand to her cheek, revealing a smiling face. "I'm afraid you *are* seeing her now."

Wayne's grin disappeared; he didn't understand. "Oh, you're...um...I don't..."

The woman chuckled. "I'm Ruth Guilford. You're talking to her."

Wayne didn't think he'd heard right—maybe *she'd* misunderstood. "Oh, yeah, I mean I'm looking for the one who moved—"

"From Philadelphia a while back," she finished for him. "Yeah, that's me. Came a couple years ago, almost."

Wayne thought she must have been kidding. But a quick glance into the tiny apartment behind her told him otherwise—she was indeed the only one there.

"And somehow, I don't think we're even *cousins,*" she added, her expression quickly growing more embarrassed.

Wayne suddenly felt like a fist had struck him—no, he felt worse, *much* worse than that, like he'd been totally unraveled, torn apart, ruined. He was *shattered,* he was *devastated.* He stood there expressionless, frozen in position, his mind struggling, racing to counter the numbing shock—

"Would you like to come in anyway?" The woman seemed to sense it.

Wayne barely even heard her. Yet somehow—he couldn't even remember doing so—he said yes. Maybe it would put his mind on pause, maybe it would temporarily stop the horrendous emotional onslaught until he could deal with it. And that was something he was desperate for right now.

He followed her in.

Chad walked in with him; Wayne was doing exactly as he'd said.

Ruth showed him to a small, wooden rocking chair in the living room and disappeared into the kitchen. Wayne slipped the pack off and sat down, trying to behave just as he would have moments before; he blinked to keep himself from staring in shocked silence, looking around at the bare, drab white walls and sparse, old furniture, breathing the wonderful cookie smell. But he suddenly wasn't hungry. Just *sitting* here like this was already growing difficult...

Shhh. Chad stood beside him, a hand on his shoulder, speaking quietly into his ear. *Relax, Wayne. Don't think about it right now.*

Wayne shut his eyes and relaxed. The soothing *calm* came over him in an instant, as if a life saver had been thrown to him in the waters of despair. His mind was at peace again, at least for the time being.

Thanks, Lord.

Ruth appeared from the kitchen again, holding a small cookie tin. She walked over, slowly, and set it on Wayne's lap; it was warm, almost *hot.* A nice change from the weather.

Wayne felt the hunger come back. "Thanks," he said weakly, clearing his throat.

"Just made 'em." Ruth took a seat on the footstool across from him. "So...you're looking for your mother?"

Wayne nodded.

Ruth smiled and laughed quietly. "So then, how did you come across *me?*"

Wayne took a long breath—then he told her. She appeared to listen with keen interest, her smile growing bigger as once more he found himself sharing his life story with a complete stranger. It was a slightly *different* story this time—now that he could add a new and wonderful event that rendered all the lousy stuff totally meaningless—yet one that tempered by the fresh knowledge that no, he wasn't *clear* out of the woods on this whole thing. But as with Doug, he felt entirely comfortable telling her; the *calm* had completely filled his mind, insulating him from the shock he'd just experienced and letting him speak without even crying. And he was grateful *beyond* words for that.

A quiet chime sounded. Wayne looked over at the little clock on the coffee table. Five-thirty in the afternoon. He'd been there almost a half-hour already.

Chad laid a hand on his arm. *Come on,* he said. *We need to start going now.*

Ruth saw him look at it—she seemed surprised, too. "Oh, you need to leave."

"Uh, well…" Wayne felt awkward leaving right *then;* as much as he'd said, it still seemed like so little. He wanted to *do* something for her, something of value.

"Uh, is there anything you need…anything I can really do?"

"You've already done plenty, Wayne." She leaned forward on her cane, beaming. "Just a visit from anybody, especially a brother in the Lord like you, is more than enough for me."

She laughed again. "We *are* related, you know."

Wayne nodded. Her hand came out to rest on top of his, the one on the tin.

"You remind me a lot of *my* son, Wayne. I still don't know where he is—he left me so long ago, ran away just like you did. And I still wait for him. I pray every day that he's safe, that he'll find what *we've* found and come back."

She looked right at him.

"I'm glad you came. Your mother would be very happy to know you're all right and that you've made the most important decision you can possibly make in your life."

Nodding was all Wayne could do. Chad repeated himself. *We have to leave now. We can't stay here any longer.*

"Well, um…" Wayne slowly rose. He helped Ruth to her feet and picked up his backpack in one hand, the tin in the other before making his way to the door.

Ruth followed him.

"Thank you." Wayne turned and faced her from the

hallway. "Thank you so much. Just talking with you has helped me a lot. I do hope your son comes back, and soon."

Her hand came up and landed softly on his arm. "And I hope you find your mother, too, Wayne. I'll pray for you."

"Thanks a lot. I'll never forget you."

She smiled warmly again and reached for the door. Wayne heard it shut quietly behind him as he headed for the stairs.

Chad stayed close by him. He would need to guide Wayne *extra* carefully from this point on.

Only now, back outside in the cool evening air, did the full impact hit Wayne. Somehow, miraculously, it'd been quelled in his mind; making another person so happy had indeed helped. Yet as he trudged along in the fresh layer of snow, completely alone in the cool winter dusk, he couldn't ignore it anymore.

He *hadn't* found Mom.

And he was no closer now than he'd ever been.

The reality came back on him so hard he was thrown into another blank daze almost at once; everything became a blur. He literally saw or heard nothing, he was oblivious to his surroundings. He couldn't remember walking to the street, or getting on the bus, or getting off at the next location on the list he'd hoped so fervently he wouldn't have to use again. He couldn't remember getting the key or taking the elevator to his room. All he knew was that he was sitting on the bed, his head buried in his knees, crying hard.

Chad sat down right beside him; he laid an arm around his shoulder.

Wayne felt *awful.* So awful, in fact, it nearly rivaled how he'd felt a couple of nights before, at the red light in front of the concrete wall. He didn't *want* himself to feel that way, but he couldn't help it. He figured it was coming so *close,* so sag-blasted, *wonderfully close,* and then finding out he'd made no progress at all, he was right where he'd started. Which was pretty far from anything. It *had* all seemed too good to be true, from that first moment of euphoria on the telephone—but he'd stifled the feeling. Sure enough, though, it *had* been too good.

I haven't found her. I haven't found her. The fact was all he could think about. And here he was, sitting on yet *another* bed in *another* room, after *another* grueling day, with no evidence or clues to go by this time—Mom had vanished, without a trace, off the face of the earth. And *now* what time was it? Good grief, almost six-thirty Friday. His order would be lifted in less than six hours and the moment he'd been waiting and waiting and *waiting* for would finally arrive…and he had absolutely nowhere to go. His money would run out in another couple of nights, and he'd be stuck in the city again, just as before, only with the addition of a *contract* on his head, and hit men closing in all around him.

Please, God, he prayed. *Help me. I don't know what to do. Please show me what to do…*

He sobbed.

Chad's grip around Wayne strengthened, his hand tightened on his shoulder. He himself blinked back tears. Wayne couldn't make a single plea, or feel a single emotion without *him* hearing and feeling it as well. *Whatever* Wayne felt, he felt. Being so near to him, being completely aware of his safety every second of every day made *that* relatively easy. And sharing in his emotions was a *wonderful* ability, indeed.

But Chad *didn't* like seeing Wayne bothered or saddened or hurt by anything—especially something like this, and to this extent. It made *him* feel the same way, too. He could feel it all, just as intensely, just as deeply as Wayne himself. He hurt *with* him, *ached* with him. He knew exactly what Wayne was going through and felt all his pain, every last little bit of it. He was *that* bonded, that remarkably *close* to him. All the devastating disappointment and despair that Wayne was feeling, *he* felt.

And Chad *wanted* to relieve him. He wanted *badly* to end the agony and sadness and uncertainty for him, once and for all, tell Wayne what he needed to know and let him rest. One simple phrase would do it. But he couldn't say anything yet—he'd have to wait just a *teeny* bit longer.

Besides, Wayne was also *safe,* at least for the time being.

And his prayer had certainly been heard.

Wayne took solace in the *presence* once more, and the comfort it brought. And again, he was deeply grateful for it. Heartbreaking though this whole thing was, he still had nothing to complain about. He had *not* squandered his time thus far; he'd done all he possibly could. And he'd brought some of the comfort and warmth he was now feeling to another person who had desperately needed it, as well. He actually managed to smile, even *laugh,* through his tears. Time well spent was certainly not a moment wasted.

Chad smiled, too. *No doubt about that, Wayne.*

Even so, finding Mom would certainly be a big, big relief. And Wayne just *didn't* know where…

His smile dissolved into a frown, his chuckle into a quiet sob once more.

Chad stayed right beside him.

He'd soon be busy again.

Down on the main floor, safely out of view in the dark stairwell, Slasher waited impatiently. The guy in the little snapshot he held had never passed through; he hadn't gotten the chance to use his knife like he'd been promised and he was disappointed. But he was determined to have his fun *sometime* that evening. And the sooner, the better—it was much more thrilling when the prey was still awake and could scream more.

He brushed his black, flowing hair back over his shoulders, pulling his dark plaid coat down tight over his belt and walked out to the front counter with the plastic badge he always carried. He showed the snapshot to the desk clerk— suddenly leaning forward inconspicuously as a half-dozen or so members of the Guardian Angels sauntered through the lobby behind him—and asked if the person pictured had checked in. He displayed the badge and explained that he was an undercover narcotics officer; the guy in the photo was wanted for possession and distribution of illegal substances.

He laughed silently at the flowing sound of his own voice. He was so *good,* so convincing.

Yes, he was told, the guy *had* checked in, almost an hour earlier. Slasher's gold teeth showed as he grinned broadly; he thanked the clerk profusely for his help in the fight before turning for the elevator.

The Guardian Angels were just crowding into it.

Slasher stopped. He *couldn't* get in with them—they unnerved him. He'd have to wait until they were safely gone.

He watched the numbers above the elevator light up, one after another.

Three...four...five...

It stopped at six.

Crud.

The very floor *he* was going to.

He walked over to the stairs' entrance once more and waited. He'd give them a few minutes to get where they were going, then head up and do his work.

Wayne ate a couple of the chocolate-chip cookies from the tin. They were delicious, and they *did* make him feel a little better. But he was still plenty depressed. How were things going to work out *this* time? If he could only—

He heard people walking by in the hall. He automatically drew back, tensed, as they neared his door...no, they kept on walking. He breathed a sigh of relief and continued eating. *Mmm*...yes, they *were* very good.

Chad slowly lifted his hand from Wayne's shoulder. He didn't *want* to, of course; he wanted to remain at his side for a long, long time. But he *had* to get up. He knew what was coming and what had to be done.

Wait here, Wayne. I'll be right back.

He made his way to the hall just outside the room and surveyed (Sir Veyed?) it. He saw the soda machine down at one end, by the stairs' entrance, and the restroom right across from Wayne's door; the Guardian Angels were just arriving at *their* room on the other end.

Chad grinned. This would be *funny!*

He ran to the machine and whistled to them as they disappeared from view. *Hey! Come here, friends. I can use your help.*

Slasher approached the landing on the sixth floor, tiptoeing, ever so silent. He drew the twelve-inch hunting knife from under his coat.

It was time to kill some nice, fresh meat.

He laughed again. This would be swift and easy; he'd be in and out in minutes.

He pushed open the door and slipped into the hall.

The knife immediately went up his sleeve as he came face-to-face with a man—a much *larger* man—in the Angels uniform, who eyed him suspiciously as he stood at the soda machine.

Damn!

He grinned at the guy—who only *stared* back—before making a fast U-turn for the stairs again.

He'd give it another shot in a few minutes.

"Hey, Jose!" The guy at the machine was suddenly all excited. "Check this thing out!"

"Yo!" answered a voice down the hall. "What is it, man?"

"There's a sign taped over the money slot," he hollered. "It says, 'Free, help yourselves!'"

"Seriously?"

"Yeah, and it's *open,* too! The inside's packed—I mean *packed*—with cans!"

"Hey, guys," the second voice continued. "Ricky's struck a gold mine! What kind of soda you people want? I'm goin' down there now."

"Ha, you *never* get the right kind," said a third voice, from the same room. "Go on ahead, and we'll come down one at a time and pick 'em ourselves."

A chorus of other voices echoed the plan.

Chad chuckled. Just *exactly* as he wanted.

Inside *his* room, Wayne could hear the racket. *I wish*

they'd hold it down, he thought. *Just a little.* He didn't mind hearing people *talk;* in fact, he *enjoyed* the company of other human voices when he felt so depressed. Only not so *loud,* that was all. He didn't *need* the yelling.

Slasher again approached landing number six from the stairs and drew out his knife. Again, he slipped into the hall.

The same thing happened as before.

He waited a few more minutes and tried again.

The same thing happened.

He waited several more minutes.

Same thing.

Chad was laughing hysterically.

"Wow, this is *great!* Want another one, Delmar?"

"Sure, Jose! Bring me one!"

"What an end to a busy day of crime-busting, huh?" Jose got two more cans out of the machine. "I can't *believe* this!"

And neither could Wayne. *Jeepers,* they were loud. And up and down more than a berserk kangaroo. Didn't they have anything *better* to do? He grimaced, now longing for silence in his misery. There could *not* be any reason for that much activity, he figured; it couldn't possibly serve any useful purpose.

He flopped down on the bed and covered his ears.

And *Slasher* couldn't believe it, either. How much *longer* would he be kept from his fun?

He slumped against the wall on the ground floor landing, out of breath from the endless trips up and down. He'd *had* it. Enough was enough. *This* time he'd wait a full *hour* before going up. But he *would* do it. He was *determined* to outlast this little distraction.

"Aw, *shoot.*" The guy stood dejected at the soda machine.

"What's the matter, Perry?"

"We're down to the last two," he shouted back. He pulled them out and strode off down the hall, chuckling. "Too much is never enough, I guess."

Chad laughed, too. He shut the front of the machine once more and peeled off his handwritten note. There. The rest of this thing would play itself out in due time; right now he had to rejoin Wayne.

Ahhh. Wayne slowly removed his hands from his ears at the sudden, new silence. *Now* maybe he could proceed with his work.

He instinctively reached for the telephone, on the little nightstand beside the bed.

He didn't feel anything.

Startled, he looked over—there *wasn't* any phone. In his distraction, he'd paid so little attention to the room that he hadn't even noticed until now.

Rats, he thought as he got up. *Must be a pay phone in the hall or something.* He walked to the door and peeked out— indeed there was. Ready and waiting for him to use.

He started for it and then stopped. What was he *doing? Who* was he calling? In a wonderful moment of habit, he'd completely forgotten. He *had* no one to call. Mom wasn't anywhere and he was sunk.

The sudden recollection brought the hot tears back in a flood. He went to the bed and sat down and cried again.

Chad drew close to him; his arm went back around his shoulder. *Don't lose hope, Wayne...don't lose hope...*

But I have none left. Wayne tried not to sound rude in his thoughts. *Of finding her, I mean...she's gone...she's gone...*

Keep the faith, Wayne...always remember, your faith is very powerful...

I know it is...but it's still so hard...

Just trust the Lord, Wayne...never lose sight of what He can do...

Please, God, Wayne prayed. *Please show me where Mom is...please...*

Chad heard a calling. Immediately he folded his hands and knelt.

Yes, Lord.

He got the message.

It was *time!* It was *okay* to now!

He raised his head, a big, *big* smile spreading across his

face. He'd been waiting *so long* for this moment! And he *couldn't* wait to see Wayne's reaction—quickly he stood and laid a hand on his arm...

Wayne was almost *startled*—the thought had popped into his mind out of absolutely nowhere.

Take care of your mail now.

His mail. He'd completely forgotten that he'd remembered it. But why he was thinking of something so insignificant, at a time like *this*...

He didn't care. He desperately needed a distraction to preoccupy his mind, and he wasn't about to brush off something that might do just that. Besides, what *other* pressing matters did he have?

He reached into the backpack and felt around...yes, his fingers closed around the battered stack. He pulled it out and set it on his lap.

Take care of it now...take care of it now...

The words kept running through his mind over and over as he breezed through the whole pile once again, tossing aside flyers, Penny Savers. There was absolutely *nothing* of value...

Take care of it...take care of...

He came across the crumpled little coupon booklet, the weird one addressed to "COW JENKINS."

Take care of it.

His eyes centered on the first name. *Funny,* he thought, studying it. *Looks almost like...*

Then it struck him. That was *exactly* what it was.

Care of.

Run together with his first initial to form a single word, the two letters had totally slipped past him unnoticed. He stifled a chuckle.

But then what was the *second* name?

Jenkins. My last name isn't Jenkins.

Then *another* thought struck him, this time with such force he almost fell over.

Good grief, I wonder if...could it be...?

Quickly he stood and grabbed a pen; he raced to the door,

flung it open and ran to the phone in the hall, a sudden, new, seemingly unstoppable surge of *hope* rising within him—

Yes! Yes! Could it be?

He trembled as he once again dialed directory assistance for Philadelphia, Pennsylvania. *Could it be? Oh God, please...*

The connection went through. He asked his question and was momentarily put on hold; the few seconds of adrenaline-building suspense were almost unbearable.

Then his answer came.

First suspicion confirmed.

He squelched a yell of triumph as he hung up and again dialed the main branch of the Philadelphia post office. He asked his second question and was put on hold once more; never in his life had a wait been so tough.

Then his second answer came.

Again, suspicion confirmed.

He almost dropped the receiver—his heart *leaped* inside of him!

"WHOOOOAAAHH! YAAAAHOOO! YAAA—!" It took him a moment to realize he was shouting almost at the top of his lungs. He had to bite his lip to stop himself. "Uh, could you repeat the town, please?" He lowered his voice as he tried to regain his composure—yet he could barely jot down the information.

"Um, uh, thanks! Thank you!" He trembled as he hung up and ran back to his room. He closed the door behind him and slumped against it, tears of joy streaming down his face.

Mom! I've found Mom! Finally! Finally! He looked down at the revealing little piece of mail his sweating, shaking hand still clutched, the one he'd just taken his notes on. He shook his head and smiled. Of all the screwed-up, switched-up, *wonderful* mistakes! Leave it to a simple mailing-list error to have his mother's maiden name, the one he'd never known, on the front. He'd been *right*, before—she *had* left him a P.O. box to trace her with. He'd simply been using the wrong *name,* until now! What an *incredible* mailing error. How on earth that name had ended up with his own...

It hardly mattered at this point. He kissed the thing. *Thank you, Lord! Thank you thank you thank you!*

Chad laughed. *Boy,* it was good to see Wayne happy again!

Wayne could scarcely believe it. In a single instant, through a simple prayer, everything had changed for him once more. How could he have *ever* doubted at all? He'd *always* had hope, he'd *never* been neglected, never once. His cry had been answered immediately, his biggest need met. He'd yet to comprehend, he figured, just *how* seriously his requests were taken, and how utterly *miraculous* the responses could be. And this was one of them. The power of a prayer was awesome, and the Answerer even more so.

I've found her. I've found her. He kept repeating it to himself over and over, as if it would make the fact even more true.

Again he sat down on the bed, his head in his knees, as a tremendous, *overwhelming* wave of relief swept over him. He felt like a huge anchor had finally been cut loose. He'd certainly *intended* to find Mom, and for a while, earlier, he'd thought he had succeeded. Somehow, though, when it all came down to it, he hadn't *really* expected to.

But he had. *He had!* And the big clue had been right under his nose the whole time. Mom had simply changed her last name back again. *What an answer!*

Thanks, Lord, he repeated, almost giddy. *Thanks so much! Thank you!*

Chad beamed. *He* was happy, too—happy to see Wayne's spirits lifted once more, happy to see his mind *finally* at ease on the matter, happy to see Wayne be Wayne again. Most of all, he was happy to see Wayne, his best friend in all the world, so thankful to the One Who had worked this miracle for him, the One Who was *ultimately* responsible for his safety—and most importantly of course, the change in his life that made all this possible. It made The Big Guy Himself happy, too, and *nothing* could make Chad feel better than that. He could feel every *bit* of Wayne's joy; it *tickled* him and he laughed.

But at the same time, he couldn't allow Wayne to get *too* distracted by it. He slipped him another reminder.

Wayne looked up with a start. In his euphoria—justified though maybe it was—he'd momentarily forgotten.

He wasn't *in* Pennsylvania yet. He had to get out of *here* first.

But what was so hard about *that,* really? All he had to do was go downstairs, out to his car, and drive away. In fact, that was the easiest part of all...

Wait a minute.

His *car.*

He couldn't recall parking *here*—where *had* he left it, anyway? He combed back through his near-blackout period of distraction, trying to reconstruct the events.

Again, Chad helped him out.

Wayne suddenly gave his eyes a roll and blew through his mouth. *Jeepers, now I remember.* He'd left it in the gravel lot near the bus stop, when he'd gone to see the wrong mom. He was amazed at himself. He'd been *so* distracted by the whole thing afterwards that he'd taken the bus *all* the way back and left it there. And that was a *long* way off.

What a dummy I am, he thought. *I'm too young for this kind of senility—I forgot my own car, for cryin' out loud!*

Chad grinned. Of *course* Wayne had. Purposely and for a reason. *Don't worry about it,* he said. *What you did was just fine.*

Well, maybe so, thought Wayne. *But I still want to leave at once.* He stood and put his mail in the backpack, rearranging it, tying the thing shut. *I'll take the bus over there right now and get out...*

No, said Chad. *Get some sleep and take the bus later. It isn't safe yet. Leave the car there and wait.*

He laid a hand on Wayne's arm. *Hold back the urge for now.*

Wayne stopped and looked at his watch. *Shoot, I'll have to hold it back. My restraint's still got almost three hours left.*

Chad grinned again and shrugged. *Well, that too.*

Wayne yawned—he *was* a little sleepy. *Guess I can manage to lay down for a little while,* he thought. What was three more hours, anyway? The car would be safe until then, certainly—the old thing fit in with the surroundings almost perfectly with its rustic beauty and nobody would bother it. Yes, he'd drive out of the city just after midnight, when he could legally do so.

Of course, this would take some planning ahead. If he was to *reach* the car as close to the big hour as possible, he'd need to catch the last bus at ten of, which meant…he'd want at least *five* minutes to walk from here to the curb, out front…all right then.

He set his watch alarm for eleven-forty.

Good shot, said Chad. *I'll make sure ya wake up for it.*

Wayne unleashed another huge yawn as he once more undid the string on the backpack and pulled out his radio. Heck, getting up then would be easy, considering how late he'd slept into this morning. He was actually *glad,* suddenly, for all that noise he'd endured the night before!

Chad watched him plug in the radio and set it on the nightstand. He was happy that Wayne was listening so much more now, and that he was beginning to see how little, everyday "annoyances" could often be a *lot* more than they first seemed. He was really starting to understand, and even *appreciate* them, something *most* people were incapable of. And it only strengthened Chad's fast-growing, *deep* admiration of his best friend.

Wayne flicked on the radio, tapped it lightly to get it going and stretched out on the bed. *Ahh.* Now for some nice, quiet music to go to sleep with.

Nothing but static came on.

Oh, rats. He sat up and played with the dial; he tried the other band. Same thing. In fact, he could find nothing but a stupid talk show.

He adjusted the antenna and moved the radio around. The talk show came in loud and clear, but he could still get nothing else.

Jeepers, what a weak thing. He reached for the switch.

Chad clamped a hand over it. *Naw,* he said, *you wanna leave it on for now.*

Hmm, maybe I should just leave it alone. Wayne drew his hand away and flopped down again; the talk show quickly became a background noise as he laid there in anticipation. He couldn't *wait* to get out of here and get home. In a way, strangely, he was glad he hadn't found Mom sooner—the temptation to leave a little *early* might have been too great. It was plenty strong *now*...

Shh. Chad whispered to him. *Don't think about it, Wayne. Just go to sleep.*

Yeah, of course I should. Wayne chuckled. It was foolish trying to plan everything right this minute. He knew where Mom was now, and that was all he needed to know, for the time being. But still, it was hard to sleep...he wished he could tear himself from his own mind and *sleep*...

The hour was up.

Slasher stood and cringed in pain—both his legs had fallen asleep from squatting on that step so long. He stretched and started up the stairs once more. Now to get it *done* this time.

"Man, I gotta go *bad!*" Ricky started down the hall from the Angels' room. "I can't wait on Jose anymore—he *always* hogs the john! I'll use the public one down here!"

"Haw!" laughed a voice behind him. "What's the matter, Ricky? Can't hold *four* cans?"

"*You* otta talk, Robby!" he shouted back. "You had *six!*" He entered the restroom across from Wayne's door.

Once again, Slasher arrived at landing number six. He pushed open the door and looked around.

There was no one.

He smiled as he pulled out his blade and approached Wayne's door; he jumped as another one opened behind him.

He whirled around and the same guy he'd first seen in front of the soda machine was just coming out of the restroom, tugging at his pants. The blade went back up his sleeve as he got another suspicious look.

Slasher smiled again. He stuck his hand into his pocket and rattled his change—like he was dropping in a key—then turned back for the stairs. He *scowled* as his face went out of view.

Ricky watched him a moment longer before strutting off toward his room; he laughed as he passed Robby. "See? *Told* ya you were worse off!"

Slasher waited several minutes. He again entered the hall and approached Wayne's room.

The same thing happened as before.

He waited a few more minutes and tried again.

The same thing happened.

He waited several more minutes.

Same thing.

Chad was laughing hysterically.

"Man, how many gallons did we put away, Delmar?"

"I dunno, Perry," he answered as they passed each other in the hall. "But wait 'till *Hudson* goes! He must have had *eight,* at least!"

Wayne could hear the new commotion outside as he slowly drifted off. It was so *nice* to hear other voices, with his mind so at ease. What a *wonderful* sound. He felt like going out and hugging every one of them.

Naw, said Chad. *That isn't necessary.*

Wayne smiled. He fell asleep.

Slasher was *furious.* He was *going* to do this, if it took him forever! He'd try again, and *this* time he wouldn't stop even if he *was* seen. He'd climb out the *window,* if need be.

He started for the door, but not before a huge hand grabbed him by the arm. Terrified, he turned around.

It was Moose.

"You little pip-squeak!" he bellowed down. "We've been watching you! You've been in and out of there like a stinkin', walkin' *ping-pong* game! And the G ain't very happy about it!"

"Yeah, well I've been avoiding—"

"Your job!" Moose interrupted.

"—*witnesses!*" Slasher fumed.

"And you're *scared* of 'em!" Moose shot back. "Get out to your truck and join that jerk friend of yours! *I'm* goin' in there and do this myself right *now!*"

He grabbed Slasher's knife and gave him a kick as he stumbled down the stairs, muttering.

Moose threw open the door and thundered down the hall, covering the distance to Wayne's room in less than five steps. He drew back, ready to smash his way in.

Another door slammed behind him and he stopped. He turned around, slowly, and the largest dude he'd ever seen stood in front of the restroom across from him. He was a *huge* black guy, clad from head to foot in the Guardian Angels uniform, easily two or three inches *taller* than Moose, with arms like cedar trunks and a stare that could cut through marble.

Moose felt like he was *melting.* He swallowed and tried to smile.

The guy only let loose with a *belch* that whisped his fiery-red hair, steamed up his sunglasses, and sent him scurrying back down the stairs in a hurry, tripping and stumbling over himself.

The guy started back toward his room to the sounds of laughter and applause. "All *right,* Hudson! We all heard that! Don't anyone light a match for a while!"

More laughter. "How many *did* ya have, anyway?"

The guy's booming voice filled the hall.

"Ten!"

Eleven-forty.

The quiet, high-pitched beep sounded from Wayne's watch; Chad reached over from the chair and lightly shook him.

Time to get up now, buddy. Time to go.

Wayne stirred. Groggily he raised his arm in front of him and activated the watch's light, silencing the alarm. Was it really twenty 'till *already?*

Man, it got here fast. He could still hear the radio, faintly, in the background; an engine quietly idled somewhere outside the building. Getting up was a lot harder than he thought it would be. He fought the sleepiness, struggling to push himself up and get on his feet.

Chad pulled on his arm. *Come on, we have to leave now!*

But I'm sooo sleepy... Wayne struggled to rise but it was no use; he dropped back down onto the pillow again. *Just a few more minutes won't matter...*

Yes, it will, said Chad. *You must get up now!*

Wayne didn't budge. *Just a few minutes more...please...I'll get up soon...*

He drifted off to sleep again, only vaguely aware of the muted roar outside as the last bus of the night revved its engine, ready to pull away...

His eyes shot open to the rude blair of the radio; it had suddenly become louder and far more staticy.

Jeepers, he thought. *Now the knob's going funny.* He reached for the thing, feebly, to shut it off. Why couldn't his last few minutes of sleep be quiet ones?

It was beyond his reach. He rolled sideways and folded the pillow over his head; he couldn't believe the same, dumb talk show was *still* on!

He tried to ignore it. Chad scooted the radio back farther and increased the volume a little more.

"So what *happened,* anyway?" The crackly voice filtered right through the pillow, loud and clear. "(phzt) I thought your boyfriend there was supposed to be the *best!*"

"Shut your face, stupid!" retorted another voice. "You didn't fare so well *yourself* this afternoon, so I've been informed. (phewzz) You couldn't even wire his car, or tap his phone line, let alone *find* him!"

Another crackle. "Well at least I looked, greaseball! (brwzt) *Your* man had the bait in *front* of him and he couldn't even bite! Does he need dentures, or what?"

Wayne's expression grew funny, his eyes opened wide. What a *strange* program for the *radio...*

"Hey, *I* didn't ask to get dragged into this friggin' mess with you clowns! So cut the bad-mouthin'!"

"*Cork* it, guys," said a *snarly* third voice.

Wayne's eyes opened wider—he *knew* that voice.

"Just mind yourselves," it continued. "Your bosses and I agreed this is to be friendly cooperation among business competitors(crackle)to eliminate a common deficit, (frzz)gardless of how long it takes."

Wayne shot up, suddenly *wide* awake. His eyes moved over to the radio, staring at it as if it had suddenly become a monster.

It was *Glitch's* voice.

"(buzt)member, the rat stiffed *you* boys, too," he continued. "And you're already signed. So let's forget our different blood types for now, all right?"

"It's *just*(crackle)for the time being, G. We still don't like each others' breath—or yours, either! And...(phewzz)listen! You *sure* this channel's secure?"

"*Course* it is!" snapped Glitch. "I'm not *stupid!*"

There was a brief, pregnant pause.

Wayne was flabbergasted. It took him only a moment to realize that he was picking up cross talk by his would-be killers. And they must have been *close,* too—it certainly wasn't a powerful radio, not indoors, six stories up.

He sat there and looked at it, jaw quivering. He swallowed. Yes, it was indecd Glitch. But who were all these *other* guys?

Just keep listening, said Chad, his hand still on the volume knob. *I know it's hard to, but keep listening.*

Glitch's voice crackled on again. "I'll repeat, this is only for a tiny bit longer.(pfft)So let's keep it *bearable, okay?"*

"Hey, Noyes!" blurted one of the other voices. "The Slash just got back here from his cool-down walk—too bad he(phzt)missed all your nice comments about him!"

"*What'd* he say about me?" a fourth voice chimed in.

"(crackle)Nothing untrue, ya dumb screw-up!"

"HEY!" Glitch's voice bellowed over. "You all either shut up or you're out with *no* cut right now!"

A smattering of static, crackles, and half-audible profanity followed before he continued. "(brzz...garble)listen up—I'll say the game plan once more. I head up in fi(garble)minutes. He slips out past me, Noyes, I'll let you and Kutz know. Then you watch that front entrance and take him."

"What about *us?*"

"I'm *gettin'* to ya, Slasher! You and Dolati are Noyes' back-up, remember?(phewzz)If *you* have a problem, then *my* people are coverin' the back(garble)give 'em a horn."

Noyes' voice came on. "Just hurry up! Kutz is fallin' asleep over there!"

"Hey, I said(fwzz)minutes," said Glitch. "Sit tight and wait. You'll *all* be reimburs(pht) regardless—this is one to enjoy."

Wayne was *terrified.* They were coming after him again— *lots* of them, all at once. He shivered as menacing laughter crackled over.

"Hey, G, we'll *enjoy* having some *fun* with him, like you said we could!(buzz)Slash is still peeved that he couldn't(phewzz...garble)and that yellin' he took sure didn't help any!"

"Gosh, I wonder *why?"*

"Shut up, Noyes!"

A sigh was heard. "Don't worry, Dolati.(brzt)If there's anything left when *I* get done with him, I'll hand-deliver it to ya."

"How about *us,* G? Kutz and I have been out half the day tryin' to nail down this slippery seed!(crackle)I've been itchin' to use my potato peeler—"

Wayne shut it off, sickened. He'd heard *enough.* They were coming; he had to leave for the bus at once.

He caught a glimpse of his watch as he drew his hand away—was it only *eleven* o'clock? He checked again; to his horror, it was a *single* digital 'one.'

It was *one* A.M.

Good heavens, he thought. *What happened?*

He'd missed the *bus, that's* what happened. The last bus until dawn. Right then and there, as with so many other times, he *knew* he should have listened to the urge, he *knew* he should have gotten up when he'd been told to. But he still had to leave at *once!*

He suddenly felt panicked, nauseated. *What* had Glitch said? He'd be up in…*five* minutes? *Fifteen?* He didn't know. But how could he *leave,* either? They were *waiting* for him, *everywhere.* He thought maybe he could chance it, barricade himself in the room until daybreak, then make a mad dash for the first bus; at least that way he'd be more visible…

No, no that would be futile. They'd wait as long as it took. They'd nail him before he even stepped away from the building. So what could he *do?*

He blinked back tears. *You've done it to yourself again, Wayne. You should have listened, you should have listened!*

Chad laid a calm hand on his shoulder. *Just get ready to go, Wayne. Please don't let that bother you.*

But it *did* bother Wayne. It was *inexcusable,* missing his chance like that. Especially after he'd been *warned!* He'd been listening so *well,* and then he'd blown it again. *Big* time. And now his life was endangered more than ever because of it.

And it *infuriated* him.

He pounded the nightstand repeatedly with his fist, bouncing the radio right off. "Wayne, you *fool!* Why can't you *listen?* When are you gonna *learn?*" He slammed his knee and laid his head forward on his palms.

There's not a moment to lose, the voice repeated. *Get your stuff ready and let's go.*

Wayne couldn't believe he was having such a thought at a time like this. But indeed, he was.

Get ready to go.

He couldn't shake it. If only to put it at ease, he stood and picked up the radio, stuffing it into the backpack, quickly scanning the room for any other personal objects. But he knew where his actions were leading. He knew, deep down, that this *was* it, there was no going back. He was going to walk out that door, and as soon as he could.

He couldn't help feeling that maybe he was a little *crazy*

as he contemplated what he was about to do. He was about to *knowingly* walk outside, into a hornet's nest of desperate, vicious, bloodthirsty killers who were waiting for him to do just that. And even *if,* by some miracle of heaven, he made it past *them* alive, he still had to reach his *car.* And it took him only a moment of mental calculation to realize it was parked almost *nine city blocks* away. He'd have to go that distance on foot, through a slightly-less-than-upper-class neighborhood, at one o'clock in the morning—an hour in which few people, few *sane* people, would be out and about.

Wayne shook his head in disbelief as he continued packing. *Was* he mad? Yes, maybe he was. And maybe he'd make it, maybe he wouldn't. But he *had* to do it. What other choice *was* there? The car wouldn't get up and walk to *him.*

He breathed out long and slow through his mouth. It would take strength and stamina he just didn't have to get him through *this* little venture. But his sheer determination, he hoped, would rise above it. He'd just have to look over his shoulder constantly, and…

And who was he *kidding,* anyway?

He stopped what he was doing; the bag slipped from his hands and fell to the floor. *He* didn't know how to leave safely; heck, he didn't even know how to *start* trying. It'd take every angel in *heaven* to get him out alive.

A cold sweat suddenly drenched his clothes as he realized, really *realized,* exactly what he was facing. He took yet another seat on the bed, burying his head in his hands, paralyzed with fear.

What am I doing? he thought. *I'm nuts!*

Chad laid a hand on his knee. *Wayne, you're fretting again.*

Wayne raised his head. He *was* fretting again. And even now, in the midst of this latest—and indeed, biggest—crisis, he could see how utterly *silly* it was. In his frustration at not listening to the urge, he was again doing exactly that—not listening. His eyes moved to the floor; he actually managed to smile at himself again.

Chad giggled, too—but precious seconds were slipping away. He knew Wayne had a decision to make, and he had to make it now.

He stood directly in front of him. *Please, Wayne, listen to me.*

Wayne looked up again; he suddenly felt like he was being *addressed,* almost like a parent to a child, only somehow…it felt the other way around. He couldn't explain it, but…he listened closely.

Chad laid both hands on Wayne's arms, his gentle blue eyes gazed directly into his friend's. He spoke slowly and clearly, his voice unmistakably calm.

I'm here. I'm right here with you, Wayne. And I'll guard and protect you, no matter what happens, here or anywhere else. If you let me, you have absolutely nothing to fear.

For a moment, neither of them said anything. Chad slowly lifted his hands and lowered them in front of him; he'd said what he needed to say.

The rest was now up to Wayne.

Wayne knew it, too. He'd heard every word, clearly and distinctly; he understood completely. And it was only then that he could see, really for the first time, what the source of his lingering worries and troubles were. *He* had been doing the thinking, he'd been following his *own* advice on how to handle matters. The more *he'd* tried to avoid them, the more they'd found him. True, the much more powerful and intelligent guardian watching over him (Chad laughed at the choice of adjectives) had used his many careless errors to save his hide more than once. But nevertheless, Wayne had never *completely and totally* let go and let the Divine Guidance from above take charge. And he knew he would now *have* to do that if he was going to survive the night.

He also knew doing so wouldn't be easy for him. A lifetime of bad habit wouldn't go away in one night. He'd literally have to hide his mind from itself, leave it in neutral, shut it off. He would have to discern what were his own thoughts and what weren't, what to do and when, where to go and how. So many things could happen…there were so *many* possibilities…

I'm here. I'm here.

Yes, Wayne felt it and right there he decided.

The *Lord* would get total charge of events tonight, with the special agent He'd placed with Wayne handling all the specifics. And it couldn't be just another time where he pondered before reacting; he would not, he *could* not hesitate. No, that would leave too much room for his own thoughts. He had to make a commitment, he had to place total and complete trust for his protection, right now, in the same One Who, by virtue of changing his own life only so recently, was capable of *any* miracle.

Wayne was fast getting there. *Pray, Wayne,* Chad urged him, a smile creeping over his face. *Pray!*

Wayne was ready. He lowered his head and folded his hands; Chad did, too.

Lord, I place my safety, my life in Your hands right now. Please get me safely to my car, no matter what may happen. Please guide me with the angel You've given me. Please keep me from thinking for myself. Please stop whoever's trying to hurt me. Please let me get home, safely and soon. Amen.

Amen, said Chad. He looked up at Wayne, beaming. He'd done it. He'd done it!

Wayne looked up at Chad. *He* beamed, too—this time with a confidence and calm he hadn't felt as strongly since his life-changing evening at the church. He'd been right—he *didn't* have the strength for this undertaking. But he also knew his angel would improvise.

"Pennsylvania's pretty this time of year," he said.

Really? Chad was curious. *I've never been there before.*

"Oh, *yeah.*" Wayne nodded. "It sure is. The winters are nicer than here. You'll *love* it."

Chad felt closer to his best friend now than ever before. They were inseparable—not only by virtue of his job, but now by attitude, character, and respect for each other. Yes, he *would* improvise. It would be the easiest piece of cake in the world for him.

Then let's go now, he said. *I wanna see Pennsylvania for myself.*

"Me too," said Wayne. "My mind's already there. I want to go join it."

Chad stepped aside as Wayne stood and strapped on the backpack. Wayne didn't know *what,* exactly awaited him outside, nor did he want to. He *already* knew enough. But he'd be looked after, taken care of, and watched through it all. He could *feel* it.

He walked to the doorway, eyes straight ahead. His objective was clear, his mind fresh, his adrenaline pumping.

Chad walked beside him, silent, unseen, yet so present.

"I'm ready," said Wayne. "You ready too, buddy?"

I sure am, said Chad. *I've been waiting for this moment.* His hand reached out and took hold of Wayne's wrist. *Let's do it, big guy. Let's get out of here and get home.*

Wayne felt his grasp. "That's a *wonderful* idea. From this moment on, *you're* doing the leading."

Chad's smile remained, his expression grew stern. *Follow me, Wayne.*

Wayne took a deep breath.

He walked out the door, Chad in the lead.

16

The first priority was to get Wayne out of the building at once; Glitch had already entered through the back and was about to come up in the elevator. Chad made sure the room door was locked—that'd stall him a few extra minutes before he discovered his prey was gone.

Use the stairs, he said to Wayne. *Take them to the lobby and be very quiet. Hurry!*

Wayne did. He swallowed as he walked down, floor after floor, acutely aware of the silence, the absence of any other people as his footsteps echoed off the walls. He knew the seriousness of the situation; the overwhelming sense of caution and the need for alertness, both of which he felt, merely underscored it. If Glitch knew he'd been an informer, then he'd probably also learned of his deal with the cops. He'd *also* know the restraint would expire tonight, he'd know this would be his last shot ever at Wayne. And considering how *mad* he probably was from missing so much already...well, that would explain the elaborate set-up outside.

In *addition* to the nine blocks he had to survive.

But Wayne knew he wasn't in charge now. *You lead, angel. You lead.*

He reached the lobby floor and entered. *Head straight outside,* said Chad. *Don't say anything.*

Wayne tossed his key onto the counter as he made a beeline for the front doors. He clutched a backpack strap in his hand; he could see it had stopped snowing out.

Chad saw, too. Good. That would only work to Wayne's favor.

His hand tightened around his wrist. He knew what was coming and what he'd have to lead Wayne through. *Keep going,* he said. *When you get outside, keep your head down and your eyes in front of you. And don't look back at anything. Ignore everything you see and hear.*

Wayne swallowed as he reached the doors. He went through and was immediately enveloped in bitter-cold night air. A full moon was out; save for a slow-moving line of clouds, the sky was dark and clear, almost a neon black. It was outlined by a hundred even darker buildings, and they were visible only because of their difference in color. The ghostly, naked frame of a new skyscraper loomed over the street a ways ahead, its base ringed with blinking construction flashers. Wayne lowered his eyes at once, his vision momentarily blurred by his breath.

This way, said Chad.

Wayne followed, veering left down the sidewalk toward the flashers, off in the distance. As his eyes swung straight around with his body, he saw a dark, black *car,* with heavily-tinted windows and a layer of half-melted snow on the roof and hood, parked along the curb up ahead of him. Its engine was quietly idling, the passenger window was down.

And it was the *only* car on the street.

Wayne knew it was them. Or at least *one* of them.

Keep walking, said Chad. *Ignore it.*

Wayne did. He ignored his own mind, every instinct he had as he stayed his course, hearing the quiet crunch of snow under his tennis shoes. He got closer to the car...closer... *passing it...*

He jumped as a loud *snore* met his ear. He walked a little faster, suddenly faint from the scare yet more at ease. Shoot, the guy was fast asleep! He almost chuckled.

So did Chad—it was just like Saint Peter in the prison. But Wayne *couldn't* be distracted. This certainly wasn't all.

Ignore it, he repeated. *Ignore everything you see and hear.*

Wayne listened. And indeed, he needed to—he was already being trailed. From the corner of his eye he could see the reflection of the black Jeep 4x4 in the window beside him; it was slowly following him along the curb across the street, like an old movie, visible every couple of seconds in the sickly yellow blink of the flashers. He kept his head forward, his eyes now focusing on the chain-link fence rapidly materializing out of the darkness ahead of him. He could now tell that it was stretching *completely* across the road, blocking off an equipment storage area at the new building's base. There was no way through. But he couldn't *backtrack* now...

Keep walking, said Chad. *It's your only way out.*

He loosened his grip on Wayne's arm. *Get ready to run.*

Noyes brought the Jeep to a stop. He still couldn't tell if it was the guy or not; the little bits he'd picked up in the pulsating lights weren't enough to go by. But he hadn't yet heard from Glitch, either. He'd wait here until his suspect passed right by one of the flashers—he'd know then.

He caught a glimpse of his own wispy, strawberry-blond hair in the rearview as he ignited the lighter; he picked up the snapshot with the same hand, balancing both in front of him as he scrutinized the thing by the flame. His other hand carefully aimed the Uzi through the open window at the moving figure across the street, ready to pull should there be any resemblance...

Chad was way ahead of him. *Be very careful,* he whispered to Wayne. *Wait until this next blinker goes off, and then get past it before it comes on again.*

He pointed ahead. *Keep running to that gap in the gate and go through it.*

Wayne *could* see it clearly now—a small space between the two large, chained cargo gates in the fence, where they came together unevenly. But was it *wide* enough for him?

Never mind that, said Chad. *Just go through it.*

Noyes leaned forward, waiting; the guy's face would be visible any second now. He glanced at the photo once more and then back outside, carefully keeping his aim pinpoint accurate—

Rats.

The guy either stumbled, or adjusted his step or something—all Noyes saw was his back, first silhouetted, then illuminated as the stupid light went off at the one critical moment.

The guy started running.

Noyes hesitated. Should he fire? No, he couldn't—if it *was* the wrong person, this whole thing would be blown.

Grumbling, he drew the gun back inside and tossed it onto the seat next to him. He ignited the lighter once more and studied the photo—where *was* that guy...?

The two-way crackled on. "G here! He's gone! Look for him! He'll be goin' out the *front* way!"

Noyes panicked—it *was* the snitch he'd seen! He dropped the lighter as he lunged for his gun; it fell on his lap and sent him jumping, yelling, scrambling to brush it off as he thrust the barrel back out the window, aiming wildly at the rapidly disappearing figure—

Wayne reached the gate as a clatter of loud *pops* went off across the street; he heard a window behind him shatter as the deadly barrage quickly spread out, striking fence poles all around him, thudding into things on the other side, ricocheting, whining. He turned sideways and tried to slip through—

No! The backpack wouldn't fit. Chad dropped the bullets

he'd caught and bent the pole back, allowing Wayne the room he needed; he snatched a half-dozen more slugs from the air before joining him.

Noyes was furious. The little sneak had walked right *past* him and he'd done *nothing!* Why couldn't he be told *sooner?* And what was *Kutz* doing all this time?

No matter, though—the target had run straight into *another* trap.

Noyes ripped his CB from its perch. "All right, big shot!" he hissed. "He's in *your* cage now! Try not to *avoid* him this time!"

Slasher's voice crackled back over. "We're ready and waiting for him."

Wayne weaved around cement bags, wheelbarrows, and garden hoses, racing unimpeded through the blackness as if it was broad daylight. The strange *sound* was steadily growing louder; he couldn't tell if it was an engine, or machinery, or *what,* but the vibrations were growing stronger, he was getting closer to whatever it as. Yet he was too preoccupied to notice. He continued on his course around the edge of the skeleton's base, almost within eyesight of his goal—yes, there was the gate on the other side of the area, vaguely visible now between two huge stacks of steel girders up ahead.

Look out! Chad pushed Wayne's head down as he guided him under a board jutting from a lumber pile. He continued steering him through the blackness and around the multitude of dangerous obstacles; he grabbed a large roll of heavy, industrial cable and slung it over his arm. He'd soon need it.

Slasher leaned out the driver's window, his ear cocked. He heard running footsteps approaching and flashed his headlights; Dolati did the same from *his* rig, not fifteen yards in front.

Both men threw the huge tractor-trailers into gear and started moving toward each other. They laughed. They had a puddle of grease to splat.

Keep running keep running keep running! Wayne again ignored the hailstorm of natural instincts as he followed the orders. He could see the other gate clearly now between the girder stacks. The strange beams of light spanning the gap had cut out twice and then remained steady; they appeared to be getting *brighter.* Wayne picked up his speed, aware that the *noise* had grown louder, the vibrations stronger—he could feel the air growing warm, smell the acrid exhaust fumes as he neared the small channel. *What in the world—?*

Ignore it, said Chad. *Keep your eyes straight ahead and don't look either way!*

He let go of Wayne's arm and moved in back of him. It was useless running in *front* of him, with his stride; he'd have to pull this off from behind. But he *had* to stay with him—it would take perfect timing.

Dolati flashed the lights once and both semis picked up speed, rapidly closing the space, slamming toward each other like two giant hands about to smash a bug.

And here it came.

Wayne bolted through the gap, Chad right behind him as the monsters bore down from both sides. Chad's arms shot out at full length—

Both vehicles smashed into his outstretched hands, instantly stopping as if they'd hit a solid wall and throwing the drivers into the windshields with such force it shattered the glass into a million pieces.

Wayne hadn't even seen them. He stayed his course toward the fence.

Dolati screamed with rage. He knocked glass from his eyes and face, groping, feeling for the gear shift, determined to swat the fly he'd started after. He repeatedly threw it into reverse, then forward, smashing over and over into the other truck, ramming it out of the way, knocking it aside, sending Slasher staggering from the cabin and falling drunkenly to the pavement amid bits of grid and headlights. Dolati swung around to the gate—yes, his precaution had worked. There was the fly, trapped against it.

Now he had him.

Wayne was panicked. He could hear the truck coming

behind him, but there was no other way out—stacks of girders completely covered all the rest of the fence. He tried again to slip through the crack; it was no use. Not wide enough. He threw himself against the gate, he pulled on the chain. It didn't budge.

The truck was almost on top of him.

Help! He slammed himself into it, desperately—

Chad snapped the chain. Wayne stumbled out.

The tractor smashed through the fence right behind him, sending poles and barbed wire flying all over the road.

Run, Wayne!

Wayne did; he ran for his life.

Dolati was now crazy with rage. Forget ramming. Forget locks and chains. Forget all the conventional stuff.

He was going to run over Wayne.

He laughed dementedly as he pressed the engine to the limit, rapidly closing in on his prey.

Then he noticed it. His target was getting *farther away, not closer!*

He glared at the gear shift, still in drive. *"What in—?"*

He was moving *backwards!*

Of course he was. Chad was pulling him backwards. He had one end of the cable tied on the trailer's bumper, the other slung over his shoulder and he was simply dragging the thing along behind him and chuckling. No tug-of-war was *ever* this fun—or easy!

He walked all the way back to the building, tossed his end up over one of the girders and pulled. Then he looped it again over the bumper, leaving the rig's back wheels hanging several feet off the ground.

It wasn't going *anywhere.*

And neither was Dolati. Cursing, he tried to open his door; the handle had been ripped off and it wouldn't move. He crawled over and tried the other door—the same thing had happened.

He cursed some more. He started to lower himself out through the shattered windshield, but quickly climbed back in; completely surrounding the cabin, neatly arranged in a U-shape, were three rows of jagged metal pipes.

And a lot of small, tennis shoe footprints.

He was stuck.

Glitch's voice crackled over the two-way. "I don't *hear* anything! What's happening over there with you guys?"

Dolati grabbed the receiver. "I'd *tell* ya if I knew!"

"—thought *they* had him!" Noyes finished, answering at the same time.

There was a pause. "No, no, I don't even *wanna* know!" Glitch bellowed. "Just keep after him!(phewzz)Take your cars or whatever! Anything that moves!"

"I *can't!* " Dolati shot back.

"Then go the hell on *foot!* " Glitch screamed. "Just *kill* him! Death on sight!(buzt)Over and out!"

The two-way went silent.

"SLASH!" Dolati shouted out the window. "Get the car and come get me outta this!"

Wayne kept on running. It was incredible—the truck had *vanished!* He had to resist the urge to look back.

Don't, said Chad. *It's not over yet!*

Wayne didn't look. He kept going, cutting back his speed ever so slightly to conserve his energy. Two blocks down, seven to go.

The street suddenly became dark as the moon disappeared behind the cloud bank. But it didn't matter. It was pretty much a straight shot from here on out…

The sound of another, lone *engine* suddenly filled Wayne's ears; he could suddenly see his own shadow, quickly swelling in front of him. He made a quick glance over his shoulder—above the blinding glare of the headlights, he could make out the familiar shape of the *brown car,* the same one he'd seen only too recently, as it fast approached.

No, please, he thought. *Not again!*

Afraid so, said Chad. *This way, fast!* He jerked Wayne right, down a side alley—just before McKernan's car zoomed past—then left up a small parallel street as the headlights of *another* car, this time the black 4x4 appeared in the distance. He steered him down another alley, then up another street as the brown car swung around a corner ahead, facing him; a third, *different* car appeared behind him as he ducked into yet *another* alley...

The two vehicles veered to the sides to avoid each other, sending sparks flying as they scraped the rough concrete walls and hitting garbage bags and trash cans—both mirrors were ripped off as they passed inches apart.

They stopped and backed up. The drivers glared at each other.

"Seen him?" McKernan tried to ignore the sigh from his back seat as Moose sat next to him, scowl-faced.

"Nothing," answered Dolati. Slasher sat beside him, holding his head in his hands.

"Well *keep* looking," said McKernan. "We saw him go in here *somewhere.*"

Both cars screeched off in their separate ways.

"I *saw* him come in here," said Kutz's gravely voice. "I *saw* him! *I* should be the one doin' this, ya know. When are ya gonna decide to *find* him."

Noyes cringed. "You just let *me* do the drivin' tonight," he said, turning another corner. "I don't need ya dozin' off behind *my* wheel, for God's sake!"

Kutz's burly frame remained perfectly still, his glaring eyes stared straight ahead. "It wasn't like I *planned* to," he retorted. "It sometimes *happens* after spending all afternoon lookin' for a stupid car that probably doesn't even exist, anyway."

"I'm drivin' this time," said Noyes.

"So when are *you* gonna *find* him again," Kutz repeated, continuing his annoying tradition of saying all his questions like statements.

The same thing kept happening over and over—Wayne kept slipping down one alley and up another street, down one and up another, in a seemingly endless, deadly game of zig-zagging leap-frog as the three cars combed section after section from both directions.

Chad knew this cycle would have to end soon; Wayne was getting farther and farther off course, and closer and closer to being seen.

And that's exactly how he *would* end it. With Wayne being seen.

Stop here, he said as they passed some trash cans in one of the streets. He pointed to them. *Hide here and don't get up until I say.*

Wayne squeezed in between the cans and squatted down, his coat quickly becoming sticky with a residue from the cold, rusty metal. His ears could already pick up the sound of a car coming.

His forehead dropped onto his knees. *Jeepers,* he thought. *All I wanna do is go home. I didn't know it'd be so tough.*

He waited, yet again, for the vehicle to pass.

Okay, Wayne. Chad pointed across to the alley they'd just come through. *Get up and run back over there.*

Run across? Wayne was flabbergasted. *But they'll see me!*

Yes, said Chad, urgently. *Get up and run!*

Wayne swallowed. He shot to his feet and bolted across, literally diving over the car's hood as it swept past and sending Dolati and Slasher ducking and yelling as he continued back down the alley.

"What was *that?*" Slasher bellowed. "Was it him?"

"I don't know!" Dolati brought the car to a stop. "That alley's too narrow for this thing—but I'm gonna go see, though!"

Slasher sucked in through his teeth, gently feeling his temples again. "You didn't have to smack me so *hard* back there! It made me groggy and I can't see for *spit!*"

"That's *your* problem, pansy!" Dolati left the engine running and jumped out; Slasher feebly did the same and followed him toward the alley.

Good. Exactly as Chad wanted. He slid into the driver's seat...

Dolati reached the alley and gasped before drawing his gun. "It's *him,* all right!"

"Shoot!" yelled Slasher.

"I can't! He just turned the corner down there!"

"Well *I'm* goin' after him!" Slasher drew his blade and started off down the alley.

Dolati motioned toward the car. "What about—"

"Take it around," Slasher called back. "I'll find ya somewhere!"

Dolati raced back and climbed into the driver's seat. *"What—?"*

The keys were gone.

He scoured the dashboard and checked the floor.

They were nowhere to be found.

Chad ran alongside Wayne once more, laughing as he tossed the keys down a sewer grate. It would hold Dolati off for a *few* minutes; Slasher wouldn't show up right away, either. He was already going the wrong direction, having forgotten to ask Dolati which *way* he'd seen Wayne go.

But it was *only* temporary, and there were still two *other* cars to deal with. And the second one would be coming along any time now…

Stop here, Wayne.

Wayne stopped as he crossed another intersection of alleys—so suddenly that Chad ran smack into him nose first.

Wayne felt it. "Oops! All right there, buddy?"

Oh, yeah. Chad giggled and rubbed his nose. *You're listening good! Wait here for a second.*

Wayne did.

Kutz looked over at Noyes as they rounded another corner with a screech. "Boy, I hope we find that little twerp soon!" His voice cracked with rage. "He's really, *really* made this a bad day. And I *hate* gettin' yelled awake by that grouch!"

He cocked his .223-caliber rifle, his finger on the trigger.

"We'll find him." Noyes kept his eyes straight ahead. "And when we do, we'll make sure he *knows* just how hard it's been, right?"

Kutz nodded and rolled his window down a little more. He

almost laughed, but he was too angry for it. He scanned ahead
as Noyes swung around yet another corner...

Wayne saw the 4x4 appear up the street to his right; he was
standing directly in the headlight beams. He heard a yell and
saw someone lean out the window with something—

Start running again, Wayne!

Wayne took off in the same direction; Chad snatched the
barrage of slugs from Kutz's gun as the vehicle swooshed past.

He dropped them and walked back into the road, waiting
for it to come back.

Dolati heard the blasts as he searched for Slasher. "Yo,
Slash!" he called out.

No answer.

"I know where he is!" Dolati yelled. "I'm goin' after him,
Slash!"

He ran back to the car and dragged the full, five-gallon
kerosene can from the back seat.

Now to use the short cut.

"Stop, Noyes! Go back!"

Noyes slammed on the brakes and tried to make a U-turn;
the Jeep slid on the wet snow, spun around, and slammed into
a wall, blowing out all the windows on one side.

"You *idiot!*" Kutz yelled, knocking glass from his shoulders. "Why didn't ya *follow* him back there."

"Cuz I didn't see the alley!" Noyes yelled back. "Why
didn't *you* hit him?"

"Shut up and drive!"

The vehicle pulled away and roared back toward the alley
Wayne had just used. Chad's hands shot out as it passed and
ripped the back tire off.

Again it spun around, crashing into the opposite wall and
blowing out all the remaining windows.

Both men staggered out, dazed.

"Fool!" shouted Kutz. He grabbed the rifle and stalked off
down the alley. "Search on foot! I don't care *where* ya go!"

Wayne cut left, then right, then left again, going back along the exact same path he'd just taken. It was useless trying to retrace his footsteps—the snow had already melted away in some places and they were gone. But he *knew* where to go. He was being led.

He didn't know if he'd lose the *hit* men or not; maybe they'd get lost among the maze of other alleys. But he wasn't about to question his guidance. He'd learned.

Chad grinned—that he had. And now for that *third* car.

He drew close beside Wayne as they approached the last little intersection before the main street again. *Be careful,* he warned. *This one's gonna be a close call. Don't stop this time. Run straight through and keep going.*

Wayne did, trusting completely.

"Shouldn't we be lookin' somewhere *else?*" McKernan gestured in front of him as he drove down the side street. "We've already been here. And where are—"

"Keep driving and keep your mouth shut." Glitch's voice drifted from the back seat. *"They* can do what they want. But *we're* gonna drive until we find him."

McKernan sighed. "I dunno how *much* longer we can. There's an awful lot of streets, and the gas is gettin' low…"

"Then you'll get out and *push,"* said Glitch. "So for *your* sake, let's hope he shows up soon—"

Wayne suddenly appeared, not more than thirty feet away, bolting across through an alley.

"It's *him!"* Glitch screamed. *"Smash* him!"

The car surged forward like a rocket.

Chad caught the front end with his hands just as it reached Wayne and lifted it high into the air, standing the whole thing on end and sending Glitch and McKernan tumbling out of their seats into the back window; he swung the car sideways and propped it against the building, rear bumper on the ground.

Then he rejoined Wayne.

• • •

Kutz ducked back into the alley, gun ready.

Someone was coming.

He peeked out. Someone carrying something—a big gas can, it looked like—ran across the opening at the end of the little street.

Kutz scrutinized him for the second he was visible; he checked the little snapshot with his pocket flashlight. He couldn't tell—*was* it the guy, or maybe…?

He didn't know, but he followed him anyway.

Wayne reached the main street again. Chad took hold of his arm once more as he started back on course.

Keep on this street, Wayne. Don't change your path until you hear me say so. I'll be right back.

Wayne kept running. *You're in charge, angel. You're in charge.*

Chad dropped back and took off down the alley again. He had a few minutes to further confuse them before Wayne was discovered.

"Get *off* me, ya brick!" Glitch's muffled voice bellowed. "I can't breathe!"

McKernan tried to climb onto the back seat, but it was no use—he was too big, too heavy.

"Moose!" Glitch pleaded. "Climb out and help me!"

Still strapped in the passenger seat, Moose carefully undid his belt and opened his door. As he gingerly twisted around to lower himself out, he bumped the release lever on the seat; the back instantly dropped, plunging him down on top of the two and smashing them through the back window onto the pavement. The sudden shift of weight disbalanced the car, sending all three men scrambling to get out of the way as it tipped backwards—the roof landed beside them on the ground; they were sandwiched under the trunk, with Glitch on the bottom.

"Get off!" he wailed, pounding his fists. "Get off get off *get off!*"

• • •

Slasher's ears picked up the *footsteps* as he raced down the alley, toward the main street again. So *that* was it, he figured. The guy was simply doubling back to where he started.

He followed them.

Chad grinned. *Keep following me,* he said. *Just a little farther...*

Slasher was rapidly catching up. He came around a corner and there was his prey, against a wall, looking around nervously. Slasher laughed. He *finally* had him right where he wanted him. He drew his hand back and threw—

Noyes jumped with a shout as the blade whizzed past, ripping his sleeve and lodging in the boarded window next to him. *"What* the—?"

Slasher came into view.

"You!" Noyes yelled. "It was *you* I heard! What are ya *doin'?"*

"What do ya *think,* idiot? *He* just ran through here!"

"Nobody was here!"

"But I heard—"

"Nothing, that's what!" Noyes pulled the knife from the wood with a snap. "You hear him when he *ain't* around, and ya can't even get him when he *is!"*

Slasher grabbed it from his hand. "I wish I'd hit you!" he yelled, shaking the point under his nose. "I otta right now!"

Noyes whipped out his pistol. "You wanna *try,* screw-up? You're damn lucky it's *this,* and not my baby in the car!"

Chad was laughing hysterically. He wanted to do it again. He took off down the same alley.

Slasher whirled around. "There—there it is! Hear it *this* time?"

Noyes pushed him out of the way and raced after it.

Slasher followed him. "No! No ya don't! He's *mine!* I've waited too *long!"*

Wayne approached another intersection along the main street. Never before had he been so glad to see traffic lights, street lights, *any* kind of lights. He walked across it, catching his breath, savoring that one moment of brightness before racing into the darkness once more.

He was now halfway there.

Moose suddenly dropped McKernan—leaving him halfway under the trunk and still on top of Glitch—and whirled around to the intersecting alley Wayne had just passed through.

He'd heard something.

"What are you *doing,* you fool?" Glitch muttered. "Get him off me!"

Moose stooped again and yanked McKernan out with a single pull, then walked over to the corner.

Glitch dragged himself out. "What is it?"

"Shh," Moose whispered. "Someone's coming. It sounds like *him.*"

"How *could* it be?" McKernan sat up and shook his yellow hat into shape. "He just went *through* here. Why would he come back—?"

Moose waved a hand at him and stood flat against the wall, ready to pounce; both Glitch and McKernan drew their guns.

Chad laughed. He wanted to stay and watch this, but he had to rejoin Wayne at once. He'd already succeeded, anyway—he'd indeed set them back at least a *few* minutes.

And Wayne would need every extra second he could get.

Wayne kept running along the dark, cold sidewalk, ever aware that every step brought him closer and closer to freedom. But he wasn't there yet. And he was tiring rapidly from the *endless* running…

He stopped momentarily to catch his breath, and then he heard them.

Footsteps.

He was being followed. *Again!*

Afraid so, said Chad. *I know you're tired, Wayne. But we can't stop yet.*

He laid a hand on his arm. *Get ready to climb.*

Climb? thought Wayne.

Moose grabbed the person as he came around the corner and flung him to the ground; Glitch and McKernan aimed—

"*Hold* it!" Noyes yelled. "It's *me!*"

Glitch's eyes grew wide and his face turned red with fury; he dropped his gun and stormed over, pulling Noyes part-way up by the shirt collar.

"What are *you* doin' here?" he screamed. "Why aren't you driving around looking?"

Noyes pried off his hands and motioned toward the car. "Well at least *mine's* still right-side up!"

McKernan stifled a laugh.

"You'd better *pray* the others had more luck," Glitch hollered. "Otherwise I'm gonna be—"

Slasher stormed around the corner, breathless, knife ready to throw. He stopped cold and looked around, his face dropping in total confusion.

Glitch looked his way; his head cocked and his eyes grew even wider than before. He started to shake—everyone drew back from him, as if he was a volcano about to erupt.

He rose to his feet and stood there, swallowing, stuttering. Then, slowly, his face returned to normal. He scratched his lip and looked down.

"Just find him," he said with a sigh. "He's here somewhere. Just *find* him."

He stalked off down the alley, gun in hand, as everyone else fanned out in all directions.

Dolati stepped into a doorway, out of view, and paused from his awkward running; he set down the kerosene can and massaged his aching arms. He scanned the block ahead. Yes, the rat *must* have been heading back here to the main street, from the sound of those shots. But had he made it?

He caught sight of someone, standing in front of the large, brick warehouse on the other side of the street, a little farther down—he was leaning forward on his knees, panting.

It was *him*.

Dolati grinned; now to have some *real* fun. It was payback time. *He'd* do the job and leave everyone else in the mud.

He looked at the can by his feet, then scanned the buildings beyond where his target was standing, past the point where the street angled to the right. His eyes traveled along the various rooftops and grids...

There. He saw the one he needed.

He picked the drum back up with a grunt and started toward it, carefully staying in the shadows.

All right, Wayne, start climbing now.

Wayne stood straight again, suddenly realizing just how *sweaty* he was. *Climb what,* he thought.

That, said Chad, pointing. *We have to go up there, before you're seen!*

Wayne looked behind him. Through the darkness he could make out a black metal grid against the warehouse, framing the building about twenty-five feet up; it was part of an elaborate fire-escape system. There was a metal stairway leading down from it—

It descended only halfway.

Wayne's mouth fell open. How could he climb to *that?*

Don't worry, said Chad. *I'll help you. Come on, we have to now! Someone's coming and he'll see you anywhere else!*

Wayne followed the guidance once again as he made his way to the building's wall...

Kutz cocked his rifle as he approached the main street from the side street. Yes, it *was* Dolati he'd been following. Where was he *going,* though? There was no way of telling. But it was best to be ready—

He aimed from his hip and swung around the corner.

Nothing.

Dolati was nowhere to be seen.

Kutz lowered his weapon, muttering. Just *another* wild goose chase. And he'd probably lost the prey for *good* this time.

He started to roll his eyes in frustration and then he saw

Wayne. He stopped, his attention suddenly fixed on the warehouse down across the street. At least it *looked* like him. It was hard to know for sure, through such heavy darkness, but...yes, he could indeed make out the shape of *someone* against the bricks, scaling the wall.

He started toward it, slowly.

Hurry, Wayne! Climb as fast as you can!

Wayne raced, struggling against the backpack's weight as he hooked his leg over the next ledge in the vertical row of bricked-up windows; he lifted with every ounce of strength he could muster...

Chad gave him a boost.

Wayne felt himself ease onto it as Chad effortlessly scaled the wall ahead of him and pulled him to his feet; he did the same as Wayne reached for the next ledge, then the next one, giving a boost then a pull, a boost then a pull...

Wayne reached the platform at the base of the stairs. He clamored onto it and momentarily lost his balance; Chad seized him by the coat and pulled him away from the edge.

Hurry, now! Wayne bounded up the metal steps two, three at a time, already aware of someone crossing the street below, coming toward him...

Kutz saw the guy appear on the grid. It was his target, all right; he could see him clearly now. But how had he gotten up there so *fast?*

He shook his head as he stormed toward the place. It didn't matter how. The only thing that *did* matter was that the rat's extraordinary *luck* was about to end.

He reached the building and ran alongside it, following the grid above with his eyes and scanning through the patterned holes in the metal floor, trying to pin down the exact location of Wayne's footsteps as they echoed noisily. They suddenly stopped—right at a fork in the grid.

Kutz stopped, too; his gaze was fixed on the spot. He started to raise the rifle, slowly...slowly...

Wayne's eyes shot back and forth. He was panicked. He

hadn't even seen it until now—the warehouse was actually two *separate* buildings close together, connected by the grid; one path branched left, down the side of the second building, the other continued straight, around its front.

Which way?

No time for that, said Chad. *Just run!*

Wayne took off again.

The footsteps bolted down the left grid—Kutz swung his aim and fired.

They kept going.

He'd *missed!* He cursed and resumed the pursuit underneath, this time *directly* under—he could see someone through the holes.

The footsteps slowed to a walk; Kutz aimed again and fired.

They kept going.

He fired again.

They kept going.

Another shot.

No change.

Wayne heard the blasts and looked over his shoulder. He didn't know why the guy had gone *that* way, or who he was shooting at. But he was suddenly glad he'd stayed his course.

He kept running.

Glitch heard the shots, too. He looked all around, suddenly realizing he was alone.

"Everybody!" he screamed at the top of his lungs. *"To the main street!"*

Moose was already on his way there, having started with the first crack of the shotgun.

Kutz's eyes widened in disbelief—he kept on firing again, then again, then again, rapidly, one right after the other, his target directly in his sights, blowing hole after hole after hole clean through the bottom of the grid.

Yet the footsteps kept walking!

Of *course* they did. It was Chad he was shooting at.

He was distracting Kutz, walking down the grid and drawing his fire, laughing as each successive blast inflated his baggy white shirt like a parachute; he was leading him clear around the building, as far as possible from Wayne, until he was safely beyond range or the guy's ammo ran out, whichever came first.

The latter did. Kutz clicked the rifle several more times before throwing it to the ground, cursing vehemently.

Chad straightened his shirt and laughed again. Now to get back to Wayne.

There's gotta be some other stairs around here, somewhere. Wayne looked closely as he approached the end of the grid…yes, he could see the railing, leading downward.

Ahh, there they are. He started toward it and the whole area in front of him was suddenly ablaze in unnaturally brilliant, white moonlight, so crystal clear it seemed at once the middle of the day. He shielded his eyes from the brightness—and then stopped suddenly.

There *were* no stairs at the end. They'd been completely broken off and his feet were inches, *millimeters* from the edge.

He jumped back. Then the light shifted, exposing the makeshift stairway going down from the *side.*

Wayne hadn't even seen them. He bolted down, as the moon disappeared behind the clouds once more.

Chad looked at his immaculate white clothes and smiled. Pretty good *reflective* material! And they'd be needed again before long, too.

He joined Wayne's side as he reached the ground and ran. They were back on track.

Moose reached the main road and charged full-speed toward the warehouse; he stopped abruptly as Kutz appeared from around the corner of the place, dejected-looking.

Moose didn't even ask—he didn't *need* to know, it was becoming so routine. "Which way?" he yelled.

Kutz pressed his lips together and pointed in the direction Wayne had just gone.

Moose took off.

"Hey!" Kutz called after him. "What should *I* do?"

"Stay *there,* idiot!" Moose yelled back. "If ya see the G or anyone, send 'em this way!"

He disappeared around the bend.

Wayne could hear Moose coming; he'd grown to know the heavy, menacing footsteps. He picked up his pace along the rapidly narrowing street, quickly growing weary again, coughing as his lungs reacted to the sudden new demand. He wiped at his running nose, he could feel his ears burning in the crisp air.

Chad was looking ahead, to the place where construction fencing had narrowed the street to a sidewalk's width. *He* knew Moose was coming, too, and also catching up—but that wasn't his immediate concern. Something much *more* deadly was fast approaching.

He got ready.

From his position on the grid high above the sidewalk, Dolati watched as his target approached the little channel.

He raised the match and laughed.

This would be so fun, so right, so *fitting,* the *perfect* ending for this walking piece of trouble he'd had to mess with for so long. He couldn't *wait* to hear the screams.

He struck the match with his thumb, carefully holding it as far as possible from the now-lidless kerosene drum perched on the railing in front of him. Just a few more seconds...

Chad threw a hand on Wayne's back. *Duck down,* he yelled. *Keep your arms in and your head low and don't stop!*

Wayne obeyed.

Moose was almost on top of him.

Now! Dolati tossed the match down over the sidewalk and spilled the entire drum after it, immediately transforming the clear waterfall into flaming lava as it crashed down on Wayne—

Instantly Chad leaned over him, shielding him from the torrent of liquid fire as it flowed off his outstretched garment, engulfing everything in sight, setting trash cans, brick walls, even the pavement ablaze amid the steam of vaporized snow...

"Aaagh!" Moose leaped sideways over the fence to avoid the gushing, liquidy fire; he stomped frantically on the unpaved gravel as some burning kerosene splashed onto his boots.

Chad steered Wayne into an alley, unscathed.

Moose checked himself as the fire quickly dispersed and started to burn out. He *glared* up at Dolati.

"Get down here—!"

"All *right!* It'll take me a minute!"

"—so I can kill you!"

"Hey, it wasn't *my* fault you were—"

"I *had* him!" Moose interrupted. "I *finally* had him and you almost fried me like a hot dog!"

"Yeah? Well I almost had him, too—"

"Ya *missed* and ya made *me* do the same!" Moose yelled. He stalked off down the alley. "You better pray we don't get near each other down here!"

Wayne couldn't understand it—he'd entered yet *another* maze of alleys and back streets, even darker and more sprawling than the first. He knew he had to lose Moose, but this would put him off track *again,* and who knew for how long? Hadn't he done *enough* of that already?

Why did I do this? he asked himself, almost angrily.

His mind stopped. Because he'd been directed to, that's why. He was already sorry for questioning it. And besides, time was too precious, his energy much too limited to be wasted on fretting. He was *already* struggling to keep running—his weary legs were growing heavier and heavier.

Come on, said Chad. *Only a little farther, Wayne!*

He *had* to press Wayne now. This was *the* critical stage of this whole thing. They were down to the last three blocks, Moose was rapidly closing the gap again, and the rest of the hit men were about to regroup and come this way, too. Wayne had to reach his car, and fast.

But Wayne *couldn't* go fast. All the endless running and danger and constant state of alertness had taken their toll. Each step grew harder...harder...*harder*...

"Ha! *Gotcha,* vermin!"

Wayne looked back. Moose had seen him and was coming after him.

No! Wayne turned and tried to bolt again, but the fatigue wouldn't let him...it was *useless...*

Chad took charge.

Wayne suddenly found himself being pulled along, ducking right onto another side street, then right again into...

A dead end.

Nothing.

Just a dirty old alley with a *wall* at the end of it.

Moose's cold laugh echoed through. "You're *mine,* stoolie! It's *over!"*

His footsteps grew louder.

Wayne turned around. He slumped down against the wall, almost...*reserved,* withdrawn, wholly accepting of some awful thought his troubled mind had only just deemed inevitable. He froze, his throat tightened as the giant appeared from around the corner, looking straight ahead; he abruptly stopped.

So *this* is how it would all end, Wayne thought. Trapped against a cold brick wall in an alley in New York City in the middle of the night in winter. After all he'd been through. And so close to getting out. He blinked back tears as Moose's body turned with his head...around...around...

Wayne saw his whole life over again, everything that had ever happened to him, all the neat things, all the bad things. *And now I'll never see Mom,* he thought. *I'll never get home.*

Moose's eyes landed directly on him.

Please, Lord, just end it quickly.

Moose kept *turning,* looking past Wayne until he had made a complete circle of the area. He smacked the wall with his fist before crossing the alley and running on.

Wayne couldn't believe it. He hadn't *seen* him. He sat flabbergasted as he listened to the heavy footsteps steadily grow weaker.

He hadn't seen him!

Of course he hadn't. Chad was standing in front of Wayne.

He waited until the footsteps could no longer be heard before lowering his arms and letting his shirt hang loose again.

You can get up now, Wayne, he said.

Wayne only sat stunned.

Chad took him by the hand. *Come on, friend. Let's get to that car.*

Wayne raised his tired body and followed Chad again.

"That way!" Kutz shouted to Noyes as he approached the warehouse, Uzi in hand. "He went that way!"

"*Which* way?" Noyes stopped, breathless.

"Over there." Kutz pointed toward the bend in the road. "But we better move if we're gonna do this—that big oaf's already gone!"

Noyes loaded a clip into his weapon. "Well, we'll beat him to it. I think I know where the rat's headed—*and* a quicker way to get there."

He handed Kutz a revolver from his coat. "Come on!"

Kutz followed him across the street and down another alley. "Just glad ya came by when ya did," he said. "I didn't want to let all those *other* losers know first!"

Slasher followed them from a distance.

Glitch and McKernan followed *him*.

Wayne continued down the alley a little farther, gasping, staggering...

He reached the end; his mouth fell open in wonderful disbelief. He was on the *main street* again, by the icy banks of the Hudson River!

And he'd cut almost two blocks by going this way!

Now he felt even sillier for questioning it. *I'm sorry, angel,* he thought. *I did it again.*

Chad grinned. *No problem, Wayne. Just keep going.*

Wayne *tried* to keep going. And he knew he had to *now* more than ever—this last little stretch was by far the most dangerous, with nothing but big, empty lots and garbage-strewn fields. It was one vast, open area, with hardly any structures; there were really few, if any places to hide. If he got caught out here in the open like this, he'd be fair game for anyone with anything, even a slingshot.

But it was growing incredibly difficult to move at *all*. Even the boost his spirits had gotten from his latest escape was rapidly fading; he was simply running out of energy.

I've gotta get away from them, he thought. *But I can't keep going...only one thing I...I can do now...*

He slowed to a jog.

No, Wayne! Chad tugged on his arm *You can't stop! You can't do that!*

Wayne kept slowing. His stride quickly became a fast walk, then a slow walk, then a mere *shuffle...*

Wayne, no! Keep going! Don't give up yet!

Wayne slowed to barely a creep...then he stopped entirely. He leaned forward on his knees, hyperventilating, breathless, completely *exhausted.* He could hardly even stand.

Wayne, come on! Chad pressed a hand on his front, trying to push him up straight again. *We're so close! We have to keep running!*

Wayne only stood there, head down, eyes shut, breathing hard. He could already hear the distant, distant footsteps in the alleyways behind him.

Chad *had* to get him moving again. If not, then it *would* be all over.

He stood in front of Wayne, laying both hands on his arms once more. *Please, Wayne. You've listened well so far. Listen to me now! You can't stand here like this. I know it's hard, I know you're tired, but you've got to...*

Wayne was praying.

Oops. Chad immediately fell silent; he dropped his hands to his sides and listened.

Lord, I'm tired. I can't go another step. Please intervene right now. Please work another miracle...

Chad drew close beside his best friend—his eyes sparkled with admiration as he listened intently. *Wayne* knew what he was doing.

...Please give me the strength to go the rest of the way...
Wayne felt the soothing *rejuvenation* at once. So swiftly, in fact, that he bolted up straight and tall—alive with a flood of energy that both filled his body and calmed his mind.

Thanks, Lord.

His strong arm tugged on the backpack; his newly-alert eyes focused on the road ahead. He finished his prayer.

Please stop these killers once and for all. Amen.

Chad looked up at Wayne, startled. He had just made *the* big request—

A calling came.

Immediately Chad knelt, a huge smile crossing his face. He already knew what it was.

Yes, Lord.

Wayne felt *great!* "Look out, car!" he yelled. "Here I come!"

He sprang forward, bounding down the road like a gazelle, faster than he'd ever run before. He felt like he could run a *million* blocks now.

Wayne would be safe for a while. Chad stayed put, carefully listening to his instructions. Good old Wayne! He'd *finally* asked it, *finally* done what Chad had been waiting and *waiting* and *waiting* for him to do. And now all he needed was the *Official* go-ahead.

He got it.

Take 'em, he was told. *Take all of 'em.*

Chad raised his head. He stood up, slowly turning and facing the alleyway, silhouetted by the moonlight, his shadow extending far into it. A look of utter determination was etched on his face, a fierce glare burned in his eyes. His teeth showed, his fists *shook* with emotion.

He was absolutely *livid.*

In fact, he was downright *furious,* angry, madder than he'd ever been before.

Enough was enough!

They had consistently threatened the Lord's property, the property *he* was guarding. They had intended harm for *his* best friend. And they were *not* going to anymore. They were *not* going to follow him or harass him or endanger him *ever again!*

Wayne had asked, and that's all in the world it had taken— now Chad had the permission he needed.

Now it was between *him* and them.

Now it was *personal.*

He stalked off down the alley, suddenly a hunter.

He was given one more bit of instruction: *Have fun doing it.*

Chad laughed. Oh, would he *ever!*

Dolati stopped cold as he felt his way along the dark, narrow alley.

Something wasn't right.

He didn't know what, exactly, but he suddenly felt... *uneasy,* apprehensive, two things he'd never felt before. It wasn't just Moose's threat—though that *was* enough in itself. No, it was *more* than that. It was a deep, uncanny *fear,* almost like...he was being *tracked.*

He swallowed nervously, glancing behind him into the blackness as he continued following the *three* sets of foot-prints—Moose's, the prey's, and *whoever's*—rapidly vanish-ing in the melting snow. He approached a corner...

"Ooof!" Slasher barreled smack into him as he came around, knocking them both to the pavement.

"Damn you, Slash!" Dolati pulled himself to his feet again. "Ya scared me to *death!*"

"What?" Slasher staggered up. *"You* scared? *That's* a first!"

Dolati glanced around him. "Well can't you *tell?* It's...it's this *place,* here. Something—"

"I don't know what you're talking about!" Slasher snapped. "Where were *you,* all this time?"

Dolati sighed. "Don't ask—"

"Forget I ever did!" Slasher interrupted. "Here!"

He tossed Dolati a small roll of the cable that had ensnared the truck. "You'll finally get to use it the way it *should* be, and *I'll* get to cut some worm meat! Now come on! I've lost those other jokers and I want 'em to *stay* lost!"

"How'd ya manage *that?*"

Slasher laughed. "No one knows these 'short cuts' better than me. Now let's move it—"

He stopped abruptly. His eyes shot up the alley ahead; his hand closed around the large knife handle protruding from the leather case strapped to his hip.

Dolati craned his neck, trying to see where he was looking. "What is it?"

"Shh!" Slasher held up a hand. He looked uncertain for a moment, then his eyes widened, his mouth broadened into a gold-toothed smile. He laughed again, quietly.

"It's *him,*" he whispered.

"But how do ya kid?" Dolati whispered back. "It might be one of the others—"

"I just *know,* that's all." Slasher drew out the knife. "I've been after this little snake so long I've memorized him."

"So what are ya—"

"*You* wait here." Slasher crept forward, his gaze fixed on another corner farther down. "I'll stick him just a *little* bit, then bring him back with me—then we'll *really* have some fun! You choke and I'll cut."

Dolati grinned, too. That *did* sound good; maybe it'd help calm his nerves.

He stood and waited.

The alley around the corner was pitch black, darker than any others so far—nothing but the faint outline of the buildings against the sky were visible. And the *footsteps* were rapidly approaching. But from which way? Slasher couldn't tell—were they *behind* him, or in *front?* The front sounded louder.

He held the blade loose as he moved silently along the wall. Shoot, he didn't *need* to see; he'd simply wait until the right moment and then aim for the legs. He drew his arm back...

Now! He stepped forward to throw and *something* grabbed his arm, instantly jerking him backwards to the ground and knocking the air out of him.

"Uh!"

He raised his head and felt a sharp crack across his temple.
He passed out.

Yes! Chad stood over him, laughing, rubbing the fist he'd
just used. This little wimp was merely practice.

Now for the next guy.

"Slash?"

Dolati tried to keep his voice below a whisper as he called
out again.

"Slaaash!"

Nothing but the quiet moan of the wind echoing through
the black maze.

Dolati was growing edgy. Slasher was taking too long;
something must have happened.

He gulped. He'd have to go see.

He wrapped an end of the cable firmly around his hand
before starting for the corner Slasher had disappeared around,
only vaguely aware of the quiet clatter as the excess cable
dragged along the wet pavement behind him. He gave it a yank
and picked up his speed, a little faster, a little faster...

"Ouch!" He was jerked to a stop as the cable stretched
tight. Cursing, he backed up and looked—the other end had
caught in a broken window, high above the pavement in the
brick wall. How had he flipped it up *there?*

He mumbled some more and tugged lightly.

The thing didn't budge.

Chad stood on the ground floor inside the building, hands
tight around the cable. He grinned and tugged back.

"What the—?" Dolati gave a harder pull.

Chad didn't move. He pulled back again.

Dolati's face grew red. "Come on," he muttered. "I don't
have *time* for stubborn mules!"

He pulled hard.

Now Chad was *really* having fun. He wanted to keep the
game going, but he still had work to do. He'd have to end it
early.

Oh, well.

He reached forward and drew his arms way back in a single, powerful yank, ripping Dolati into the air and clean through the wall with a crash. For a moment he lay dazed—then he staggered back up, eyes rolling around.

"Uh...uh...*ow,*" he muttered, then fell face forward, out cold.

Yes! Another one down. Chad laughed and moved on.

Moose whirled around as he reached the main street. Was that a *wall* crumbling he'd heard? He wasn't sure, but the rat was certainly nowhere to be found...yes, it must have been him. So *that* was it. The little twerp had gone back the other way!

He reentered the maze of alleys.

"You *sure* that's where they're comin' from?" Kutz squinted into the darkness ahead. "With the acoustic screw-ups this place is full of..."

"Yep, I'm sure." Noyes readied his Uzi. "It's *him,* all right. He's doublin' back from the main street. Moose is probably on his tail."

"Then what was the bang?"

"Aw, he probably hit some cans or something." Noyes pointed to a side alley. "You go off that way in case he gets back out there again. I'll go *this* way and try to spare ya the work."

"Gotcha!" Kutz snickered and took off toward the main street.

Noyes started forward into the blackness. *Man,* it was dark. He could barely see ahead of him—only the dim forms of the walls lining the alley were visible. But he kept going. He was determined to hunt down the snitch, and make him pay for escaping so much and being such a *phenomenal* problem.

The footsteps grew louder. Here they came, rapidly approaching him in the dark—only now, suddenly, they didn't sound familiar. They were strange, different from any he'd ever heard before.

Noyes stopped, at once uneasy. Who—or *what*—was it, then?

He took a couple more steps and then stopped again, frozen in horror. Now he could *see* it. His eyes widened as *something* appeared in the distance, racing directly toward him with a pale, white glow. Or *was* it? He couldn't tell—was he merely *hallucinating?*

His senses told him otherwise. The *something* was still coming, the footsteps were getting louder—

Noyes screamed. He aimed wildly and pulled the trigger.

Instantly the alley was ablaze in a dancing yellow light as the Uzi's barrel lit up in a deadly fire; the quiet was shattered as dozens upon dozens of rounds struck the walls and street, ricocheting in every direction, screaming, whining, peppering boarded windows and trash cans, exploding garbage bags, hitting anything and everything there was. Noyes kept on firing and firing and firing, repeatedly switching clips, using his entire supply in a panicked, desperate attempt to stop the advance of the *thing...*

Moose dropped the unconscious Dolati onto the pile of bricks again and whirled toward the sound of the fire. He shook his head in confusion. First Slasher, then him, and now *this*—what was going *on?* It wasn't the *rat,* that was for sure.

He ran off toward it.

"This way!" Glitch shrieked. *"This way!* It's Noyes! They *got* him up there!"

He bolted down the alley toward the sound of the gunfire. McKernan gasped, struggling to keep up.

Noyes inserted another clip and fired frantically, but *something* was still coming...closer...closer—

Chad reached him and grabbed the Uzi's blazing barrel, bending and twisting it out of shape, sending Noyes flying backwards as it misfired in his hands and exploded.

Noyes was terrified. He sprang to his feet and tried to

run—his eyes met Chad's outstretched fingers and he covered them, yelling in agony; he doubled over as a knee was thrust into his groin, then landed flat on his nose from a leg brought down across his back. He rose up on his knees, moaning, only to be knocked backwards into the wall as Chad backhanded him across the face.

Chad laughed. He cast a glance skyward and winked. *Thanks, Mike. Thanks for the lessons.*

He laid on his side on the ground, head propped on his fist, as he watched Noyes stagger up again, barely able to walk, blinded, gasping, moaning.

The poor fool. Time to put him out of his misery.

Chad raised his head as Noyes passed, then swept his legs out from under him. He toppled forward onto Chad's fist—still propped in place—bouncing right off and landing flat on his nose again.

Out cold.

Yes! Three down, four to go. Chad laughed again—this was so *incredibly* fun.

And now for Kutz.

Chad started after him and then he heard a familiar, *snarly* voice.

He stopped. *Glitch,* huh? The one who'd *started* this whole thing.

He altered his course.

"Come *on,* ya dumb bouncer!" Glitch fumed at the sound of McKernan's wheeze. "If you'd lose some of that extra mountain, maybe you'd *function,* every now and then!"

McKernan muttered as he reached Glitch's side.

"Now stick *with* me," said Glitch. "It's dark in here and I want you nearby with that gun!"

McKernan gasped, trying to catch his breath. "Why…does it *matter,* if…if they got him?"

"Cuz I don't *trust* anyone, that's why! Stay over there and take it slow."

They both started forward, Glitch moving along one wall,

McKernan along the other.

Chad was waiting for them.

His feet closed around the long, thick, metal pipe he'd broken to just the right length. He took a couple deep breaths, his attention grew concentrated. He'd have to be very precise about this...everything had to go just right for this to work...he'd get no second try...

The goals moved into position.

Shoot-in time!

Chad picked the thing up and spun around as the two men passed, sending Glitch crashing forward, McKernan backwards as their legs were swept out from under them—

"Ow, my *calves!*"

"Aw, my *shins!*"

They sat up, moaning, clutching their aching legs. "Moose!" Glitch hollered. "Get over here!"

Chad laughed. Now *they* were the helpless ones.

Double-shoot-in time!

He again took the pipe with his feet and jumped high into the air, this time spinning the other direction—cracking McKernan directly in the forehead, Glitch in the back of the head and sending both flopping to the ground in opposite ways.

Out for the count.

Yes! Chad planted a foot on Glitch's back and clenched his fists. Oh, *yes,* it felt so *good!*

Now for those last two.

And lo and behold, here came one of them.

Moose raced from Noyes' prone body toward the sound of the pained voice he'd heard. He shook his head in puzzled disbelief—no, it couldn't be the *G* this time, could it?

Yes, it was. Moose stumbled over his body in the dark— both his *and* McKernan's—and crashed into some cans.

Moose was utterly flabbergasted. *What in the name of heaven was going on, here?*

There could only be *one* explanation, he figured; only one person in the world could have done all this.

It was *Kutz,* that's who it was. Yes, of *course* it was him—
he was the only other one left. He must have gone flippy,
taking everyone else out of the way, even his own teammate,
so he could grab the prize for himself.

Moose snarled. *The little bastard!* He'd pay *dearly* for
this. And the rat, too—that elusive, slippery...*person* had
caused enough trouble to last a *thousand* forevers.

He tore off down the alley toward the main street again.
Now he'd hunt down *both* of them. He'd stay up as long as it
took; he'd keep going as long as necessary. He'd use his bare
hands, if he had to—and that was really all he had left. But he
would find them.

Chad followed him. *You're mine, tall boy.*

Moose's mouth watered; he *savored* what lay ahead. Oh,
what he'd do to that rotten snitch! He already had a hundred
different ideas, some he'd tried, some he hadn't, but none
seemed appropriate. Maybe one of each would do...

Moose stopped. He turned around, squinting into the
blackness behind him.

Had he *heard* something?

No, there was nothing there. He started running again, his
mind picking up where it left off. The rat. Yes, the *rat!* That
was it—he could drag him back to the hide-out and toy with
him there for a while, before...

Moose stopped again. His ears were fooling him for a
second time. He looked back; there was still nothing there.
Well, he *was* groggy from all the chasing.

He took a few more steps and then stopped again—*this* time
he heard them clearly. Sharp, heavy footsteps, slowly approaching from somewhere behind him. Ones he'd never heard before.

Moose swallowed. He took a few more steps and looked
back; the sounds did the same. He tried it again, the same thing
happened.

Now Moose was growing a little uneasy. He hated being
followed, especially so *close,* and by someone apparently
invisible—whoever it was must have been wearing a cloaking
device or something.

Time to outrace it.

Moose shot forward at top speed, covering huge distances with every step as he ran on and on and on into the blackness; he took a left turn, then a right one, then a left again, feeling in front of him, sliding on the layer of slush on the pavement, working his way deeper and deeper into the endless maze of alleys.

He finally stopped, sweating, panting, leaning against a wall for support as he bent forward to catch his breath.

A smile crept over his face as his ears picked up nothing but the sound of his own tired breathing echoing off the walls. He'd done it. No one, *no one on earth* could have stayed with him at that pace. He gave a smug chuckle, wiping his forehead on his black sleeve as his breathing slowly returned to normal. Now to get back to business—

Moose stopped cold again. His eyes widened, his mouth dropped open in horror; he couldn't believe his senses. It started quietly, barely audible, but...it was *them.*

The footsteps.

Here they came, slowly, heavily, methodically.

Moose shot to his feet. Now he was scared. For the first time in his life, he was really, *really scared.* He stood there, petrified, a cold sweat suddenly blanketing his face as the footsteps grew louder...closer...

They stopped directly behind him.

Moose was terrified. He turned and swung his fist—there was *nothing there!* Yet already a pair of *hands* were grabbing at his shirt, pulling him forward, down, down to his knees, locking around his neck in a choking grip, suffocating his screams as he swung wildly, frantically at nothing but space—

The grip suddenly let go and the most powerful fist he'd ever felt slammed into his jaw.

He spun around and crumpled to the pavement, out cold.

Yes! Chad leaped with euphoria, jumping up and down, clenching his fists in triumph. *Oh, yes,* it was so *fun* being a guardian angel! And on the *Lord's* side, too!

Now to deal with Kutz and rejoin Wayne. He took off, glancing down at his immaculate white high tops.

He laughed.

He hadn't known they could be so *scary!*

At last. Kutz grunted as he reached the ladder's end; he hoisted himself over the rim and onto the roof of the flat, one-story garage. Yes, at long *last* he'd caught up with his prey. And he had him right where he wanted him.

He crawled to the edge and spotted Wayne as he ran down the street below, so out in the open, by himself and unprotected, without so much as a mailbox to duck behind. And the river would make such a convenient dumping ground...

Kutz laughed as he fastened the scope onto the revolver; he was so *glad* he always carried a spare with him. He aimed, bringing the cross directly across Wayne's back, squeezing ever so gingerly—

The trigger wouldn't pull. It was stuck.

What? Kutz tried again, squeezing hard.

Still it wouldn't pull.

Of *course* it wouldn't. Chad had his finger jammed behind it. He chuckled as he cocked his fist, ready to pop him on the head.

Then he stopped. He looked behind Kutz...was that who it *looked* like coming...?

Kutz was growing desperate. He looped both index fingers over the trigger as he peered through the scope once more, taking aim at Wayne's rapidly shrinking figure. He gritted his teeth, pulling with all his might—

An *eye* suddenly appeared in the scope. "BOO!"

Kutz jumped with a shout and fell backwards as a foot pinned him down; the gun was pried from his hand.

"*Sykes!*" he yelled, furiously. "What are you—!"

"And just what do ya think *you're* doing, sir?" Sykes leaned right up to his face. "Aimin' at my *friend* over there?"

Kutz tried to raise himself on one elbow as he grabbed for the gun. "He's *mine*, Sykes! Leave it alone! He's mine—*uh!*"

He was knocked out as Sykes brought the pistol hard across his temple. "Ha ha! Haven't ya heard my new *policy,*

Butts? Ya just said it *yourself,* in your own way!"

He stood and tossed the gun over the side behind him. "It's a real simple policy, my friend: If ya don't know it, don't touch it!"

He laughed jovially, then turned around to the direction Wayne had just gone. His laugh quickly turned into a smile; his face grew calm and warm and his eyes looked as normal as anyone's. He laid an arm on the rim and shook his head. He couldn't help but admit it, after trailing his ex-prey tonight: the guy *had* something he didn't. It had only taken a short while of mere observation to convince him that any further hostilities on his own part would have been futile; all plans of revenge had quickly dissolved into a journey of fascination at the miraculous happenings surrounding his one-time nemesis. There was something there he'd never seen before. Such a new, obvious, and *awesome* power—a concept he *himself* was so used to commanding from everyone—could only draw his respect, and needed to be left alone. Yet the power he'd seen was so…so different, so *likable,* that, well…maybe it was time to seriously reevaluate some things.

Sykes' hand rose to his forehead and he saluted Wayne.

"Godspeed, young man," he said. "It's been real."

Then he laughed again and vanished into the darkness once more.

Chad stood in amazement. *Holy wow! Who'd have thought?* He rejoined Wayne.

The last block.

Wayne tried to blank out his mind as he focused every bit of attention on covering the remaining distance as safely as all the rest. The task had been done *for* him, quite miraculously; but now the sudden, new curiosity at why he was no longer being followed threatened to puncture the insulation against his own thoughts. And it was literally the fear of that happening alone that drove Wayne on, carrying him forward, as if he were somehow in a race against himself, as if *he* was now the enemy. But he was slipping. Already the urge to look back was growing stronger. Something had *happened* behind him—all his pursuers had seemingly *stopped,* dead cold, as if they'd reached an invisible wall that *he'd* somehow slipped through.

His prayer had worked, and like a kid with a new tool, he wanted to see how.

He uttered another silent prayer. He prayed that he *wouldn't* think for himself in these last critical moments—or the rest of his *life,* for that matter—that he'd put complete faith and trust in the Divine protection he'd already experienced so much of.

Thanks, friend. Wayne instantly felt the gratitude, the warm presence of a guiding hand locked firmly around his wrist. He ran on through the night, miraculously moving where he needed to, leaping clear of dangers in his path as he came across them—holes, fire hydrants, dozens of thing he couldn't even see. It was incredible. It was like wherever he went, he *wanted* to go there. Like he knew where to go before he even thought of it.

Chad grinned. *My thoughts are quicker than your mind.*

He was leading his best friend, aware of every little detail along his route, every possibility, every danger. Nothing was hidden from him; his eyes scanned everywhere, seeing everything, penetrating the thickest darkness. *Anything* that even remotely threatened Wayne's advance—even so much as a bump in the sidewalk—he steered him clear of. *Anything* that would harm Wayne or distract him, he guided him away from.

He saw the snarling pit bull and heard its inaudible growl before Wayne even knew it existed; he momentarily let go of Wayne's arm and came to a halt, swinging around in an offensive position, facing the animal with a piercing stare as it approached, slowly circling…

The animal stopped. It sensed something—its ears drooped and it slowly backed away before turning around and scampering off, whimpering.

Chad rejoined Wayne and took hold of him once more.

Never before had Wayne felt the *presence* so strongly as right then. And it was a *good* feeling. The cold winter wind blew his clothes against his thin frame, but he ignored it; his nose was running all over the place, but he ignored it.

He reached the parking lot. The moon reappeared from behind the clouds and his path was suddenly illuminated as the white snow lit up all around him.

There was the little blue car, dead ahead.

The only car in the lot.

Without a *bit* of snow on it—it'd been *brushed clean!*

Wayne surged forward with a new burst of adrenaline at the sight of the tired old vehicle, now the most beautiful sight in the world. The hidden puddles spattered under his weight as he got closer...closer...

He reached it!

Breathless, gasping, he leaned forward on the roof as he inserted the key and unlocked it; he slid the backpack off and got in, tossing his load into the back seat. He started it up.

*Pennsylvania...Pennsylvania...Pennsylvania...*He could think of nothing else as he sat and revved life into the cold engine.

Time to go home.

His hands gripped the wheel and he slammed his foot down; the car screeched as the pedal met the floor and he was going...going...

Nowhere.

He rolled down the window and looked out. The back wheels were dug deeply into the slushy mud.

No, please, he thought desperately. *Not this close!*

He gave it another go. The car went even deeper.

I don't believe this! Wayne threw up his hands. *Does someone wanna get out and push?*

Chad grinned. *Sure!*

He climbed out of the passenger seat and went around back. *Okay, Wayne! Give 'er some gas and hang on!*

Wayne floored the pedal again. He felt the back end start to move...lifting up...slowly...

"Go, car, *go!* Come on, baby! Let's *do* it!"

A little more...a little more...

He broke free. The car took off like a rocket.

And he was on his way.

Finally!

"YAAAHOOO!"

Chad laughed—it wasn't so heavy at all. He clamored onto the back and planted his high tops firmly on the trunk, leaning forward on the roof as the car sped down the road. His eyes continued to scan, ever alert; he would stay his post until Wayne was safely beyond the city's borders.

And here it came.

Wayne let another cry of joy go up as the car crossed the bridge over the Hudson and reached New Jersey; Chad laughed and settled back into the passenger seat.

Wayne couldn't believe it. He was *out. He was finally out—and alive, too!* He never thought it would happen, but it had. And he was *happy.* In fact, he was *overjoyed!* It was so *fantastic* to be *rid* of a long, sorry chapter in his life where *nothing* had...

His mind drew a breath. He looked in the rearview and watched the city lights growing smaller and smaller.

He was wrong.

Those six years hadn't been *entirely* bad; after all, it was during that time—albeit only recently—that his life had been changed forever. And if for no other reason but that, it had *all* been well worth it, every single, last minute, everything that had brought him to that one critical turning point. And that was *everything.*

For but an instant, one fleeting, *unbelievable* moment, he was almost...he was almost *sorry* to leave. Almost. In a way, it *was* his home town, he *had* grown up there. And he'd certainly seen more action than anyone could ever hope for. And now...

His eyes moved back to the road ahead of him. He chuckled. Now it was déjà vu. Now, for the *second* time in his life, a whole new start awaited him. Only this time, he *knew* he was ready. He now had something he didn't have before—an *assurance* that was fathomless, bottomless, *endless.*

"Thanks, Lord," he said aloud. "Thanks for answering my

prayer and getting me out safely. You gave me one *super* angel!"

Chad laughed again; his face grew red. He drew his feet up and retied his high tops, which had become undone during the last chunk of action.

Pennsylvania...Pennsylvania... Wayne had to struggle to keep his speed down on the wet roadway. Good though he felt, he still wouldn't feel *absolutely* satisfied until he was back over the border in his home state, where he belonged. He couldn't *help* feeling that way; somehow, he saw the border as a turning point, a line between him and more permanent safety. And he wouldn't let it *all* out until then.

Chad said nothing. He knew better, he knew there was *no* place—save for one—that was *permanently* safe, that would be without need of his aid. And where they were going *wasn't* the exception. But he also understood the reasoning behind Wayne's feelings, given all that had just happened.

He smiled. Who could blame him?

He joined Wayne in his anticipation, staring through the windshield at the highway in front of them, watching each dotted line pass through the dim glare of the headlights...

The hour or so went quickly. Then the large, white sign came into view; both Wayne and Chad leaned forward, suddenly breaking into *goose bumps* as the big, black letters spelled out the news they'd been yearning for:

WELCOME TO PENNSYLVANIA
WHERE YOU ALWAYS HAVE A FRIEND.

The pavement changed as they passed the sign—and then both of them went bananas.

"WHOOOAAHOOO!"

Chad whistled loudly, cheering and clapping and drumming his heels rapidly and clenching his fists in triumph while Wayne honked the horn and banged the wheel and cheered at the top of his lungs.

"WAAAAHOOO! WE DID IT!"

Wayne looked over at the passenger seat. "We *did* it, angel! *Put 'er there!"*

He held out a hand and Chad gave him a five. Wayne felt the smack and looked at his palm—it felt so neat it made him *tremble!*

"Whooo, *boy!* I feel like a million *dollars!*"

Chad laughed hysterically. *Don't set a limit, Wayne!*

"Well, I feel like...*whooo!*"

On and on it went. Chad was giggling and laughing, Wayne was pounding his fists on the wheel and dashboard and both of them were yelling and cheering and carrying on in a tremendous surge of euphoria, joy, feel-good adrenaline—so loudly that Wayne had to roll down his window just so his own ears could bear it. *Oooooh, yes, it felt sooooo good!*

They passed the tiny green marker indicating the first mile; it started all over again.

Ahh, Pennsylvania. The yelling gradually subsided as they *both* found themselves losing their voices. They inhaled deeply as the fresh, crisp country air blew in through the open window.

*Where you always have a friend...*Wayne again looked over at the passenger seat and smiled. *He* felt the presence; he knew who was there.

"Thanks, friend," he said through suddenly misty eyes. "I couldn't have done it without ya."

Chad's eyes grew misty, too. Never before had he been so happy to see *his* best friend so alive and well, and where he wanted to be. It made him *just* as happy.

No problem, Wayne. Thank you.

Wayne sniffled. He wiped his nose on his sleeve and looked back out the window, blinking rapidly. *And thanks again, Lord. Thanks for letting me get here. You sure can do a lot more than crossed fingers ever could.*

He took another deep breath. *Boy, I'll never get enough of that air.*

The car fell silent for seemingly a long, long while. Wayne finally looked over beside him once more.

What an angel I have, he thought. *He's magnificent! It'd sure be neat to see him. Just once.*

Chad looked at Wayne, somewhat surprised. Then he glanced upward and smiled. *Hmmm...*

"Gimmee another one, pal!" Wayne held out his hand again. "Only not *too* hard—a guy *your* size'll knock me right over!"

He laughed and Chad did, too. They exchanged another five and Chad settled back into his seat again.

He couldn't wait for daylight. He still wanted to *see* Pennsylvania.

Scranton.

Wayne would stop here for the remainder of the night. Or *morning,* really—he checked his watch as he stopped at the small motel on the outskirts. It was almost five o'clock, Saturday morning.

He didn't *want* to stop, he desperately wanted to keep driving until he got *home,* but he could not—the adrenaline was subsiding now, and the grueling events of the night were rapidly catching up once more. He was on the verge of collapsing—he *had* to rest, just enough to get him the remaining distance.

Chad followed Wayne inside; he grinned broadly. He was again following his instructions to the letter.

Wayne grabbed a road map as he headed up the stairs for his second-floor room. Shoot, he wasn't sure exactly *where* he was going, anyway; he only knew it was in the western part of the state. But a good guess probably put him at least another three or four hours on the road...

It didn't matter. He'd figure all that out later; right now he wanted to sleep. He entered his room and staggered toward the bed...the backpack slipping from his hand as he fell straight onto it...

He passed out at once.

Chad laughed. He closed the door, picked up the backpack, and laid it neatly on the little, round table before moving one of the chairs over and taking his vigil at Wayne's side.

Dawn was just beginning to break.

17

Ahh, what a fresh smell…

Wayne turned over and breathed in deeply. The bliss of sleep was so enjoyable!

What a fresh, cool smell…almost like the country…

He thought he was dreaming until he felt the light breeze on his face. His eyes slowly opened—he *was* feeling wind!

He raised his head and looked down past his feet, into daylight—the heavy curtains were pushed aside, the sliding glass door was open just a crack; only the thin screen door remained shut. Wayne could make out a small terrace on the other side.

A *terrace.*

He blinked rapidly against the sudden, new brightness—

he hadn't even realized his room had one.

Oh yeah. Chad stood next to the bed and looked at it, too. *Isn't it great? I thought it was getting a little stuffy in here, so I fixed it.*

That is neat, thought Wayne. He started to get up and then realized he was under the covers.

Jeepers, he thought. *I don't even remember doing that. I must have really been out of it last night.* He chuckled and whisked them off.

Chad laughed, too. *Just didn't want ya to get too cold.* He followed Wayne to the screen door; Wayne slid it open and they both stepped out onto the tiny, covered balcony.

The sights, the smells, the memories.

It all came back to Wayne in an instant as his eyes made a slow, panoramic sweep of the surrounding fields and distant hills. He stretched, setting off an *enormous* yawn—and then stood in silence once more, taking in the scenery he'd long forgotten.

Spring had arrived early. There were blossoms on most of the trees; they were *everywhere,* really. The air had grown warmer yet—though it was still crisp—and fresh, green grass was poking through the last remnants of snow still visible here and there. Wayne watched the mist slowly rising off the parking lot below.

"So, angel." He leaned forward, crossing his arms on the damp wood railing. "You said ya wanted to see it, and, well...here it is." He motioned at the scene with his eyes. "How do ya like old P-A?"

It's beautiful, said Chad, as he stood gazing beside Wayne. *I like it a lot.*

"Yeah, it's *fabulous.*" Wayne shook his head and grinned. "I can hardly believe I'm standing here now."

But indeed, he *was* there. He *had* made it. Despite all that had happened the night before—which already was starting to seem like another world—he was *there,* alive and safe. Certainly he would have preferred a little less *excitement* in the process—especially when the outcome might have been so different, so often—but that was all irrelevant now. He was here, and *that* was all that mattered. To imagine how anything might have gone differently was hypothetical and completely silly and besides, he *knew* it was the best way it all could have happened. Tiring, grueling, dangerous as it was, he wouldn't have made it any other way.

His angel— and the Lord Himself, ultimately—had done it.

"Thanks again, buddy," he said. "Thanks for gettin' me here."

No problem, friend. Chad continued gazing. *No problem at all.*

Wayne took another deep breath and wet his lips. *Mmm, that smells good. I feel like some hot chocolate.*

Chad looked at him funny.

"Yeah, I know," Wayne said through another big yawn. "It sounds weird in warmer weather like this. But it's my favorite drink— I haven't had any for so *long.*" He stretched again. "And I'm gonna need *lots* more sleep, sometime. I *know* the full brunt of this whole thing still hasn't hit me. How long *did* I sleep, anyway?"

He checked his watch; it was almost one o'clock in the afternoon. "Whoa! Almost eight *hours!* I better reconfirm Mom's address and get going."

He turned and went back in. "I was so shook last night when I found out where she was that I couldn't write straight," he said with a grin. "Practically garbled everything except the state!"

Chad followed—he'd have to stall him.

"Let me make sure I have that now." Wayne balanced the receiver between his ear and shoulder as he held the slip of paper up in front of him, scrutinizing his own scrawl. "That's 927 Mountain Spring Road, in Rolling Falls? And that's...right...and that's near Allegheny National Forest? Yes...uh-huh...okay, thanks a lot. Bye."

He hung up and smiled. Bingo. Now he had it, clear, confirmed, and definite.

Now to go.

He shot to his feet and reached for the backpack—a sudden wave of lightheadedness struck him and he sat down on the bed again. "Wow! Guess my circulation's not up to speed yet!"

Stay here and relax for a while, said Chad, seizing on the moment.

I know I'm tired, thought Wayne. *But I want to get moving. I'm so close now…*

Naw, you don't need to. Chad laid a hand on Wayne's shoulder. *Stay here and unwind for a little bit.*

*Well…*Wayne thought for a moment. A check of the map *had* showed him it wouldn't be as long a trip as he'd originally planned on. And now that he wasn't *pressed* quite so much…

Guess I can wait a little more, he thought. *I'm close enough now for a breather.*

He slowly rose to his feet, chuckling. *So what should I do?*

Chad laughed. He raised his hands and shrugged as Wayne stood ponderizing…

Ah, I know! Wayne reached into his back pocket and pulled out the worn poker deck. He sat down at the table and removed the frayed rubber band.

"Forgot I even *had* this," he said, giving it a few shuffles.

Chad was surprised—*he* hadn't known, either. He silently pulled the other chair back away from the bed and sat across from Wayne, watching him intently as he whisked card after card off the stack and neatly arranged them, design up, in overlapping vertical rows in front of him. The smell of the deck filled his nose.

"Mountain Spring Road." Wayne whistled over the quiet sound of the things slapping the tabletop. "That's a *pretty* name. Probably a pretty town." He turned over some cards. "I never really *did* see anything outside of Philly. But I wonder why she's way out *there?*"

I don't know, Wayne. Chad crossed his arms and laid them on the table, bringing his chin down on them. He was enjoying this immensely. He *loved* watching someone play cards.

His eyes followed Wayne's hands, darting back and forth, scrutinizing every move, watching him go through the motions as he flipped over some more in a fast, set pattern...

"Oh, *bats.*" Wayne had stopped and was staring down at the complex layout of hearts, diamonds, clubs and spades. He looked puzzled. "I *always* get stuck like this."

Chad wanted to help. He raised his head and glanced upward.

Could I try?

Sure, came his answer. *Give it a shot.*

Chad scratched his chin as he studied the situation. *Hmm...how to do this...*

He reached forward and laid his finger on the ace of clubs. *There,* he said to Wayne. *Take that one.*

Wayne cocked his head and looked at it, oddly. He started to reach for it—then moved his hand over and lifted the jack of spades.

"Ha!" He smiled triumphantly and folded his hands on the table. "Beat the deck at itself!"

Oops. Chad only smiled weakly. *Guess I still don't really understand that game.*

He watched as Wayne played again.

"Well!" Wayne gathered the deck into one stack and slapped it down. "I've had enough of *this!*" He stood and rattled the car keys in his pocket. "I'm gonna go down and warm that old thing up. It needs to get running for a while first—something I sure didn't let it do *last* night."

He walked to the door, chuckling. "Watch my stuff, will ya buddy? I'll be right back for it."

Chad stayed in his seat. It still wasn't time for Wayne to leave yet, but everything had already been taken care of. He chuckled, too—yes, Wayne *would* be right back.

And the upcoming scenario was going to be *fun!*

It had suddenly grown darker.

Wayne looked around at the sky as he stepped outside—

clouds were gathering over the surrounding fields. A light breeze had picked up, and a familiar smell hung heavy in the air. He breathed deeply.

Rain.

It was going to rain. A nice, cool, springtime-in-Pennsylvania thunderstorm was rolling in.

He smiled. *Boy, I love these.* He reached his car and felt for his keys.

His smile vanished.

The keys were gone.

Hmmm? He reached deep inside his pocket, turning it inside out. He checked all his other pockets.

No keys.

Suddenly concerned, he scoured the pavement around him, slowly walking back toward the building. Where had those darn things *gone?* He'd *had* them, he'd *felt* them in his *hand* only minutes, *seconds* before. They *had* to be somewhere. Maybe he'd dropped them inside…

He reentered and checked around the base of the stairs. Had they fallen *here?* No, there was nothing. He scanned each step as he climbed; he reached the top and searched the entire second floor hallway, both in front of his room and everywhere else, walking the entire length, eyes down, combing every inch. Still no keys. He scoured the stairs at the other end from his vantage point above (not really sure why—he hadn't even *been* there), slowly looking all the way down, across the floor, to the backdoor at the bottom…

He stopped. Someone was just entering—or *was* there?

Wayne looked closely. A little kid was standing just inside the door, holding some kind of large, white cardboard box with a lid on it; he was craning his neck, trying to see behind himself, reaching vainly at something…

Now Wayne could see what his problem was. His baggy white shirt had apparently caught in the door when it closed behind him, and he seemed unable to twist around and free himself without first setting the box down—but the snag was preventing him from reaching the floor. He was stuck.

That looks familiar, thought Wayne, glancing at his own excess shirt which often gave him the same trouble. *I can relate.*

He almost chuckled. Nevertheless, it pained him to see the poor little tyke struggling with the thing; quickly he made his way down.

"Need a hand there, buddy?"

"Yeah." The kid looked embarrassed. "I guess I'm kinda caught."

Wayne pushed down the bar and opened the door a crack. The kid was leaning forward slightly and almost fell over as his shirt suddenly came loose; Wayne caught him by the arm and stood him up.

"Whoa! You okay?"

"Yeah. Thanks a lot." The kid brought a knee under the box to steady it, then lifted the lid and peeked inside. "Good. None of 'em spilled."

"Oh, ya got *liquid* in there?"

The kid nodded. He tried to push it shut again.

"Here!" Wayne lifted the box from his arms. "I can hold that for ya."

"Gee! Thanks again." The kid pushed the lid down tight.

"Wow!" Wayne steadied his grip under the pressure. "This thing's got some *weight* to it! Isn't it a little too *much* for someone your size?"

The kid grinned. "Naw, I can handle it all right." He straightened his shirt and brushed his thick, dirty-blond hair back over his ears. He looked up at Wayne.

Wayne looked back at him; it was the first time he'd really *seen* his face. And he'd never seen a more gentle one—such a deep, quiet stare, such calm blue eyes. He couldn't have been more than nine or ten, but already he had a character more appealing than any *adult* Wayne had ever known.

There was something *different* about him.

Wayne tried to break his own stare. "Are—are you going anywhere in particular?" he asked, blinking. "I could sure carry this for ya, wherever."

The kid looked over and nodded toward the steps. "Up there," he said. "*That's* where I'm going,"

"Really? That's where *I'm* going, too—"

Wayne heard a low rumble. He glanced through the glass in the door—it had grown even darker.

He looked back at the kid. "Would you like to come in, for a little bit? It's gonna get awful wet out in a hurry."

"Sure," he replied. "That'd be fine. I won't be missed right away."

Wayne felt concerned. "Oh, I don't want to keep you from anything—"

"Don't worry. You're not."

"Are you with someone?"

"Yeah, but he's not going anywhere for a while yet."

"Oh, all right."

They both walked up. Wayne tightened his grip on the box, careful to keep it as level as possible. He was actually *surprised* to hear the kid accept. He sure was *trusting,* considering they didn't even know each other. Yet somehow, Wayne felt they did.

"Here." He tried to point in front of him. "It's this door here—oh."

The kid had already opened it. Wayne made his way in and set the box on the table; the kid followed him and shut the door.

"Thanks," said Wayne. He walked to the sliding door and stared out. It was now *quite* breezy—the dark clouds were nearly overhead and a few lightning flashes were visible. The sporadic, low rumble of thunder continued.

"Wow," he said. "We're really *in* for it."

"Want some hot chocolate?"

"*Huh?*" Wayne turned around. The kid was holding a large, styrofoam cup out to him, steam rising off the top.

Wayne was startled. "Oh...*sure.*" He reached out and took it and the *richest* aroma of chocolate he'd ever smelled met his nose.

"*Jeepers!* Where'd you get it?"

The kid walked back to the box on the table. The lid was

off and Wayne could see a half-dozen or so other cups inside—so *that's* what he was carrying.

Wayne didn't know exactly what to say. "Uh, um…thanks! Uh…how much is it…?" He reached for his wallet.

The kid giggled and shook his head. "Nothing. I don't need anything for it at all."

"Well…" Wayne motioned toward the box. "Get some for yourself, then. Please."

"Naw." The kid looked at him. "It's not *for* me."

Wayne stared in amazement. What a *likable* little guy. *And boy, he seems…he feels familiar.*

Wayne couldn't stifle the curiosity any longer; he *had* to ask. "I—I haven't ever seen you before, have I?"

"Not that I'm aware of." The kid fit the lid over the box again.

Wayne took a sip of the chocolate. *Mmm,* it was *heavenly.* He'd never tasted anything like it. He took another sip…

"Wow! You like those, too?" The kid was looking at the deck of cards.

"Oh, yeah." Wayne shrugged. "Gives me something to do in my spare time—which I haven't had much of, lately."

The kid smiled. "Did ya ever play crazy eights?"

"Only once or twice in my life, I'm afraid." Wayne felt embarrassed. "Believe it or not, I don't remember how."

"Really?" The kid looked surprised. "I can show ya."

Wayne grinned. He'd been searching for a reason—*any* reason at all—to lengthen the kid's stay; he wanted to be around him for as long as he could.

"Sure," he said. "I'd like to learn."

He sat down across from his young guest and handed him the deck. "Go ahead, give 'em a shuffle."

The kid looked hesitant. "Well…okay."

He divided the stack in two and leaned the piles together on the tabletop. Then he placed his thumbs in the middle of each and tried to mix them together with his fingertips; they spattered all over the place.

"Oops." His face got all red. "Sorry."

Wayne chuckled and gathered them up. "Don't worry. I learned the secret." He straightened the deck and divided it in two again. "See? Ya gotta put your thumbs *under* the stacks— like this."

The piles shuffled together, evenly and neatly.

"Oh, *that's* it?" The kid watched the procedure with wide eyes.

"Yep! That's it." Wayne handed it back to him. "I know because *I* always did it the first way, too."

The kid took the stack with a new look of fascination. He divided it and shuffled the way he'd been shown. It worked perfectly. He looked up at Wayne and beamed; Wayne smiled back.

"You're a quick learner," he said.

He gulped down some more chocolate as he watched the kid shuffle again, then deal out seven cards to both of them. He'd *never* tasted anything so good.

"Mmmmm! This stuff's a *godsend!* Where did you *get* it from?"

The kid didn't look up from his dealing. "It was given to me."

Wayne could see him smiling; he got the point. *He* wasn't saying.

The kid explained the rules to crazy eights and they played a couple of games. The kid won the first, Wayne won the second.

"You're a fast learner, too," said the kid.

Wayne finished his drink and set the cup down on the table. "And that was *delicious!* I gotta say, you sure know how to look after me."

The kid grinned. "That's my job."

It thundered and the sound of rain hitting the pavement drifted in. They both looked out.

"Well, it finally got here," said Wayne.

"Wanna go watch it out there?" said the kid.

Yes, thought Wayne. *He's gonna stay some more!* "You bet," he answered. "Let's go!"

They both stood and carried their chairs out to the balcony.
They sat and watched the rain for a little while.

"You really like watching thunderstorms, don't you?"
said Wayne, finally.

"Yeah." The kid's gaze was fixed ahead of him, almost
captivated. "A lot."

"Yeah, they *are* fun." Wayne was lost in thought, too. "I
liked to do this same thing when *I* was younger. I think
thunderstorms run in my family."

They both chuckled.

The kid started sniffling a little bit. "Mm—guess the
weather gets *to* me, like this."

"Oh, here," Wayne handed him a tissue. "Let 'er rip."

"Thanks." The kid blew his nose.

"Still a little cool for ya, huh?"

"Yeah, but a lot warmer than it was."

"That's for sure." Wayne stared at the sky. "At least it's—"

A brilliant flash, followed by a sharp crack of thunder,
momentarily interrupted him.

"—at least it's *raining* now, instead of *snowing,"* he
finished.

They watched the dark clouds roll by.

"Listen, you sure *you're* not thirsty?" Wayne felt hard-
pressed to do *something* for his young guest.

"Well, I am a *little,* but—"

Wayne got up.

"No, no, you don't have to…"

Wayne didn't even hear him. He had already gone in and
was feeling inside his backpack. He pulled out one of the three
cans.

"All I have is root beer, if that's all right with you."

"Really?" The kid's eyes lit up. "That's my favorite
drink."

Wayne brought it to him and watched as he momentarily
struggled with the lid. "Oops…*there* we go." He got it open
and smiled. "I'm sorta used to bottles."

He brought it up and drank almost half the can before

taking a breath. *"Mmm!"* he gasped. "Thanks!"

He hiccuped as Wayne took his seat again.

"Wow! You must really *like* the stuff."

The kid paused between gulps. "I haven't had any for a long time."

"Since they still had it in *bottles?"* Wayne tried not to giggle.

"Yep. Not since." The kid grinned and continued gulping; he took another pause. "Have ya ever made a black cow?" he asked.

"A *what?"* Wayne didn't understand.

"A root beer float."

"No, I haven't found one that light yet."

The kid stifled a laugh.

"Seriously, no I haven't," Wayne continued. "Are they good?"

"Sure are. Nothing like 'em."

Wayne nodded. He watched the thirsty little tyke drink down the rest of it; he thought back to when *he* was that age. He'd loved root beer, too—he felt good, watching the little guy enjoying himself.

The kid tipped the can upside down and sucked out the last bit. He looked at it, burped quietly and sighed.

Wayne smiled at him. "Need any more, there?"

"Sure, thanks!"

Wayne rose and walked back in, but not before he lightly bumped his foot on the door track.

"Aaah." He sucked in through his teeth and shut his eyes against the sudden, throbbing pain; he walked with a limp, trying to avoid putting any pressure on the foot where the heavy table had landed. He pulled out another can.

Ooo, that's sore.

The kid noticed. "Is something wrong?"

"Oh…" Wayne tossed him the can and slowly walked back out. "I, uh, sort of *dropped* something on it yesterday."

"Mm! Sorry it happened."

"Oh, it's all right." Wayne sat down again, drawing his

aching foot up and rubbing it. "It's only a bruise. I'd completely forgotten about it until now. It's perfectly fine."

"Sure?" The kid looked concerned. "I mean, I *know* it must
have hurt."

"Oh, it *did.*" Wayne recalled the moment vividly. "But it
was just another one of those times—"

Wayne stopped as his mind pieced together all the events,
before and after the fact. He looked at his foot and smiled.

It was just *another* one of those times where everything
was perfectly planned," he finished quietly, talking to himself
more than anyone else. "*My* angel knew what he was doin.'"

"*Angel?*"

Wayne looked up, startled. The kid seemed surprised to
hear it.

"Oh, yeah," he replied. his smile returning. "My watcher.
This was *his* work, I realized just now. He's taken good care
of me, and I'm never, ever gonna question his methods."

The kid smiled, too—he exhaled deeply. He seemed very,
very happy, almost *relieved* at something. "You believe in
angels?" he asked, popping open the can.

"Certainly." Wayne crossed his legs and propped them on
the railing. "After all I've been through, my angel's the only
reason I'm still around."

The kid listened intently.

"And I've kept him plenty busy," Wayne continued.
"That's for sure. If ever an angel can get tired, *he* probably is."

The kid kept listening. The rain was gradually diminishing
to a drizzle.

"He's *great,*" said Wayne, shaking his head in amazement. "He really means a lot to me, more than he'll probably
ever know. Next to the Lord Himself, of course, he's my best
friend in the whole world."

Now the kid's grin was turning into a big, *big* smile.
Wayne drew his legs back off the railing.

"I was just thinkin' last night how much I'd love to see
him—if only to…to *thank* him."

The kid's smile remained strong. His face grew red again;

he looked down for a moment and swallowed. Then he looked back over at Wayne with the deepest gaze he'd seen yet.

"He hears you," he said, speaking with the same calm Wayne had already come to greatly respect. "He hears you and he appreciates it a lot. I *know* that."

Wayne was startled. Such a confident and genuinely *heartfelt* answer, especially from someone so young and—as he would have thought, *unaware* of such things—had caught him totally off guard. He smiled, too, thinking how silly it must have sounded, an older person talking about his angel with a little kid. But he admired—he was *surprised,* really— at the kid's response to it; not only his willingness to listen, but the utter *respect* he showed for the topic. There wasn't a trace of the confusion or uncertainty or humorous, cynical doubt he might have expected; rather, he seemed to understand completely, he really *did* seem to know. And it was yet *another* neat thing about him, yet another thing that made him seem...*familiar.* Wayne almost asked again if he'd seen him before, but no, he'd gotten the answer. He believed the kid completely, and he wasn't about to question his honesty by doing so.

The rain had now subsided; brilliant afternoon sunshine had broken through the cloud cover. Wayne was almost surprised when he noticed—he'd been so thoroughly enjoying his company that he'd become nearly oblivious to his surroundings. He stood up, savoring the fresh, cool air on his face.

"Wow! I can see my breath again!"

The kid remained seated. "Mm! Don't ya love that crisp smell?"

"You bet!" Wayne leaned on the railing and took another deep breath. "The aftermath of a spring thunderstorm in Pennsylvania."

He surveyed the area beneath him—everything was so rain-washed and clean and rejuvenated; even his old blue car suddenly looked much *newer...*

Then he remembered.

His *keys.*

Oh, rats. Why'd he have to think about *that* right *now?* He bit his lip and sighed.

The kid noticed. "Oh, what's the matter?"

"Well, I can't seem to locate my car keys." Wayne stared at his palm in frustration. "I don't know where they went. I had 'em in my hand just a little while ago."

The kid took a long drink from the can; he glanced away for a moment. "What time is it?"

Wayne's mind was still probing as to where the mysterious keys could have gone. He had to break his train of thought—only this time it didn't bother him. "Excuse me?"

"Do ya know what time it is?"

"Oh, sure." Wayne glanced at his watch. He was astonished to learn they'd been on the balcony for almost half-an-hour.

"It's seven minutes after two."

"Mm." The kid looked back at Wayne. "Have ya checked your pocket?"

"Oh, yeah," said Wayne, instinctively reaching into them as he spoke. "Several times. But they weren't—"

He stopped abruptly as his fingers closed around his car keys. He looked at the kid as he slowly drew them out. Then he stared down at them, an astonished grin spreading over his face.

"I looked in there before and they *weren't* there," he said. "Now they *are.*" He broke into a chuckle. "It's like they were *hidden* from me or something."

The kid chuckled, too. "Little things get lost sometimes, but there's always a reason for it." He took another long drink.

Wayne looked at him with admiration. What an *optimist!* He wished *he* had that kind of attitude more often.

The kid finished the can, then slowly rose to his feet and stretched. "Well…"

Wayne knew what he was going to say and his heart sank. He'd *not* been looking forward to this moment.

"Sure ya can't stay any longer?" he asked, trying not to let his disappointment show.

The kid smiled. "The guy I'm with is leavin' real soon. I've gotta go with him."

Wayne nodded. "I understand." He didn't *want* him to leave—in fact, he could have *begged* him to stay—but he knew they couldn't be around each other forever. They both stepped back in and crossed the room, slowly.

"Where are ya headin', anyway?" asked Wayne.

The kid picked up his box. "West. The Allegheny area."

"You *are?*" Wayne's heart leaped, his spirits lifted again. "So am *I!*" He thought fast. "I could give you a lift there."

"Well, I'm already with someone..."

"Oh, that's right. I forgot." Wayne's excitement fizzled once more. The kid's gentle gaze had cushioned his answer, but he still wanted to help him, somehow. "Could...could I give *both* of you a lift, then?"

"Well, he's got his own car." The kid brushed at a dirty area on his old, white shirt with his wrist. "Besides, I've gotta go change first. I can't go like I am and I'm really never supposed to leave him."

"Oh, I'm sorry!" Wayne suddenly felt concerned for him. "I didn't realize...I mean, I hope you're not in any trouble—"

The kid was chuckling. "Naw, don't worry. He's within walking distance."

"Oh...oh, *good.*" Wayne chuckled too, relieved. *The guy's probably his guardian or something,* he thought.

He followed the kid to the door and opened it for him. "Is there anything else I can do for ya?" he asked. "Want me to carry that down again?"

"Naw, I can handle it now." The kid turned and faced him; he carried it with such ease it...it almost looked *empty.*

"Besides," he added, "you've done more than enough for me already."

"Boy." Wayne gazed down at him, shaking his head. "I'd *sure* like it if we could see each other again sometime. You've really been fun to be with."

The kid shrugged. "Ya never know when or where we might. Like I said, I can only be so far away from ya."

Wayne tried not to look puzzled. *When did he say that?*

"Well, *here.*" He pulled the pack of gum from his pocket and dropped it into the kid's shirt pocket. "I want to at least leave you with *something.*"

The kid looked down at it. "Wow! Thanks a lot!"

"Ya like spearmint?"

"Sure do! It's my *favorite!*"

"Great."

They looked at each other a moment longer; Wayne just didn't know how to say goodbye. He swallowed.

"You take care," he said, finally.

The kid's eyes traveled from Wayne's head to his feet, then back to his face. "I will," he said. "Don't you worry about that."

He swung the box under his right arm—not a *sound* came from within.

Wayne extended his hand. "Thanks," he said. "Thanks for everything."

The kid's free hand came out and grasped Wayne's. It was a long, warm handshake.

"No, Wayne," he said with a sparkle in his eye. "Thank *you.*"

He smiled broadly and winked before turning away.

Wayne smiled, too—he watched him go down the stairs toward the front door. He heard it open and hurried to the balcony, expecting him to appear in view in the parking lot below.

He didn't.

Hmm. Wayne carried the chairs back inside. He realized he hadn't even asked the kid his name. Then he realized he hadn't told him *his* name.

Then how had he known—?

Wayne stopped, perplexed. *Jeepers,* he thought. *That's really...*

He wanted to say "strange," but it didn't fit the way he was feeling right then. *Neat* was the only word he could think of.

Chad leaned back in his chair and laughed.

He *really* enjoyed that root beer.

Boy, what a likable little fellow. Wayne felt as rejuvenated by his visitor as the outdoors did from the rain. He walked to the big wall mirror by the bed and gazed into it.

Chad walked over beside him.

Now that's the kind of angel I'd like to have, thought Wayne. *Fun, curious, neat to be around, a laugher. Someone seemingly so small, with a job so big—immortal innocence in a world where there isn't any.*

He stared at Chad's reflection. *I can see him standing there at my side right now. My little protector. My guardian angel.*

Chad laughed again.

And he thinks it's funny. Wayne couldn't help laughing himself. *I guess I do, too.*

He started to reach for his backpack—then diverted his hand to his shirt pocket and pulled out his wallet. He removed the old, battered, expired restraining order, and, as if to seize the newness of the moment, tore it up and threw it away.

There! And good riddance!

Now for one last thing. He pulled out the dusty answering machine and plugged it into the wall.

He erased the tape.

He shouted with joy as it whirred and came to a stop. What a moment, what a *perfect* moment, to officially end it all. Now the threat against his life, and everything it encompassed—and all *memory* of it, so far as he was concerned—was gone forever. And that was that.

He packed the machine away and tied the bag shut again before slinging it over his arm. Then he pulled out his car keys, his *beautiful* car keys, and headed out the door.

"Come on, Shortstuff!" he called over his shoulder. "Let's go!"

Chad giggled. Now his stuff *and* his stop were short—it seemed he was a little short on everything!

He started to follow and then he stopped.

Now *he* felt something in his pocket.

Slowly, he reached down inside and felt what it was. A huge grin spread across his face as he pulled out the brand new, crumpled white *baseball cap. Perfectly* white. To match his uniform.

Holy wow!

For a moment he just stood there, speechless, looking at it and feeling it and smelling it and turning it over and around in his hands. Then he looked up.

Thanks, Lord, he said, barely able to utter it. *Thanks a lot. The best present I've ever had. It tops this whole day off just right.*

He shook it into shape and set it on his head—backwards, of course.

Makes me look brand new, he said, casting a wink skyward.

He rejoined Wayne. Hot *diggity!* Now for the *really* exciting part.

18

Wayne couldn't help trembling as he got into the car. *This is it,* he thought. *The last leg of this whole crazy thing. I'll finally be home.*

For a moment he just sat there, trying to relax in his seat. He couldn't. He was almost *afraid* to, so accustomed was he to having *something* go wrong. Residual paranoia, he figured.

Chad noticed; he reached over and gently laid a familiar hand on Wayne's shoulder. *Don't, Wayne. There's no need to fret.*

Wayne instantly felt the soothing *calm* come over him. He relaxed. The comforting presence reminded him of what had just happened inside, and astounded him at how fast he could forget in a moment of uncertainty.

He smiled big.

I have a guardian angel, he thought. *My own personal one. That's neat. I guess I knew before, but now it just seems…that much more real.* He looked over, already relishing his new perception of the close friend he could neither see nor hear. *What a kid—one of the Lord's special agents, sittin' right beside me.*

He gave the other seat a pat. "Hey! Good to have ya along, buddy!"

Chad grinned. *Good to be along, Wayne.* He settled back, then crossed his legs and propped them on the dashboard. Wayne would have a nice, safe ride for a while.

The car pulled back onto the highway. Wayne sighed—he was glad for this chance, this little stretch of time where he could just…*sit,* uninterrupted, and listen to the dull hum of the engine and let his mind clear. Driving was one of the few times he *could* reflect. He smiled again, feeling the heat of the sun on his knuckles as he clutched the wheel.

My own little guardian. Boy, has he been busy.

He glanced over again. The passenger window had already started to fog up—it looked almost like someone had drawn a *car* on it. His eyes moved back to the road.

So, so busy. And what a time it's been for both of us.

Indeed, for literally the past seventy-two hours straight he'd been riding an emotional roller coaster that had taken him through every danger imaginable, from the four corners of New York City and everywhere in between to the rocky hills of western Pennsylvania. And it wasn't even quite done *yet.* For seemingly the hundredth time he shook his head in amazement. *What a week!* It started so drearily; it ended so differently.

"But I've been looked after well." Wayne didn't sound like he was speaking to anyone in particular. Chad paused from his steam drawing and listened.

"I sure have." Wayne busied his mind reviewing the past several days, randomly sifting out of the blur what few specifics it could remember. *"Jeepers,* I have. You've done good, little friend."

Chad blushed again. *Thanks, Wayne. Anytime.*

The car slowed as it came to a railroad crossing—the muffled *bump* of metal under the tires sent Wayne shivering as he recalled, vividly, his *not-*so-pleasant experience of only a short time before. He shook his head.

"Ooof! I guess ya got me out of *that* one, all right. And lots of *other* stuff, too!" He chuckled. "Shoot, you were probably the one who showed me that thing with Mom's name on it, weren't ya?"

Chad drew his legs off the dashboard and grinned.

"But maybe…naw, ya couldn't have. You're a *protector,* not an information center."

Chad's grin turned into a laugh.

"But then, if lettin' somebody know something will get 'em out of danger and where they belong," Wayne reasoned, "then *that's* guarding, isn't it?"

Chad nodded. Wayne was beginning to understand. And he admired and appreciated his desire to know, his simple curiosity about when he'd been watched. He *was* aware of some of the times, but not *all* of them. He probably never would be. But then, he didn't need to be.

Chad finished his drawing.

"Ya know, you're a *neat-*lookin' little kid." Wayne's voice had a reminiscent tone. "It'd have been nice to have known ya when *I* was a kid."

Chad smiled at the thought.

"See, I didn't have any siblings," Wayne continued. "And I really didn't have any friends, either. You'd have made a *great* one. But I guess I just wasn't ready for an angel then— I hadn't made *the* decision yet. But…"

He sighed, then smiled again. "But I have nothing to complain about, because you're here *now*—and you'll never know how *glad* I am for it!"

And I'm glad for you, said Chad. *I'm glad I have you, Wayne. You've been just as fun and important to me.*

"Thanks, buddy. You're an answer to prayer, nothing less." Wayne glanced upward. *"He* sure heard me. He's really kept me safe with you right there, and, well…"

He paused and looked back over at Chad. *"That* must've been planned, too, because I've always wanted a kid for a guardian angel."

Chad's mouth fell open; he stared back at Wayne. *Really?*

Wayne was grinning. "Yeah, I have! And the kid I saw was absolutely *him*—right down to the high tops."

Now Chad *really* felt good.

Wayne started to laugh. "Aw, good grief. Here I am talkin' like I *know* or something!" He laid a hand on the passenger seat once more. "You'll have to excuse me for givin' ya an assumed appearance…"

Chad chuckled.

"…because ya probably don't really look like that at all. You may be a husky *grown-up,* for all I know!"

Chad roared.

"But *I* think you're a kid. And I think you're a neat-lookin' angel. *You* don't mind, do ya, little tyke?"

Chad looked warmly at him. "Tyke" was yet another new name. But it was a good one—it made him feel like…well, like the kid he was.

Naw, he answered. *I don't mind a bit.*

The wail of a siren suddenly broke the quiet. Wayne looked in the rearview—then pulled over as a firetruck, then an ambulance raced past, horns blaring. They were soon followed by two other firetrucks.

"Whoa!" Wayne squinted ahead. "Something big must've happened *somewhere.* "

Chad looked over at him, happy once more to see the Lord's property alive and well. *It sure did, Wayne. It sure did.*

The car pulled onto the road again.

Wayne was startled to see all the flashing lights, the flares, the commotion as he approached the bridge over the narrow, muddy river. Or *was* there a bridge? Through the small crowd of rescue workers in front of it, he could make out a broken guardrail…

The whole area had been roped off; a state trooper in a raincoat was directing what little traffic there was back down the highway. Wayne rolled down his window as he neared.

"What happened up *here,* officer?"

"Bridge collapse," he replied. "Washed out in that thunderstorm that passed through here."

"Jeepers! Was anyone on it?"

"No one that *we* know of, thank God. Pretty unusual, considering it happened about two o'clock."

Wayne nodded. He got brief detour directions before making a U-turn and backtracking to another highway. He'd have to drive through some back country for a little while.

"Mm! Two o'clock!" Wayne thought aloud as he drove. "Heck of a time for *that* to happen, huh, tyke?"

Chad said nothing. He looked at Wayne.

"Wow! I guess *I* could have been..." Wayne paused as his mind calculated time and distance; he suddenly broke out in goose bumps. My gosh, I would have been on that bridge, if it weren't for...

Now his mind stopped dead in its tracks. For a moment, his face went expressionless—then his eyes widened and his mouth opened slightly; he bore a look of surprise, of disbelief, of someone who'd just put two and two together and realized something no words could describe.

...if it weren't for my little visitor, his thought managed to finish.

The clean smell of spearmint gum filled the car as he slowly looked over at the passenger seat.

Chad only grinned at him.

It...it was...it really was... Wayne didn't exactly know *how* to feel. Muted embarrassment, awe, wonderful *shock*— all struck him at once. Not simply a comforting thought any longer, or a pleasant idea, it was real.

He had a neat-looking, likable, laughable, *lovable* ten-year-old guardian angel. His alone, sitting right beside him. Someone he could now see, hear and feel, as clearly as anyone.

And despite the other emotions, he felt like the richest person in the world because of it.

The road seemed long and endless, but the country was beautiful. On and on he drove, through small town after small town, past fields, meadows, wood-covered hills, *beautiful* country—more of such than he'd ever seen at once in his life.

He took it all in as best he could, but he was distracted; his mind was still busy absorbing the fact that had eclipsed all other thoughts. He kept looking over at Chad.

Finally, he shook his head. "I've gotta stop for a while, little tyke. I've got to."

That's fine, Wayne. Whatever helps ya. Chad chuckled— he knew it was probably the best thing Wayne could do. Such a whirlwind of events, combined with what had just happened, would probably be too much for him to handle otherwise.

Wayne approached a place in the road overlooking a grassy meadow, surrounded by distant hills. He slowed and pulled onto the shoulder, angling the car toward the edge before coming to a stop.

He shut it off and slowly got out, nearly oblivious to the country splendor he'd missed all his life. Slower still, he walked to the front of the hood and sat down, drawing his feet onto the bumper.

Chad sat down beside him, exactly the same way. He spit out his gum and tossed it.

For a time they both stared out over the field and said nothing. The distant sound of a crow and the wind rustling the winter-dried weeds was all there was to be heard. Wayne shut his eyes and listened to it. What a *pretty* sound.

He put his hands in his tattered coat pockets; his fingers closed around it and he remembered. Slowly, he drew out the small brown Bible that Doug Waters had given him. It had somehow remained unscathed, *miraculously,* through everything.

The Bible. *His* Bible. The first chance he'd had to read any of it. The first time in his life he'd ever read it.

He began to flip through the pages in no particular order, not really sure where to look. But even so, he felt...*led.*
And he was startled.
Do all things without grumbling or disputing, that you may prove yourselves to be blameless and innocent.
Wayne chuckled. *I'll try to complain with a good attitude from now on.*
Man looks on the outward appearance, but the Lord looks at the heart.
He sure had to look hard, thought Wayne. Because I didn't have any.
The Lord knows the way of the righteous, but the way of the wicked will perish.
Wayne was amazed. He'd never realized there was so *much* in it.
How blessed is he whose transgression is forgiven, whose sin is covered!
Chad was enjoying every minute of this; his face beamed with happiness. *Keep reading,* he urged.
And He Himself bore our sins in his body on the cross, that we might die to sin and live to righteousness, for by His wounds you were healed.
On and on Wayne read, and he was *astounded.* This book was *fascinating.* Far from the dull, drab image he'd always harbored, it was the most vibrant book he'd ever read before. And he'd never seen anything quite so *personal*—it was almost like an instruction manual, written just for his life.
And the Lord will continually guide you, and satisfy your desire in scorched places, and give strength to your bones; and you will be like a watered garden, and like a spring of water whose waters do not fail.
Jeepers! This is the best book I've ever seen!
Oh yeah, said Chad. *It's my favorite, too.*
The Lord will protect you from all evil; He will keep your soul.
And He's certainly done that. Wayne looked at Chad. *Wow! What a thing to remember.*

It's all neat to remember, said Chad. *Every bit of it, from cover to cover.*

Wayne glanced at his watch; it was time to go again. He found it hard to put down his book—but he had to, if he was going to arrive home before dusk.

He started to get up, then took his seat once more.

Chad knew what he was doing. He put his hands together and lowered his head.

Wayne looked out over the field, watching the wind bend the dormant grass and sunlight run across between the shadows of clouds.

Lord, he prayed, *thanks for everything. Thanks for saving me. Thanks for watching me. Thanks for taking care of me and helping me. Thanks for everything I have—this Book, my car, my health, my family...*

Wayne paused. He breathed deeply, then his eyes lowered to his lap.

And thanks, Lord, for the little fellow You've given me, to guard me everywhere I've been and will ever be.

A big grin spread across Chad's lowered face.

Thanks so much, Lord. Amen.

Amen, said Chad.

Wayne looked up to find that an extraordinary *calm* had settled over the area. He smiled. Inside and out, he felt brand new.

Chad laid a hand on his shoulder. *Let's go home, Wayne. Let's go home.*

Wayne patted his friend's shoulder in return. They both stood and got back in the car.

"Well!" Wayne felt as if he'd settled all but one important thing; he glanced at Chad. "You've *gotta* have a name. Now what would *that* be?"

Chad said nothing. He'd let Wayne guess.

"Oooh, a *silent* man, huh?" Wayne playfully cocked an eyebrow. "Okay, let's see…um…*Gabriel?*"

Chad laughed. *Naw. There's only one Gabe, and he's a great guy to know.*

Wayne shook his head and smiled. "You're right—of *course* it couldn't be that. Besides, it's too stereotypical."

Oh, ya think it sounds like two at once?

Now *Wayne* laughed. "No, I mean it sounds too *normal.*"

Oh, that's what that word means.

"Yeah, I'm looking for a more *unusual* name," said Wayne. "One that wouldn't come to mind right away."

Chad listened eagerly. This was getting interesting. He drew his knees up under his elbows and rested his chin on his fists.

"How about...*Erastus?*"

Chad roared. He'd never even *heard* of that one.

"Jeepers—what am *I* sayin'?'" Wayne sounded almost exasperated with himself. "It's gotta be a *kid's* name, of course!"

You're gettin' warmer, said Chad. *Keep tryin'.*

"Okay, you're a...a *c* name, I can tell. Mmmm. What is it now...Chris?...Cory?...Chuck?...no, no, now wait a minute. Hmmmm...what's the one I'm gropin' for? There's *one* I'm really, *really* lookin' for...hmm...oh, I'm *so close...*"

Chad was enjoying this immensely. He leaned forward on his hands, waiting.

"Let's see...what *is* it? Is...is it Ch...oh, *gee!* I *almost have it...*it's...*Chad? Bingo! That's it!*"

Yes! Chad smacked his hands together and laughed. It was the first time Wayne had ever called him by name.

"Jeepers. *Chad.*" Wayne felt as if he'd just discovered a long, lost item. "That's a good, strong, down-to-earth name. No pun intended, seriously."

He extended his hand to the side. "Hi, Chad. I'm Wayne. 'Course, you *already* know that."

Chad didn't care. His hand reached out and grasped Wayne's. *Hi, Wayne. I'm Chad.*

"Good to know ya, buddy."

Good to know you too, Wayne. Chad grinned broadly. He liked his newly-discovered name a lot.

He looked up. *What do You think of it, Lord?*

He paused, then laughed. *Yeah, that's what I thought, too.*

Wayne consulted the map frequently. The detour alone, he figured, would put him back a good forty-five minutes to an hour. But no matter. In fact, he welcomed the slight adjustment of pace. And he could enjoy the country scenery—plus his time with Chad—a little more this way.

"Well, Chad!" Wayne was busy trying to refold the map with one hand. "It's really been something, all of this. I can't really comprehend…"

The dumb thing wouldn't fold. "Aw, come on, here." He struggled briefly with it, them moved the whole thing onto Chad's lap. "Here—all yours." He ran a hand down over his eyes. "Never *could* refold 'em right. Besides, readin' in a car makes me sick."

Chad refolded it; he also avoided reading the words.

"Anyway," Wayne continued, "like I was sayin', it's only *now* I'm really starting to comprehend just how busy you *have* been—so *much* has happened."

That's for sure, said Chad. *It's been kinda wild.*

"Yeah, we've been through everything! I mean, there's nothing we've seen that we haven't already seen."

Chad gave him a funny look; Wayne paused and tried again.

"I mean, there's not much that we haven't already seen."

Chad laughed. *You're funny, Wayne.*

Wayne's mind again drifted through the past three days, where he'd nearly been shot, crushed, chopped up, ground to bits, axed, run over, flattened, burned alive, strangled, obliterated. And yet he'd found his family again, he'd found a peace and happiness that nothing could conquer, he'd found a warm, personal friend and guardian who'd be right there with him for as long as he lived.

Again, he didn't know what to feel.

He smiled haltingly as he began to realize just how *strong* a love and commitment it must have taken to get him through everything—and how many times he'd made it tougher by thinking for himself instead. And then, suddenly, he felt…*silly* for doing so all over again, awkward, uncomfortable, *apologetic* for being in the presence of the little guy who'd faithfully done it all despite his stupidity.

"Aw, *jeepers,* Chad! I'm sorry!" Wayne's embarrassment grew as every single instance of worry and panic came back to his memory. "I gave ya such a *hard* time. I *fretted* so much! I didn't *mean* to…"

He shook his head in disdain over his own shortcomings, then glanced upwards. "I just wasn't trusting Him to handle things."

But ya are now, Wayne. Chad's hand came to rest on his shoulder once again. *And you're alive and safe and happy, and that's all that matters to me. All those times when you didn't listen are in the past now. The Lord's left 'em there—and He wants you to leave them there, too. They don't matter anymore.*

"You're right, Chad. You're right." Wayne laid his hand on Chad's. "And I'm just as silly to remember them as I was to *do* 'em."

A determined look came over his face. "But I'm gonna try *not* to so much from now on, by gummy! And with *His* help, I won't!"

He looked over again and smiled. "He sure *did* handle everything. And he chose just the man for the job. Thanks again, Chad—for bein' there, and for bearing *me.*"

Sure thing, Wayne. Anytime.

"My own personal *guardian!*" Wayne chuckled. "What a side benefit of knowing the Truth, huh? I never realized so much would *come*…I mean, from that one moment when I prayed in that little church." He sighed. "Some things change for the better, some things change forever. Just lookin' back at my life—my *B.C.* life, that is—could prove it to anyone."

Chad was beaming. *He's a Life-changer, Wayne. Nothing's impossible for Him.*

"*That's* for sure," said Wayne. "I know *I'm* not the same anymore. I'm just *not.* And I never will be again. And I gotta say, I wouldn't ever *want* to be!"

They both laughed.

"It's nice to be at peace, and *in* one piece, too!" said Wayne. And suddenly he felt good again. His mind was back on the road, back at rest, back on the *neat* feeling that came with simply remembering what, and *Who,* he had. He was thinking ahead once more, anticipating what awaited him.

"So much to do, so much to catch up on. *So,* so much I wanna do. *You* have any favorite activities, Chad?"

Sure do, Wayne.

"This quiet country." Wayne rolled his window down a little. "Breathin' fresh *air's* one I like."

Same here, said Chad.

"Or a nice, quiet *walk* in the country," said Wayne.

Or an evening bike ride, said Chad.

"Or just...takin' a nap."

On a screened-in porch.

"*Ahhh.*" Wayne was deeply lost in a daydream. "*That* sounds great. Got any other ones?"

Oh, yeah. Lots of 'em.

"I do, too, come to think of it. Like skiing. I've always wanted to. I've never even *seen* a pair up close."

Or how about horseback riding?

"Or fishing."

Or camping in the timber.

"Or hiking up a woodland trail."

Or thunderstorm-watching.

"Or Wyoming."

Chad gave Wayne another puzzled look. Wayne looked embarrassed again. "Sorry, bad joke."

Chad laughed.

"Anyway, I want to do *all* that stuff sometime, at least now that we're in the right country for it. All those and a countless million others. To just...get out in the open—*this* open—and see it all."

He looked hopeful. "Maybe someday."

Chad smiled at the idea. Both he *and* Wayne had the same vast list of wanna-do's; yes, maybe someday. But...

"But not to jump *too* far ahead," Wayne finished for him. "We've gotta get *home* first."

And I can't wait, said Chad.

Home. What a *lovely* word, thought Wayne. Ironically, though, he also found it dredging up the same, tiring concern once again.

What would he *say?*

It was a concern he'd expected to subside; hadn't Mom, after all, *helped* him find her? Certainly that would indicate she *wanted* him back. But supposing...what if she no longer felt that way? After all the years of no communication or goodbyes or *anything,* how could he face her...?

He found himself slipping again and he stopped. He was determined not to fret.

"Pray for me, Chad," he said, urgently. "As always, I'll need it—both for when I get to the door *and* now. I can't fight the worry on my own."

Sure, Wayne. Chad lowered his head and prayed.

Wayne felt the relief at once.

"Thanks, friend." Now he felt *really* good. In fact, he felt *great.* He noticed there were no other cars for miles around and looked over once more.

"The road's ours, Chad. We still have a little ways to go— let's make a ride of it. Whadaya say?"

Chad smiled and nodded in approval. Yes, that sounded *fun!*

Wayne slowed a bit and rolled his window down all the way. He drove for a while longer...

"You don't mind if I ask ya something, do ya?" he finally said, turning to Chad once again.

No, not at all. Ask away.

"Well, uh...how...how *did* ya ever get stuck with a person like me?"

He'd said it only half-seriously, but still, he honestly wanted to know. Then it struck him and he laughed. "Shoot! What a *silly* question *that* is!"

Chad only grinned. He knew—as Wayne was beginning

to understand—that if you're the *Lord's* property, it doesn't matter what make or model or type you are, because you belong to *Him,* and he will protect you. And Chad was Wayne's guardian angel and that was that. And he loved every minute of it. And he'd grown to deeply respect and admire Wayne all the more as they'd been with each other—a learning experience for *both* of them, in a way.

Wayne grinned, too. *"I'm* sure glad you're with me, Chad. Not only for all you've done, but…well, because you're a laugher. It's good for *me* to hear someone laugh. I guess the Lord laughs a lot, too."

He glanced at himself in the rearview mirror. "I mean, look at how He made *me!"*

Chad giggled.

"I'm so thin I have to jump on the scales to register anything," said Wayne. "I lose half my weight when I burp, and I'd run in the negative if I ever did it twice. I know I should put on some extra weight, but I have no extra weight to put on. And forget using belts—a *twistie* is all I need." He paused to chuckle. "I'm so light I can't even register an *opinion!* I could win an oxygen look-alike contest, for all *I* know."

Chad roared. Wayne chuckled some more, too.

"Aha! Maybe *that's* a reason you were put with me, Chad. Angels *love* to laugh, don't they?"

Oh yeah, said Chad, between gasps. *They sure do. All of 'em.*

To his own astonishment, so did Wayne—his sudden new ability to laugh at things he once found extremely *dis*likeable was exhilarating.

He noticed his speed had crept back up again. "Whoa! I better slow down—I can't even read the speed limit signs."

Again Chad roared.

Wayne wanted to hear more of it. Quickly he thought and thought…

"Hey Chad, did you know Sir Isaac Newton had a brother named Fig?"

Chad laughed. *Figures,* he said, barely able to draw a breath.

"Or that William Tell had another kid named Pray?"

Another laughing fit from Chad.

This was getting fun. "Come on, Chad," prodded Wayne. *"You've* gotta know some, too. Let's hear 'em! We're on a roll!"

Chad regained his composure. *You really think I...I should?*

"You bet! Shoot!"

Well...I knew a guy who was so short he couldn't reach his own height...

Chad's face grew red with embarrassment—until he heard Wayne laugh.

"Good one!" he said. "My turn, now—it was so cloudy in my old neighborhood all the time that we used to paint the phone poles gray and watch people walk into 'em."

Back to Chad. *Did you hear about the guy who starved because he didn't want to get his teeth dirty eating?*

"Well, I bought a dollar bill for a buck one time and got cheated, because I didn't end up with any more than I started with."

And left-handed people are the only ones in their right minds.

They *both* roared.

"Good job!" said Wayne. "Let's keep goin'! I feel *great!"*

Chad did, too. He thought of some more...

I knew an electrician who refused everything.

"And I saw a shirt that was too loud, so I turned it down."

And I got bored in a lumber factory.

"And *I* tried to plug in a guitar chord."

Did you ever try to join a golf club?

"Naw, but I tried joining a whole *ace* of 'em, once."

Wayne's watch beeped. "Oops! I've gotta watch that thing—"

Every second, said Chad.

"—all the time," Wayne finished. He paused. "You're right, I like 'every second' better. Anyway, they have ticks in 'em and they'll latch onto your wrist, if you're not careful."

Their laughter subsided. This was getting too easy—and

frankly, too *dumb*—for both of them.

Time to get complex.

Did ya hear about the two ranchers' sons, who bought their own cattle ranch? said Chad. *They named it the Focus Ranch—it's where the sons raise meat.*

Wayne pondered it, momentarily bewildered. Then he laughed. "Ha! A *triple* pun! Good one! Really, *really* good one!"

He took a deep breath. "Now try *this* one. Did you hear about Lou Minum, the guy who metaled with everything? He liked to steel irons, which lead a copper wearing tin to zinc him. His wife went to the brass in her Mercury, and he solder help—and that's the rust of the story."

They both roared. Now *Wayne* was really embarrassed.

"Holy *mackerel,* Chad! I'm just as screwed up as that whacko the other day!"

As screwy as calling someone to get their phone number?

"Or writing someone to get their address." Wayne reminisced between laughs. "I actually *did* that once, you know—when I was a kid."

I thought the lotion was vanilla pudding one time—only it didn't taste too good.

"And I tried to play the Scotch tape in the recorder."

They both wiped at their eyes; Wayne turned and smiled once more. "No doubt, Chad. You're a laugher!"

Chad did just that.

"And what a *neat*-sounding laugh it is—it's so contagious! *It's* what makes me laugh, more than anything else." Wayne grinned. Indeed, it *was* neat, hearing his little protector laugh.

Jeepers, I used to think I was gettin' old and cranky," he continued. "Now…"

Now he felt *younger,* yet more like he'd grown than ever before. It was almost like a late childhood, in a way. Again, he wished time would pass more slowly—so he could enjoy times like this.

"Life is great, Chad. Never did I *ever* think I'd say that."

It sure is, Wayne. And He makes it that way.

"He does indeed. And what a scene *this* is! An ex-runaway driving *back* home with his ten-year-old guardian angel. Who'd have thought?"

They both laughed again.

"Well, Chad—I guess that leaves just one *last* thing to ask ya."

Chad turned, curious.

"Do ya ever wear it forward?"

Huh? Chad didn't understand.

"Your *cap,* I mean?"

Oh, that. Chad reached up and swung his cap around.

Wayne reached over and flipped his hand down through the air; Chad grinned and pushed the bill back up over his eyes.

Wayne chuckled. "Didn't think so. I always wore *mine* backwards for the same reason."

Chad giggled. *Should've seen that one coming.*

"But they're *neat,* all right," said Wayne. "I think they're special gifts, too."

Chad reached up and felt his prize possession. *They sure are, Wayne.*

"Among *other* things, of course." Wayne looked straight ahead and sighed. "You know, Chad, you and I are near opposites in everything, but we have so much in common. We're really, well…the *same* opposites. We're so different, but we're almost identical. It's kinda funny."

Chad nodded.

"But I tell ya, you're the best insurance I could ask for, Chad. Never a dull moment with ya—never once."

He laid a hand on Chad's knee. "Life'd be a lot more dreary—and *short*—without ya, friend. You're kinda like… well, like air. I don't always think about ya, but I'd sure notice if ya *weren't* there."

And I'll always be right here with ya, said Chad. *Wherever you are, whatever you're doing, wherever you go, for as long as you live.*

"Whew! What a great thought *that* is!" Wayne exclaimed. "Makes *me* glad to be around *you.* It's *another* ironic thing, really. If you weren't around, I wouldn't be here. But if *I* weren't around, then *you* wouldn't be here. Guess we kinda need each *other.*"

We sure do, said Chad. *And there's no one else I'd rather be with, doing this. I've learned a lot from ya, Wayne. You're one for me to follow.*

"Thanks, Chad—thanks a bunch. But if ever you may look up to me, I look up to you even more. *You've* really been the trend-setter in this whole thing. A lot of times *I* was the kid, and *you* were the grown-up; you told me what I should and shouldn't be doin', and I didn't always listen, and I got in trouble for it."

He looked at Chad. "You're *more* than a guardian to me, tyke—you're my *family* now. You're a little brother to me."

Chad swallowed. He didn't know what to say.

"You and the Lord are the only family I've had all through this whole thing," Wayne continued. "You've really kept me going. And *He's* made my life worth living again."

He paused.

"It all kinda makes ya wonder what *heaven's* gonna be like," he said.

Chad beamed from ear to ear. *Ooooh, way better than you can possibly imagine, Wayne. It'll be the thrill of your life.*

"I guess it will be." Wayne looked hopeful. "I'm really looking forward to it."

He settled back into his seat, his mind focused on the road once more.

Chad settled back, too…then sat up again. He had to burp. *Mmm,* that root beer.

He leaned back once more, the carbonation tickling his nose.

Wayne had been right. The full brunt of all the excitement *hadn't* yet hit him—until now. Every bit of the sleepiness had suddenly crashed over him like a wave; he yawned a *looong* yawn.

So did Chad. He couldn't see anyone do that without doing it himself.

"Good *grief,* Chad! I've *never* been this tired before. One thing I'm gonna get sooner or later is a normal, good night's sleep!"

He glanced over again. *"You've* gotta be a little draggy, too!"

Chad chuckled. *Naw, not really.*

"I'm so completely *spent,"* said Wayne. "So, so sleepy." He didn't want to be, considering he was still driving. Yet somehow, he didn't mind. It was a *pleasant* kind of sleepiness—perhaps because it was the first he'd felt, without any big distractions, in a long, long while.

Before he knew it he'd let himself go…the moving lines on the highway became a blur as he slowly drifted off… sleepier…*sleepier…*

Chad took the wheel.

For what must have been a good two or three minutes, *he* was driving the car—seated on Wayne's lap, foot on the pedal (though he could *barely* reach it!), hands firm on the wheel, a good booster seat under him so he could see the road. He eased it to the right, then the left, careful to stay in the lane…holy *wow,* it was easy to drift. Driving was a new, fun, yet slightly *unnerving* experience. But he *loved* it! In fact, he didn't know which had been the *most* fun job so far—the night before or this.

But Wayne *did* need to wake up. Chad smiled. *Oh, well.* Save but one, no good thing could last forever.

Sorry, Wayne. I don't wanna, but…

Wayne was jolted awake by an icy cold feeling on the back of his neck—*"Whoops!"* He grabbed the wheel as the car drifted onto the shoulder.

"Holy *mackerel!"* His adrenaline raced as he rubbed his neck—and then a smile crept over his face. He looked over; Chad was just settling back into his seat.

"Ya did it *again,* ya little rug rat!"

They both laughed as Wayne reached for the radio. "I tell ya, Chad—it just keeps on happening. I can try all I want, but I won't last a day without you—"

He stopped as he realized the radio was echoing his words in song. "Ha! What more can I say?" Wayne motioned toward it. "Couldn't have put it any more bluntly myself."

A different tune came on. "Oooh, this is one of my favorites! I grew up with this one!"

Chad grinned. *Turn it up a little, Wayne.*

"Just a little before your time, I imagine." Wayne adjusted the volume knob. "So you've probably never heard it before. But then, bein' an angel, you probably know a lot more than *I* do."

Chad couldn't help laughing as the familiar lyrics of "Sing" uttered their simple, happy instructions. He relaxed in his seat, drumming his thumbs on his lap and singing along with the words he knew so well.

Soon he and Wayne *both* were singing, as brilliant sunshine flooded the countryside.

"Whew!" They finished, and Wayne smiled big—the second biggest one he'd ever made. *Three days ago I had nothing,* he thought. *Now I have everything.*

He looked beside him again.

"Best friends, Chad?"

Best friends, Wayne.

"Then gimmee *five,* brother!" He lifted both hands off the wheel and held them in the air.

Chad laughed. He smacked Wayne's right hand with his left, then the reverse, then both at once—then *left* on left, then the other way around, then both again.

And then their hands met in mid-air, and embraced in another long, firm clasp. Wayne smiled as his palm grew warm.

Thanks, Chad. You're a great angel, and a neat kid, too.

Their grip strengthened.

"Good to have ya along, buddy."

Good to be along, Wayne.

"And besides—if that *wasn't* you I saw in that room, then it was a darn good look-alike!"

They both roared.

19

Rolling Falls, Pennsylvania.

And what a sight it was. Wayne was awestruck by the wooded beauty, the rocky hillsides and calm stillness; there was even a small woodland stream running right through the middle of town under a plank bridge, which vibrated all through the car as he slowed and drove across. With its quiet streets, set-apart houses (which were a beautiful blend of brick Victorian and cabin-style structures), huge yards and a *forest's* worth of trees, it seemed less a town than a collection of country dwellings. Its tiny size only added to the feeling; situated on the outer edge of the Allegheny, it was by far the prettiest place he'd seen yet on his drive—or in his entire *life,* for that matter.

Next best thing to the country, he thought.

277

Next best thing to heaven, said Chad, grinning. *Only there's a little more of a gap.*

He looked at Wayne. *This is gonna be a fun place to live, ya know.*

"It sure is." Wayne nodded, then squinted ahead, scanning the road signs. "Where's that street, anyway…?"

The car approached the last intersection in town.

Mountain Spring Road.

"Whew, had me concerned there for a minute." Wayne took a right off the highway. "I was startin' to think maybe it didn't exist or something." He began to scan the houses…yes, he was going the right way; the addresses were getting larger.

"Well, this is it, tyke. Whadaya think?" Wayne shook his head. "*I* have absolutely no idea what's in store for us here."

Chad shrugged and threw his hands up. *That's a good question, Wayne. I dunno, either.*

Wayne looked over, somewhat surprised.

Seriously, said Chad. *I don't! I'm as in the dark on this as you are!*

He laughed. *The Lord doesn't quite tell us everything.*

Wayne grinned and looked back out his window at the houses, now growing farther and farther apart. "We'll soon find out, I guess."

Or *would* they?

The numbers were still getting bigger, but…they were already out of town.

"Uh-oh, don't tell me I took a wrong turn—"

Ya didn't, said Chad. *I've been watching. We're still on the same road.*

"Hmm! Then it must be out…"

In the country, said Chad, dreamily.

"Jeepers," said Wayne. "I hadn't even *thought* of that."

The dwellings were at least a mile apart now; the trees had become much sparser—gathered in small patches of timber here and there—and had been replaced by hilly, grassy meadows. Wayne caught another number; he was only a couple of houses away.

The sudden realization of just *how* close he was instantly brought the anxiety back.

Again, he wondered—how would he be received?

Here he was, suddenly showing up at Mom's door, without a chance to write ahead or anything. Her very help in his search was seeming more and more insignificant; for him to even *ask* for shelter, after leaving in that manner...well, in a way, it was the prodigal son all over. He could only *hope* it would have the same ending.

His heart began to sink at the prospect of...

Wayne, you're fretting again. Chad laid a hand on his shoulder once more. *Don't think about that. It isn't worth it.*

"Aw, I know, Chad." Wayne reached up and patted his hand. "I know. All this letting go has been good for me. And I *want* to keep it up, 'cause it's payin' off. But still, it's really tough at this point..."

Chad gazed at him. *I'll be right beside you, Wayne. I'll be right here with you all through whatever comes. Just don't fret. Nothing—nothing at all—is worth fretting about.*

"Thanks, Chad." Wayne already felt more at ease. "You make everything so enjoyable."

You bet, Wayne. So do you.

Nine Twenty-Seven
Mountain Spring Road

The stained wood mailbox, situated on a post above a decorative covered-wagon wheel, spelled it out in gold-leaf letters on the side.

The dusty, dirty, mud-spattered Toyota pulled to the shoulder. Wayne looked across the road—and stared in disbelief at the one-level, ranch-style house.

It was *beautiful.*

Red brick and white wood, set just to the right at the end of a medium-length driveway with a double-car garage, framed in red rock and plants, and surrounded by *acres* of gentle green meadow. A post-and-rail fence set the left yard apart from the driveway and road; two big, brown horses grazed on the other side.

Horses.

For several minutes, Wayne only sat and gawked at it. He didn't know if being in the city so long had done it, or never really seeing the countryside, or both. But it didn't seem real, let alone *possible*...he just couldn't comprehend that something so beautiful could have anything to do with him.

Slowly, he undid his seatbelt and stepped out onto the silent roadway. He looked again at the address on the mailbox, then at the piece of paper with his scrawl. They matched, all right.

Boy, the Lord's full of surprises, he thought. *I never expected this.*

Me neither, said Chad, already at his side. He was *just* as pleasantly shocked.

Come on, Wayne, let's go over there.

They walked across and up the driveway. Wayne stopped as they passed one of the horses; it stared back, studying him with equal curiosity. Slowly, haltingly, he reached out and stroked the animal's nose.

A horse.

He'd never seen one that close before.

He turned and slowly crossed the driveway to the red brick path that led to the front door.

He took a deep breath.

"Ready, Chad?"

Ready, Wayne.

They walked down the path together, side by side.

Wayne's stomach tightened as he stepped onto the little front porch. He felt like it was all a dream.

Could this really be the right place? It couldn't be...

Go on, said Chad. *Ring the bell.*

Wayne pressed it—he heard a quiet, harmonized sound go off somewhere inside.

Now he'd done it.

Now he'd find out for *sure* if this was it.

Quickly he tried to remember what he'd been planning to say, what rough outline he'd been rehearsing a million times over in his mind. He couldn't—it had left him completely. He almost panicked as he heard short, light footsteps walking across a wood floor. The *anxiety* had come back. Chad's faithful, relentless work had safely delivered him to the door, but here it came again...

Shhh. Chad laid an arm on his back. *I'm right here, Wayne.*

Wayne cherished his touch; Chad's presence at that moment could only be described one way.

Heart-warming.

His anxiety subsided a little.

The front door opened. A little blond kid in dark soccer clothes and holding a ball under his arm was standing there, peering up at Wayne through the screen door.

"Um, is...is Ruth Jenkins at home?"

The kid looked like he didn't understand.

Wayne swallowed. He could now see an older woman sitting in a recliner in the living room behind the kid; she was also looking over at Wayne through thick spectacles. She'd obviously *just* sat down—she was pulling a TV tray on wheels up in front of her and Wayne could make out what appeared to be a photo book on it.

He cleared his throat and looked back down at the kid.

"Is Ruth Elizabeth Jenkins at home?" He said the words slowly and clearly.

The kid still looked puzzled. He turned around to the woman in the chair.

"Go find your mother," she said, still scrutinizing Wayne. "She's in the kitchen, I think."

The kid disappeared into the house. Wayne could only figure Mom had company over, although he was hesitant to think so—he recalled what had happened, all too recently, the *last* time he had. He stared at his shoes, shifting his weight from one leg to the other as he tried to look inconspicuous. He knew it was useless, being on display as he was, but he felt uncomfortable at having intruded on such tranquil privacy.

He'd have to endure it, though; after all, *he'd* knocked on *their* door. Still, he found himself again fighting the *feeling* that he had the wrong house…

He heard the kid's voice from somewhere inside. "Mom? Hey, Mom! There's a guy here who wants to see ya."

Wayne's initial apprehension turned to confusion. *No,* he thought. *I don't want to see his mom, I want to see my Mom!* Now he was *certain* he had the wrong house. His face sank as he braced for the numbing disappointment.

Then he saw someone.

A woman had stepped into view from a doorway in the hall, wiping her hands on her kitchen apron. She leaned over and nodded as the kid said something to her, then started walking toward the front door; the kid followed closely behind her, as if to shield himself from the stranger on their porch.

She entered the living room, and through the orange beams of evening sunlight from the picture window, Wayne could now see her face clearly.

It was Mom.

He jumped. His eyes widened, his mouth dropped open— it took him a moment to realize *she* was reacting the same way.

"Wayne?" she said.

"Uh…uh…h-hi, Mom," he sputtered through his shock. "I, uh…I'm…uh…h-here."

"Wayne?" his mother said again—this time with more emotion, as if reality had just hit.

"Uh, yeah, Mom…i-it's, uh…it's…i-it's me. I'm here." Wayne felt like a total stutterbug.

He swallowed again as she slowly opened the screen door. She stared at him a moment longer—and then they were in each other's arms.

"Wayne!"

"Mom! I'm back, Mom!"

"Wayne! Oh my God! *Wayne!*"

For what seemed a *wonderful* eternity they hugged and kissed, laughing, *crying,* talking at once, asking each other questions they didn't even hear, embracing in long-awaited, joyous reunion. For Wayne, it was the second-best moment of his life.

Thank you, Lord, he uttered silently. *Thank you thank you thank you!*

Chad laughed heartily. Indeed, the crowning moment of everything that had happened so far...and the *best* one, too.

"Oh, Wayne! Come on! Come inside!"

Wayne stepped in through the front door after her, wiping at his face with his coat sleeve. Now he *was* really embarrassed with himself. They hugged again.

"Wayne! You're *here!*"

"Oh, Mom! I'm so *glad* to be back!"

The fresh smell of homemade cinnamon rolls filled his nose as they shared yet another long embrace; they held each other at arms' length, silently gazing into each others' faces through red eyes. Only then did Wayne remember there were others in the room!

He looked over. The kid who had answered his knock was standing there, wide-eyed, taking in the scene with a look of curious and absolute bewilderment on his face. Wayne felt sorry for him—he couldn't imagine what he must have been thinking.

But who *was* he?

Mom's hands slowly lifted off Wayne's arms and lowered in front of her. She looked first at the kid, then at Wayne, then back at the kid, stepping out of the way as if to give them a clear view of each other. She smiled warmly.

"Wayne, this is your little brother Josh."

Huh? Wayne's mouth fell open again; he thought it'd hit the *floor.*

"Josh, this is your big brother Wayne—the one in all those old pictures, the one I've told you about."

The kid looked up at Wayne, a new spark of *awe* in his eyes.

Wayne tried to speak but he couldn't. *A little brother! A sibling!* Something he'd waited, *longed* for all his life. And now he had one. They stared and stared…

"Hi, Josh," he said, finally breaking his surprised silence. He held out a hand.

"Hi." Josh reached out and shook it.

"Aw, what am *I* doin'?" Wayne dropped to one knee. "Come here, you!" He held out his arms, and then *they* were hugging and laughing—Wayne stood again, lifting him right off the floor, holding him in the air.

"Josh!" Wayne squeezed him and rubbed his head. "What a *neat* name!"

Josh giggled. "Careful! Don't get my soccer clothes dirty!"

Wayne glanced down—indeed, the front of his pants were all white with flour from Mom's apron. He laughed and gave Josh another hug.

But it wasn't over yet. Mom still had the same warm, anticipative grin on her face; she was nodding toward the hallway with her eyes.

Wayne looked, and for a moment…he thought he was staring into a mirror from the past. Another kid—a little older this time—was standing there, gazing back at him with the same wide-eyed expression Josh had just had. He was holding a school textbook.

"Wayne," said Mom, "this is your *other* brother, Caleb."

Wayne had to set Josh down before he dropped him. The book slipped from Caleb's hand and fell to the polished wood floor.

"*Jeepers!*" they both exclaimed at once.

Holy wow! Chad clutched his cap—*he* hadn't known, either. And he was just as surprised, just as delighted as Wayne himself. He watched, grinning from ear to ear, as yet another warm embrace was shared.

"Good grief!" Wayne stood misty-eyed, each arm around a brother. He looked at Mom. "There…there aren't any *more* of you, are there?"

"Well, *one* more," said another voice.

Wayne looked over. He'd completely forgotten about the

older lady. She had risen from the chair and was beaming at him, her eyes narrowing into little half-moons.

"I'm your grandmother," she said.

Wayne was astounded—he was absolutely as speechless as he'd ever been. His arms remained around his brothers; he looked at the floor before facing Mom once again. *Her* eyes were misty, too.

"I was finally able to make arrangements to come home and live here with mom—your grandma," she explained. "She'd been raising the boys…I'd been saving to get you back out of the foster system and bring you with me, so we could *both* join them." A weak smile came over her face. "It seems getting you out again was a little harder than I'd anticipated."

She was suddenly fighting tears. "It was the biggest mistake I've ever made, Wayne. You shouldn't have *ever* been in that place, to begin with."

"Don't let it bother you, Mom," said Wayne. "It doesn't matter to *me* anymore."

Mom sniffed, then smiled once more. She looked at Josh and Caleb. "Your brothers were your surprise."

"And *what* a surprise!" Wayne gazed into Caleb's face. "You're *me!* You're me all over again—except ya still have full-length hair."

They both laughed.

"When…when's your birthday, anyway?" asked Wayne.

Caleb's face grew red. "December three," he said, flashing a shy grin.

"Really? I'm November twenty-nine! How old?"

"Fourteen."

"Ha! I'm twenty-two." Wayne chuckled. "Wayne and Caleb. Identical twins, born eight years apart."

"My birthday's *tomorrow*," said Josh. "I'll be *ten.*"

"*Seriously?*" Wayne exclaimed. "Well, happy birthday, Josh!"

"Thanks." He looked up at Wayne and smiled. "I already got a good present."

"Yeah, now there are *three* of us." Caleb laughed triumphantly. So did Wayne—he hugged them tight again.

"Hey, ya wanna come with us tomorrow?" said Josh. "We're goin' to see Uncle Lynn and Aunt Barb for my birthday."

"Uncle *who?*" said Wayne.

"They live near Portland Mills," Josh continued. "And they have a great big house, and a big playground next door with a soccer field in it." He picked up the soccer ball and handed it to Wayne. "Can you play it with us?"

"Well, uh…" Wayne stared at the ball. "I've never really played it *before.*" He glanced at Chad, standing in front of him and grinning. "But maybe with a little *help…*"

Chad laughed—help he'd get. *I'll teach ya the shoot-in, Wayne.*

"Awesome!" Josh was all excited. "Then you can be on our team. I'll tell 'em *nobody* can beat us, with my big brother on the team!"

"*Us?*" said Wayne. "You mean there are more…"

"Oh, yeah. All our cousins will be there."

Cousins? Wayne's mind was swimming—what a *huge* family!

"Some of 'em live there and some are coming like us," said Josh. "And they're all as old as I am. Nicholas and Jeff and—"

"Whoa!" Grandma had a hand up and was laughing. "Don't *overwhelm* your brother, Josh! He *just* got home." She looked at Caleb. "Why don't you show him his room?"

"My *room?*"

"Yeah," said Caleb. "Come on, it's back here."

Jeepers, Wayne thought. *I can't believe this!* He ruffled Josh's hair and tossed him the ball.

"I'll be there tomorrow," he said as he followed Caleb. "Count on that!"

Josh's eyes sparkled. "Oh, boy! I can't *wait!*"

Wayne grinned—he sure was a *cute* little guy. He slipped off his coat and hung it on the rack in the hall, pulling at his excess shirt to cool himself. "*Whoo!* This is the *warmest* March I've ever felt!"

"Yeah." Caleb stopped to pick up his book. "We keep the

thermometers on standard time year round so it always gets warmer earlier."

Wayne chuckled. They even had the same dry sense of humor.

That's for sure, said Chad, between giggles. His high tops echoed off the polished wood as he followed them to the little room at the end of the hall, the one with *music* coming from it. "Unforgettable," in fact—he'd recognize the tune anywhere.

They entered and Wayne couldn't believe his eyes.

There was all his stuff.

His old wood-frame bed, neatly made with all his old stuffed toys lining the wall next to it; his race car set, fully assembled on the floor beside it. His favorite Spider-Man towel hung neatly over one end of the bed; every book he'd ever owned was carefully arranged and propped between his old school globe and ancient, leather baseball mitt on a small shelf above.

And, of all things, even his old, white baseball *cap*—looped over one of the bedposts.

Every little thing he'd ever owned, loved, personified, cared for—*every* little thing—was there, exactly as he remembered it, in the exact same condition in which he'd left it.

He looked at Caleb.

"We took care of 'em," he said. "We didn't know, but we always had a feeling you'd come home. Wishful thinking, maybe, but…"

Wayne blinked back tears. *My gosh. Stuff I had before they were even born and they're watching it for me.* He walked over and lifted the cap off the post, turning it around in his hands, feeling it, smelling it.

"Mom always considered you *here,* really," his brother continued. "Any cards, or forms, or anything she got, she'd always write your name down with ours—you were just one of the kids at home, to her."

He grinned. "She even kept a box in Philadelphia that you could find her with…she never gave up hope."

That's Mom, all right, thought Wayne. *That is absolutely her.* He shook his cap into shape and tried it on—the strap was set too small and it sat on top of his head like a bottle cap.

He laughed. *How does it look on me, Chad?*

Chad laughed, too. *Kinda gwerky, but I like it.*

He watched as Wayne adjusted the thing to his new size and put it on again—backwards, of course.

"I...I don't know what to say to ya, Caleb." Wayne faced him once more. "This is...it's *great!* I suddenly show up out of nowhere and you all have everything...I mean, well..."

He took a breath. "You're the best brothers—the best *family*—I could ever ask for," he said, summing up his feelings.

Caleb chuckled. "Well then, you'll be able to stand us a *little,* I guess." He nodded toward the other side of the room. *"We're* in here, too, ya know."

Wayne looked—he'd been so taken in by his own memories that he hadn't even *seen* the bunk beds right across from his own, or the window in between with a view of the wooded foothills, or the little music center, or the desk with the computer on it.

A *computer!* Chad stared at the thing, marveling at the brilliant, full-color charts and graphs on the screen.

Wayne did, too.

"Aw, I was just workin' on that before I came out to see what was goin' on." Caleb smiled. "Homework assignment."

He walked over and laid his book down, then pressed a key on the typewriter-like buttons; Chad watched spellbound as the graphs instantly dissolved into another set of colorful pictures and charts.

"Just a little geometry course," said Caleb. His hand moved to the strange black *machine* by the record player and pressed a button; the music stopped. Chad cocked his head— what was *that* thing?

"I'll *love* sharing this room with you guys." Wayne laid an arm around Caleb's shoulder. "My two brothers, who look, act, and think a lot like *I* do. 'Course, I don't know if that's a compliment or *insult...*"

They both laughed. Wayne felt something on his leg and looked down; a small, brown cat was rubbing against him.

"Oh, that's Jeremiah," said Caleb, as Wayne stooped to rub his back. "We call him Jerry. Seems he knows ya already."

"Well *sure,*" said Wayne. "He's just another member."

Jerry walked over to Chad and rubbed against *his* leg. He purred as Chad stroked the shiny black fur.

Wayne followed his brother back out. His belt loop caught on the door latch; Chad was right there to muffle his fall.

"Whoops! You *okay?*" Caleb helped him to his feet.

"Oh, yeah." Wayne felt his ears growing hot with embarrassment as he brushed himself off. "I'm all right."

Caleb chuckled. "Don't worry. It happens to *me* sometimes—only *I* don't usually land that soft!"

"Just *another* way we're alike," said Wayne. "You and I really aren't *that* far apart, ya know. We're practically the same age. I don't really remember much of the years before you were around, anyway..."

Chad laughed as he watched them go to a different part of the house. And *what* a house—between that *computer* and *this...*

He walked back over to the little black machine, the one the music had come from, and stared at it—marveling at the blinking arrow and bright, digital numbers on the tiny screen. It looked *sort* of like a calculator, only *neater.*

Could I try? he asked, glancing up.

Sure, came his answer. *Give it a shot.*

*Mm, let's see...how to do this...*He pushed a button and jumped back, startled, as a tiny, narrow drawer popped out with a whir. He was *astounded.* He'd never seen a record so small—or *shiny!*—before. But how did it *play?*

He tried some other buttons...

"...and this is the kitchen," said Caleb.

Mmmm. Wayne breathed deeply as he scanned the picturesque, country-style room with blue-checkered wallpaper and almond countertops. A rolling pin and scattered flour covered an area near the canisters and the stove light was on; the smell of cinnamon sweet rolls had never been finer.

Music suddenly started from the bedroom again.

Caleb sighed. "Aw, that thing *always* does that."

Wayne grinned—*he* knew what had happened. He looked through the open doorway on the other side of the kitchen and saw the screened-in porch, overlooking the same meadow where he'd seen the two horses.

"We watch thunderstorms out there," said Caleb. "It's really fun. We had a whole front of 'em earlier today."

"Yeah, I know, I watched it myself. Well, not *myself,* really…"

Wayne continued to study it; he spied the card deck, on the coffee table between the two wicker seats. "Wow! You like those, too?" he asked.

"Oh, yeah." Caleb shrugged. "Gives me something to do in my spare time—which I haven't had much of, lately, thanks to *school.*"

Wayne grinned again. "Did ya ever play crazy eights?"

Caleb looked embarrassed. "Only once or twice before, believe it or not. I don't even remember how."

"Really?" Wayne was surprised. "I can show ya sometime. I just *re*learned it."

"Sure! I'd like to."

"All right! Maybe after we work on your geometry together, we can do it!"

Caleb looked surprised. "Wow, thanks!"

Chad rejoined Wayne. *Did I hear something about cards? You sure did, little tyke.* Wayne nudged him in the ribs. *Come on, let's go see Mom again.*

They followed Caleb back to the living room.

I can't believe this place, said Chad, barely able to contain himself.

Josh ran up to Wayne as they came out and took hold of his hand. "Did you like it? Did you like your room, Wayne?"

Mom was sitting on the arm of the recliner, looking over Grandma's shoulder as she continued flipping through the photo album; they looked up at the sound of Josh's voice.

"I *loved* it, Josh." Wayne took him under his arm again. "It's beautiful." He shook his head in near-disbelief. "You guys must enjoy it here immensely. I've never seen anything *like* it."

"Oh yeah," said Caleb. "We've been out here our whole life, Josh and me."

Grandma chuckled. "You must have given your brother the grand tour," she said, eyeing Wayne's cap. "Welcome *home,* Wayne."

"Thanks, Grandma."

And what a home it is, said Chad. *You're gonna love it here!*

It's your home too, Chad. Wayne felt just as good for his little protector. *It's yours, too.*

Josh laughed as Wayne playfully clamped an arm around his neck and gave his head another rub. They walked to the TV tray; Wayne craned his neck as he gazed down at the assorted photographs, neatly arranged on the thick, white pages.

"Who's *this?*" He pointed to a photo of a little blond kid sitting on the steps of a big, gray house, a dandelion propped behind his ear. "Looks a lot like Josh."

"That's *you,* Wayne," said Grandma. "When you were still lap-size."

Wayne was shocked—he couldn't even remember it. "I guess I'll have to get re-acquainted with myself," he said.

He reached into his shirt pocket and pulled out his wallet; he removed the old photograph of himself and Mom.

"Here." He handed it to Grandma. "This can go with the rest of 'em. It was a godsend for me."

Grandma took it and studied it for a minute, then smiled. She found a place for it, right in the middle of some others.

"Oh, Mom, has it really been *six years?*" Wayne's voice cracked with emotion. "Have I really been gone that long?"

Mom nodded, then sniffed again. "Things have changed a lot."

Wayne couldn't comprehend it. Where *had* all the years gone? He felt like they'd run clean over him. He looked at his two new brothers. To them—and *him,* really—it had been an entire lifetime.

"Uh, Wayne…" Mom stood once more, gazing at him with a look of both curiosity and relief. "Where…where have you *been?*…Where *were* you all this time?"

"Yeah, and what happened to your *coat?*" Josh was looking toward the rack in the hallway. "It's all black!"

"Oh, *gee,* I haven't even *told* you yet, have I?" Wayne sighed. "It's a long and strange and *complicated* story. But it would have turned out a *lot* differently without Chad."

"*Chad?*" Everyone looked puzzled—except for *Grandma.*

"Oh, I guess I didn't introduce ya to him." Wayne glanced beside him and grinned. "He's my guardian angel."

Chad laughed and started back toward the bedroom. He *had* to check out that computer.

"You have an *angel?*" Josh stared wide-eyed at his brother. "How'd you *get* one?"

Wayne picked him up again; it was the question he'd been waiting to hear.

"I can *tell* you how, Josh."

"You *are* different, Wayne." Mom's gaze had turned into a perplexed stare of her own. "You're *completely* different. I noticed almost as soon as I saw you—it's as plain as night and day." She shook her head. "I thought I'd *never* see you again, you were so bitter and angry. But you're not the Wayne *I* knew anymore. What…what *changed* you so much? What brought you back?"

Wayne took Caleb into his other arm again; he, too, seemed curious to know.

"I'd *love* to tell you," he said. "Come on, let's sit down."

It was now dusk.

Epilogue

Morning in Pennsylvania.

Chad sat on the fence along the driveway, stroking one of the horses and breathing the fresh, clean air; he watched as his best friend stepped into the brilliant sunshine with a big suitcase in his hand.

"*Mmmm! Five* homemade sweet rolls!" Wayne sighed and patted his stomach. "*This* otta be interesting, huh? Goin' to a birthday for my brother, who I've *just* met, at my aunt and uncle's, who I've *never* met." He looked at the suitcase and grinned. "Talked with 'em on the phone—never even *seen* 'em and they already want me to stay overnight. I'll have to start renting myself out, at this rate."

Chad laughed.

"Oh, that's *right.*" Wayne smacked his forehead. "I gotta remember—I don't *own* me anymore!" He started toward the family's white minivan in front of the garage. "But we'll enjoy it a lot, Chad. Josh is gonna stay over with us—*I'll* be takin' him to school tomorrow."

He chuckled, too. *"Another* world to explore today."

Then Wayne stopped halfway down the brick path. Slowly, his smile vanished; he set his load down and stared all around him, an awestruck look developing on his face.

"In *addition* to this world, here." He shook his head in disbelief. "This is gonna be *home* from now on, Chad. This is where we're going to live. I guess it hasn't really sunk in yet."

Chad was equally as spellbound. This was *exactly* the kind of place, the kind of home, the kind of family he wanted to be with.

He stroked the horse's mane. *Wayne's life sure is gonna be fun.*

"A life out in the country," Wayne continued. "It's so *quiet!* I've never *heard* anything so quiet." He looked back at the house. "And I haven't ever *slept* that well before in my life. *You* must have dozed a little *yourself,* didn't ya?"

Chad grinned. *Not really, but the chair was comfortable.*

Wayne chuckled. He picked up his luggage and continued walking. "And the grocery guy in town's already called me with a job offer…I mean, it's just…*great.*"

Yes, it *was* great. Chad could only watch him and reflect—so many things to do, so much to look forward to in Wayne's lifetime. Chad liked it so far. And he still had so much ahead of him.

His grin remained. He couldn't *wait!*

Wayne looked back at him; he cocked his head and gave Chad a *look.*

"So—you comin' along, or what?"

Chad laughed. He hopped down from the fence and joined Wayne as he lifted the suitcase onto the vehicle's luggage rack. "What a fun day," he said. "Grandma will be coming a little later on, with a friend of hers—"

The suitcase started to slip off, falling down on him before he could react.

Instantly Chad was sitting high on his shoulders, pushing it back into place. Wayne clutched his legs in a steadying grip and glanced up.

"Thanks, Chad."

He put his hands together in front of him for a step; Chad climbed down off his shoulders.

"Thanks again for bein' there," said Wayne. "And *here, too!*"

I always will be, said Chad. *I always will be. That's my job—to guard and protect you for as long as you live.*

He would always be with Wayne and would always be his guardian angel. And there would *never* be any shortage of work.

"Yep, it's an eight-seater, all right." Wayne had a hand cupped beside his face and was peering through the tinted windows of the vehicle. "Good. We're gonna need every one of them."

Huh? Chad was puzzled. *Now wait a minute,* he figured. *His mom, his brothers, him and me. That makes, uh...five.* So what was...?

Then he noticed Wayne was grinning. Only this time it was a *different* grin.

Wayne knew something.

Chad was perplexed. What *was* it?

"Well..." Wayne had a sparkle in his eye. "I said earlier that I'd like to do *something* for ya, so..."

Now Chad's curiosity was really aroused. *What* had he done?

"...I got together with our Boss, and we thought you'd like some *extra* company."

He nodded toward the front door.

Chad turned around. He saw Wayne's mom come out, then Josh, then Caleb...they all looked very different, even happier and more at peace than the day before.

And then three more figures appeared.

All Chad's size, all his age, all in the same immaculate white from backwards baseball caps to high tops.

All fellow guardian angels.

Holy wow! Chad's mouth dropped open. *Drew! Brandon! Jeremy!*

Hi, Chad! they all answered. *How's it goin'?*

Wayne's grandma stood in the doorway behind them, smiling; another small figure stood partially hidden beside *her,* flashing a calm grin of his own.

Hi, Chad, he said.

Micah! Chad couldn't believe it—he looked up at Wayne.

"I told 'em the Good News last night," he said. "They wanted to know what—*Who*—changed me. They were so *eager!* And well, déjà vu." He gave Chad a wink. "Grandma was a *big* help—seems she and I had something in common already."

You told 'em? Last night? Chad was both euphoric and shocked. How had he missed his coworkers until *now*—with one of them there the *whole* time?

Micah started to giggle, ever so quietly.

Chad looked at him, then a knowing grin slowly covered his face…he started to giggle himself. *Aw, gee! You were all in on it, weren't ya?*

Micah nodded, beaming. *We sorta hid from ya—me first, and them as soon as they came.* He motioned upward. *I talked with the Boss, too, before ya got here. We kinda knew this was gonna happen and we thought we'd surprise ya.*

Ya sure did! exclaimed Chad. *Thanks, guys…and thanks, Lord.*

Anytime, Chad, answered a chorus of voices—including one from above.

"I *knew* he'd make it fun for ya," said Wayne, casting his own glance skyward. "I know first hand—He's *good* at it!"

Chad laughed. Wayne scooped him right off the ground and held him in the air, and then they embraced—Chad gave him a big bear hug, as big as could be expected of a ten-year-old.

I love you, Wayne.

"I love you too, Chad."

The strong arms set him down again. "Come on, tyke. I wanna learn that 'shoot-in' thing!" He tugged on Chad's bill and helped his family find their seats.

Gee whiz, Chad, exclaimed Brandon as they climbed in and sat down by their assigned properties. *You guys really like each other!*

He looked at Josh. *Wonder if he'll ever pick me up like that?*

Chad laughed again. *Sure, he will. He's Wayne's brother.*

"Goodbye!" Wayne's grandma called out. "You all stay out of trouble, now!"

See ya in a while, Micah called, quietly. *I'll be there a little later, with her.*

He broke into another quiet chuckle, then stepped out of view once more.

Wayne looked his direction as he got ready to slide the car door shut—then looked back at Chad with half-a-grin on his face.

Chad smiled, too. *Micah's real shy,* he said. *He doesn't talk very much. Today's the most I've ever heard him say!*

I understand completely, thought Wayne, a reminiscent look on his face. *I know what it's like to be shy.*

But he's fierce when he needs to be, said Chad.

Oh, yeah, I know all about that, too. Wayne gave Chad another wink before closing the door.

Chad laughed yet again. He pulled out his pack of gum and popped another piece in his mouth.

Wow! Jeremy's eyes grew wide. *Is that spearmint?*

Sure is! Want some?

You bet!

Could we too, Chad? asked Drew. *Brandon and me can split one.*

That's okay, I've got plenty! Chad passed them each a whole stick.

Whew, thanks!

Wayne climbed into the driver's seat. The vehicle slowly backed out of the driveway and started down the road—quickly filling with the smell of spearmint gum.

"Jeepers, Wayne. I'm-I'm so *new,*" said Caleb. "I'm *brand new!* It's not just some empty words, it's *real!*"

"Yeah, now you're my big brother *twice,*" said Josh. "And *now* I have my own angel!" He laughed. "Wait 'till I tell everyone what I know! They won't *believe* it!"

"I'll bet they *will,*" said Caleb.

Wayne's mom said nothing; she only smiled in silent agreement.

Wayne himself gazed at the beautiful spring countryside as he drove. He thought of his mom. Of his grandma. Of his brothers. Of the family he hadn't yet seen. And, of course, of Chad.

All this and heaven, too, he thought. *What more could I ask for?*

A calling came.

Special Agents number Seventy-seven, Twenty-four, Fifty-eight and Thirty-five lowered their heads as He spoke.

Just take care of that property, and don't forget to have fun doing it!

They all raised their heads and laughed before exchanging a big round of high fives.

Score three more for The Big Guy.

The Beginning